UNKNOWN

A hard male voice rang through the room. "Unknown, you have one standard unit to come out. After that we will take action."

It meant nothing to DonEel. He mounted the three steps, reached out cautiously toward the silverness, into it. It was like holding the wind back, resisting and yielding, there and not there. As if his hand was not there. He jerked back, unnerved by the sight of his arm ending at the wrist. It had not been like this on the other side, only black and empty. Some deep and buried instinct said this was not a door now, but a trap, a danger. Yet he had come through.

One last option remained, and he took it, leaping hopelessly through the mute silver nothing of the gate....

MINDSONG

JOAN COX

AVON
PUBLISHERS OF BARD, CAMELOT AND DISCUS BOOKS

MINDSONG is an original publication of Avon Books. This work has never before appeared in book form.

Cover illustration by Esteban Maroto.

AVON BOOKS
A division of
The Hearst Corporation
959 Eighth Avenue
New York, New York 10019

First Avon Printing, April, 1979

AVON TRADEMARK REG. U.S. PAT. OFF. AND IN
OTHER COUNTRIES, MARCA REGISTRADA, HECHO EN
U.S.A.

Printed in the U.S.A.

MINDSONG

ONE

HE was a dead man.

Turning from the woman on the bed beside him, warned too late, he had finally seen the man in the doorway. Halpor. Her husband. Lord Mayor of Scarsen. Once past the shock and humiliation of discovery, he had known there was no escape. He had taken the gamble and lost.

The long night of his captivity had brought acceptance of a sort, and a sometime preparation. He'd known how it would go—the predawn accusation before the people, the sentencing, the clean dawn-arc of the sword. She hadn't been worth it. But then, it hadn't been her, but the risk itself, a chance to do the forbidden thing and take pleasure in knowing he had done it.

He *should* have been dead. That he wasn't was a thing he could not adjust to. Trying once more, futilely, to ease his position, he knew he was as dead now as when brought before the people, knew that his life was still forfeit. But the sword stroke so carefully prepared for had not come. It was important to understand why, but it was difficult to think around the cramp of overstretched muscles. For a moment his eyes dwelt on the black hole at the base of the cliff thirty paces before him; then he looked away. His head ached from the tension in his shoulders, though his arms, bound in reverse embrace about the stone pillar, had long ago ceased to be a part of him. Bound erect and alone in the grove, he felt a thrust of anger

1

threaten the apathy he was trying to hang onto. What was this for? Why this? No one had bothered to explain.

During the long night of self-condemnation and fear, he had come to some kind of resignation, so he had been able to follow the guards quietly through the predawn dark, mounting the raised platform empty of any feeling other than a distant pride and certainty that he would not disgrace himself beyond his crime.

Torches had been lit, and, stripped of all save the useless scrap of rag about his loins, he had stood aloof, knowing the court of five had only to hear the charge and pass sentence. He ignored them. It was cold, and he focused his attention on an effort not to shiver, so the watchers would not think him afraid.

Halpor himself had come forward to accuse him, robed in fur against the cold, but before he could speak there was a cry, cutting the dark like the cry of the dawn bird, breaking into the quiet, coming closer, making itself into words. "Lord Mayor! The church lays claim on DonEel of Erl!"

Surprised by the interruption, he had glanced at Halpor and known this was expected and not entirely pleasing.

"Who will speak?" This question from the court.

"Ronan, the Elder." This voice of all voices was familiar, and he had held to his calm with difficulty, searching the flame-dancing shadows.

Leaning on his twisted staff, Ronan, robed as Halpor in furs, had come up the rough steps to them, seeming as magic at this hour as the old tales told around the winter fires. For a moment his pale eyes had touched DonEel, bringing the first tentative twinge of fear, for the eyes had not known him. Yet of all the people of Scarsen this one DonEel had called friend.

Now, needing to understand the purpose of his position, he tried to recall what had been said. Perhaps the old man had explained it. It seemed like a long time ago, and faint in his memory, a time of cold and dark and red-flamed torches dancing on the edge of vision as he kept his head up. There had been talking, but he had been apart from it. His only purpose there had been to die, and nothing apart from that had any meaning. He had not even heard the call summoning him before the priest until someone pushed him forward, roughly, so he stumbled and would have fallen, but the old hand had reached out to steady him. A normal human act. But he had been afraid again, for though Ronan had often touched him, this time the hand, like the eyes, had not known him. He'd felt only a distant impersonality. The movement, and the awareness it woke, made him feel the cold burning him, stinging his flesh. Would they never get to it? he thought as he heard the voice of the priest.

"He must be one of us and without blemish, and adult. And we must not be impoverished by his sacrifice." The voice had dropped these nonsense words into the breeze-stirring air as though they meant something important. "If he fails in these things, the church quits its claim. Examine him."

Two of the guards had come to him then, enjoying their part in it. The examination had been physical and rough, humiliating him, as he remembered it now. Then he had been dead, and so submitted, letting them outrage his pride.

"There is a scar," one had said, running his hand over the jagged line that marked shoulder and chest.

"He took it going unarmed against a treecat to aid Loham." Some unknown voice had supplied the information. So it was an honorable imperfection.

"What of his obligation to Scarsen? Will we lose more than we might gain?" It was growing light, and the faces of the people were rising out of the dark below him. The breeze had quickened; he shivered, and the chattering of his teeth interfered with the

3

voices, until the one question of all the questions that had meaning for him: "Has he any issue to survive him?"

"A son!"

For the first time then, he had been aware of where he was, of his buried anger and fresh humiliation and the burning cold. Looking for the voice, he'd seen the woman being pushed forward near the platform, had heard her voice clean against the crowd's stirring. "Elder Ronan, he has fathered a son, coming a year this spring."

"A bastard."

"Yes. But his. And fit."

It was Sharill, and she'd looked only at Ronan, as though he stood alone before them. A son, begotten and forgotten in one night. He had not known. But he did not doubt her.

"The conditions are met." Ronan had ignored the question of legitimacy. "People of Scarsen, what is your will?"

A roar had surged up like heat, breaking into words against his face. "Aye! He is the one! DonEel of Erl!" He had felt it more than heard it, and now, in spite of muscles knotting to pain, he thought of the strangeness of the sound and wondered why it scared him still.

Still shouting, they had cleared a path and the guards had prodded him to follow old Ronan down the steps. The sun was nearly up and he was still alive, but the only thing in his thoughts had been a fear he might stumble and make a fool of himself for their pleasure. His feet were so cold he had scarcely felt the rough steps.

They had walked through town and beyond the wall while the sun came up, not warm, but promising it for later. And he had felt the people following. Warmed by the exercise, he had finally begun to question what was happening to him. He had yearned to ask Ronan, the one who had always answered his

4

questions, but something in the bent old back was too frightening, so he had held silent, reaching for what remained of his resignation, supposing he would know soon enough.

He had recognized the grove more by the feel of it than by watching where they were going. This was forbidden ground. One of his earliest memories was of punishment for coming here. Not that that had stopped him, but it had made him careful. As a child he had run down the path into the cuplike depression to prove himself to some of the older boys. As a man he had been content with sitting on the cliff above the hollow, feeling the mystery of the place and the black hole at the base of the cliff, knowing there were things here beyond his understanding.

Ronan had ignored the ban this time, and the guards had pushed DonEel to follow, and it was as it had always been, heavy with mystery, greening now with spring, the white pillar thrusting up suggestively from the new grass, drawing the eye beyond to the black hole and the feel of something that had no name for all its realness. The people hadn't followed this far, but had stood above, on the lip of the hollow.

Eyes closed now, remembering, it seemed he had thought that for some reason they had decided on this place to do the thing that must be done. Now he knew that he could have escaped them, had he tried. He had been free, only following because he had accepted death and nothing else mattered. So he had stood still until they had pushed him back against the shocking cold of the pillar, drawing his arms back, binding them too tightly. He had been prepared, offering himself up in his own mind, but the guards had turned away from him and started up the path. His confusion hadn't found a voice until Ronan also turned and moved away from him. "Ronan," he asked then, almost too late, "why this? For what?"

"For the people." The old voice was quiet; none could have heard it save him.

"What is to happen to me?"

"I do not know that, DonEel. Only that at sunset it will be done." Finally, the old eyes had met his, and something in the look had said trouble and uncertainty and farewell. Then the old man had gone, and there was nothing in the grove but himself, bound on the pillar, and the black hole, and he still did not know why.

Perhaps he had dozed, or wandered in his thoughts, for the sudden sounds of birdsong brought him back to himself and his pain and confusion. His feet felt swollen, and he moved them, trying to restore circulation, waking the pain in his shoulders. The sun was at his back now, and he looked at the shadow stretching before him, pointing to the round blackness. Sunset, Ronan had said. Something would happen then, but he did not know what. Perhaps then someone would come to do the thing he had prepared for. But he began to believe it would not be one from Scarsen. There was a feel of something waiting. . . .

He swallowed often, troubled by thirst. The sound of water, always part of the grove, became the only important sound, and he looked toward the spring trickling from the side of the cliff, flashing wet sparks where it caught the sun. A clumsy woodcat ambled along the cliff, unaware of him, stopped to wash itself and drink before moving up into the brush. He wished it had stayed longer, giving him something to watch and think about.

He felt paralyzed now, rather than bound, only his head alive and able to feel, aware of time racing the sun down too fast. The long night behind him might never have been. He was not resigned to death. Not like this. Did the ones who brought him here think of him now? Wonder how it was with him? He recalled the guards, the ones who had touched him, taking pleasure in doing a thing by law they would never have dared had he been free, and he knew them again, as they had once been. Playmates as children, they had accepted his lead. Growing to manhood, they had hunted together, fought and laughed together, even shared the wonder of women and the delights they discovered. Could they have forgotten? Or was it because he had gone away from them, refused to be bound to Scarsen, preferring the shadowed trails and dangers of Blackwood to the high-walled town, wanting his freedom above all things.

The black hole drew his eyes, and he fought it, but he felt a change in the grove, an excitement like that he had known in the hunt when the game was his and nothing remained but the taking of it. Only now he was the prey. He wanted to be out of this. He was no coward, but the smell of his own fear came to him and he breathed too hard with the need to move, to be away from here, to be free. . . .

His legs were cold and he looked down, pulling at stiff neck muscles. Shadow cut across the grass a few feet in front of him. So soon. This could not be. It was not real. He searched the familiar land, the trees and grove he had known all his life. He could not be meant for this.

Then he saw the man, seated comfortably among the twisted roots of the great oak that crowned the cliff, sitting where he himself so often sat pondering the mystery of the grove. He was motionless, legs folded, chin resting on fisted hands, and something told DonEel he had been there a long time, watching. For a moment then, he was angry. Bad enough they should bind him here, helpless. But to be made a spectacle. . . .

The watcher saw him looking and moved, putting a finger to his lips and shaking his head slightly.

Doubting his own vision, DonEel looked away, then back. He was still there. And he was a stranger to Scarsen. Then he was gone. DonEel looked, wondering if the man had been real, or his own imagination.

Then it didn't matter. Silence fell in the grove. The shadow line touched the base of the cliff, and the hol-

7

low filled with cool blue light. Sunset. It was time. He no longer questioned his fate. He could feel something malevolent near, approaching, and sudden fear turned his insides to water. He would have bent double against the cramps, but the thongs held him falsely erect and brave against the cold stone. He was helpless. His heart pounded in his head, pressing at his eyes as if to escape.

"DonEel, be still." The words, breathed against his ear, jerked his head back against the stone, and he nearly cried out, feeling a fumbling touch on distant, forgotten wrists. Freed, his numb arms dropped away from the pillar. He would have fallen forward but for the quick, strong arm across his chest, holding him. "Move to me, slowly," the whisper commanded, and somehow he forced his clumsy legs to move him, sidling around the stone.

For the first time then, he saw him close, and perhaps his vision was affected by relief, for he seemed one of the mythic heroes, tall and flame-haired. But the strange gold-flecked eyes stared toward the black hole wide and direct, challenging something only he could see.

It was not easy to get away. DonEel had to depend entirely on the strength of the other to get out of the hollow, and then, as circulation returned, pain claimed all his attention, so he stumbled awkwardly.

He had no way of knowing how long they moved; it took too much thought just to keep going. Until, finally, they stopped, and he knew there was brush and rock about them. "Rest here." It was voice now, not a whisper, warm and confident as he was helped to sit and a warm fur robe was laid about his shoulders. "You are safe here."

DonEel shivered violently. Warm hands held him until the spasm passed, then produced a cup of cool water from somewhere, holding it to his dry lips. It was impossible to refuse the matter-of-fact ministrations; all else was confusion and thirst.

8

He rested against an old log, wrapped in the warm robe, and after a time the pain receded from his limbs, leaving only the hard ache in his back where the stone had drawn out the warmth and stiffened the muscles. He dozed.

"DonEel?" Soft as starlight, the voice ran close to his head, and he woke, realizing the stranger had been gone for some time. It was full dark. "Come." A hand slid under the robe to grasp his arm and help him up, and he felt the cold outside the robe.

They moved to the north, away from the grove and Scarsen, following the cliff to the west. His feet were cold again, so he felt the roughness of the trail, but he said nothing, walking until a glow over the trees to the east said the first of the moons was rising. Then the hand reached out to him, guiding him toward the shadow of the cliff, and a cave.

Inside, there was warmth from a small fire burning to coals, and camp gear set out. This, then, was where the man had come while he rested. There was a smell of food, and he realized he had not eaten since some forgotten time yesterday.

"Sit here, with your back to the fire. It will warm you."

He did so, holding the robe across his lap more from modesty than for warmth, suddenly conscious that his only covering was scarcely sufficient. Built up, the fire warmed the stiffness from his back and he was deeply grateful, but not sure of what was happening.

Listening to the man moving about behind him, he finally spoke. "My Lord, I was justly condemned under the law."

"Some justice." The voice was easy, touching humor, and he came around the fire to where DonEel could see him. His unusually light hair was reddened by the fireglow, and he was both younger and more human than DonEel had supposed. The lines and planes of his face were bold, and the thick coppery curls on his brow gave him a reckless look denied by

9

quiet eyes. His mouth held laughter and other things leashed and waiting. "If they had wanted you executed, they should have done it quickly," he said, and smiled, becoming beautiful. "That sentence outweighed one man's honor, whatever his rank."

"You know of that, My Lord?"

"Aye, DonEel. I know. And I am not your Lord. My name is Pollo. Of Delpha."

"Pollo," he repeated, feeling something stir in his mind. The memory refused to surface, and after a moment he turned to more personal thoughts. "Why did you free me?"

"Would you rather I had not? In your crime there are necessarily two guilts, unless you had your way by force. Yet the woman is free and being tended in her own house. Anyway, you were absolved of your guilt before the people. By the old man." There was a questioning in the strange eyes as he looked at DonEel a moment before turning to fill wooden bowls from the pot heating on the coals. "Do you not know the purpose of your being offered?"

"I expected to die, but at dawn, and quickly." The proffered stew tasted of rabbit, strangely flavored with herbs, and thicker than he expected. He ate gratefully. "I asked Ronan," he said after a little, remembering. "Maybe he told me the reason. I don't know. He said it was by the people."

"For the people, rather. You are of Scarsen?"

"I have my house there. Yes. They are my people. But in most seasons I am in Blackwood taking meat and furs. And I have not kept to the church."

"So you would not know if there had been changes." Leaning back against the rock, Pollo considered him thoughtfully. "I went to the town after they had bound you, and listened to the people. It was the church put you there. There was much I did not understand, but the talk was of dreams and signs that had come to the priest, the Elder. He hopes to end

10

the disappearances of the people by offering you as sacrifice."

"To what?"

Pollo shrugged. "It was not said. Only to something in the grove."

"The church does not sacrifice. Nor does it accept dreams or prophecy. It is the law."

"Perhaps it has changed."

DonEel shook his head, doubting it. He had known Ronan too long. The old man was more realist than priest; that was how he had come to hold the position of Elder. He had also heard of the missing people, five at least in the winter season, and privately he thought the mystery surrounding the reports was due more to the imaginations of the townspeople than any reality. It was hard to believe they could have pulled Ronan into their fear. Still, the old man was politic; it might have come to the point where he would yield to popular opinion. And he had been under sentence of death.

"I would not have waited so long, but the old man said sunset. They might have kept watch, and it would not have done for them to see you leave the grove."

The man's words recalled the waiting, recalled also the challenge he had seen in those gold-flecked eyes. "There was something there," he half-questioned.

"Aye. There was. You felt it as I did. And I nearly misjudged the time."

In that, then, old Ronan had been right. What did the old man know that the others did not about the grove and the power in it?

The fire was loosing his muscles, and the food in his belly made him sleepy, so the question seemed complex, sliding away from him. He turned to something easier to think about, closer. "You are a stranger to Scarsen, and the south people are as dark of hair and eye as we of Scarsen, or darker. Whatever brought you here on this day, I am grateful."

"It was not entirely accident, DonEel." Laughter

11

danced in the direct eyes. "You said your church and law forbid dreams of prophecy."

"They do."

"And you?"

Habit born of early punishment and later caution halted DonEel's reply, and he looked away, feeling he had already betrayed himself.

"Please, I would not try to trap you with words, but there was talk in the town that you once— I only meant to say that not all people follow that law. My people see such a gift useful, and so it is encouraged. When I left Delpha to come south on our Council's business, I was told I might find one with a gift, from Blackwood. And three nights ago I dreamed I would come to the aid of one who would be a companion to me."

"You were looking for me?"

"Not exactly. Or perhaps I was, and did not know it. But when I saw you bound in the grove, it seemed to fit."

Instinct told DonEel this man was from a different world. "Are you asking me to go with you?"

"You cannot go back." Gentleness ran through the logic of the voice, and DonEel knew he had no argument. He had nothing, not even a people. As though following his thoughts, the man from Delpha rose, stretching. "Is there anything you need from your house?"

There were things he would have liked, but nothing he could not live without. And it was too dangerous. There were dogs in town to give warning.

"You would be recognized," the Delphan continued. "But I am a stranger off his path. I'll go."

Left alone with the fire and the security of the cave surrounding, DonEel wanted to think on the strangeness of the day, and, more especially, the appearance of the one from Delpha. But this comfort, after the long and sleepless night and difficult day, overcame him. He wrapped himself in the warm robe and slept, waking once to see Pollo returned, bending to add wood to the fire, then sleeping again to dream of the black hole and his own helplessness as some nameless thing reached out for him. He woke sweating, and, going out of the cave to relieve himself, he saw that it was near dawn, and clear. A good day for travel.

Pollo was rebuilding the fire when he returned, and by its light he indicated the bundle he had brought from Scarsen. There were clothes and his fur robe and boots, and atop the pile lay his blackwood flute and a leather-bound book. Seeing them, DonEel paused, then picked up the book. It was one he had bound himself, a secret part of himself no one knew. In it he had recorded the dreams and visions and forbidden thoughts he had been prevented from sharing. Those dreams of proved prophecy had been marked. "Did you read it, then?" He did not look at the other, but felt his eyes on him.

"Enough to know it was yours, and important. I did not mean to violate your privacy." The voice was flat, giving nothing, and because he was indebted, DonEel masked the quick irritation he felt. But Pollo did not let it go. "DonEel, all Scarsen knows the child is yours. He would have suffered had it been found."

There was no arguing that, and the tension between them evaporated in the activity of leaving.

They traveled fast, due north, crossing the steep canyons as they went, climbing higher with each ridge mounted. Pollo set the pace, and DonEel did not protest, though he watched the man and wondered about him and his reason for haste.

It was a long march that day, with no stops save for quenching thirst at the many cold springs, so both were glad for dusk and a chance to rest without the burden of the packs. They were high on the flank of West Range, and Pollo chose a place in the protection of broken rock and trees for their camp. DonEel questioned the man's caution. "If they expected me to be gone, they would not pursue, and even if they suspected I had got away, they would not come so far north of Scarsen. It is forbidden to travel here."

"I was not thinking of the people of Scarsen; they knew before I went into town last night that you were no longer in the grove. But there is another people in the Blackwood. The Zonas. They have no towns, but live in groups that travel at will. And they do not like others moving through their hunting grounds."

"If you mean the wild people who dress only in skins, I have seen them here. They usually do not come so far east until later in the spring."

"I thought travel here was forbidden your people." There was humor in the voice as Pollo began preparing a meal from his pack supplies.

"It is. Our Council knows of these wild people, and there is some fear they would make war on Scarsen. So we hunt to the south and east. I come here alone. One man is no threat to a whole people."

"You have little liking for Scarsen's laws, it would seem."

"Perhaps. They are mostly laws of not doing, made by a fear of learning and growing. A cage for the people. And they know my feeling. Maybe that's why they found it so easy to take me to the grove." He smiled now; the grove was a thing of the past. He would remember it, but, like Scarsen, it was behind him, out of reach to the south.

"A quick execution would have served them as well," Pollo reminded before dropping the subject and returning to the Zonas. "Do they come here every year?"

"I believe so. But not always to the same place, and sometimes not so many as other times. I've wondered where they go when they are not in Blackwood."

"To the west, in summer, we think. In the cold season they probably go into the southern mountains where it is warmer. Maybe even as far as Warm Sea. But we don't know. We Delphans are more scholars than anything, collecting the knowledge and laws of

14

the different people. It's what we trade, by setting up schools in the towns to teach the children while we learn from them. We hope one day to know the whole history of man, and perhaps join all people in one law, sharing all knowledge. Of those we know, only the Zonas refuse to allow us to teach their children, or learn of them."

"Are you at war with them?"

"Hardly. We do not war. The problems between us are not so simple." Letting the fire burn down as they finished their meal, the Norther told of his people and how they moved among the people of other states, though they had their own town to the north, a place of research and study. Their reputation for knowledge and fairness had led to strong political involvement, with Delpha acting as mediator and sometimes judge in the disputes between states. Now, outside teaching and study, their activities were primarily diplomatic.

"For several seasons we have been involved in a dispute between the Beachers on the coast of Long Sea, and the Plainers, an inland people who raise the greater portion of the grains. Because the Beachers control the ports, all grain sold must go through their hands, and they set the price. They have become wealthy from it, and are gaining control in other areas, but the Plainers, who raise the crops, are unable to sell for a profit. They have asked us to arrange an agreement giving them access to the sea in trade to the Beachers for a route through Plains to West Range, where there are mines. It would be a good thing for both, and there would be less anger to breed violence. But the Beachers refuse. They have put out word that Delpha herself wishes treaty or union with the Plainers, and now they threaten to work a treaty with the Zonas."

DonEel listened, fascinated. He had heard, vaguely, of the teachers of Delpha, not knowing if it was a true tale. All his life had been bounded by the wild people to the north and west, and the people to the south-

15

east who were far away and, like the people of Scarsen, not given to travel or trade. "Would the Zonas treat?"

"A year ago I would have said no, but there have been changes. We cannot know what they have been told of us, but I believe they think Delpha is bidding for power, wanting to control not only the central lands and crops but the road north and south, and so into Blackwood."

"Couldn't you do as the Beachers have said and join with the Plainers?"

"Delpha does not treat. We cannot. We would lose everything we value and become one more like them. Besides, if we did, we would force the Beachers to the Zonas, and we would be cut off from all travel south of Plains. We think there are other people on the coast of Warm Sea, maybe even bordering the unknown lands to the west, but there is already difficulty getting to them."

"The Zonas?"

"In part, yes. And I would as soon get out of Blackwood before they know I am here and there is more trouble with them."

"They know of you, then?"

"Perhaps. But it would be enough for them to know anyone of Delpha was in their land. The Gods know what they would make of it, but it could mean trouble in our dealing with the Beachers. Word was sent south through Plains that I would travel at the end of the planting season, a month from now."

They were moving again at daybreak, leaving the narrow east-west ridges for the broader slope of the foothills, high above Scarsen and thickly wooded. Before midday they had passed the northernmost point of DonEel's solitary journeys from Scarsen, and he began to mark the land in his mind, noting there were no trails here save those made by animals.

At ease in the woods, he let his thoughts dwell on

16

his companion. Pollo of Delpha was not like the people of Scarsen. He called his people scholars, concerned with knowledge and the law, and that brought to mind Ronan and the student priests. But there was nothing of them in this man; he seemed free and unbound, more warrior than scholar. Perhaps he, too, felt at odds with his people. There were questions, but he could not ask them; he was too much indebted, and in Scarsen one did not pry into another's private affairs.

His own gratitude could not mask the mystery of the Delphan's coming near Scarsen on that particular day. He said he came south for his Council, but he had come farther than the task required, endangering himself, to reach the grove at Scarsen. He had postponed his task and risked failure of a mission that must be important, for his Council had put out false information to protect him. Had he come only because of a dream? Instinct said yes, that there was no hidden purpose in the man, but old habit controlled much of his thinking, and he wondered.

They stopped early, choosing to camp above the wooded valley that stretched north and east before them. Neither wanted to risk camping below, where a fire would mark them easily. In the last of the sun, the forest below looked more black than green, with accents of emerald and yellow-green where new-leafing oak and river trees marked watercourses on the slopes winding down to the silver ribbon of a river.

There was time here for leisure, and a creek provided a place to wash away the sweat and dust of their hurry. Alone at the water while Pollo struck a fire and began to prepare the now-familiar meal, Don-Eel used a trick of patience and cold hands to take a pair of wide-striped fish from the pool. They were fat and firm-fleshed, better always than fish in the lowland water that ran slow and quiet, a welcome addition to their meal and ease for his pride. Even neces-

17

sity and circumstance did not banish the fact that he was living on the Norther's charity.

As the fish, split and spitted on green boughs over the coals, began to swell and run juice on the way to doneness, DonEel touched on the things he had been thinking. "You risked much to come so far south because of a dream."

"Not only a dream." Spreading the sleep robes, Pollo glanced up, grinning. "Some might argue it, but even I have some understanding of duty. The start of the matter was when I was leaving Delpha. I was told to look for one, a prophet and dreamer from Blackwood, who would be of help to the people."

"To the people? Which people?"

"I didn't ask. Any people. Or all people. It is not the sort of question one asks Dioda. Besides, it is the way of Delpha to be of help to any people, if they can. Anyway, Dioda said all he could say. All he knew."

"Is this Dioda a priest?"

"No. A historian, for the most part. We do not have priests like your Ronan, with his sort of power over the people. We do have our religious scholars and teachers, of course, and more temples than you might believe." It pleased him to talk of Delpha, and while they ate, he told of its history and way of life.

Even before the city of Delpha was founded, according to the legends, the people had been scholars, moving from place to place seeking answers to their questions, and ways of doing and thinking. They collected and copied the ancient writings they found in almost every town. "You write and read," he pointed out. "You've probably read from the ancient works."

"Aye. There were some in the basement of the church building. No one bothers with them now, but once I took some of the pages." His blue eyes flashed with curious humor, remembering. "It won me a public whipping by Ronan himself. Then he asked that I be sent to him as student. Perhaps he thought to make

18

me one of the faithful and spare the town some trouble." Now, thinking of the writing he had stolen, he recalled where he had heard the man's name. The story had mentioned one very like it.

"Apollo, yes." The Delphan laughed, drawing his robe about him, preparing for sleep. "The scholars still argue if he was a god or a more than commonly beautiful man. It is said my mother liked the name, but changed it a little so it should not offend if he is truly a god."

Years of sleeping by choice in the open, alone and vulnerable, had developed a watchful sense in Don-Eel, something that warned of trouble even in sleep. He did not know what it was that wakened him, only that he was awake and alert, and something held him still. He lay with his head pillowed on one arm, letting his eyes move over the area he could see without moving, looking for something that could have wakened him. All three moons were overhead now, casting confusing shadows, creating shapes out of the imagination that would not be there in daylight. He let his eyes tell him only what was there, not really knowing what he saw, waiting. Something was near—he could feel it—but it took a moment. Twice his eyes noted the bulk of shadow and ignored it. Then, looking away, he caught a hint of movement on the edge of vision. He tensed, not looking at it, waiting for the shape to come to him in outline. It was moving, not much, but enough to become something other than the general pattern of light and shadow. It took on the form of an owl, but larger, triple the size, unless his idea of distance was off. It moved again, a sudden jerky hop toward the long shadow that was Pollo, lying asleep. A portion of the shadow-shape seemed to lengthen, to extend toward the sleeper—

"Pollo!" He barked the warning, already moving, reaching for the blade near his head. But there was nothing to use the weapon on. For a moment there

19

was movement and sound, then Pollo brushing against him, reaching for the hand that held the knife.

"DonEel! Wait—" There was urgency, not fear, in the voice, and his grip held the Souther long enough for him to realize that whatever the shape had been, it was gone. "Lie down and be still. It was Aree. He might not have gone far if we are lucky."

There was assurance in the whisper, and, wondering, DonEel let himself be pushed back onto his robe to lie quiet, senses keyed to the man moving away quickly beyond the dead fire. A low, melodic sound stirred the silence, sending an answering ripple across his shoulders before he realized the sound had come from Pollo, a summoning. If there was a reply, he didn't hear it, and the Delphan was gone into the shadow.

He dozed when the waiting became long, and knew when Pollo returned more by his own relaxation than any conscious thought. He slept deep then, but not long. Before first light, he was brought back from sleep by dreams of shadow-threat.

As the last moon set, signaling the pink blush of dawn in the east, he was up, building the fire, setting water to heat. To pass the time, he put a fine edge on his blade, and, squatting near the warmth of the fire, he scraped away the rough stubble on his face. Unlike most men of Scarsen, he had never worn a beard. Pollo lay quiet, sleeping soundly, one hand outstretched on the ground. Glancing at him, DonEel puzzled over the events of the night. What was it Pollo knew that he did not, and why had he not told him? It was one thing to know this as a land of danger to them both, but he could not be well prepared to defend even himself if he didn't know what else was here, and if it were friend or foe.

"There was no danger, DonEel."

The sudden voice startled him. "You knew what it was." There was a touch of accusation in his voice, and, hearing it, he was annoyed.

"Yes. Aree. Though how he knew where to find me is more than I can answer." Ignoring the accusation, he got up, stretching. Rubbing his face, he came to where DonEel still crouched by the fire. "You have a good blade." His hand reached out and for a moment the backs of his fingers brushed DonEel's shaven cheek. It was a casual touch, meaning nothing, but he stiffened and felt his face grow warm, the flash of confusion holding him still. In Scarsen, men did not so easily touch other men. Pollo did not mark the reaction, already testing the water to see if it was hot.

Leaving him to shave, DonEel retreated to the creek, which repeated its bounty of the previous night.

"About Aree," Pollo said, sprinkling coarse salt on the fillets. "He is a message bird of the east land, tamed by a friend. He came to bring word that we can slow our pace. There's a company of Afs moving up the river today. Jania, Aree's master, knew I would be somewhere near the Zona border, and he has asked us to join him."

"What was he?"

"Aree? A sort of owl, I think. Jania says there are many of his kind in the east land, as pets. The Afs make pets of everything."

Afs. DonEel had never heard of them. Either. How much had he missed of the world? And he wondered if Ronan or any of the others of Scarsen knew more of the world outside of Blackwood. He had a sense of being poised between cage and freedom, eager, because he had known as much as Scarsen that he did not belong. Eating and preparing to leave, he listened to Pollo's stories about the Afs, traders from across Long Sea who brought goods from all places, trading their way through the land when weather permitted.

"They are allowed to travel at will because they want nothing of land beyond their island homes. But they travel armed—they are wealthier than most.

21

Jania will be pleased to learn of Scarsen—he could send an envoy to open trade."

Privately, DonEel thought the Council and church would be less than pleased by contact with the outside world, but he said nothing.

They moved down to the valley floor while Pollo talked of the Afs, and it was clear he held them in a special regard. In spite of the differences, he said, there was much similarity between Delpha and the Afs. Neither took part in the complex politics of the other states, but each had become an important part of all in the impartial services rendered. Although lately even the Afs had been pulled into the dispute between the Beachers and Plainers, much as Delpha had. Wealthy as they were, they depended on the grain from Plains, and the Beachers controlled it. Also, as far as the Afs were concerned, there was a good market for the minerals taken from the mines in West Range. An open route, controlled by the Plainers and Beachers, would increase trade possibilities.

The ford was deserted when they reached the river, with no sign the Afs had crossed. And it was hot. Below the ridge, the trees seemed to catch and hold the spring sun. It was good to put off the packs and find shade among the close-grown willows near the water's edge. They lay against the packs, talking over the drowsy insect hum, their conversation wandering without direction until DonEel found himself talking about Scarsen and his life there.

"From the first, Ronan had great plans for me. He thought I would become a priest and follow him." He laughed shortly, but Pollo did not share his humor.

"A priest? By the Gods, I forgot. That's what Dioda said."

His excitement surprised DonEel, and he looked up, about to question him, but before he could speak, his eye caught movement beyond the soft green screen of brush. He hissed a warning, and Pollo went still, waiting, his back to the movement. DonEel's hand went to the knife lying between them. Before he could more than feel the leather sheath, the brush parted. For a moment, shock paralyzed him. A black mask, bearded and fierce, thrust into the opening, and brilliant black eyes fastened on him. He grasped the knife convulsively, would have gathered himself to attack in sheer animal instinct had not Pollo's hand flashed to his wrist, holding him with an unbreakable grip.

"Pollo." The mask spoke, came to life.

"Aye, Jania. You're late." The Delphan still gripped DonEel's hand, and his eyes gave warning as he rose from his position before releasing him.

Then they were out of the brush and Pollo's hands were clasped in hands as black as soot. Stunned and watchful, DonEel followed him, watched the big black man embrace him. Impossibly, the man was all black—or all that could be seen of him. Not until Pollo touched his shoulder did he realize he was staring like a fool. Then the hands he had not known he was extending were clasped in the black ones, and they were warm and real and as human as his own. And the black eyes were watching and laughing and dancing to Pollo as questions were asked. It was too much to take in. He put his attention on himself, gathering shattered control, breathing deep as he turned to watch the activity around them. All the men were dark of skin, though not all as dark as Jania, and they were setting up camp in a vivid swirl of noise and color.

Pollo's hand brought him back to himself. They were, the Delphan said, to gather their belongings from the willow grove and join Jania at his fire for supper.

DonEel appreciated the seclusion of the grove. He felt he had made a fool of himself and Pollo in his ignorance. He would have apologized, but Pollo cut him off.

"It was my mistake, DonEel. Forgive me."

He looked at his companion blankly. "Forgive you?"

"I did not mean for this to happen. My only excuse is that I have known him so long I do not think of his color. I should have told you."

It helped nothing that he should take the blame, and DonEel smiled somewhat ruefully. "Anyone else should have known, I think. I can see he is your friend. Thank the Gods you stayed my hand. I might have killed him out of fear."

"Not likely. He knew your intent before you touched the knife."

Suddenly DonEel understood his concern. Pollo had feared for him in those moments. Embarrassed, he busied himself with his pack. "Will he understand it was only surprise and ignorance in me?"

"Aye. But they will watch you awhile. Expect it. Jania and I have been fight-mates a long time, and he takes his duties seriously."

"Surely he does not think I would harm you?"

For a moment the words hung in the green air, and Pollo looked down at him, bright eyes still. Then he bent to his work, smiling slightly. "No," he said. "Surely not."

TWO

THEY did watch him, and even though he knew it was for Pollo's sake, it made him self-conscious. But his curiosity was as great as theirs, and he watched them also, holding back but listening close to their soft voices that changed speech so it lay easy on the ear and carried meanings beyond the sound of the words.

He stayed on the fringes of activity, watching and

watched, until smoke and the odor of roasting meat mingled with the dust in the thickening sunlight slanting down from West Range. Then Pollo came looking for him. They had been given quarters near Jania's large tent, and Jania expected them to share the meat cooked at his fire.

They ate well of roast venison and strange coarse bread and cheese, and there was a strong foamy ale, better than any made in Scarsen, that warmed and loosened him until he heard his own silliness and fell quiet again, listening to the talk around the fire. There was much he would have liked to ask Pollo, but he felt through the general gossip that the two friends had much to say, so he excused himself. The camp had quieted with dusk; the men gathered in groups about the fires. So, taking his flute, he moved down to the river seeking silence and privacy.

Sitting beside the curling water, he played softly without thought to what, if anything, he played, only liking the sound of the notes changed by water and darkness. There was something lonely in the sound that recalled him to himself, so he knew he played his own feelings. In the short time since his intended sacrifice, the world had become a different thing from what he had known before. He felt cast adrift and unsure, unable to see ahead. Scarsen had caged him; now he was anchorless, without purpose or people, save the stranger to whom he owed his life. And what did Pollo want of him? This was his world. Under the influence of the strong ale, he was tempted to pity himself, so he turned his attention away, seeking interest in the simple melody he cast across the water. It was a good melody, and he repeated it, adding and changing, but keeping true to the original.

Lost in thought, he remained there, playing and silent in turn, until the first moon rose. His thought returned to Pollo, and he felt his dependence on the man. It was not in his nature to be dependent, but he knew he could not deal with this new world without the companionship of the Delphan. He owed him for more than his life, and he wondered what Pollo must think of him. He imagined him sitting now with the black Jania by the dying fire, talking and laughing about his reaction to the black man. For a time that imaginary humiliation ran through his music, muted and minor-key, until—half-fearing it might be true— he fell silent.

It was some time before he realized he was not alone. Someone sat motionless on the bank to his left, close enough so the moonlight glittered from eyes brilliant in the dark, unbearded face. A youth, then; there were a few in camp. He stared, trying to see clearly, and his attention must have touched the other, for he moved restlessly and finally spoke, his voice no less clear through the silver air than the voice of the flute. "Your song was meant for solitude, DonEel of Erl. I beg forgiveness for intruding without leave, but it is said that sharing the heart through music is a gift of the Gods and one must attend. I thank you for it. I, too, am far from home."

The music of the voice ceased, and in another moment the figure had risen, graceful as a dancing girl, and gone into the shadow. As well, for DonEel had no words of his own. He was touched by the feeling, but he could not have said so.

"I did not suspect you played so well."

The familiar voice, softer, touched by something he could not believe was his music, startled him, turned him quickly. Pollo, half-silver, half-shadow, stood behind him, though he had not heard him approach. It occurred to him as he looked up into the still and pensive face that the Norther had been there for some time, listening. Then Pollo stepped forward and offered his hand to help him up.

"I didn't know you were there," he said, trying to put distance between himself and the knowledge that Pollo had been listening. He could feel a mood on the other, a quietness and thinking, and he wondered if he had somehow brought trouble.

But Pollo's thought ranged far beyond their companionship and its responsibilities. "Jania has news of the east," he said as they walked back to camp. "Somehow word of my coming south early reached the Beachers. They are saying I came to work a treaty with the Plainers in secret. They have closed our schools there, and our people are leaving. It is foolishness. They oppose us for no reason. They have never been friendly, but they have always valued knowledge. Now Jania tells me there is fear among the people that Delpha works to control all the states and their wealth. Maybe because it's what they would do if they could."

Much of what he said meant nothing to DonEel, but he couldn't help pointing out that Delpha had sent false information about his trip south. "Whatever the reason for it, it gives weight to what the Beachers say. It looks as if Delpha has something to hide."

"But it has nothing to do with them." Pollo spoke sharply, then relented and touched his shoulder. "Forgive me, my friend. You are right, of course. But it seemed a wise thing at the time, for my safety. We are seekers after knowledge, first, and the thing I came for is only that. Proof, perhaps, of something we think true. If it is, it could be a means of power for some. The Beachers want power, and with enough, they would upset the peace between all states. They do not yet understand that they are dependent on the others. If there is truth in what we think, then all should share equally, and through Delpha, all will." He pulled back the flap of the tent, and for a moment light spilled across his face, showing lines of worry that had not been there before. Then he grinned and was young again. "Maybe this is a good thing for Delpha. The Council should remember that it can make mistakes like the others."

There were cots for them, and sleep came quickly

27

to DonEel, carrying him into the depths where a dream waited, and it seemed he traveled yet with Pollo, but the land was like none he had seen, for all it was wooded and wild. There was a path, clear and well-traveled, but they were alone and silent, hurrying toward their goal, a goal he had forgotten, or did not yet know beyond its importance to them.

"DonEel of Erl."

The dream voice came from behind, and he turned, surprised, to see an old man robed in white from neck to ankle. The face was closed and stern below hair as white as the robe. DonEel did not like him. "I must go."

"You must turn back. You cannot follow Pollo; you do not know his path. You must go your own way."

The voice angered him, and he stayed to argue, though he could feel that Pollo had gone on as though he did not know of the old man. "He has asked me. I am in his debt, and he must not go alone."

"All men travel their paths alone, DonEel. You can see he does not need you." A long arm extended, and he turned to look. Pollo was far up the path now, and a mist thickened through the trees, dimming sight. But he could tell Pollo had changed. He no longer wore the dark woods clothing, but a short tunic of white that reached to his knees, clasped at one shoulder and leaving the other bare. Somehow this was right, and he was not surprised, but the mist worried him. There was a bend in the path, and he knew Pollo would soon be out of his sight.

"Go back while you can; you cannot go with him." The cold face seemed to take a sort of pleasure in that fact, and for a moment it seemed to DonEel that he truly could not go, his feet refusing to take him away from the old man.

"I must go. He has heard my music." The idiocy of that remark shamed him, as though he should not have admitted it, and the old man frowned.

"As you wish, then. I have warned you." He turned

28

and walked back along the trail, and mist was so thick about them he seemed to disappear, white melting into white. The mist closed in solidly; yet there was no feeling of moisture or chill. He turned and could not see the trail; even the trees were lost. He began to walk forward, feeling for the path with his feet, knowing he must find Pollo. He stumbled, trying to hurry. He called, but the mist drank his voice like fleece, so he called again, louder, and this time, on the edge of hearing, it seemed he heard a laugh as cold as the face of the old man who had stopped him. It had been a trick, a way to separate them, and there was danger, not only to himself but for Pollo. Real and deadly danger. "Pollo!" For a moment, the mist thinned and he saw the familiar figure far ahead, not pausing but striding on purposefully. He must hear; he must! He began to run as the mist closed in, stumbling against unseen rock and dead limbs, brushing against trees as he lost the path. "Pollo, wait!" he called, breathless. "I must go with you. There is danger!" He was lost, and the blood pounding in his ears sounded like cold and distant laughter.

"What is it?" Familiar voice, close, and strong hands staying his arms. "DonEel—"

Stranded in the dream, yet waking, he looked up through moon-shattered darkness. "Pollo." Panting from the dream run, sweating, he could not put down the urgency. "You must not go alone. Let me come with you."

"Of course you shall come with me." The mooncast face smiled. "It was a dream."

"A dream. Yes." He repeated it, breathing in the silver heavy air through a dry mouth as Pollo released him and stood up. "I'm sorry. Someone was trying to—" He let it drop, not knowing how to explain, and sat up, knowing movement would dispel the last traces of the dream and return him to sanity.

"It's too early to get up." Pollo returned to his cot.

"Go back to sleep." And later, when they were wrapped in their sleep robes and warm again, "DonEel?"

"Yes."

"If you choose to come with me, do so because it pleases you, not out of debt. I want nothing owed between us."

The words took him by surprise, and he lay silent, thinking of replies he might make and discarding them until sleep came and he forgot.

One of the younger Afs brought hot water at first light, and an invitation to join Jania when they were ready. Clothing was provided from the caravan stores, and their own travel-stained garments taken to be cleaned at the river. It was a generous gesture, but in DonEel's opinion the Af costume was too colorful and fine for woods traveling. Pollo laughed at his protest, remarking that with his dark hair and fair skin he should wear colors more often. "Besides," he added, "now we are less conspicuous."

"Certainly," DonEel agreed, looking down at himself, then at Pollo's brilliant hair. "No one would suspect we are not Afs, like the others."

This brought more laughter from the Delphan, who clapped him on the shoulder, half-pushing him from the tent. "Come, Jania is waiting."

The camp was astir about them, subdued still by the chill river mist lying above the ground, and there was a good fire and hot food waiting in front of Jania's tent, where they were greeted with grins and salutes. While they ate, Jania told them they would be spending another day and night at the ford. They had not taken time to collect proper stores before leaving the Beachers, having heard Pollo was in the south and wanting to catch up with him before their paths separated.

Around other fires, the hunt teams were being selected by lot, and DonEel was invited to join, but he declined. His way of hunting was solitary and certainly quieter than the voluble Afs'. Instead, he wandered about the camp, leaving Jania and Pollo to talk.

With a day off, the Afs didn't rest. There were animals to be fed and groomed, and DonEel found his way to the makeshift pens. They were strange beasts to his eye, smaller and somehow rounder than the horses of Scarsen that were used for plowing and drawing the heavy wagons. The men caring for them were friendly, laughing and storying, and they took him into their company as readily as one of their own. He asked about the animals and was told that they were mules, offspring of mares and asses, hybrids that did not reproduce and so were valuable for use as pack animals. The thought of breeding unlike animals was a strange one, and DonEel wondered to himself about the value of animals unable to reproduce their own kind.

The morning passed quickly for him with so many willing to talk, and it was well past noon when Pollo found him watching a game of chance in which the number of sticks to fall crossed was guessed.

"Jania is asking for you, my friend." The tone and face were sober, but there was a suspicious glint in the bright eyes that made DonEel pause. "Come, DonEel. He is our host, and he did not say why." The hand on his back was reason enough to obey, and, shrugging, he did so.

"DonEel of Erl," Jania greeted him, loudly enough to catch the attention of a dozen or so men standing before the tent, and they gathered about as he stepped forward.

"You wished to see me?"

"Yes. My son claims he owes you a debt."

DonEel shook his head. No one here owed but himself. "What could he owe me?"

"For a sharing. He asks the privilege of settling."

This made no sense, and he glanced at Pollo for a clue, but the Delphan only grinned and remained silent. Hearing no protest, Jania gestured, and a beardless youth came forward with a flat box. Something in the way he moved was familiar to DonEel, but it was not until he spoke that he remembered where they had met.

"DonEel of Erl, as I took from you unasked and on my own, I beg you allow me payment. Will you accept?"

It was the boy who had listened to his flute on the riverbank. "You owe me nothing" was all he could think to say.

"I am richer for it, and so the debt is made. I would settle this between us."

"As you will. The gain is surely mine." The seriousness of the boy's face eased, and DonEel thought he had done wisely. Bowing, the boy held out the flat box, and as DonEel took it, he flashed a startlingly white smile. That was all there was to it.

Turning away, he noticed a commotion up the river from camp and a man dressed for the hunt coming at a run for Jania's tent.

"Wait for me in the tent," Pollo said quickly, moving to join Jania. He went, feeling the beginnings of unidentified threat in the tightness of his belly. Something was happening, and he was involved.

Alone in the blue dusk of the tent, he opened the box. Surprise held him for a minute. It was a knife, and beautiful, somehow like none he had ever seen. The blade was perfection—like new-forged metal it glowed cool in the close warmth—and the handle was the honey of well-polished horn, chased with some exquisite metal that could have been, but surely was not, gold. It was the shape and beauty of deadly purpose.

Meaning to test the balance and weight, he lifted it from the box. It fit his hand perfectly, and the finely etched design, almost unnoticeable on the hilt, was comfortable. It would not slip easily in palm wet with sweat or blood. The blade flashed blue-silver against his eyes, and staring at the weapon and his own hand holding it, he had a sudden confused sense of dislocation, a vertigo that set him down on the cot unawares. He felt split, staring, breathing quick and shallow, trying to follow the feeling, to fit together the knowledge that what he held was long familiar and returned to him with strange memories of nonsense and time that scrabbled for hold in his brain, against the absolute assurance that both hand and blade in his sight were alien, some utterly unexplainable combination apart from the man whose arm owned the hand. Even the feeling itself was dual, both familiar and unfamiliar.

"DonEel?"

Startled, almost guiltily, he jumped and dropped the knife. Pollo stood in the tent with him. "You heard, then?"

"Heard?" He bent to retrieve the knife, feeling his heartbeat.

"About the attack." Pollo moved closer, looking. "Are you all right? You look pale."

"It's nothing. What attack?"

"On the hunters. Two, at least, were killed. Others wounded. The Zonas ambushed them. For no reason. They have attacked the caravan before, seeking goods. But never the hunters. There was some thought that you, being from Blackwood—" He sat down on the other cot, leaning toward DonEel. "What's the matter with you? Are you ill?"

"No." The feeling had passed, and memory of it felt slippery. He shrugged it off, still holding the knife. "What of my being from Blackwood?"

Pollo told what he knew, that the hunting teams had been attacked without warning, though always before, the Afs had been allowed to hunt here when they traveled the shorter southern road inland from the Beachers. Happening now, it was natural that some suspicion should turn to DonEel; he was unknown and from the almost mythical Blackwood.

"Jania does not credit the idea. He sent this as

33

assurance of his trust." It was a leather sheath for the knife, finely made and worked with brass rivets along the side where a sharp blade often parted regular stitching.

DonEel took it, knowing it had been made for the gift knife, and the thought came to him that the knife was older, that the bright blade itself had flayed the hide. A swift, romantic thought that pleased him beneath the concern Pollo brought. Then it passed as a voice outside called to the Delphan.

They followed Jania's son through the press of men to Jania. There was another with him, and he was wounded—it showed in his eyes and the peculiar ashen pallor beneath the dark skin. There was blood, dark and drying on the sleeve of his tunic above the elbow, and he clasped the place of injury as he talked. It struck DonEel that the wound must be only in the flesh of the upper arm and not severe; yet the man was obviously in great pain and ill. He watched closely, aware of the suspicion against him, but was unnoticed. When the man was done speaking, some-one began to pull off the soiled tunic, probably one skilled in tending wounds, and Jania turned away, began issuing orders to break camp.

"There is more to the attack than you said," DonEel guessed when Pollo came from Jania's side.

"Aye. Mesal says it was not Zonas alone that attacked, that there were Nomen with them. And the wound bears him out. It does not appear serious, but already he is showing fever, and the arm has begun to swell and blacken. Come, we must pack." It did not occur to the Norther that DonEel did not understand what he had said of the attack; he was surprised when he questioned him.

"The Nomen. You don't know of them? No, maybe you wouldn't. But I'd wager your old priest Ronan does. They are animals that think and reason, or so we believe. They are not like Truemen, and they hate us. They are said to live high on West Range, and

34

they do not deal with Truemen except to kill those they meet."

DonEel worked silently, listening. Except for Pollo's concern, he was tempted to think the story fable. Another mystery unknown in secluded Scarsen. "What is it about the wound?" he asked when he remembered.

"There is something in the way they treat their weapons, a poison that enters the body and kills, though the wound be no more than a break in the skin." His mouth was tight as he spoke, and there was a fierceness in him DonEel could feel that was not like the man he knew.

For all their numbers and equipment, the Afs were mobile. The camp disappeared quickly, and the animals were packed and moving. The river was forded with a minimum of confusion, and DonEel's respect for the dark people grew. There was no panic; they were simply going about their business. Accepted as part of the caravan, both men took their share of the work, and DonEel noted the placement of the men gave protection to the animals carrying supplies and trade goods. Jania and his son, Tarhel, led the way, setting a quick pace as they left the river.

The rest of the hunting party rejoined them at dusk, with little meat. They had been too busy trying to return unseen to hunt. When they met with Jania, DonEel and Pollo were asked to join them, and listening to the soft melody of their speech, DonEel revised his opinion of the dark people. For all the grief they felt for their lost comrades, they had enjoyed the conflict and danger. They reported all they had seen and heard, and their tales mentioned the Nomen. But there was no reason for the ambush.

"Perhaps the hunters came on them before they could attack the camp," DonEel suggested.

Jania thought it through, then shook his head. "The time to attack was when we reached the river. Or at dawn. They knew where we were; they always know."

For a moment his eyes touched the light-skinned men, but he said nothing of the thought that brought the look, only turned to his son and gave orders that they would move on through the night. "They know us, and experience has told them we are not easily attacked on the march." Teeth flashed as he grinned and resettled his broad belt. "So we march."

The caravan moved from the low river meadows into woods so thick the trail was a tunnel where overhanging branches wove into a roof shutting out the sky and giving strange form to the shadows. Shortly after second moonrise, DonEel felt the watchers pacing them beyond the trail. It was a feeling he didn't like, not being able to see them. His back tensed against unknown weapons, and his hearing strained but told him nothing. The animals felt them, too, crowding closer together. Adding to the tension, a low moaning sounded from the center of the troop. Mesal. The fever had invaded his brain, and he was no longer aware of the need for silence.

As quietly as they moved, there were too many for silence, sounds of metal touching, of footsteps; even breathing, hurried by movement and tension, interfered with the sounds of the dark beyond the trail. DonEel felt muffled and enclosed, yet at the same time exposed to the threat he could feel moving with them. Alone, he would have moved unencumbered through the shadowed woods, not target but hunter, more lethal in his solitude. Here, penned by watchful eyes and the rising fever cries of the wounded man, he paced beside the nervous mules, trying to hear beyond, to know the position of the threat carried on the air. This drawing together for safety and comfort was not his way.

"DonEel." Faint as breath, the sound came to him, and some small tension in him eased. Unseen, Pollo had come back from the group near Jania. "I doubt they will attack an alert caravan."

"They are here. Beside us."

"You're sure?"

He felt Pollo half-turn to scan the darkness around them, and limited his reply to a nod. Mesal, carried now on a litter in the midst of the troop, whined like a rabbit, shrill and full of pain, and DonEel's back rippled. The man was dying—it was there in the sound—and knowing it made him angry. It was such a small wound. A man should not die of so simple a thing. He thought of the dart that might have caused it and felt more vulnerable.

The dark hours were long, pulling him tight with the need to keep alert, to be aware of things just beyond the trail, invisible and soundless. His thoughts became woven around the shrill sounds from Mesal, the warm sweet-acrid smell of the animals, the movement of the Afs and Pollo near him. He wanted to be free of it, to move at his own whim, but he dare not leave the trail. He was already suspect in some minds, and Pollo would surely follow.

When they decided, they came quickly. There was one clear instant of knowing, of feeling the tense peace about to break. "Pollo!" He hissed one warning, grasped the still-hesitant shoulder, and moved instinctively to place the animals between them and the attack. A man behind them cried out, then was silent. It was warning to them all.

"Arms!" Jania's voice, commanding, rang out, and there was no other voice. There may have been some sort of order to the defense; DonEel did not know. He sensed-felt the swift rush, the closing in of movement. They came from both sides, dropping among the animals. There was confusion and a sudden fear of who— Then his nose brought him the smell of them, and he could tell friend from foe.

In the milling press of men and animals, there was little enough he could do. Once a strong grip caught at his shoulder and he reached out to snare tough leather. The gift blade felt good to his hand, and the solid shock of striking with it pleased his arm. The

37

weight fell away, and he ignored it, turning to keep his back to Pollo. There were other hands and rushes, but the main focus of the conflict was away from him, sound and movement in darkness.

It ended abruptly, a shrill, whistling signal, and the attackers melted back into the dark and were gone. There was no attempt to follow. It was the Afs' way to stand firm and defend the whole of the caravan. In a moment, Jania's voice came back to them, calling for names. In quick order, the names sounded.

"Three lost," the Delphan said quietly as the Afs searched for the silent. DonEel felt new respect for the Afs. Discipline and pride were strong weapons. Not one had run.

The word came to march, and it was as though the attack had never come. Oddly, Mesal lived still, and his sounds stirred the troubled shadows like death wings. He died finally just at first light, and DonEel was profoundly grateful. Jania called a halt as dawn brought light enough to see the trail and some little way into the forest. They buried the dead quickly and then were moving again.

With light, the need for hurry evaporated. DonEel could feel the release of tension and knew the caravan was alone, and he was content to move with the others.

THREE

MIDDAY found the caravan at the second river crossing. The land had changed again, running in a long, broken slope to the east where there was a sound of fast water and falls. To the north there was a slight rise above the river leading to the long plateau along the flank of West Range. They had passed beyond the land of the Zonas and that forest called Blackwood, and there was evidence here of regular travel across the shallows. They were safe here and could take time to rest and tend their wounds.

The Afs pitched camp and were soon moving by twos and threes to the river above the ford. About to join them, DonEel saw they were discarding their clothing entirely before entering the river. Embarrassed, he held back. For all the distance traveled, he was a man of Scarsen, and the law that had governed his life was yet a part of him. Nudity was forbidden, a mark of shame. Criminals were stripped before the people to humiliate them. Even understanding that these people did not live by those laws could not remove his feelings.

"DonEel! I was waiting for you. Come to the river with me." Pollo's voice caught him unprepared. "You do swim?" Golden eyes, too direct and offering to understand anything, held him, and there was no way he could explain.

"Yes," he said after a minute, "I swim."

He had, like most of the youths of Scarsen, indulged his interest in nudity. But he was no longer a child. He envied Pollo's easy manner and tried to copy it, but he felt obvious and awkward until safely in the water.

Among the Afs, laughing and splashing one another, he felt that he and Pollo were the only ones exposed. Somehow the dark-velvet skins were a different thing from his own white nakedness. The water deepened into a long pool toward the ford, and he struck out, swimming strongly, feeling the water slide cool and clean against his skin.

Seeing him leave the group, Pollo followed, laughing as he caught up where they could touch bottom. "You do indeed swim. I shouldn't want to race you."

"You flatter me. Swimming is not considered a necessary skill in Scarsen, but it's good to know when a child falls in the river."

"I would imagine. In Delpha we learn young to

39

love the water. There are even heated pools for winter use." He swept dripping copper hair from his eyes and became more serious. "We leave the Afs in the morning, just beyond the ford. They must take the east road. Jania has offered us an escort to Loos."

"To protect us?"

"Aye. He does not understand the attack, but our being with them might have had to do with it. He thinks we would be too vulnerable alone."

"We were alone before, and in the Zonas' land. They must have known we were there. Maybe it was not the Zonas that pressed the attack."

"You mean the Nomen. But it isn't like them to join with any Truemen." He squinted up toward the heights of West Range, splashing water over his sun-hot shoulders. "I would rather think it was a mistake of seeing in the heat of battle. As for Mesal's wound, it is possible the Zonas have learned some of the Nomen art. They're closer to them than any other people. And there were none but Zonas at us last night, and only clean weapons."

The hot sun and cool water flowing about him relaxed DonEel, and he thought of the people called Nomen. It was strange that those of Scarsen knew nothing about them.

"No one knows them, really. They avoid the lands of Truemen. We know only what we have seen exploring, or what others have told. The companies that go up to work the mines in season have made contact and battle. It is said there are many kinds—not like man but formed like beasts, with furred bodies, or feathered, maybe even scaled. But they have common speech and they build weapons. If they have homes or towns, they must lie beyond the mountains."

"But they aren't beasts."

"They look to be. I saw one. Alive. A female captured by a party of Beachers at the mines. They killed her, of course. She was nearly dead when I saw her. I'm not sure I'd like to see another. There is

40

something in them that is like us, but changed and made evil. Like the ogres in children's tales." He grinned at his admission of dislike, and his hands cast diamonds through the air as he splashed water over his shoulders, then turned quickly, laughing, to splash DonEel. "Come, Jania will want to talk of Scarsen before we part." He struck off across the pool, and DonEel followed.

Interest in Pollo's talk had all but obliterated his self-consciousness, and it was the Delphan who recalled it to him, hesitating in the water as he came up. "DonEel, had I known this would trouble you, I would not have asked. For us, it is a thing done without thought."

"I hoped it wouldn't show. I guess I have much to learn before I leave Scarsen entirely."

"So it is your choice, DonEel, and not done against your nature. Our way is ours, but not necessarily the best or only way. Each man lives his own law in himself." His ready grin flashed as they dried themselves before dressing. "We are taught young to exercise our freedoms, and sometimes we forget they apply differently to others."

The afternoon was a time for talking and rest. As Pollo had said, Jania was interested in Scarsen. It was not often now he learned of a new people. And there was talk of other places the Afs had gone, and people who lived in ways DonEel had never imagined.

By nightfall all preparation had been made for their journey. The Afs supplied them with the dried trail rations he had first tasted in the cave outside Scarsen, and their clothing was returned, cleaned and mended. Pollo refused the offer of escort, and DonEel was glad Jania didn't insist.

It was good to be moving alone after the busy company, setting their own pace on the road to Loos. They traveled quickly again, mindful of Jania's concern, and by nightfall the land had begun dropping

41

down toward the inland plain. After meeting the Afs, DonEel was curious about the town that was their goal. Pollo told him the people of Loos were simple folk, not given to pleasure, like the Afs. Theirs was a life molded by work in the fields and the seasons. DonEel drifted to sleep imagining a town not too different from Scarsen.

They came out of the forest at dawn, and the land lay below them, flat and open. A world of black earth beginning to steam in the early sun, stretching away into blue and misty distance. It made him uneasy. He was used to seeing the sky through the high branches of Blackwood, and feeling mountains surrounding him, enclosing vision. Here was naked emptiness.

Perhaps Pollo sensed his uneasiness or also felt exposed. He shifted his pack to a more comfortable position and walked closer, so they could talk quietly.

The land, he said, was not so flat and empty as it looked from here, but lay in broad steps, this being the highest and so last planted. "Loos is down on the next plain. When the mist is gone you can see the mountains to the west and north, and the trees planted to protect the crops from the big winds they have in the summer. In a month this will be green and growing and easier for travel."

The road was straight and empty, with nothing to ease the eyes until the distant mountains appeared like dreams through the thinning mist. He would have turned to see the green of the forest they had quitted, but Pollo did not look back, so he continued forward, listening with half an ear, wondering about the people and where they were, wondering if the Zonas had followed them from the last ford and were even now watching from the shadows of the big trees.

The edge of the plateau came suddenly, and he realized he had been lost in his own thoughts, withdrawn from the monotony of the land, for a long time. They stood at the top of a long slope a hundred feet above the next level, and water flashed silver strips back to the lifting sun. The road turned east along the face of the slope, and the ground here was hidden in a mat of shrubbery already green with new growth, giving off an herby fragrance as the dew dried.

Loos was a disappointment. There was no protective wall or fence, only a collection of low white buildings crowded together as though threatened by the emptiness about them. The small shade came from fruit trees beginning to blossom. There were cattle and draft animals everywhere, in house yards, in corrals, walking untended through the streets, but there were few people about.

"This is planting time," Pollo explained. "All the people who can work are out in the fields. Some of them travel a full day's journey to the planting and do not return until the crops are in. Then it takes a great number of people to keep the water flowing where it should."

The children and the occasional adult they met as they entered the narrow road between corrals eyed them without curiosity, merely seeing them.

There were shops, of course, those of leatherworkers and smiths, and at least one where honey-sweetened baked goods were sold. DonEel was struck by the dullness of their work. He had supposed Scarsen a poor place after talking with the Afs, but there, at least, the craftsmen worked in color and design, for all the fabric was rough. And the metalsmiths adorned even the plows with their ornate mark to show pride in their work. Here was mere utility; the wares were as simple and undecorated as the people.

Pollo stopped to talk to a man near a large building smelling of horses, and DonEel stood a way off, listening to their voices. The Plainer's words were slow and deliberate, with many pauses. As dull as the town. Recalling the music of Af speech, he wondered how he had sounded to them, and he missed their clamorous, happy company.

"We have mounts for the journey north." Pollo interrupted his thoughts. "It is an agreement Delpha has with most towns. Loos may lack many things, but not horses or cattle."

"They look a sad people."

"They are poor and bound to their work. The Beachers could do much to change this if they would. Of course, not all Plainer towns are like this."

Pollo's goal, the school of Delpha, was near the center of the town. The trees were larger here, giving shade to the central courtyard, and a high, thick wall shut out the clutter and sadness while holding in the peace and clean simplicity. They were met at the gate by a youth in a long white tunic, who led them to a small garden before asking their mission.

"I would see the master of the school. It is a matter of Delpha."

To DonEel, the request had the ring of formality. The youth bowed and directed them to a small building—a private apartment, DonEel supposed. "Rest here, I will see if the master may be disturbed."

Left alone, the two men looked about the room. It seemed almost familiar to DonEel, like the room in which he had studied with the priest Ronan, but more cluttered. There were shelves along the white walls piled with books and rocks and odds and ends, even bones. Maps were hung on the walls or lying half-rolled on the long table along with bottles and boxes. One such box, beautifully carved, caught his eye, and he picked it up. Inside, lying on dark, soft cloth, was a large honey-brown stone with flashes of red and green and gold moving in its depths. Cut and polished to perfection, it was framed in a web of red-gold clasped to a heavy, intricately worked chain of some length. He was tempted to take it up and feel the weight of it, but before he could, the outer door opened.

"Nephew." The voice broke the spell of the pendant, and DonEel turned to confront another mystery, nape hairs stirring. "I expected you days ago. And

44

alone." The voice rang familiar against DonEel's hearing as Pollo stepped forward to greet the white-robed man.

"I am here now, Uncle. With my companion, DonEel of Erl." And turning to present him, Pollo said, "DonEel, my uncle, Kylee of Delpha."

The look in the eyes was unfriendly challenge, though the straight mouth curved in a smile. "Not of Delpha, I see."

"No." He held voice and face carefully free of the tension and illogical anger growing in him. He knew this man. He had met him before, in a dream. He almost expected to hear that chill voice again command him to leave Pollo. He fought the feeling, familiar from other dreams and times. But he did not like Kylee any more than the old Delphan liked him. And the feeling between them was near the surface.

He caught Pollo's eyes on him, frowning, but he could do no more to help it than turn away.

The awkward moment passed somehow, and there was an offer of food and the exchange of news, edited by Pollo for reasons of his own. No mention was made of Scarsen or his manner of meeting DonEel, and the talk went on to the trouble between the Beachers and Plainers, leaving DonEel to sit silent, watching Kylee. And wondering.

The meal, brought by the youth who had met them at the gate, was simple: cheese and bread and dried fruit, it being too early for fresh. Good food, in quantity, with sweet, cold milk. Kylee seemed to regain his good humor as they ate, trying to draw the Souther into conversation, but Pollo had not mentioned Scarsen and DonEel was guarded. There was not much to talk about until Kylee mentioned the jewel-stone DonEel had been looking at when he came in. Pollo had not seen it, and Kylee got the box, holding up the stone on its chain so the light struck through it.

"Where did it come from, Kylee? Not here, surely."

"It was traded for a cow. I doubt it has real value, but the workmanship is interesting. I have heard a man from Plains, a mineworker, made it. If so, we may be able to establish a new trade article." He laid the stone back in the box, changing the subject. "There is room here at the school, should you wish to spend the night."

"Thank you, Kylee. But as you said, we are late. The Council will be anxious. And I have already secured mounts. We must leave within the hour. We could use provisions, if they are available."

"As you will. Calm will see to it. I had hoped you might speak with the Lord Mayor Gail. He is anxious about our Council's position with the Beachers. But I know your time grows short." Somehow the cold eyes seemed to blame DonEel for that, and many other things. "Will you travel together to Delpha?"

"We travel together." Pollo's voice was pleasant, but the smile he turned on DonEel was betrayed by a shadow in his bright eyes, and a question he could not ask there.

The reason for Pollo's journey south was brought from another room, a flat package well wrapped in cloth and oiled skin to protect it from moisture. There was also a letter from Kylee to the Council of Delpha giving his assessment of the package, but there was no conversation about it, and DonEel wondered if his presence prevented an open exchange between them.

As promised, their mounts waited outside the school, saddled and eager to be away. DonEel looked at them dubiously. He had ridden in Scarsen, but there the horses were big, heavy-boned animals, used more for pulling and plowing. Still, he was as eager to go from here as they, and he supposed it would be faster to ride than walk.

"It's been awhile," Pollo laughed, seeing DonEel's hesitation. "I'll wager we have regrets tomorrow."

With sleep robes and provisions tied behind the saddles, there was no reason to delay. The horses moved into a steady lope without urging, and soon they were beyond the dusty little town, riding through fields shadowed with new green. When the animals got the impatience worked out of them, it was pleasant to ride side by side with an opportunity to talk.

Pollo brought up the subject of Kylee, showing he had been aware of the mutual dislike. "I apologize for him, DonEel. He is known as a cold man and not easily friendly. He has no children of his own, and being my father's brother, he often watched over me when I was little. He still worries about me."

"He does not want me to go with you." It was not the meeting at the school that spoke, but the dream, though he had not planned it. Pollo laughed off the idea, checking the thongs that held his pack, but DonEel turned to look back toward Loos, and his dark brows drew into a frown. Perhaps it had been only a dream, but it rang in his memory now like a warning. He was glad to be away from the school, and it came to him that leaving might have been less easy if they had spent the night there.

They rode through plowed land, sweating in the damp heat, heading for the upper road where there were trees for shade and the unplowed land was easier for travel. Clouds built above West Range, billowed high, and began to drift heavily down the slopes. The air grew heavier and hotter, and the horses were content to pace steadily, tails switching.

The storm broke as they reached the road cutting north along the ridge. Rain came suddenly with quick flashes of lightning and rolling thunder. It was cooling, and they rode through it, heads down, content with their own thoughts until it drifted beyond them to the east, leaving the sunlight crisp and pleasing. A soft wind stirred the heavy air, chasing the clouds, and as the sun slid to the peaks of West Range, it drew a vivid double bow across the eastern horizon where rain still fell in curtains, making the land more beautiful than DonEel had thought it could be.

They were glad to halt at sunset near a spring, their muscles stiff and tired. But they had covered a lot of ground, and Pollo thought they could make it to Delpha in less than two weeks with luck and if the weather held. The farther north they went, the cooler it would be. Now the pleasant sleep came quick and deep.

The horses gave warning, stamping and snorting, bringing DonEel quickly awake to moon-splashed darkness. He lay quiet, listening, seeking some clue. But there was nothing, only the feel that they were not alone, and the restlessness of the animals. He sat up after a minute, searching the shadows. The horses, calm again, watched him in turn, and an arm's reach away, Pollo was sleeping undisturbed, one arm across his eyes as if to shield them from the bright moons. Knife beneath his hand, DonEel listened and watched until he had to fight off sleep, but there were no further sounds, only the occasional shifting of the horses.

Dawn brought birds to wake them, and substance to DonEel's suspicion that they had been visited during the night. Bending to wash in the cold spring, he saw a footprint, neither bare nor booted, as he and Pollo were, and smaller than either of them could have made. He called the Delphan, pointing to the track, and told him of the night's disturbance.

"Were we south of Plains, I would guess it to be Zona-made. They wear a soft boot sewn to fit the foot. Perhaps some of the Plainers have taken the style." He shook his head at DonEel's suggestion the Zonas could have come so far north. In spite of the rumors connecting them with the Beachers, the Zonas were not welcome in the more settled lands. And the Plainers dealt harshly with those who trespassed their lands without leave of their Council. The land was all they had, and they protected it.

They were mounted and riding north again as the sun lifted above the mist-shrouded horizon. Days of riding lay ahead, but now the road was above the tilled fields where they could ride in comfort looking over Plains, seeing an occasional town in the distance or people working—sowing or plowing with the large plows pulled by oxen. No one shared the road but a few Plainers come up to see to the irrigation canals. It was yet early for travel, but Pollo said the road would be busy when the first crops were ready for harvest. He was familiar with the land and full of stories about the people and teachers here from Delpha who lived in the towns they passed.

It was a good journey, and they forgot the silent visitor of the first night out from Loos. They rode side by side, talking, sometimes laughing, kicking the eager horses into a run through cool dawns. And at night there was the fire and peace and not having to move. Their goal lay days in the future, and there was nothing to press them but their own will and desire.

This was a freedom Scarsen had never allowed her people, and DonEel reflected occasionally on his pleasure, thanking his unnamed fate for the strange circumstances that had brought the Delphan south. This was what his spirit had hungered for unaware, this companionship, and he was alive and strong with a world to see and touch and know.

They left Plains on the sixth day, the road climbing onto a shoulder of the mountain thrusting out to the east from West Range, bounding the flat and fertile land. It grew steep and rocky, a barren land, raw and broken, supporting little life. The road had been carved in places from the rock itself, and Pollo said that though no one claimed the land, Delpha had convinced the Plainers and the Shepherds to the north that it was in their own interest to keep the road in good repair. The only other route to the north lay far east, through land claimed by the coastal people such as the Beachers.

"Beyond that ridge is a special place," Pollo said at

49

midday, pointing to where the road curved above them. "It is known and loved by all who travel this road. It pleases me to be the one to show it to you for the first time. We call it Beauty."

They topped the ridge, sweating in the fierce sun, and DonEel understood the name. Below them, in a deep circular hollow, lay a garden of trees and flowering shrubs about a green, oval pool. Two springs rose in the rocks above it, one steaming gently in the hot sun, and they flowed together, striking sun sparks on the way down to the pool. After hours of climbing the harsh, barren rocks, the place was balm to the eyes and spirit, waking senses dulled by austerity. The horses, scenting grass and water, needed no urging, and they came into the garden at a gallop.

They let the horses free, knowing they would not wander beyond the grass. Sleep robes were laid out, and wood gathered for a fire. Finally they turned their attention to the pool.

The water was warm silk, different from any water DonEel had known, melting away tension and fatigue. It had a slightly bitter taste on his lips, and Pollo told him of the minerals that came from the hot spring above. The other was sweet and ice-cold, yet they seemed to flow from the same rock. It was a mystery never solved.

Swimming gave way to lazy floating as warmth soothed, seeping into muscle and bone. Pollo talked of other times here, even in the coldest season, when the warm pool was hidden in dense steams and the hollow full of green and growing things even when the rocks above were buried in ice and snow. Finally, reluctantly, they pulled themselves up onto the moss-soft bank to dry in the warm air, half-yielding to the desire for sleep.

The indulgence trapped them. Dulled by security, days away from any thought of trouble, they had left their weapons out of reach with their clothing and saddles. The shrill whistle erupting through the golden light woke them too late. Shocked into action, DonEel lunged toward his knife and met a leather-clad foot. Grabbing instinctively, he pulled, rolling toward the pool, and the Zona toppled over him, bruising ribs and belly, knocking the breath from him. He held on, sliding into the water, drawing the other down, glad there were no shallows. Lungs aching, he tried to stay down, to hold his attacker, but lacked strength. The Zona struggled, pushing him away, and was out of reach. Surfacing, he saw confusion on the bank. Pollo was struggling with two others, and the one he had dragged into the water, obviously unable to swim, fought to climb the wet bank, weighed down in sodden leather. For a moment that struck him funny, so there was a wolfish grin on his lips as he struck for the opposite shore near where his weapon lay.

Streaming water, he was out of the pool and armed without pause. Trusting his eye and the superb balance of the blade, he threw. A Zona went down with a cut-off cry, and he turned to help Pollo. He never made it. A shadow flashed across his eyes; a rough leather loop settled over his head, snapping tight about his neck. Jerked off balance, he seemed a long time falling, long enough to see the wild bearded face and recognize victory in the dark eyes. Then something very near and very loud happened in his head and he knew nothing.

Waking was a struggle spurred by a necessity he could feel but not honestly remember the reason for. It took some time to realize there was no need for struggle, that the arms holding him quiet were soothing, not restricting. Head aching violently, neck sore, he lay still, grateful for the moment and willing to take advantage of it until the pain receded. When he finally opened his eyes, it was to see Pollo's face bent close over him, to understand it was Pollo's arm beneath his shoulders.

"It's over, DonEel. Lie still. Your head's still bleeding."

He obeyed the soft voice, giving himself over to noticing the sun had gone from the hollow, replaced by the flickering glow of a fire.

"Have they gone?"

"Aye. But the one dead. And I feared the same for you. How is it now?"

"Not so bad." He tried to smile, to ease the shadow in the clear eyes above him.

"I thought you dead by my carelessness. By the Gods, it was like feeling my own death."

"I am not so easily dead." But he might have been, he knew. And he was yet glad for the arm supporting him.

"So I see." A gentle finger traced the zigzag scar over his shoulder. It was curious comment, becoming something other as the hand flattened, palm warm and faintly moist, stroking lightly over dark curls, small concave nipples. Everything had changed. He saw it in the golden eyes, gone dark and wondering; yet he could not move, only lie there, waiting, as the head bent to him. For a moment, warm lips touched his; then understanding broke the spell. With an inarticulate sound, he twisted away, stumbling to his feet.

"No," he said distinctly. Then, taking refuge in outrage, fleeing the moment, he turned toward the horses. But he could not leave. The saddles, as well as his clothing, lay behind Pollo near the fire. So he stood still, a long white mark in the green dusk of the garden, feeling the fury run out of him, leaving him weary and with the dull pain of head and throat.

"DonEel, forgive me. I did not intend—" The soft voice struck him like a blow.

"Pollo—" He couldn't turn to face him, afraid of what he might see, what might be said. "Don't."

"I cannot leave it so between us. Is it so wrong that

52

I love you? You cannot, must not, believe I would shame you."

"Let it be." He almost shouted it. Action became his only buffer against that voice, and he moved finally, going near the fire, taking up his clothes.

"Will you go, then?" The gentle voice rode across the gulf between them, calmly insistent.

"Must I?"

"It is for you to say, DonEel." The watching face and eyes gave nothing. Cut adrift, forced into thinking, he almost did go. In his mind he rode away from this place, from this strange man he knew and did not know. But imagining himself going, alone, he realized he did not have a destination other than that which included the Delphan.

"I cannot leave you. Not now," he said into the long silence. "There is danger for you until you reach Delpha. We have proof of that now. And I am in your debt. Again."

"There is nothing owed between us now. It must be your choice. Made freely."

"Do you wish me with you?"

Pollo's unexpected laugh stirred the shadows. "Need you ask? Aye, I wish you with me. Could you believe otherwise? I have said I love you." Some expression in the other's face warned him, and he shook his head. "DonEel, a man does not choose to love, it is thrust on him. Gift or curse."

"We are different from your people. In Scarsen no man would speak so to another."

"Is what is unsaid less real, then?" Getting up finally, he went to put wood on the fire, laughing again, shortly. "Never mind, my friend and companion. It is not your doing. You are right. We are of our own people. Yet do not judge me too hard."

"Pollo, I don't judge. I only acted out of surprise. I have never—" He broke off, unable to put words to the thought.

"Nor have I. Of my own choosing. In that, we are

53

alike." Unasked, the question not yet realized was answered, and what had come between them was somehow eased. They ate in peace, trusting an understanding too new to be named, and they were relieved, as though they had skirted the edge of some abyss and come to safer ground.

There was the unpleasantness of the dead Zona to tend to. Leaving Pollo to take care of the horses, DonEel went to reclaim his knife. He saw, with grim satisfaction, that the blade had gone true, sunk to the hilt in the thick throat. As he bent to pull it free, his eye caught a glint of gold, a thick chain tangled in the matted hair and beard, with a pendant suspended inside the leather shirt. Curious, already almost knowing, he drew the chain over the head and held it up to catch light from the rising fire. It was the stone Kylee had shown them in Loos. Almost. The colors shifting beneath the faceted surface were subtly different, but the workmanship and design were identical.

For a moment, feelings too fast to fasten meaning to roughened his back and shoulders; then recognition of the jewel faded before an older, deeper familiarity. He stiffened, breathless, almost understanding, reaching for something. . . .

Looking up from the fire-shimmered stone, he did not recognize this place, the fire, or the man bending over it, busy. But he did. It was—

He was—

Wavering between realities of knowledges that did not fit, he touched fear. Ice-cold, he made the effort. "Pollo!" There was desperation in the word, and hearing it in his voice gave him back to himself, shattering the spinning web.

Startled by the call, Pollo turned, fire-blinded. In the time it took him to reach DonEel's side, the strangeness had gone. Unable to speak of it sensibly, he held out the pendant.

"The Zona's?"

"Yes."

"But it's Kylee's stone."

"No. Only like it." Taking up his knife, he moved away, to the fire. "The color is different, I think."

"Yes. I see it is. But it is the same. The work is unlike anything I've seen. Made by the same hand, I would say."

Crouching near the fire to clean his blade, DonEel didn't answer. Staring at the weapon, he felt another chill of strangeness. The fine metalwork about the hilt was the same as the golden web encasing the stone, delicate lines and spirals, repeated in the nearly invisible carving on the handle. Still silent, he showed Pollo.

"The same," he agreed. "We must remember to ask Tarhel how he came by it." He considered the coincidence of three articles of unknown manufacture appearing so closely related in time and place, but it was clear he considered it nothing more than coincidence. His thoughts were more fully occupied with the Zonas. Jania must be right, he decided. On their own, the Zonas would not leave their land. "It would take something important to get them this far north. And even they know of this place and the law of all people that holds that Beauty shall not be violated by battle. Perhaps they yearn after the Beachers' wealth."

Maybe he was right. But looking at the necklace lying fire-warmed near his knife, DonEel frowned. Something more was involved. Somewhere beyond Pollo's practical knowledge of politics he recalled Kylee and the other stone, and the dream he had had of Kylee before they met. This was all of a piece.

"You must keep the jewel as a trophy. It is yours by right of victory," Pollo said, perhaps mistaking DonEel's attention on it. The other thing between them had passed, not forgotten, but out of reach.

"Perhaps your Council will want it." It surprised him that he should feel a fear of the stone, but memory of the feeling that had taken him when he first held it still troubled him.

"If they do, you can give it to them." Smiling, Pollo bent and picked it up. "For now, wear it." He dropped the stone into DonEel's hand, and it was only a piece of jewelry, nothing more. After a moment, he slipped the chain over his head and felt the stone slide cold and hard against his chest inside his shirt.

They were away from the pool at sunrise, climbing through the barren, broken land surrounding the garden. Both felt the need to reach Delpha quickly, and they were watchful as they had not been since leaving Loos. They rode in silence, side by side, and DonEel's thoughts were on Kylee and the stones. He wished now he had told Pollo of the dream, but the habits of Scarsen were hard to break, and Kylee was not only Delphan, he was related to Pollo by blood.

"Your thoughts must be troubled to make you frown so. Or does your head pain you?" Pollo's voice surprised him.

"No. It's nothing. I was thinking of Kylee." He hadn't decided it, but the night thoughts troubled him, pressing it. "I think he means you harm."

"Kylee?" Pollo laughed; then, seeing the Souther's face, he reined his mount. "By the Gods, you mean it."

"I do. There are the stones—"

"And your knife." Gold-flecked eyes held steady.

Wishing now he had kept silent, DonEel nodded. "Kylee knew you would come south early; he expected you. And he knew we left Loos quickly, and mounted."

"So did others, DonEel. Kylee is of my blood. He has never wished me harm. Don't make too much of his dislike of you. He thought more between us than is, and he feels duty should be my first obligation."

DonEel's face warmed at the memory called up in the quiet words, but having gone so far, there was no choice but to continue. "I knew Kylee before Loos. He came to me in a dream and warned me not to go with you." He waited for the laugh to come, but Pollo only looked at him a silent moment.

"You're sure it was Kylee?"

"I knew him, by voice and look."

"That night in the Af camp, by the ford, when you called out to me. But why did you not tell me?"

"Many dreams mean nothing, and I could make no sense of it."

"Nor can I now. But Dioda has taught me that all dreams carry meaning. It is only waking we do not understand. Alchia must be told of this."

"Alchia?"

"Our Council Chief."

"But it might be as you said, a personal thing between Kylee and myself."

"I did not say that, my friend, only that I can see no reason he would wish me harm." Smiling a little, he urged his mount into movement.

By afternoon they had crossed the barrens, but it cheered them little. The weather changed, with cold winds and low gray clouds slipping down from the peaks of West Range. This was the land of the Shepherds, but this early in the year it was deserted on High Road; the people had their flocks down in the winter lowlands yet, busy with shearing and lambing, readying their flocks for the trip to High Pasture.

The stone and sod huts, built for the herders, were waterproof and open for the needy traveler, and they found themselves comfortable as the storm broke. At least they would not spend the night wet.

The weather continued cold and wet for two days, and there was nothing for them to do but ride through it, wrapped in their fur robes for warmth, pushing the horses as fast as possible without wearing them down. Then they were leaving High Road, riding east toward the coast and Delpha, two days earlier than they had hoped.

FOUR_____

VIEWED from High Road, Delpha was a pearl set
white and clean between the emerald of Greenwood
and the sapphire of Long Sea, pleasing the eye with
balance, and the spirit with the promise of peace.
Pausing to rest the horses, grown thinner now and
too tired to press, the two men enjoyed stillness, savoring the journey's end.

"Much has changed, DonEel of Erl," Pollo said
thoughtfully. "For both of us, I think." He looked at
his companion a moment, then grinned, rubbing the
coppery bristles on his jaw, as thick as the black
bearding of the other. "It will be good to be home.
Come, let us go down."

He pointed out his house as they came down the
mountain, a lesser pearl set away from the town, and
for the first time DonEel thought how little he knew
of his companion outside what they had shared on
the road. Seeing the world of Delpha, knowing it
would be different, he felt a gulf between them and
wondered what he would find at journey's end.

The buildings lost nothing of their beauty up close,
only gained in detail and clarity. They were simple
in line, with curving and sturdy arches of some
dressed stone he had never before seen. The effect
was not so much simplicity as it was elegance and
something else that touched the mind and made one
think of wisdom and learning.

A woman appeared on the roofed porch as they
rode into the yard. She paused there a moment as

they dismounted, then came running down the wide steps in a flurry of blue and gold, to be caught up in the Delphan's strong arms with laughter. The manner of the embrace told DonEel this one was truly loved, and a shyness struck him, so he turned away, unsure, to tend the horses.

"DonEel, the groom will see to them. Come, meet my lady and wife, Masila."

Wife. Hearing it was a shock, for all he couldn't think why, except he had never considered the possibility. Beckoned, he came forward, feeling the weight of Pollo's eyes, schooling his face to silence, looking at her. And she was, he saw, beautiful, a creature of golden skin and hair, and wide gray eyes.

"Welcome to this house, friend." She held out her hands to him, and he took them, thinking how small she was and perfect. Her touch made him realize his own hands were rough and dusty, and he smelled of horses and his own sweat. "We had word from Jania that Pollo was well companioned, DonEel of Erl. Now do I believe it." Her gray eyes smiled up at him, and when his own smile answered, she colored faintly and turned away.

"Come," she said to them both, "I will have clothing laid in the bathhouse and a meal prepared. Then we can talk." As she turned to the house, the soft gown revealed the curve of her body, and DonEel saw she was with child.

"I shall have to watch the women around you," Pollo grinned, leading the way through open halls toward the bath. "Masila is scarce the type to blush at any man's smile."

"You are teasing me. But she is beautiful."

The bath was a luxury DonEel could not have imagined. Colored tiles lined a pool of warm, faintly scented water, deep enough to cover his chest. He sank into it gratefully, wondering what more was to come.

"Does she not care that you leave her for so long?" he asked, thinking of the woman.

"Masila? Aye, she cares. But she loves me for what I am, not what she could make of me. Did she not, she would go to another. There are enough who would have her." He pulled himself up onto the edge of the bath, dripping. "When she first came here, I doubted she would stay, for all I wanted her. Now I believe we are well and truly matched. She will have my child by summer's end." He grinned, kicking warm spray over the Souther. "Perhaps I, too, shall have a son."

A son. He remembered the long-ago questions of Ronan, and the unexpected knowledge thrust on him when there was nothing he could do or say. His son. He didn't even know his name. Blame Scarsen for that. "But not a bastard," he said quietly, out of memory.

"There are none here, DonEel. Only children of love."

A youth, blond as Masila and nearly as pretty, came into the bath, interrupting their talk, bringing towels. His look at DonEel was frankly admiring as he told Pollo the barber waited on them and their clothing was prepared in the dressing room. Something touched his wide young eyes as he asked if they would want a massage before dressing.

"I think not, Niki," Pollo laughed, drawing a towel around himself. "Let our guest become familiar with our ways first."

The clothing was stranger even than that of the Afs, a short tunic clasped at one shoulder, leaving both arms bare, snugged to the waist by a wide belt. And over it a loose cloak fastened at the neck, swinging to the floor behind. Pollo chose the colors for DonEel: soft blue for the tunic, and deeper blue, bordered with gold and scarlet, for the cloak, matching the wide buckle. He chose shades of green for himself, setting off his copper hair.

Shaved—for the first time by hands other than his own—dark hair trimmed to neatness but left long on the nape, he was pronounced ready for Delpha. In his own mind he was not so sure. There were soft sandals laced to midcalf, but his legs felt uncomfortably exposed, though Pollo said he would get used to it.

A servant appeared from somewhere to bring word the meal was ready and there would be a guest at table. The master's sister had come to visit the Lady Masila.

DonEel thought he would have preferred a simple meal with Pollo and his wife this first time, but when she was presented to him, he knew he would not have missed it if he'd had the choice. If Masila was gold, Argath was silver. Her gown left both arms bare, and the jeweled belt about her slender waist emphasized full, high breasts and flaring hips. Rising from her couch by the table, she seemed a half-tamed creature —or a huntress, perhaps, for her green eyes measured him levelly beneath the silver cascade of her hair.

"Masila spoke true, DonEel of Erl," she greeted him, and there was in her easy smile the challenge and ready humor of her brother. The sound of her voice recalled the voice of the flute, but mellower.

"Not knowing what was said, I dare not answer." He smiled, warming to the familiar challenge of a lovely woman. Here, he thought, was a prize worthy of any man.

"It was only good, I assure you," Masila laughed, reminding him there were others present, and he turned to greet her. "You do honor to our dress, DonEel."

"As I said," Pollo reminded, laughing. "One would think we never guested at table. Come, we must eat while there is time. The Council will know by now that we have come home."

The food was good; the wine cold and served by Pollo's hand. But as he had foretold, before there was time to enjoy the meal and company, a messenger arrived from the Council, bringing greetings and a summons to attend as soon as possible. Pollo sent word for the groom to bring horses, giving only enough time to finish the meal.

DonEel protested the immediacy of the summons, but Pollo laughed. "They are the Council, and Jania's messenger undoubtedly mentioned you were from an unknown state. Protocol demands they greet you as ambassador. Anyway, Father will want to meet you."

"Your father is of the Council?"

"Aye. Lord Alchia, Council Chief."

"Lord Alchia. Then you are a prince of Delpha." Standing in the spacious entry waiting on the horses, DonEel looked at him. For some reason it seemed almost obvious now, but he was surprised again.

"I suppose I am, in a way." The Delphan's voice said he had not considered the idea before. Then his mood changed to teasing. "Do you love me less for it?"

"You might have told me." Perhaps it was unfair of him, but it seemed there was much unsaid that could have been.

"But it is my father's position, not mine."

"Yet you will someday rule."

"I suppose I might. If I wish it, and the people so choose. Kylee is eldest of the brothers, and he sought the seat, but the people chose the youngest as best fit. We are not born to greatness here, DonEel; if we have it, we earn it. I am what I am. As are all men."

It was close to a rebuke, delivered with the understanding that the man from Scarsen could not be expected to know the ways of Delpha. And it served to remind DonEel that he was the one passing judgment, not Pollo. Accepting the message, he accepted also the warm pressure of the hand on his shoulder as they went to mount.

He rode by Pollo's side into a city of white and graceful buildings and open parks. Delpha was all that the view from High Road promised. The widely spaced buildings were, Pollo told him, mostly schools and places of records and research. The parks delighted both eye and ear with lifelike statues and singing fountains. The people—and there were many about the parks and streets—took note of the riders, and many recognized Pollo, raising their hands to him in salute or calling out to him.

There were no markets or shops on this central street, and Pollo explained that the craft shops and markets were located mostly on the south side of town, near the waterfront. Many people from other states brought their talents and crafts here and earned their living selling and trading articles they manufactured or by teaching their methods to others.

The Council was represented by a dozen men, who greeted DonEel as warmly as Pollo had anticipated. They asked for an accounting of the journey, and Pollo, after presenting the package from Loos with Kylee's letter, told the tale. Again no mention was made of the circumstances surrounding their meeting in Scarsen, and DonEel wondered what their reception would have been had they known he was under sentence of death.

It was over quickly, and they were being ushered from the chamber, when a white-clad youth came to them with a message for Pollo.

"Wait for me by the fountain, DonEel. My father wishes to see me."

It was a good place to rest. The newly leafed trees gave pleasant shade, and he watched the people going about their business. There were children gaming across the park, throwing a hoop and laughing, and he watched them, wondering if they were as free as they seemed, or if they also had duties in this city.

"My Lord, DonEel of Erl?"

The gentle voice startled him, and he turned to see the messenger who had come for Pollo.

"Lord Alchia would see you now."

63

The Council Chief was a surprise, lean and supple as a youth, though he must surely be approaching middle age. His curly hair, lighter than Pollo's but boasting a touch of copper, showed no gray, and his face was unlined, serious, but not severe. "I am in your debt, DonEel of Erl, for the safe return of my son."

We are what we are, Pollo had said, and looking at the father, DonEel thought that here was one born to greatness, to rule by the strength of being himself and drawing men to him in love and respect.

There was no ceremony here—Alchia bade him be seated as an equal—and DonEel could not help comparing him with Halpor, Lord Mayor of Scarsen. He knew without thinking that though it might cost him more than he could yet reckon, he wanted nothing less than honesty between them.

"There is no debt, Lord Alchia." He felt Pollo's attention and ignored it as he told the true manner of their meeting. Alchia listened gravely, without interruption, glancing once to where his son sat on a wide window ledge bathed in golden sun.

"They sound a stern people, my friend," he said when DonEel had done. "There is none other I know that holds with sacrifice."

"Nor did they. Until this time."

"Could it have been but vengeance?" No word was said of his crime; it might have meant nothing.

"Not with Ronan's agreement."

"This was not an old thing." For the first time, Pollo spoke from where he sat in the window. He told what he had heard in Scarsen that day, of the disappearances and the dreams and visions of some of the people. "Nor would they have managed his death by their own hand. There was a feel of power in the grove, and something you have spoken of, Father. The feel of Nomen."

Alchia frowned slightly, then changed the subject.

"My son has said you sometimes foretell the future. Is it a willed thing?"

"Would it were, My Lord. I should not have ended in the grove."

Alchia smiled at the obvious logic, and the change in his face was remarkable. DonEel wondered if he realized just how effective that smile was. "So I should have known, DonEel. Unless there was some special destiny bound to those acts that started you on the road to Delpha. Pollo has told me of the message Dioda brought to him, and the dream of his own that took him south beyond his destination. It seems all things have conspired to bring you to my son, and so to us."

It was a thought he had considered, but put to him by Alchia it brought a question. "Is it my destiny, then, or Pollo's?"

Hazel eyes held him fast for a moment; then Alchia smiled and looked toward his son. "Perhaps, DonEel of Erl, they are the same. Or a larger purpose involves you both. We at Delpha are seekers, and we do not yet know all that may be known of purpose. Perhaps the chain of events begun in Scarsen will bind us all. But I speculate. You must be weary from your journey, and I have duties of my own." He rose, and DonEel with him. "We will speak again; you bring us much of interest." He took the Souther's hand and led him to the door where Pollo waited, and for a moment he took his son's hand also. "Tell Masila I will come when duty permits. Surely within the week."

For all the peace of Delpha, it was not an idle city, and Pollo had Council affairs to attend to. His duties took him into the city early in the mornings, leaving DonEel master of his own time except for those few hours spent with the scholars who were students of the different peoples and wanted to learn of Scarsen. He had the freedom of the city and Pollo's estate, and the people were kind to him; yet somehow that very interest and approval hemmed him in. There was a restlessness in him. He went to the scholars and talked with them, glad now for the long hours of Ronan's special attention, and he learned more in idle conversation with the teachers and students than the Council and churchmen of Scarsen would have dreamed possible. Still, the very perfection of the people and their city was confining.

When he went into the city, he found himself hoping for sight of Argath, and told himself that was foolishness, and worse, for she was Pollo's sister and a citizen of Delpha. So he marked the looks of interest received from unknown people, both men and women, and played with fantasies behind his dark eyes, understanding the subtle tensions that had once nearly cost him his life. And it was Argath who disturbed his sleep.

When the restlessness pushed too hard, he took a horse from the stable and rode alone up into Greenwood, away from people, wondering where any of this was leading, toying with the idea put to him by the scholars of bringing Scarsen and Delpha together, but unable to feel any real interest. He had gone from Scarsen a longer distance than he had traveled with Pollo, but he had not yet come to another place. He was stranded in limbo, and keyed up, waiting for something he could not name. Even his dreams became confused and vague.

Alchia came, as he had promised. And Argath with him. It was a pleasant evening, made more so by the fact of her eyes on him as often as his glance to her, and her eager interest in all things of Scarsen. But soon after the meal Alchia indicated he wanted to speak to the two men, and they retired to another room—a library, perhaps—with many books and papers about, and a small fire laid against the chill spring night. Alchia's manner was serious, and he did not keep them waiting.

"We have word from Jania there is trouble abroad." The Council Chief himself poured a light wine for them, more host than guest in this house. "He will be in Delpha before long, but he thought we might be sending out teachers and others before he could talk to me. He puts no name to the trouble, except he thinks it involves the conflict between the Beachers and Plainers, and the Zonas are involved. You told the Council of the attacks made on your journey north, but they have been unable to put a reason to them, unless, as you said, it could have been to prevent you from returning with word from Plains. Or to keep the thing you brought from Kylee from reaching Delpha."

"What is it?" Pollo asked. "Kylee did not say. I understood it to be a thing of historic interest, and the Zonas do not deal in history."

"It is old, but of more than purely historical importance. We are not yet decided on the real value of it; the Council and scholars are divided on the question. It is a map—not entire, but a large fragment —that appears to show a road that leads from north of Delpha to south of Blackwood. Even perhaps to Warm Sea at the south land's end."

"The old High Road?"

"One before it, if we read right. It seems to show passage through part of West Range above the mines, even west of Zona."

"But that would be Nomen territory," Pollo protested. "No Trueman would dare such a route."

Alchia only shrugged. The map, if indeed that is what it was, was like none they had seen before. Even the material of it was strange, and the writing so different it was impossible to be sure even of the directions. But the landmarks like West Range and the eastern extent of Blackwood fit, and the courses of the major rivers.

"In all our dealings with the Zonas we have believed them to be without learning, except in the basest form. It is possible we have misjudged them, though the scholars say we lack evidence to change our ideas. If we could understand why they broke their own traditional law and attacked you out of their land, we could better understand them. Is there anything you can tell of them that you did not tell the Council?"

Pollo was sure there was nothing. The contacts had been brief and totally unexpected.

Listening to him retell the story, DonEel sat, chin on fist, remembering. He knew nothing of these people beyond what Pollo had told him, except that they were jealous of the land they considered their own: the major part of Blackwood to the north and west of Scarsen. It seemed Alchia knew little more.

"Mesal," he said when Pollo had retold the tale. "He said there were Nomen with the Zonas who first attacked the Afs. And he died of their poison." He could not remember if they had told the Council.

"But the weapon could have been used by a Zona. They are closer to the Nomen than any people we know, and they are clever enough to adopt a method of doing, once it has been done to them." Alchia used the same argument Pollo had.

"But if they had weapons that could kill at a distance—" He glanced at Pollo, thinking of the attack at Beauty. "They could have killed us without coming out of hiding while we slept if they only wanted you not to return to Delpha or to get the map brought from Loos. And they need not have waited until we reached Beauty. That first night out of Loos, they were there while we slept."

"In the center of Plains?" Alchia frowned.

"I did not see them. Only the horses gave warning, and there was the print by the spring."

"Perhaps they were afraid to attack you in Plainer territory. The Plainers allow no misuse of their land, especially against Delpha." Alchia's explanation made sense, but his mind was on other things, and his gravity troubled the younger men.

"There was another thing," DonEel remembered after a moment. "The Zona killed at the pool wore this." He drew the stone from inside his tunic and slipped the chain over his head, handing it to Alchia, who held it a moment up to the light so the fire struck changing lights from the faceted surface. There was a strange, almost waiting, expression on his face. Then his eyes darkened and he looked away into the flames, closing his fingers on the jewel.

"It has a feel to it," he said quietly.

"Yes." A small excitement stirred in him, and he wondered that Alchia should have felt what his son had not. The hazel eyes moved to him and seemed to question what they saw, as if knowing the Souther had felt the power and not spoken of it.

"Were I a mystic, DonEel, I should say there is a spell on it. Some magic I might touch and use, with study."

"Better to wonder and leave the study to those who deal in it."

Alchia smiled a little, perhaps hearing a more personal concern than had been in the words, and he looked at the stone more closely, wondering now, as his son had, at the workmanship. "I have seen nothing like this before, but the piece does not have the feel of newness."

"Kylee has such a stone," Pollo said, and DonEel was glad he had been the one to say it.

"It is the same?"

Pollo described it, but Alchia's eyes went to DonEel, asking more than the simple question, and he nodded, knowing, and wondering a little that he should know, and Alchia accept his knowing.

"I shall ask Kylee to send his stone here for study. Perhaps Dioda—" He left the thought unfinished and, rising, went to DonEel and slipped the golden chain over the dark head. "This one you must keep and wear. It becomes you."

There was nothing of value learned of the Zonas that night, but long after Alchia left them, Pollo and DonEel sat before the small fire and talked as they had not since coming to Delpha. Pollo was certain there was more in the message sent to the Council by Jania than Alchia had told them. The Afs were more aware of Delpha's role in the political interaction of the states than any other people, and they did not carry tales for the sake of it. If Jania thought there was trouble brewing for Delpha because of the Zonas, he had good reason.

As the night aged, the talk became more personal, and Pollo spoke of his father. "I have heard that in his youth it was thought he would choose to become one like Dioda and dedicate himself to the disciplines that help men touch the unseen world. But he was popular with the people, and not the type to withdraw from living. Still, there is a depth to him, and more than a touch of mystery. He is a man born to greatness, and it is not I alone who say it."

For all Delpha's pride in democracy, there was yet some virtue in having friends in higher places. The second day after Alchia's visit, a messenger came from the Hall of Council requesting DonEel's attendance. Pollo had already gone, and, wondering a little, DonEel rode into Delpha alone.

At the door of the Hall of Council, he was greeted by name, in a manner that indicated his position had risen somewhat above that of an interesting curiosity. He was shown into a large, airy room filled with quiet activity. Here, scholars were studying the map sent from Loos. Alchia came forward to meet him, accompanied by a smaller, bearded man. Alchia told him it had occurred to the Council that as the only one in Delpha having any real knowledge of Blackwood he could be of value in determining the accuracy of the southern part of the map.

Surprised, he protested that he was not a mapmaker, but Alchia laughed, indicating the busy room. "Mappers we have, but none from Blackwood. It is your knowledge we need, not your art with pen and ink."

Not sure he could help, DonEel agreed. He was curious about the map. And this, at least, would be more interesting than talking about Scarsen.

Almost as an afterthought, Alchia drew the bearded man forward, away from the main group, presenting him to DonEel simply as Dioda.

There was much to learn and study and argue in the old map, and throughout the day he was caught up in speculation and alternative explanations. It was well past the middle hour when he finally had time to study the old chart for himself. On the surface it was unremarkable, well drawn on heavy, probably oiled, parchment, cracking with age now. The drawing was done in black and green, and it was obviously a map of something. He ran his fingertips over the faded tracings, and it occurred to him that there was a strangeness, something not right, about it. Not that it was false; just not right.

Looking up, he found Dioda's eyes on him, and for a moment he thought he detected the beginnings of a smile and the briefest of nods. Then the quiet one turned away to his work of copying a section of the original and enlarging it, and DonEel wondered if he had imagined his interest and attention.

After a break for food and relaxation, during which the conversation never left the map, he was given a section they thought to represent the northern boundary of Blackwood. By itself, drawn several times larger than the original delicate lines, and without the confusion of detail and extended lines, he could place himself fairly close. The two rivers they had crossed

71

with the Afs were in the right place, and memory said there were the correct number of ridges and canyons crossed by them after leaving the grove. After hours of studying and even trying to draw his own map from memory, he was sure of even the long, curved valley where Scarsen lay.

He went back to the original to try to place his section in the perspective of the whole, and thought he might see in it now some correspondence to reality. There were sections of High Road, but the marks formed no continuous line from north to south. But another tracing, in green, winding among the black lines and writing, came near High Road at certain major points—one he was certain was the pool Beauty. Then it angled away sharply to wander through what must represent West Range, touching the land beyond and returning to High Road.

"It would be a longer journey," he remarked to no one in particular.

"Then you do agree it is a map, intended for use." The gentle voice was Dioda's; he was standing beside him.

"It must be."

"So we feel. But come, it is late, and Pollo waits your company. Until tomorrow, DonEel of Erl."

Pollo was not surprised by the Council's invitation to his friend, and was glad for him. "Were my father less an open man, I would be tempted toward jealousy. Already they speak of you as his friend in the Hall of Study. There is other news today to please you, DonEel. Jania trades with the Shepherds for two days, then turns toward Delpha. A week at most and we will guest him."

It was good news. For all the troubles during their short journey together, DonEel thought the Afs more lively and enjoyable than any other people he had seen. And, Pollo pointed out as they luxuriated in the bath, Jania would know what was happening abroad. He might even have information that would help

72

them understand why the Zonas had attacked so far north of their own land.

"There is business concerning Scarsen before the Council, too. They talk of sending a delegation. Partly because it is unknown and we are always curious, but more immediately important, it is closer than any other town to the Zonas. Contact with Scarsen now might tell us if Zona is truly against Delpha."

The idea pleased DonEel, and he laughed to himself, relaxing into the barber's care, imagining the Lord Mayor trying to deal with Delpha's life-style. Understanding, Pollo laughed with him.

"By your example we have decided to be circumspect concerning their law. Women of our own will be included in the first contact. In fact"—his golden eyes laughed a more personal laughter—"my sister has asked to be included."

"Argath?"

"Why not? As a member of the College of Human Studies she's more than qualified. In fact, she's been asked to meet with you to become acquainted with any special problems that might arise because of our different customs and laws. If, of course, you are willing."

"I'm willing to bet you had a hand in this." At the moment he couldn't have said if it pleased him.

"But you will help?"

"Could I not? She is Alchia's daughter."

"I accept the rebuke, my friend. For my father's sake I am pleased, and I thank you. As his daughter will. She has asked to company with Masila a few days to help prepare for the arrival of Jania. She will be at table with us tonight."

Clowning now, they bowed formally to one another, then dressed quickly, laughing. And it was Pollo who had the last word, speaking as they entered the dining room. "I think, my shy friend, that you will find the women of Delpha a different sort from those of Scarsen."

Indeed, he already believed it. Often enough he had been greeted familiarly in the city by women whose manner alone would have won them a public shaming and punishment in Scarsen.

She was as beautiful as his dreams of her, and smiled, greeting him as her friend. But if she was eager to be with him under the guise of study, she hid it well. She spoke to him casually, touching on his work with the Council, but the rest of the time she seemed more concerned with the arrival of the Afs, and she and Masila told stories of other times of guesting, and the parties and music and dancing. It was an interesting description of life in Delpha he had not yet seen, and he accepted her easy attitude toward him. It was a pleasure just to have her there.

Not until long after the meal did she turn her attention to him alone, repeating the news already given by Pollo while Masila took Pollo aside to discuss the coming company.

"It is said your people are stern and have many laws," she said to him after explaining her position and qualifications. "The Council agrees it would be better if we came to them a complete and integrated company, so they do not mistake our intentions."

"You may be right." He wondered what Halpor's reaction to her would be if he had to accept her as an equal, and found himself amused with the idea. It would do the old boar good. "What can I do to help you prepare to meet with them?"

"You can teach us what is obvious to you and unknown to us. The things in daily life we must or must not do. We will be strangers, and were we to do as we do here, there would be trouble and bad feelings before we could become familiar enough to overlook differences."

There was no arguing Delpha's logical approach to problems, but he wondered how much good it would do. There were too many differences. "I have never

been a teacher." He smiled. "I wouldn't know where
to begin."

"By talking." She answered his smile so warmly he
nearly reached out a hand to touch her dimpled
cheek, but did not, quite.

"We will talk. And perhaps both learn." Before he
bade her goodnight, she promised to go riding with
him the next afternoon.

Knowing he would see her made his morning in the
Hall of Council go faster, and his own eagerness
amused him. Seeing her mounted brought back his
first impression of her as a huntress. Silver hair flowing free down her slender back, she rode astride,
dressed as the youths of Delpha in short pleated tunic
and laced scandals. Women of Scarsen did not ride
astride, nor did they bare their legs to midthigh in
public, and from the first he found the sight of her
tanned legs gripping the horse disturbing. He wondered if she knew, but her manner, while full of
laughter, was casual. She asked questions, forcing him
to examine his own people as he never had done, and
she was interested in what he said. And, more important, she answered his questions.

The hours spent with her were like none he had
spent with a woman, and after the first ride, the
afternoon meeting became ritual, something he looked
forward to. It was not all riding; there were times
spent resting in the shade when the spring sun turned
hot, but the talk was, as always, of Scarsen and
Delpha.

"The women have no voice as citizens," she said to
him. "Only the men decide and lead."

He thought about it, comparing Argath to Sharill,
or the Lord Mayor's wife, and then he laughed. "Their
voice is all the stronger for being silent. The wise
woman sees to it a man speaks for her. So it is the
man who bears the responsibility for word or act."

"You misunderstand, man of Scarsen. By choice."

Playfully, she flicked a pebble at him, and, laughing, he caught it. Impulsively she grabbed for it, and as impulsively he dropped it to grasp something infinitely more satisfying. She resisted as he bore her down, kissing her mouth as he had dreamed of doing. But this was no dream; she was real and alive and warm. Feeling her go still beneath his weight, he knew the swift strength and heat of his manhood, too long repressed. Had not the horses whinnied nearby, startling him, he might have taken her there beneath the tree, quick and savage as any forest animal. Recalled to who and where they were, he released her and moved away, face dark, muscles knotted in conflict. From a safe distance he looked at her, lying still, hair spilled silver over the grass. Her eyes, green as emerald, saying something he could not understand, held him until he must speak or lose himself.

"Forgive me, Lady."

His voice let the world move again, and she sat up, combing leaves from her impossible hair. He saw her throat work as she looked out into the forest. "It is late," she said after a time, not looking at him. "Masila will be expecting us."

"Argath, I cannot leave it so between us." Unconsciously using words from another time and place.

"It is done. Do not worry it." If it was rebuke, it was gently voiced, leaving him uncertain as they mounted their horses. There was nothing else to speak of, so they rode back in silence, unspoken words loud between them.

He didn't expect her at supper, but she was there, regal and serene in a gown of gold, and there was easy conversation between them. But thoughts of her kept him awake through the night. To his greater surprise, she was waiting for him in the garden the next afternoon.

"I thought we might find it easier to talk here," she said. "Masila is busy with preparations for Jania."

Admiring her ease in a situation he had made

difficult, he could be no less than honest. "I give my word to behave. You are, for the moment, safe."

The smile she gave him held something he could not read as she nodded, inviting him to sit with her in the shade by the fountain. "What I said of the women of Scarsen was not meant as comment on their ways, but seeking a smoother manner of contact. I have gotten the idea that Lord Halpor would not easily accept a woman as an ambassador from Delpha."

"Not seriously. Though, were it you, he might suggest a liaison through marriage." For all the banter in his tone, he was serious. No man of Scarsen would admit a woman's authority in matters of state.

Many of the scholars and students were eager to be the first to contact Scarsen, but the Council needed to know what type of individual would be most readily accepted. It was easier to be correct the first time than to have to spend time later trying to overcome unnecessary misunderstandings.

"In Delpha we revere perfection and excellence above all things. The pure Delphan, like Alchia, whose ancestors were the first teachers and scholars, are held in high esteem because they have continued to perfect their talents. Our aim is to become as near perfect as possible in mind, spirit, and body," she explained. "When we meet one who approaches our ideal, he is accepted as one of us."

It was, perhaps, an obvious compliment, but searching her face he could not see her words meant more than example, so he held his pleasure close and gave thought to Scarsen. Strength was respected there, he told her. If it was obvious. And courage and ability, but in a more limited way than recognized in Delpha. There was no place for impractical frivolity, and gentleness almost guaranteed an attempt to take advantage.

"If the Lord Mayor and Council see some visible gain to Scarsen that will increase their own power, they will welcome you. But it will have to be more than a promise of future learning. Only the churchmen are interested in schooling. But they have a strong voice where the law is concerned. If they think the ideas of Delpha will interfere, they will go against you." He described the man who had been in power when he left, and the system of polygamous marriage for the wealthy.

He was still answering questions when Pollo came to tell them Jania and the Afs would arrive late the next day. At the news all thought of Scarsen was put aside and Argath went to help Masila with preparations.

FIVE

THE Afs were greeted with celebration. There were booths set up along the beach, and fires lit, and games and food and wine. So it was late when Jania and DonEel accompanied Pollo to his house.

"We feared for your safety until word came from Loos that you had passed through," the big black man said. He told them of his roundabout trip and stops on the way to Delpha, and they in turn told of the attack made on them by the Zonas. DonEel marked the quick change on the dark face.

"We heard talk the Zonas raided north of Loos, and doubted. But at Beauty? Are you certain?"

"We buried one of them, Jania," Pollo answered. "But we don't know the reason for the attack. We hoped you might be able to tell us something about their temper toward Delpha."

"Only that it is against Delpha. I will tell you what I must tell Alchia tomorrow at Council, that two students and an elder scholar were taken north of

Loos and killed or carried off. They were never found, only marks of struggle and Zona sign."

"And Loos? Kylee's school?"

"He is well. I spoke with him about this, and he is troubled but has no answers. I have a letter from him to Alchia that I sent by messenger tonight. Perhaps there will be more in it."

Jania was inclined to believe the Beachers were behind the trouble. They were wealthy and proud, and perhaps jealous of Delpha's influence in the other states. This could be their way of trying to force Delpha out of Plains, both by threat of attack and the fear planted in the Plainers that the trouble would involve them. As for the Zonas, he thought they probably enjoyed the sport and gained whatever spoil they could, plus what the Beachers might pay them. "So long as it is only Delpha attacked, and not the town or the planters, there is little fear of reprisal. It would be easier for the Plainers to ask Delpha to leave."

The idea had merit, but DonEel found himself doubting. There was something yet hidden from them, some purpose that would make sense of it. But they did not have it. He wondered what Alchia's thoughts would be, and if this would interfere with the Council's decision to send a delegation to Scarsen.

They were late to bed that night, and given no great time to sleep. Before the sun had cleared the horizon, a servant woke DonEel with word that Pollo waited for him. He dressed quickly, feeling a push of excitement in the change of routine.

Pollo was indeed waiting, pacing the tiled entrance, and below in the yard a groom stood holding two horses.

"I'm sorry for the hour, DonEel, but there has been a summons from my father."

"Is the Council met so early?" DonEel stretched his shoulders, wishing he had had time for breakfast. He

79

felt dull and stiff from the late hour and plentiful wine.

"Not to the Hall, but his home. He did not demand your presence, but said you might come if you wished. It is your choice."

"So I choose." He smiled, guessing Alchia knew he would come. "Was there a reason given?"

"None." Pollo led the way to the horses. "But it probably has to do with the letter from Kylee that was delivered last night."

The early air and spirited horse soon cleared the remnants of sleep from DonEel's head, and he decided it was a beautiful morning. He had missed too many dawns here in Delpha. The city was making him soft.

A perfect host, Alchia had the table laid for breakfast. He greeted them pleasantly, pleased that DonEel had decided to join them. He waited until breakfast was served (by a beautiful couple who could have been twins) to explain his invitation. DonEel noted with gratitude that no wine was served, but a strange hot beverage, dark and somewhat bitter, but stimulating and pleasing to the tongue.

"Our friend Jania told you of the letter from Kylee, I imagine. It was a personal note, not for the Council. He says there is growing dispute over the mines and he has reason to believe the Beachers are considering laying a claim on the mines, even forming a separate state to control them."

"Who does own them?" DonEel wondered.

"No one. By common consent. The mines are common property, and each state mines for its own needs, or barters with others, usually Plainers, to mine for them. According to my brother, the Beachers claim they could produce more and include transport to the various states if there were a continuous operation. It seems there have been a number of accidents in the mines this spring, and there was rumor of sabotage. People are beginning to fear working in the tunnels and caves."

80

A constant and dependable work force at the mines sounded efficient to DonEel, and he nearly said so, when Pollo spoke.

"That doesn't make sense."

"So I thought," Alchia agreed, slicing a dark loaf of bread. He ate with the robust appetite of an active man, enjoying his food, and for a moment DonEel wondered how he had spent the night. Then the conversation continued, and he turned his attention away from things that were none of his business. "The Beachers," Alchia pointed out to him, "have more than half of their mining done by others."

"Does my uncle say if he believes the tales?"

"He admits to being puzzled by the situation, which is why he reported it to me without involving the Council. He does say the number of accidents they have had is so much increased that he is considering sabotage. At any rate, he suggests there would be value in knowing firsthand what is happening at the mines, and that if I thought it necessary, I could submit a personal report to the Council."

"Could he not investigate this?"

"He must consider his position in Loos; it has value to us. And he is not a young man. He did not ask outright, but only reports what he has heard. In his own words, though, he would be pleased to offer his hospitality to a brother he has not seen for some years." Alchia smiled, refilling his cup.

"No." DonEel hadn't meant to say it, and, feeling Alchia's eyes on him, his face warmed. "My Lord, you must not accept." He knew it, but a logical reason for the warning evaded him momentarily while hazel eyes waited. "Jania has told us of the trouble for Delphans in Plains now," he finished lamely.

"Even the Zonas would not dare attack the Council Chief of Delpha in another's land," Pollo said as simple fact.

Alchia might not have heard his son. "Why do *you* feel I should not visit my brother, DonEel?"

81

The subtle stress on the word made it a different question, and he gave the only answer he had. "Because when the Zonas attacked, they did not kill us, as they could have done."

"What has that to do with me?" Chin on fist, there was an almost teasing cast to the Councilman's face, but his eyes asked another question.

"I don't know." DonEel almost wished he had kept silent. "Does Kylee suppose you would come?"

"He knows I would want to." For the first time now, there was tension at the table, a sort of distance between them.

"Then others might know it also," he said, realizing finally how close he had come to accusing Kylee.

"If there is trouble at the mines, news of an investigation by Delpha would cause alarm, and perhaps more serious trouble." Pollo rearranged the topic smoothly. "You spoke of bringing Kylee's jewel to the Council. Send me for it now. I could learn more of the mines on a different mission."

"Rather me, my Lord. I am not a Delphan," DonEel suggested.

"Nor do you know the mines." Alchia smiled, shaking his head. "Pollo would have the hospitality of Loos, and such schools as remain open on the road."

"Together, then." DonEel turned to Pollo and saw agreement there.

But Alchia was firm. "I cannot send you, DonEel of Erl. As you have said, you are not of Delpha."

"Then you cannot well prevent me." Now DonEel smiled, and Pollo laughed aloud. And so it was decided.

"You did not say why he should not go," Pollo reminded as they rode toward home.

"No, I guess I didn't." Frowning, DonEel didn't elaborate, but rode silent with his own thoughts, considering possibilities.

"My friend, I cannot understand your thoughts unless you voice them." Pollo broke the silence as they dismounted. He drew DonEel into the study, where they could speak without interruption. "Is your fear of Kylee that he may be plotting against my father?"

"I don't know." Hands on hips, DonEel stared out the window, not really seeing the garden. His own thoughts seemed logical to him, but he hesitated to share them. In the eyes of the other states, Alchia was Delpha. To take him would be a telling blow. Why now, in the wake of attacks against Delphans in northern and central Plains, would Kylee invite Alchia to make the long journey there? Could he not as easily investigate the matter of the mines and send word to the Council so it could act if necessary?

"Perhaps he does wish to see him," Pollo suggested.

"Perhaps." He shrugged off the easy explanation. "We were in Loos but a month ago, and there was no word of trouble in the mines. Or Kylee's wish to see his brother. It fits too well with the trouble in Plains." He turned from the window. "And you. You are Alchia's son. Your danger is too great. You must let me go alone."

"I will go, DonEel." It was said mildly, with a silent laugh. "You were attacked also. No, I could not bear to have you go and not know how you fared. We will go together. Whatever is planned for us will have to be met."

There would be no changing his mind, and DonEel knew him well enough not to try. But he was increasingly uneasy. It could so easily be a trap.

A possible answer came to him as he walked about Delpha with Jania and Argath, explaining what he had been doing. The old map, if it was accurate to any degree, could be a safe road south. They could bypass anyone waiting to ambush a party from Delpha and still make it to Loos.

Pollo, as he had expected, greeted the idea as an adventure. The mappers he had worked with were more reserved, not sure enough about the map to want to trust Alchia's son to it. But they were persuaded, without knowing of the journey's reason. It would be the only way of knowing if the map were usable. With Alchia's less than enthusiastic support, he got them to make a copy, including present-day names and the course of High Road.

Before leaving the Hall of Council, DonEel asked for, and was granted, a private audience with Alchia.

"It is a very risky venture you propose," the Council Chief greeted him. "The map could be fiction or, at best, full of honest mistakes. Were it not that the mines are valuable and must remain neutral ground, I would forbid this."

DonEel admitted the risk, arguing the advantage of secrecy. "And we have traveled unmarked roads before," he reminded. "There is one favor I would ask, Alchia. If Jania agrees, could you house the Afs here in Delpha until word comes from Loos that we have arrived safely?"

"For a reason. They usually sail Long Sea a fortnight from Carnival."

"My reasons may mean nothing, but the fact that the Zonas spared our lives when they need not could say they intended capture rather than death. And that would have value only against you personally, or against Delpha. If Pollo is taken, you will need strong and ready allies."

"If Pollo is taken." The quiet face brooded on him a moment. "And you?"

"I do not plan on being taken. Or allowing him to be."

"DonEel, my son would not accept that sacrifice. Nor do I. Alive, there is always hope. Think on that."

They did not speak of their real plans outside the Council, but DonEel was certain Masila knew. Her quietness and the way she watched her husband betrayed her knowledge.

The map was delivered on the third day, a quick but expert job, and there was no reason to delay.

That evening, though they still guested the Afs, there was no one at table with them but Argath, who would stay with Masila. Parting was a private thing, and DonEel excused himself early, warmed by the look of gratitude in Masila's eyes.

There was music from the Af camp, but he did not go down to join them. Thoughts of the morrow's journey occupied him, and he wondered again if it was a wise thing. He thought of Masila and her joy at seeing Pollo return. And there was the child coming before long. There would be danger on this ride—he felt it. Danger especially for Pollo.

Pacing in dusk light made strange by scudding clouds, he did not see the other figure in the garden until a familiar voice called his name softly.

"DonEel, you are uneasy about this ride south."

"Aye, Argath."

She came close, and her presence warmed him. He could smell the subtle female fragrance of her against the fey night odors of dark and growing things, and they walked together, not touching until they came to the wall where the sound of singing was a whisper on the freshening breeze.

"I have heard Jania. He believes there is more than ordinary danger now in travel south."

"For your brother, yes. He should let me go alone."

"You know he cannot. I have watched him, DonEel. Do not take his love lightly; he does not give it so easily or freely as other men."

"But he has much to lose."

"And you, man of the south?"

"I have no people, and I am a stranger here." He looked down into her eyes and felt his heart beat.

"A beloved stranger, then. Can this not be a home to you?"

"I do not yet know." He dared to touch her, to put his hands on her shoulders and draw her to him. She did not resist, but answered his kiss with a fervor of her own. He forgot the journey and Pollo and Delpha

85

in the wonder of her full breasts thrusting against him, and the warm pressure of her thighs. He released her finally and felt her trembling in his arms. "By the Gods, you are beautiful," he breathed, thinking one last time that this was madness, here in her brother's house, even as his hand caressed her side, moved up to mold the roundness of her breast. As though it were meant to, the fabric slipped aside and he touched the miracle of her skin. She caught her breath, capturing his hand with her own.

"DonEel," she whispered, "you are not as other men, somehow. . . ."

"Am I not?" Laughing softly, he pulled her close against his body to feel the unmistakable evidence of his likeness. The door to his quarters was close at hand, and, bending, he caught her up easily, knowing this was the time, by her wish as much as his own.

"I am afraid of this," she murmured in the dark security of his bedchamber. Yet her hands drew him down to her. Touching the silken perfection of her, inhaling her fragrance, he knew his touch was pleasure to her, growing until it was she who demanded of him, and he gave gladly, doer and done to.

And she, he thought, when he could think again, was like no woman he had known. Breathing quieter, she bent over him, skin moist with the sweat of their exercise, her hair pouring over his face and shoulder before she caught it back. She laughed softly against his lips, hands bold and gentle on his flesh as if now, finally, she would know and touch every part of him. This was a new thing to him, and he protested, laughing slightly.

"Do you not like to be touched so?" Slowly, with teasing gentleness, she taught him that their first urgent joining had been but a prelude to possibilities, and he went from shock to arousal as her lips followed the path of her expert fingertips, leading him to a place he had known before only in lonely fantasy. Once, in the newly discovered depths of his own heat, he grasped her, but she tamed him, surprisingly strong for all her yielding softness, until when he finally mounted her, thrust deep to the melting core of her, it was as if he had never before known a woman. His final pleasure shattered the darkness, and, utterly destroyed, he spun out and down into sleep.

He woke before dawn, dull and distant with sleep, and she was gone, the disarray of the bed and her scent on his skin the only evidence of the night's pleasure. Lying still, remembering, he felt his face go hot. There were, it seemed, things he could learn from her. It was a while before he remembered his reason for rising early. He moved then, drawing a loose robe about his nakedness, and went to the bath to remove the traces of their lovemaking and prepare for the day.

SIX

WHILE they breakfasted in the quiet house and saw to their packs, a thick fog drifted in from Long Sea, obscuring distance and rendering the close-at-hand mysterious. Waiting in the yard for Pollo to make his farewell to Masila, DonEel hoped it was not an evil omen.

"Don't frown so," Pollo laughed, joining him. "Sea fog is common here in spring. We'll be above it before we reach the pass. Niki brought word from my sister," he added as he checked the packs on the horses. There was teasing in his voice, but his eyes watched. "She sent a message to you. In friendship." He held out his hand, and, feeling a thrust of guilt, then pleasure, DonEel took the folded parchment. Inside the folds lay a ring, a band of black with a design of twining ropes worked in fine gold. There were but

two words on the paper, scribed in a flowing hand:
Safe journey.

Wordless under the Delphan's eye, he slipped the
ring on the last finger of his left hand, not sure he
could name the feeling it gave him, or even sure he
liked it.

They rode through a land of brooding shadow and
echo that under blue sky would have been a familiar
road, climbing into Greenwood. DonEel didn't relax
until they climbed out of the fog into warm sun. He
turned to look back, but instead of the white pearl of
Delpha below, all was hidden under a layer of snow-
white wool rolled out to the blue of Long Sea. Delpha
might not have existed, except in a dream. The
thought depressed him, and he turned away, preferring to think of the lovely town safe and protected
in the placid cloud.

Reaching the high pass, they turned north. If the
old map was to be trusted, High Road and the older
trail came together atop a long ridge running sea-
ward. They should reach the place by midday.

Seldom traveled north of Delpha, High Road became little more than a comfortable trail, a clear path
through the thick trees carpeted with years of pine
mulch, a silent, fragrant ride in the pleasant sun.
They let the horses lope side by side, covering distance, beginning the journey.

Before noon, the narrow trail cut slightly east across
a space between the trees that—except for the
shoulder-high brush crowding it—could have been a
road running west up onto the steep flank of West
Range, and east, down to a small bay.

Together they studied the map, agreeing this was
the old road. According to the map, it should run
due west to the base of the spires, then turn and follow the mountains south. There was evidence that
here it had crossed High Road and continued to the
bay, which would make a perfect harbor, sheltered
from storms. There might even yet be evidence of the

people who had used this ancient track, and there was a temptation to ride down to the bay. But first there was the business of the mines, and Kylee.

The tangle of brush and vines made travel on the old road impossible, but it was easy enough to follow beside in the shade of the great trees where the brush did not grow. The clearing was too straight to be natural, and at every break in the trees, they could see the jagged rocks above them, becoming ever higher and more real as the sun moved to the west. The ground had risen steadily and now was broken by outthrusts of rock, and there were unexpected bogs where springs seeped or bubbled to the surface. Finally the brush in the track thinned until it was easier to ride there than beside it. And it was a road. Rocky outcroppings that would have obstructed the roadway had been broken and smoothed, making an almost flagged surface where nothing larger than grass could put down roots. More than once as the land became more rock than soil Pollo dismounted to examine the surface. It was weathered, of course, and very old. Alchia would want to see it.

Sharing something of his interest, DonEel looked up to the three spires. Huge now, they seemd to tower over them, and he felt an instant's apprehension, as if the rocks were toppling, leaning slowly, falling. . . . He jerked his eyes away, turning in the saddle to look back and down. From here the existence of the road was obvious, a band of lighter green through the dark forest, running straight to the sea.

"The rocks would be visible from the sea," he mused aloud. "Whoever built this road had ships also."

"As far back as we can tell, the Afs have been masters of Long Sea. It must have been before them." Pollo laughed lightly. "There are those in Delpha who say this cannot be, that the road does not exist. There will be some battles over it in the schools."

The turn to the south was higher than they had supposed, above the forest cover, through the jumbled mass of rock at the base of the three hands. And it was a crossroad even more obvious than at High Road. Here the stonework was even more extensive, making a wide, smooth track except where time and weather had sent down slides from the towering crags. Something about the piles of rock reminded DonEel of the road near the pool Beauty.

"If it's like this much of the way, we will be in Loos as quickly as we would be on High Road," Pollo said as they rested beside a spring, eating a late lunch and trying to translate the inked lines of the map into the reality of West Range. He had traveled high into the mountains during the fall hunts out of Delpha, but never above the timberline where they now rested. It was in both their minds to explore the road to the north where the steeps of West Range took over Greenwood. "After the mines," Pollo said, repacking the saddlebags.

DonEel laughed at him, the ring flashing as he swept back his dark hair. "We should bring Alchia to see it. Would he come?"

"Aye. If you asked it. By the Gods, what a time we shall have." He held out his hand to pull the Souther up. "Come, let's finish with Loos."

They rode happily along the wide road south, wondering that no one had found it. In many places, it was true, time had all but obliterated the road, and when rocks and steepness forced a turn to the east and back down into the forest, only the absence of great trees and the change in vegetation showed the way. But knowing what it was made it obvious.

By nightfall they were as far south as they would have been on the more familiar road, but much higher. They were glad of the fur sleep robes in the mountain chill.

They lost the road in the morning beneath a vast slide of shale, too dangerous to cross with the horses, and they were forced to pick a way down to the base of it and around through a tangle of trees and windfalls, trying to find it again. DonEel took time to mark the place as near as he could on the map. And in spite of the delay, they were making good time, moving now west and above the fertile hills of the Shepherd country.

"Shall we go down to the pool?" Pollo asked as they warmed themselves at a small fire. "If the map stays right, we should be at the fork tomorrow."

DonEel looked at him quickly, then smiled. "We could. But should we?"

"We are faster by two days. If someone planned to ambush us there, would they wait? The road is well traveled in the warm season."

DonEel shrugged. The idea of a warm bath and the beauty of the spot tempted him, but there would be time to decide.

There was no choice after all. Before they came to the turnoff, they knew they were no longer alone on the old road. The horses gave warning first, snorting and shying away from the east side of the road. It could have been one of the larger predators, a woodbear or big cat—the road had dropped enough for it—but for the first time in days, the men rode with thoughts of their own safety, gauging the road ahead more alertly. They had entered the barrens, and the road began threading narrow passages between sudden ravines and jumbled masses of rock. A good place for an ambush, DonEel thought, and his shoulders tightened as a feeling of impending disaster grew, at odds with the sun-warmed silence.

The quiet was shattered by the scream of Pollo's horse. The animal reared, pawing at the air. Forced back to the road by the man on his back, he began to buck, lunging, fighting the hard hands controlling him. Shocked into action, DonEel spurred his own mount, forcing it ahead of the other. Pollo leaped to the ground, and his horse stood, sides heaving, muscles quivering with pain, a low, unnatural moan sounding in the broad chest.

"What happened?"

"I don't— Here!" It was a dart, no longer than his finger, the color of the russet coat it pierced, protruding from the flank. Carefully, Pollo ran his hand over the shivering hide, plucked quickly. The animal started, then held quiet.

"Don't touch the point," he cautioned, holding the blood-wet thorn. He examined it closely, and his face became the face of the man in the grove, stern and watchful.

"Poisoned?"

"We'll know soon enough." His golden eyes swept to the east side of the road, probing shadows and rocks. There was nothing to be seen. "Hold him." He gave the reins to DonEel and reached into the pack behind the saddle for a small leather bag, into which he dropped the dart.

"It could have been one of us."

Pollo agreed. They were terribly vulnerable here on the open road, and a high white cliff hid the path ahead. Away from the road, the land was a trap of holes and rocks—the horses could not travel there. They had no choice but to go on.

First pain gone, the horse was willing to accept his rider and seemed as anxious to move on as the men. Both men wondered why there had been no attack, and uncertainty pushed at them. They rounded the cliff at a run and found the road ahead empty. Still, speed became flight, feeding on itself, and they let the horses run, releasing nervousness in action, seeing the fork ahead and its promise of familiarity.

DonEel was never sure what he saw, only that as he approached the narrower road to pass through a cleft in the rock, something leaped up from the road in front of him, something large and vaguely man-shaped. There was a yell or scream, and his horse reared and bolted, shouldering Pollo's mount aside in

92

panic. Then they were racing away west, neck and neck, into the barrens of West Range.

"Did you see it?" Pollo asked as he brought his sweating mount to a lope.

"Not well. Was it a Zona?" But he knew already it was not.

Distance brought calm. There was no sound of pursuit, and no one on foot could have followed so far so fast. It was time to consider the immediate future.

"DonEel!"

He knew Pollo had fallen a little behind, and the shout jerked at him. He wheeled his mount in time to see the other's horse falter, to see Pollo leap free as it fell. The animal struggled wildly, grunting with effort, until the Delphan reached its head, holding it, speaking to it quietly. Then it lay still, breath rushing, great eyes holding the familiar face.

"He's dying," Pollo said flatly.

"Like Mesal. He will be long at it, Pollo. We cannot leave him to suffer."

It had to be done, for their own safety as much as for an end to the beast's pain. It was Pollo's knife that opened the thick vein, spilled crimson steaming over the hot rocks. And the Delphan's face was closed and hard as he took up the pack.

Wordless, DonEel fastened the pack to his own saddle, and both walked, leading the remaining horse. The long run had bought them time, but not enough. Walking, he studied the map, wondering how far the barrens extended, but able to see nothing but rugged country and a series of narrow canyons and ridges running east and west before them. The road made a turn to the west, perhaps climbing far enough into the mountains to avoid the roughest terrain. Instead, in spite of the frequent twists and turns, the road was already taking them west and up toward the summit.

The way became difficult again, filled with slides

the horse must scramble over. And it was hot. Nothing green eased the harsh black-and-white landscape.

The very harshness of the land that troubled them gave warning in the late afternoon. Here the slope was almost vertical, with long, sweeping slides of shalelike rock. They had stopped to rest in the shade of an overhanging cliff when below them they heard rocks clatter, pause, then gather momentum in a slide. Each thought, but was not sure, that there had been another sound in the confusion, a short cry or exclamation.

"They follow," Pollo said. "We can't go down."

The road was clearer ahead, and for a distance the land would work for them. Boulders lined the lower east side, giving some protection. They moved quickly, taking advantage, sharing a new nervousness. There were no more sounds. The heat increased as the sun westered, and as they climbed, feeling the pull in thigh and calf muscles, they were tormented by the frequent trickles of water that seemed to ooze from the rock itself. Water that supported no green growth, not even simple lichen, but built a path of crystal and stank so evilly even the horse would not approach.

Slowly the sides of the mountain changed, became less sere and cruel. A grayish-green vegetation appeared, and the air tasted alive again. Below was waste and desolation, but they were leaving the barrens. By the time the sun slid behind the peaks, there were some stunted shrubs and oddly twisted pines clinging to crevices, and finally the miracle of a spring that boasted moss and a few blades of grass. They drank, and even talked of camp, but searching back down over the land, DonEel thought he saw movement. Hours away from them, but there. They dare not risk stopping. They went on.

With dark, the wind rose, cold, yet smelling of sun-hot rock below and tainted with the odor of the dead springs. They entered forest again, knowing it by tall shadows and clean air, and they rested there, unsuppered, lying shoulder to shoulder beneath their robes. DonEel tied the horse's reins to his wrist, so any movement would wake him.

Hunger and cold had them up before dawn, and they ate bread and cheese and some dried meat from their packs, the last of the food brought from Delpha. There was no water near, but in an hour they found an icy spring and were refreshed.

"They did not come," Pollo observed, squatting by the pool. "Maybe they lost us."

"Perhaps they only wanted us gone from where they were."

Somewhat revived by the water and rest, they continued and soon found game sign. Broadhorned woodbuck lived here in summer, then, and there were big, heavy birds, too stupid to recognize the threat of man. By noon, they had bagged two with accurately thrown rocks.

They remained watchful, but there was no sign of followers, so while it was still light they chose a place to camp where there was water and dry limbs for making a quick smokeless fire. They ate well and let the horse graze on new grass. They moved on before full dark.

Even before they sighted the division in the road, they sensed their followers. Twice in the early morning, woodbuck broke from the thick cover on the east side of the road, ignoring them in a dash for height and safety. DonEel found himself wishing for the other horse.

"They will expect us to try to turn east again," Pollo said, examining the land to the west.

DonEel agreed. Though they had no idea who the followers were, there was no doubt that they were the same as had attacked north of Beauty. The only thing that didn't make sense was why they hadn't moved against them before now. The trail entered an area of dense woods, with downed trees and branches strewing the road. Picking their way through it, they were startled by a clattering roar ahead. The horse snorted and plunged, but DonEel held it, seeing a cloud of dust rise on the silent breeze and drift up the mountain.

"That was the east trail," he said softly, voicing a sudden intuition. "They want us to continue south but not on High Road." It seemed obvious. That was why they hadn't attacked. But if they were agents of Kylee, if he was behind this (and it was logical to assume he was), they should be content to have them travel south on any road. Why would they try to prevent them from reaching High Road?

Pollo suggested that High Road might be more difficult for attack, being so well traveled. "If you're right, they shouldn't bother us so long as we continue south." And in spite of the map's uncertainty, they could see that the road continued its direct line south.

"They will expect it." Therefore it was the thing they must not do. Relatively safe here in the thick cover, DonEel took time to look around. There was only one option, as far as he could tell. "If we leave the road here, maybe we could get high enough to miss them and cut back north."

Pollo nodded. They would have to do it. And quickly. This close to the summit, the sun would move behind the mountain early, and they would need light. The horse would have to be turned loose—it could not negotiate the rough country, and it might gain them valuable time as a decoy. They made quick packs, taking sleep robes and a few necessities. Once Pollo looked up from his quick work, almost smiling.

"It is like the beginning, it is not?"

They moved to the edge of the clearing. Pollo reluctantly released the horse, slapped it smartly, and the already nervous animal bolted, galloping south.

Before it was out of sight and hearing, they had returned to the thicket, shouldered their packs, and were working their way quickly and quietly up the hill. It was slow work through the downed timber, but far better than being exposed to whatever waited below.

Well above the trees, they turned back to the north, staying to the rocky clefts and patches of stunted trees, feeling the sun slide toward the high peaks. It was coming dusk when they started working their way back down to the road.

They were actually in sight of the road when a warning came that they had been anticipated. Pausing by a broad old tree to survey the road and rest his legs, DonEel leaned his hand on the rough bark. A sharp hiss and the feel of something hitting wood jerked his eyes from the distance to see a long feather-tipped dart protruding from the tree a hand's breadth from his wrist. For a precious instant, shock held him motionless; then he wheeled and dropped, pulling Pollo down with him.

"Arrow," Pollo whispered. "They have bows." The shot had come from below them, and to the north. The message was obvious. They had been allowed this far, but no farther.

Determined not to be turned south again, DonEel looked to the west, up the mountain, measuring the terrain. Seeing his look, Pollo nodded. Above, the bare rock had weathered and broken. They could climb and still be protected from those below.

They climbed, crawling, keeping close to the ground, silent. Once in the rocks and scattering of scrub trees, they began a casual northern angle. More than once, they thought they heard sounds below them, above the road, even what might have been a voice, questioning. The growing darkness made it difficult, but would confuse the searchers also, so they continued, staying high, threading their way through crevices and thick stands of pine until their legs trembled with the strain and the darkness was complete.

"DonEel—" The cry was cut off by sounds of struggle.

DonEel grabbed for his knife, leaping back from the rock he had climbed, landing on something soft and furry, thrusting the blade deep, not thinking into what, deafened by a growl of rage and pain. Something landed on him as he turned, hands grappled, and he fought, slashing, knife blade striking.

Not animals, then, but what— Fire lanced through his thigh as he stumbled, and more blinded by pain than darkness, he struck and struck again, wondering if the cry he heard was not his own. He jerked away from the suddenly lifeless grip, listened above the pounding of his heart. To silence.

"Pollo!" he called softly.

"Ah— Gods. I thought—" Leaving the thought unfinished, he came forward from the thicker shadows. "If there are others, they will be here soon. Come." He led the way up a steep incline, and DonEel followed, knowing they had no choice, trying to ignore the fire in his leg.

They climbed through a year of darkness until the first moon leaped above the trees with a promise of light. The second followed, and they found themselves coming out of the forest, moving up a rocky ridge straight for the great summit. The ridge was sheer on both sides—any pursuit would have to come from below, and in the soft light they could see nothing moving.

A wave of dizziness brought DonEel to his knees, surprising him because he felt so good, almost sleepy and happy. Blood loss, he thought quite calmly, waiting for Pollo to turn, or for the strength to rise. I'm bleeding, and I didn't know it. The thought almost made him smile.

"DonEel?"

"Sorry. It's my leg." He didn't want to worry the Delphan, but he was grateful for the arm helping him to rise, supporting him.

"Fool, you should have said. We can rest near. There is water; I can smell it."

Somehow he found a place to stop that was backed by rocks too steep to climb, and there was a tiny spring dripping steadily into a stone basin. It felt so good to rest, to drink the icy water and lie back.

"Your wound needs care. We will have to risk a fire." Pollo was matter-of-fact. The surrounding rocks should screen the glow from those below. With the brittle branches of the small brush near the spring, he soon had a small blaze going. In the light of it he looked at his companion and held his expression quiet. Beneath sweat-curled dark hair, the face was ghost-white.

The wound was bad, but not as bad as it could have been—a clean slice through the upper thigh muscle, slightly to the inside. It had bled badly on the climb, and dark blood welled steadily. He washed it with the cold water, hearing DonEel's teeth chatter, and in a moment cold and pressure had reduced the bleeding.

"They weren't Zonas," DonEel said suddenly.

"One. The one who attacked me. The others— No." He opened the packs and drew a robe over his friend.

"One had fur." DonEel shivered as the robe began to warm him.

"Some do. Not all." Pollo's eyes said he had another question, but he did not voice it. Instead, he began to prepare a meal of the dried mixture brought from Delpha. He fed the fire slowly and brought cold water to DonEel, then sat silent with some dark thought.

It was not a sound so much as the awareness of a presence. Almost as one, they glanced up, beyond the fire. Pollo reacted instinctively. Knife in hand, he moved to attack.

"Don't!" As instinctively, DonEel stopped him. "He could have attacked." He felt as well as saw the silvery eyes turn to him.

"He could be one of them—"

The eyes turned away, searching the moon-shadowed darkness, then returned to the two beside the fire.

"You are wise to be vigilant. There is no safety here." The voice was quiet, with a peculiar resonance, almost musical.

The fire flared, and they could see the face more clearly; a man's face—but somehow different—commanding respect. The color of dark wood, every feature was clean and sharp-edged; the fire-dancing glow struck red-gold highlights along nose and cheekbone, and the thick mane swept back above dark brows seemed to capture the firelight flowing about the shoulders. Standing still beneath their scrutiny, he drew his dark brows slightly together, casting his face into sterner lines.

"There are searchers abroad who do not need light." The voice sounded warning.

Suddenly Pollo's hand gripped DonEel's arm, hurting. In the shadowed dark behind the figure was a rustling, a movement, an instant's implication of wings. . . .

"DonEel, did you—" Whispered.

He nodded, feeling the ice-burn of excitement in his belly, and the stern face across the fire seemed almost ready to smile as the eyes turned to Pollo again.

"Take time to count differences later, philosopher. If there is to be more time for you at all, you must not stay here. There are more dangers than you realize. Leave the fire to tend itself. Travel upward from here, carefully. There is a path of sorts above. I will stay awhile and see you are not followed."

"He is injured." Pollo spoke aloud for the first time, and his voice held suspicion.

"I can go, Pollo. He is right. Trust him." He felt the flashing eyes and Pollo's hesitation; then the Delphan gave in and helped him to his feet. DonEel could feel the tension in his arm like a fine vibration, and wondered that he did not share it.

Under the watchful eyes they moved back through the rocks and began to climb. There was a path, a clear place, at least, for their feet. DonEel limped now, feeling the pain of his leg, moving in a fog long after the fireglow disappeared behind them. The high rocks cut off even the moonlight, and it was just dark and pain and hearing Pollo breathe near him, until some subtle sense told him they were no longer alone.

"Here." The resonant voice turned them. "Come forward around the rock, philosopher. There is a cave here."

Pollo's hand on his chest was a silent signal to wait, and in a moment the Delphan had gone, as though melting into the rock itself.

"Come, DonEel." It was not Pollo's voice; nor was it Pollo's hand warm on his shoulder drawing him forward. He caught a faint near-spice scent as he brushed against the strange figure. "Here you can rest." The voice assuring, warmth-touching, gave him strength. He felt the cave around him, space enclosed.

"Pollo?" His voice touched rock.

"Here." Surprisingly close, and a hand reaching to touch him as they waited in darkness, hearing movement, DonEel's world a lazy dream around the core of real pain in his leg.

Then there was fire, a jewel glow rising to tongues of flame beating back the thick darkness, and the being across the fire from them, still shadow-cloaked, but more clearly seen now. He was nearly naked, only a narrow band of some fabric about his loins, and examining him, Pollo admitted the body as perfect, smoothly muscled, and—except for the suggestive darkness behind the broad shoulders—as human and male as his own.

"I am without weapons, philosopher. Be at ease. Your belongings are here. And the food." A smooth gesture indicated the sleep robes and gear piled beside the cave entrance.

101

"We are in your debt," Pollo admitted, retaining his suspicion. But why do you take on our danger? You are one of them that pursue us."

The dark head shook once. "I am Ridl. Of the L'Hur. Not of those you call Nomen." For a moment he paused, as though listening. "Those who came after you now move south, down the mountain. You are safe here."

"How can you know this?"

"I know."

"Do you know also why they were after us?" For the first time, DonEel spoke, comfortable now in the fur robe. He felt those great eyes like the touch of a warm hand, and it was pleasant.

"Only the part of it, not the base or purpose. A new thing has come into Ath L'Hur, and one called Sa'alm brings it. I came from the land beyond the western mountains to learn more of it."

"Then you are in danger from them also."

"They do not know the L'Hur here by the eastern sea. It would be well if they do not learn of us yet awhile."

The warmth of the fur and the glowing fire joined with the weakness of blood loss to draw DonEel into a passive drowsiness where he listened to the voices and watched the two as he might watch a dream, pleasantly uninvolved, beyond even the reach of the fragrant steam from the stew beginning to boil on the coals.

"Yet you came to help us," Pollo pressed, seeking some way to know this Ridl.

"It is my fate, philosopher. It was told long ago that I would join with DonEel in a time of need."

This, DonEel felt, was important, and he struggled to achieve some measure of alertness. "You know me," he said, remembering the voice giving him name. "What is there between us?"

"Life." The strange eyes held him awake and would not release him. "You are my blood. My son by the

woman Chiral of Scarsen, in the great south wood."
Strange shadows moved across the stern face.

"Your son? It cannot be!" Pollo's hard voice leaped
between them. But though heard, it was unimportant.

Above the ringing in his ears, DonEel held to a
question. Could it be? Was it possible? The eyes held
him, and he slipped into a waking sleep where the
only reality was in the fire and the dark face above
it, speaking, telling him of the woman called Chiral
who came to bathe in the hidden and secret pool,
singing. It seemed he saw her there, white of skin and
dark of hair. And he knew the desire of the great
Ridl, the loneliness and curiosity and even reverence
felt for the innocent female. And so he had shown
himself, and she had been unafraid and had spoken
with him.

"Her thoughts spoke to me, as with the L'Hur, but
she did not truly hear mine." The rich voice spoke,
singing. "I knew she loved me as a man, and so I
coupled with her after the manner of her people,
earthbound, releasing their need only in pleasure. And
I was young and careless of her. I did not know she
was with child. Then she no longer came to the pool,
and I went near to Scarsen and learned she had been
given to JatRee of Erl. So I went to Kaht, our sayer,
and he touched her and knew of you, and knew you
would be as the First Ones, and accepted by them for
a time, until you had become yourself. You would be
safe. It was then Kaht told of our coming to meet in
a time of danger."

"Why now?" He tried to ask it aloud, and the effort
woke him from stupor to realize only a moment had
passed. Ridl's eyes still touched him, but were already
moving. Pollo yet rested on one knee, head turned
toward the darkness, startled.

"A night hunter," Ridl said to him, moving now
more out of the shadows. And the darkness behind
him was a cloak of wings, furled and regal as only
DonEel had yet seen them in that dream. "The

searchers have gone below the road. In the morning they will go back along the road to the north, hoping to cut you off and turn you again to where Sa'alm wants you."

"But what does this Sa'alm want of us?" Pollo tried not to see the wings.

"That I cannot yet say. Only that you are wanted. There have been others taken to Sa'alm, by those you call Nomen. And there have been deaths. Of a type I do not understand."

"Sa'alm kills them?"

"Not exactly. Nomen, and sometimes the wildlings, yes—the Zonas—take Truemen to the mines. That is where Sa'alm is, at times. But the ones taken are not dead immediately. They are—gone, for a time. Only later are they found dead, hidden in the steeps of the rocks, or the untraveled woods." The dark face bent to the fire.

"There has always been trouble between Truemen and Nomen. Now, I think, they are allied with the Beachers through the Zonas, somehow. The killing of Delphans is a plot to push us out of the other states."

"You misunderstand, Delphan. They do not take Truemen to kill them. There is some purpose. It is this purpose that kills."

Unable to make sense of this, Pollo frowned, filling their bowls with the nourishing stew. He offered to share with Ridl, but the winged one shook his head, saying he had eaten that day and their need was greater.

"Ridl, do they know who we are?" Roused by hunger and something he was not sure about, DonEel thought around the big thing in his mind, reaching for a stable reality.

"They know."

"Is Sa'alm one of the Nomen?"

Ridl frowned, and the darkness against his back stirred restlessly. "I cannot say. That is why I came here to the east land again. Our watchers could not

104

follow that one. It is as though for many days or weeks that one does not exist, and then is there. Always near the mines to the west of Loos, where you go."

"How did you—" Pollo began, than subsided under the direct touch of those eyes, glancing at DonEel.

"Pollo," Ridl's voice came easily across the fire, "the Delphans are wise, but they do not have all knowledge. There will be a time for great sharing between us, but it is not now. Until then, do not create troubles that do not exist. Trust your heart above your head." He rose from where he had rested against the rock, and moved toward the cave entrance. "Perhaps I may learn more of those who came against you. It would be safest for you to wait a day here while they look for you. And best for DonEel's leg. I will return here before the next night ends."

When he was gone, the cave seemed empty. Both men felt a need to speak, but lacked words, and so were silent. Exhausted, no longer hurting, DonEel fell asleep, but it was long before Pollo could lie quiet. The impact of the one called Ridl came full now, with his absence. An impossibility, a dream, stranding him between wonder and fear.

SEVEN

THE day of confinement chafed Pollo, but he could see DonEel needed the rest. The long climb and blood loss had sapped his energy, and though the wound was not inflamed, it was painful, and walking would do it no good. So they rested, talking about Ridl, and finally, as they must, about his claim on DonEel.

"It is not possible," Pollo insisted. "For all his beauty he is not human. Surely you cannot believe him."

"You did not hear him, then?" And asking, he knew that somehow Ridl had given the tale only to him.

"Hear what?"

"I'm not sure. Perhaps it was a dream. But if so, then he gave it, and it was the truth."

"But it cannot happen. Surely your mother would—"

"She died bearing JatRee's child before my second winter. I did not know her." In the firelit cave, his eyes were wide and dark, watching his companion's face. "I am yet myself, Pollo. Ridl's words did not change me. Does it matter so much to you?"

"It couldn't. You know that. I think even he knew." The smile that touched his lips was rueful.

In spite of his suspicions, Pollo did not doubt Ridl's knowledge or wisdom. He knew without doubt that he was not of the Nomen. "He is like the heroes in the old tales, too magical to be part of this world. I find myself wondering if this is but a dream."

"It's real enough," DonEel assured, examining his leg. He remembered they were pressed for time. The Council of Delpha would allow them some time for exploring the old road but not too much. If this injury delayed them overlong, Alchia would insist on a search, and almost surely take the road to Loos himself.

"Ridl spoke of one called Sa'alm last night, but still, it was Kylee who sent the message to Alchia."

"And the map. Yes." Pollo had the same thought. Whatever Sa'alm and the Nomen were doing, it was almost certain Kylee was involved—only he knew of the old map. The question that needed answering was how he could gain from this, and what part the Beachers played.

"He is still my uncle, and Alchia's brother," he reminded DonEel. "Some of the honor earned by my father falls to him. Especially in the eyes of the

Council. Even I dare not accuse him without evidence." And only at the mines or Loos itself could they hope to find it.

It was well after dark when Ridl rejoined them, appearing silently at the cave entrance. "Peace," he greeted them. "It is I. How fared you?" He came to the fire, making no effort to mask his differences, as he had at their first meeting, and the great wings cloaking his back added magic and majesty to his presence. Raised by a people whose appreciation of beauty approached worship, the Delphan could not help responding to this being, and Ridl met the adoring eyes with an enigmatic near-smile, subtle, but saying enough to bring unaccustomed warmth to Pollo's face.

Before sharing what he had learned during his absence, he asked after DonEel's leg and was assured he could travel.

"As well. Your pursuers believe you eluded them and reached High Road, or turned north for Delpha. It will give you time, but not enough to waste."

"Perhaps we should return," Pollo suggested.

Ridl disagreed. "There are the islanders, those you call Afs, traveling toward Loos with message birds. Alchia could not wait overlong for word of his son. From here it is quicker to Loos."

"Unless we meet with Nomen again," DonEel pointed out. But Ridl had considered this also. The map they carried was known to others, but it was not complete. As the Delphan mappers had suspected, there was a road on the west side of the mountains, connected to this eastern route by several crossroads. One such road crossed the summit just to the north of the cave. It was not so well marked, but it was passable, and on the west side the road was easier. By morning, he promised, there would be riding animals waiting for them on the western side.

"Those who first found the map do not know of

that other road. They might, in their search for you, cross over the mountains, for some of the Nomen have lived there. But the risk is less."

"Will you travel with us?" Pollo asked it, and DonEel was glad. The thought had begun in his mind also. But Ridl shook his head.

"My way is more easily made by dark in this land. But I will be near and perhaps join you from time to time."

"Would it not be easier if there were others of your people here with you?" DonEel asked, wondering at the fearlessness of the one he dared not think was his father.

"They are with me." The quiet response carried a message beyond its words, and a feather of presence touched the Souther's nape. Almost, he understood. Then he shook off the feeling and looked up to find Ridl's eyes on him, warm and waiting. But nothing more was said of it.

Ridl came in the darkest hour before dawn to lead them over the summit, steadying DonEel where the rocks were treacherous. It was cold here in the high country before dawn, and they wondered that he did not seem to feel it. He smiled at their curiosity. "It is a L'Hur thing. Cold is a feel of the body, and the body is servant of the thought, the mind. We learn early to be master, not captive. But it is nice to be at peace and warmed beside a fire."

It made sense of a sort, and was one more thing to know of him. He bade them farewell on the crest of the mountain, telling them where the horses would be and explaining carefully how to reach the road before turning back down the east side of the mountain.

Once they crossed the summit, there was no sign of man or Nomen. Animals that in the east land had grown shy from hunting merely eyed them curiously here and went on with their feeding. The trees were giants, protected by mountains on both sides, and the road was deep-carpeted with fragrant needles. The horses Ridl had miraculously provided were good ones—Shepherd quality, Pollo thought, though there were no ownership marks on them. It was a good ride, silent in the dappled shade with the sound of birdsong and water flowing fast in the bottom of the canyon.

Silence was easy between them, and when they did speak, it was of the mystery of Ridl, of his beauty and their luck in meeting him, rather than of the more personal concern he had brought them.

They traveled steadily for four days, following the old trail through steep canyons, fording many fast streams in this lush and beautiful land, glad for, but wondering at, the lack of intelligent inhabitants. It was worlds away from the states on the east side bounding Long Sea.

There was an abundance of small game, easily snared, and firm, sweet-fleshed fish to be taken from the streams, and Pollo did most of the providing. The wound in DonEel's leg continued to pain him. Examining it daily, he was reassured that it had not become poisoned, but it refused to close like a normal wound, and he could not help thinking of Mesal. He felt well enough, though weaker than he would have liked, and the slightest exertion caused fresh bleeding.

Feeling his unspoken worry, Pollo insisted it was only lack of rest and too much use that kept the leg from healing. More than once he suggested they stop for a day. He found a large velvet-leafed herb familiar to his people as an aid to healing, and he bound the wound with the soothing leaves, but though the pain faded for a time, the frequent loss of blood was a drain on DonEel and he withdrew into silence, riding with his own unshared thoughts.

On the fifth day, the trail swung sharply east, climbing, and through the trees they could see a cleft in the skyreach of West Range before them. They were well up the slope to the south pass by nightfall, and the evening fire was welcome against the highland chill. Knowing they were approaching the territory of the Nomen, they chose a secluded place for camp, turning their thoughts once again to the concerns of Delpha.

"When we return to Delpha, we must ask permission to bring an expedition to the west land," Pollo decided. "Perhaps after the child Masila would—"

"I cannot return." DonEel finally voiced the thought that had occupied him many days.

"You'll have to. Only we two know the way."

"I mean to Delpha."

"Of course you shall return with me. Alchia would never forgive me if you did not." He honestly did not know what his companion meant.

Seeing the confusion, the attempt to tease him out of a mood, DonEel shook his head. "Pollo, you know that I cannot return. I would be an outcast, a tolerated freak at best. Simply because of what I am."

"But you have already been accepted. Even courted."

"And Argath? If she knew?"

"DonEel—" His eyes dropped to the ring flashing on the tanned hand. "Argath is a woman of her own mind. Her choices are her own. Do not try to make them for her."

"She is Delphan and proud of her purity."

"There is none to say you are not as all Delphans."

"And if I got a child on her that was—"

"You don't know this, DonEel. You already have a son who is—" Eyes shifting to the fire, he did not say "perfect." He did not want this conversation, not now. "You accept too easily. I am not yet sure Ridl is—"

"My father." DonEel gestured slightly with one hand, and Pollo saw that Ridl had indeed joined them. He stood above them in the near-dark, great wings outspread a moment, as still as sculpture in blue and jet. By the Gods, he was beautiful. Even grown familiar, his magnificence was unearthly, stirring the soul.

"You know him, Pollo." DonEel spoke softly, yet felt Ridl's attention on him. "Would you have me deny that of me that is Ridl?"

Ridl's presence halted the conversation, and, watching the tall figure approach, DonEel knew beyond doubt that he knew what had been said and was left to say. Dark silver eyes studied him as they made their greeting.

"Your leg does not heal, my son." The quiet words touched them both, saying every unsaid thing, as the L'Hur produced a small leather pouch and squatted by the fire, seeming somehow regal and mystic in the simple action.

"It is not poisoned."

"Not fatally," Ridl agreed, drawing leaves and small white roots from the pouch and breaking them into a small vessel. Seeing him thus was somehow incongruous to the men; yet he lost nothing in the action, adding water to the herbs and setting them on the coals. "The Nomen had no wish to kill. Their weapons were treated with herbs they know that prevent healing. They are much skilled in plant use, both in healing and harming."

The vessel began to boil, sending up a pungent steam. Stirring the mass, Ridl told DonEel to bare his leg. The crude bandage was blood-blackened and stiff, and it hurt more than he expected. Then Ridl crouched close beside him, and he smelled the warm spiciness of him and preferred to dwell on that, to study close the fine-grained curve of cheek and jaw, the thick fringe of lashes about the tilted eyes, the free sweep of dark brow so like the line of outspread wing. Once the large eyes leaped to meet his like a touch, and he felt warm, seeing the stern mouth soften to a near-smile. He drew a quick breath as dark fingers explored the wound. It hurt. But the hands were

111

gentle, and as Ridl bent over him, one wing lifted slightly, as easily as an arm might shift out of the way, and pressed warm, unconsciously embracing his shoulder.

"There is no sickness in it other than the lack of healing." Ridl spoke to Pollo as he dipped a bit of cloth into the warm liquid he had made. "The leaves you used were a wise choice." And to DonEel, "This will feel hot a moment," as he began to clean the wound.

Hot? It felt like ice, then warmed, became fire. He hissed between gritted teeth and he felt sweat start out on his face. Then it passed, and both heat and pain ran out of him like water. Another cloth was moistened with the liquid and bound with clean white strips of some unfamiliar material over the wound. It was gently and firmly done, and the hands were finished with him.

"Keep the herbs in your pack. They are good for all healing, and they grow also in the east land. Your people should know of them." Tall and wing-cloaked, he was again Ridl, high-mountain lord, ready to take his leave. They would reach the mines the next day, he told them, and though Sa'alm was not there now, there was no way to tell when that one, or some of the ones who had come after them, would be in the area. He advised caution, saying he would try to join them at the mines.

In the morning, the soreness had left his leg, and the wound no longer bled. Pollo's obvious relief showed how much he had worried and kept from his companion, and he was more than grateful to Ridl.

"But I do not understand him, DonEel. What he says and shows of his power to know somehow frightens me," he said as they topped the pass and started down the slope toward the mines. "I'm not sure I want to know how he knows, but I must believe him." Then he grinned his golden grin. "And I

112

swear I envied you your wound and need of him last night."

Generations of working had left a mark on the land about the mines. Stands of timber had been sacrificed for shoring in the tunnels that branched off the natural caves that were the first mines, and miniature mountains of debris hauled from the labyrinth screeded the openings, forming artificial canyons and cul-de-sacs.

But there was no working here now. A masked cat stood blinking at the interruption of its nap in the mouth of the largest cavern, then turned to amble clumsily to less busy surroundings beneath a pile of fresh-cut timbers. No smoke rose from the smelter down by the stream or from the cook area.

"It isn't right." Pollo turned in his saddle to search the rutted road leading down the mountain. It was empty. "The fires should burn here from first thaw to snowfall. The youth in Loos and other near towns compete for the positions as firemen."

More cautiously now, they circled the work area and found the camping place above the smelter where the water ran clean. It was deserted, and there were signs of a hasty exodus. Cooking utensils and some articles of clothing were strewn about the area, possibly by curious wildlife. Dismounting, they walked through the area seeking clues. But there was nothing but signs that a recent rain had erased any tracks. There was no evidence of battle.

"It has been a week or more," DonEel decided, looking at the place marked by long-burning fires, cold now, and packed hard by rain and time.

"The clothing and things are from Plains, for the most part." Dusting his hands, Pollo remounted. "Maybe Kylee's note was truth, but if the Beachers ran them out, it seems they would have stayed to man the mines as he said they wished to do."

113

"There may be some sign in the mines. If not, then surely in Loos they will know what happened here."

They would investigate the mines, but now, with the sun westering toward an early dusk behind the high peaks, it would be best to find a place for camp. They chose to move back up, away from the mines into the timber. It wasn't natural for the mine area to be deserted except in winter when the road was impassable, so a mining party could arrive at any time, and they would rather not be seen.

Gathering dry limbs for a fire, DonEel thought how easily they had come to live like fugitives, and wondered how it affected the Delphan. The little hollow was a secure camp, with abundant feed for the horses, and both men were pleased and relieved to see Ridl, come silent as always, a sudden breathtaking silhouette against the sunset sky, great wings outspread a moment, then furled and cloaking as he ran gracefully into the hollow.

"It is well you chose to remain hidden," he told them in greeting. "There are Zonas and others near. They wait on the river near the plain to keep miners away until Sa'alm returns here."

"Had we turned for Loos, we would have met them," Pollo remarked soberly. "It would be best if they did not know we had come to the mines."

Ridl agreed. Some of the ones who had hunted them on the mountain were for killing them in spite of Sa'alm's wishes. It could always appear an accident, and once done would not matter.

A hastily set snare by the creek caught them a fat bush fowl for their meal, and Ridl agreed to join them. As the bird roasted over the coals, he moved out into the dusk and returned shortly with a handful of long white tubers, wet from the creek. Arranging them in the coals, he explained that they were a food regularly harvested by the Zonas. And later, eating them, Pollo wondered that no other people had discovered them. The nutty-sweet flavor added to the meat, and if it grew wild, it could be tamed and cultivated.

"There is much to be gained from sharing," Ridl agreed, tossing bones into the fire. "Once this trouble is settled, the effort could be made. But it must come from Delpha. And there will be opposition."

"Would your people join with us?" The Delphan's desire for it showed in his face, but Ridl shook his head.

"Not yet awhile, my friend. There are differences between us greater than you yet know. But there will come a time." He turned to look once at DonEel. "It begins with you and the Delphan. Do not make choices that are not forced on you." It was his only comment on what had passed between the two men on the trail, and accepting the subtle rebuke, DonEel felt Pollo's eyes on him.

By full dark, Ridl had gone, feeling it would be useful to know when and if the Zonas on the lower road moved. They accepted this, but each knew the other shared a desire to have Ridl with them when they searched the mines.

Ridl's warning that Sa'alm could come at any time without their knowing brought them to the mines early. There were torches stacked in the mouth of the main entrance, and they each took two, though there were torches set at regular intervals in the walls. And there were marks carefully drawn in white along the rough passages that Pollo could read: signs telling where the latest work areas lay, leading them through the varied natural caves with many branching paths and chambers, to a newer, more structured sort of passage shored with heavy timbers. Now the cold, dead smell of rock and time was joined, but not erased, by the incongruous fragrance of resin.

The path led downward, and soon there were other tunnels branching off at odd angles, following slashes of ore visible in the torchlight. To DonEel, walking silent beside his companion, it seemed the weight of the mountain crowded the cold air, making it thick and unsatisfying. And the silence was deafening, so he could hear the sound of his own living heart and the breath moving in his body above the steady rhythm of their steps.

They were far below the natural caverns when they found evidence of current work. Here the scars in the rock were fresh, and the heavy timbers glistened with beads of soft pitch, like drops of gold. And there were tools—scattered as though a break in the work had been called and at any moment the miners might return and take up where they left off.

"This was not dug." Pollo's voice came echoing across a wide chamber where he was inspecting one of the many branching corridors. "They must have broken into the caves again."

Joining him, DonEel spotted torches set into the walls of the natural passage, and there were fresh scars in the rock, as though they had begun to mine this area also.

"Do the caves above join this?" he wondered, looking for the ubiquitous markers.

"I don't know. I doubt they have been explored beyond where the ore shows. The purpose here is mining."

"There must be some opening to the outside." DonEel pointed to the torch flames, leaning to the right.

The marks of exploration led to the left, so, leaving a torch burning to mark the juncture with the dug tunnels, they moved down the rougher passage. The walls glittered with metallic ore, casting back vagrant flashes of firelight, and it was, in its own way, a pretty place. But the descent here was steeper than in the mines proper, and DonEel admitted within himself a growing reluctance to continue. He longed suddenly for light to see more than a few paces. Even the air, fresh as it was here, smelled of age and

116

nothing alive. Direction had no meaning here but down, and time seemed frozen into the rock itself. There was nothing here. Even the rock scars had ceased.

The awareness of danger did not grow on him gradually; it struck like a blow, halting him. A cold, heavy pressure between his hips, chilling down and up his back like sickness.

"Pollo!" He grasped his companion's shoulder, understanding suddenly how ridiculously vulnerable they were. Helpless in darkness, they carried their pool of light, and anyone, or thing, could see them without being seen.

"What is it?"

"I don't—"

The tiny sound was loud in its simple existence here where there were no sounds. A life-sound—breath or movement, he couldn't tell, except it was ahead of them. And Pollo heard it. For an instant his gold-gilt eyes met Don-Eel's in mute sharing, then leaped back the way they had come. They dared not extinguish the light—there were too many passages and only their own tracks could lead them to safety. As one they turned back, hands on knives, knowing it was too late, hearing the rush of steps behind—and before. Trapped.

There was no time, even now, to choose darkness. They came too fast, shadow figures rushing from both sides, hands seen as strange claws, reaching, striking, strange cries as well-aimed blades struck. Too many. DonEel went down beneath a bleeding weight that smelled of Zona, fought free. . . . The torches, fallen and smoking, confused his sight. He glimpsed Pollo's bright hair in the struggling figures, leaped forward, and was again attacked from behind, arms pinned. A rope settled about his shoulders. . . . A moment of violent helplessness as his knife was knocked from his grasp . . . then freedom, and two strangled cries behind. He turned, barehanded to meet—

"Ridl!"

"The Delphan—" The winged being loosed the rope, and together they leaped forward, DonEel scooping up his knife in stride.

"Pollo!" Echo ate the sound as the cluster of figures ahead slipped around the rocks and were lost to sight. He took up a smoldering torch and ran ahead, saw the narrow opening, the hint of movement vanishing in darkness. . . .

Crowding through, he found himself in a small circular chamber with three dark passages leading out. Heart thudding, he crossed the chamber, tried to hear movement. . . . Nothing. But Ridl behind him.

"DonEel." There was warning in the voice, halting him briefly. "Do not. Sa'alm has taken him." The eyes commanded, held him like hands.

"I must, Ridl!" Torn, he favored impulse, whirled to the nearest exit. Black hit him like—nothing. Vertigo. Instant destruction . . .

EIGHT

HE stumbled, blinded by light, stunned. On one knee, he looked at the cold white floor, the lights moving in mad, colored patterns along one wall of gleaming metal. White panels provided cold, motionless light. For a long, lonely minute he crouched, felt walls crumbling, dissolving someplace inside. . . .

"How the living hell did I get here?" he (not himself) said (thought) in someone else's voice, knowing . . . something. . . .

Then it passed in a wave of fear and hot, rising anger that woke a basic instinct for survival. He stood, blade in hand, poised, recognizing enclosure. And a door. Like none he had ever seen, but he knew it. His eyes scanned the room, ignoring the oscillations of familiarity-strangeness. Behind him, a blocky square of silver-black set three steps above the floor. That, memory said, was the way he had come here. His thoughts crystallized about that. It was all he had. It was enough. They had taken Pollo beyond here. He would follow.

The door gave him trouble for a minute; then, as his palm touched the curved plate in its face, it slid silently into itself and he was looking out into a gently curved corridor, soft-lit and empty. Senses keyed alert, he dealt with the strangeness around him by accepting it. It was. His leather boots made no sound on the polished floor as he moved quickly out of the room toward the curve of the passage. They were here; he knew that. And ahead of him. But how far? How much time had passed?

The corridor continued vacant, the curve unchanging, closed and faceless doors set at regular intervals on his left hand. There were markings above them, perhaps numbers, but not any numbers he had ever seen. He wasn't sure he knew what he was looking for, and he wasn't given time to find it. A door opened silently beside him, and a man stepped out into the corridor, saw him. . . .

"Hoy, where— Prime!" A hand dropped beltward, and the head turned toward the still-open door, mouth opening to call— DonEel couldn't risk it. He moved quickly, ready blade silencing the alarm even as another voice reached out from the hidden room. "Pojon? What's it?" Oddly slurred, the meaning was unmistakable. The newly dead man had a friend. There was no choice but to retreat to the room he had just left.

He ran silently, not breathing until the curve of the corridor hid the corpse. For a moment, then, he was lost, and panic jigged in his thoughts; then he saw the door, wider, marked with red-and-yellow zigzag slashes. Already he heard outcries down the corridor, then more voices and running feet. Before he had the door open, they had rounded the corner and spotted him, calling for him to stop. He leaped through the opening, but not fast enough. A flash of red and heat and numbness in his left elbow. Then he was inside and the door whispered shut.

Panting lightly, he faced the other door and the three steps before it. Ridl stood just behind that. Of that he was sure. Yet the silver-shimmer looked impenetrable.

"Unknown." A hard male voice rang through the room, startling him. "The gate is not set. Do not approach it. Open the door and come out and you will not be harmed."

He stood silent, shaking his head. If they had to ask, perhaps they couldn't get in. Rubbing the numbness of his arm, he looked up at the door.

"Unknown, you have one standard unit to come out. After that, we will take action."

It meant nothing to him. He mounted the three steps, reached out cautiously toward the silverness, into it. It was like holding the wind back, resisting and yielding, there and not there. As his hand was not there. He jerked back, unnerved by the sight of his arm ending at the wrist. It had not been like this on the other side, only black and empty. Some deep-buried instinct said this was not a door now, but a trap, a danger. Yet he had come through before, from the mines. There were knobs and lights on a metal panel to the side, within easy reach of his right hand. Perhaps a key. All were marked, but in some script he could not read.

A sharp hissing jerked his eyes from the panel. Danger, real and deadly, filled the room invisibly. He knew he was trapped and helpless even before the rising mist exploded across the bridge of his nose, shattering his skull. One last option remained, and he took it, leaping hopelessly into and through the mute silver nothing of the gate. . . .

Darkness, real and solid as the clawing acrid fumes dragged into his lungs, and then, not that, but something nearer and more familiar, and knowing that this was what he had feared, this, and not the other thing that he could not now name. For an instant he knew everything there was to know, but the time was too short. Unlike the first trip through the gate, the agony of dissolution did not pass, but grew and became the fact of his departure, falling down and out and away, and how would it be when he. . . .

"It doesn't have to be, for us." Thinking this was their one chance. "We could run out through the Big Deep. Just go on."

The yacht danced away from the red sun, alive under his hands, and he loved the feel of her, the heady excitement of the chase still flowing in him. He was alive, his muscles sang with it, and counterpoint, the deep warmth of Zhan Llir beside him, steadier now, tempted but anchored more firmly in the bigger need they sacrificed for.

Safe, whisper-flashing through the Big Deep, away from all threat, they finally relaxed. As always, this after-battle time left them stranded, so it was good to lie back in the absolute nonlife of deep space, to let go and feel the smooth harmony of their minds flowing and folding, sharing a duality so close it was unity. What, he wondered again, would it be like not to have this, to depend on the gross deceit of word and flesh for the only sharing?

"Deon." Speech-sound startled him awake, and though he felt the word-intent, and the union was maintained so it seemed his throat voiced the sound of his name, he roused and listened to the well-known voice. "Deon, it won't be forever. Timaret and the others from Stilks say it will end, like sleep, and we will know again."

*The same? The question rose unbidden from the
secret depths of him, where his private fears lived.*

*"Deon, this is part of what you are. And I. It was
so before we knew. Est."*

*And then they were gravity-bound, and he stood
face-to-face with Timaret, knowing him wise and
sure, and strong in that, and fear clawed the walls he
had built around it, so he went first to the golden
transfer room, took the cup that held sleep, and welcomed the hand that led him to. . . .*

"DonEel!" The call thundered through fire-rained
darkness, a part of the tearing agony in throat and
lungs that no longer existed. He fought to reach it out
of terror, grasped it, and came together because he
did. Falling blind and hurting, he came through the
blackness choking, grateful for the strong dark arms
that caught him.

It was some time before he could breathe without
coughing, or see through streaming eyes, and then
they were outside, away from the threat of the strange
black door. The sun was bright and warm, slanting
down from the western peaks, and he looked around
at openness and freedom and distance.

"You brought me back," he said hoarsely.

"I called." The L'Hur looked down at him thoughtfully. "You heard, and your will brought you to me."
The great dark wings stirred restlessly, undiminished
by the bright sunlight. "I do not understand it, but
you used a L'Hur thing to return."

"Where was I?" The reality of what had happened
was beginning to surface, and it made no sense.

"Your mind knows. Before returning, you knew
something else also."

"I dreamed a strange dream."

"You remembered." Abruptly, he changed the subject. "They may come searching for you. Let us go
into the timber, to the camp."

"But Pollo—"

"Sa'alm has taken him. Come."

Wanting to refuse, DonEel rose, and Ridl led the way, climbing rapidly, his dark face closed in thought. He maintained his silence as they prepared a meal, giving DonEel time to think, to remember.

He sat quietly, looking around the hollow, seeing the horses grazing by the creek, the flash of some late bird winging nestward. All familiar and known, like the earth, solid beneath him, the smells of the wood. Yet everything was different and changed by the thing he had seen, the place he had been. Knowing it, he felt afraid and slightly ill.

"Ridl, it is with me as with Chiral, it is not? My thoughts speak to you." He risked speaking of it because the thing he feared was worse somehow. Ridl he knew, to some degree, and he was grateful when the dark head nodded agreement. "Then you know—when I went through the door, you know what I felt."

"DonEel, I could not follow until you reached to me. I only know that it was distant, and that it is a greater threat than we knew, and not only for the Delphan. Yet you do know, and you deny the knowing." A still and listening silence fell across the hollow, and staring at the winged man, it came to DonEel that he was communing, that some airy invisible presence had come into the shadows about their fire. Skin roughening, he shook off the feeling and stood up. The sun was setting, the day gone. Did Pollo yet live?

"I must go after him."

"You will not return alive. Only Sa'alm will gain."

"So be it. I must try. He did not leave me alone in danger." Death faced all men—there was no choice but in the manner of it—and without Pollo there was nothing here for him—he could not travel the path that led to Argath and Alchia, and even to Ridl, without him.

"Then you will go." A shadow moved in the great

123

silver eyes. "It is your fate. But perhaps the L'Hur can help you, can give you that in yourself that is L'Hur, that brought you back. It has never been done for any but L'Hur, but knowing of you they have agreed.

"To what?" Beneath his thoughts he felt a frightened excitement stirring.

"To help free you from that which makes you sleep, to open the doors you have locked against the power in you, the power of the L'Hur. But there is danger in it; if you cannot master it, it will destroy you."

"And if I can?"

"You will join the L'Hur as equal, knowing and known. You will no more be as you are, or think yourself to be."

"I am I, Ridl. I will go after Pollo. There is nothing for me here if I do not."

"You have life. Others have lost as much and continued. You could go back to Scarsen a hero and take the place of Ronan. You would have a people and a place, and they could grow through you. And your son is there."

Scarsen was forever away, a forgotten beginning to this life, and it felt strange to be reminded of it here. He wanted none of it and was absurdly annoyed with Ridl for reminding him.

"You also have a son, Ridl."

The stern face swung toward him in the lurid sunset, and the eyes held him long and long, letting something that was purely Ridl touch him. He felt (dimly still) the deep and powerful emotions that were the unknown qualities of the L'Hur. "But not solely mine or L'Hur," Ridl reminded finally. "You risk more than you know by accepting." And DonEel thought there was a touch of pride in that voice. He had finally to look away from the flame of the eyes, feeling yet the power of their regard.

"Would it help me now?"

"Yes. If it is possible for you."

"They—your people—would not have agreed to certain failure."

"The threat from Sa'alm touches them also. There is risk in it. But they do not request anything from you; they only offer the way. They know something of your power. It is a time for risk, but you are not like them. Or I. I know your desire for this; now you must know the danger. Once the joining is begun, it cannot halt. The doors cannot be closed and sealed by any but you. There is fear on this path; the L'Hur call it the first death." And one last time. "There is another life you can choose. You need not do this."

"You believe I will fail," the man said quietly.

"I do not know. Some who are L'Hur fail. For them it is the true death."

There was no need for DonEel to voice his decision; Ridl knew it as he did, and nodded once.

"When?"

"It is begun." The L'Hur voice held finality, but for a moment, searching, DonEel thought nothing had changed. Then he felt them touch him, knowing them, though he had never known them before. Committed, and knowing it, he felt fear loosen his legs, and he sat down beside the small fire. Just once he reached out for Ridl, but before he could know if he touched him, he became a thousand viewpoints of himself, and the L'Hur. He was everyplace they were, seeing him, and he flowed out to them, felt each of them touch the stream of himself and pour it back, a flood of selves rushing into the smallness of him. He grew large as the mountain beneath him, hot as the fire before his eyes. He felt himself entering himself from everywhere and could not contain it all; it crushed him, he hurt, his heartbeat shook the earth with its thunder, and fear built the agony in his chest.

Ridl crouched across the fire, impassive as stone, only his eyes marking the slow darkening of the pale face, the subtle bluish cast to the lips.

Pain became a sort of ecstasy, a kaleidoscope of color-taste-sound-feel, but pain still, and the fear had become a way of being, a hook pulling him back as he began to juggle seemings and realities to seek that which was his true self. Irritated, he searched for the source of the pain that had become a dark wall between himself and himself, found it, and knew it to be a wrong in this place, challenging him. Knowing and doing were one, and he set it aside and forgot it, rushing away into himself with the power song of the L'Hur, down and down and down, until down had no meaning, approaching the center of being. Memory acts flashed vivid and intangible as reflections in still water, and he dove through, becoming them and beyond at the same time; not alone things that had been and were, but might-have-beens that were not and forgotten and yet to be, more and faster, no-memory-all-memory, knowing everything, being everything, becoming a million and one beings scattered as the stars. Frightened again by his own immensity, he grabbed for vision to still the dream. Eyes opening saw flame, knew the insatiable appetite of combustion, and did not know that his flesh grew hot before his attention became him the stone, and as his eyes moved he became and became, and other senses woke, so he was sound and touch and grown down into the earth like roots, and up into the sky, his own symphony.

His head moved slowly, and finally his greedy eyes met those of Ridl, saw him, familiar comfort, protection, not-him-but-other-equal. . . . Reaching, he was reached, and knew the perfect correctness of his/Ridl's massive pectorals, the heavy bands of muscle cording his/Ridl's back, the wonder and balance of the mighty wings. . . . He was no longer DonEel, but Ridl, alive and deep-sounded and known, seeing that that was DonEel lying beyond the little flames, still, but for the wide and burning eyes. *That* was he, beloved of Ridl. . . .

His eyes closed, and he was again DonEel, knowing for an instant that he had been offered everything and all that had been for himself and the L'Hur and Ridl, and the box of time had been opened, so he had gone back and out, sported with all life, and known all loves and hates of all being. . . . Too much. Only one thing had the reality of memory: Ridl loved him, cared, hoped. . . . *Ridl! God/demon/father . . . It is too much. . . .*

Return, my son. The way is yours. Alone.

Return. To what? Where was back? He floundered, knowing panic and running from it, casting off knowings and seeings and beings until there was nothing, and darkness and stillness and aloneness, and he drifted in gratitude.

He slept, and the ground was solid and kind, buoying him up from the depths he had known, and the fur robe drawn over him smelled warm, of spice, and the gentle scent and darkness worked, healing the new openings, coming to terms with what he had become, what he would know if he chose to wake.

But Ridl sat watchful, eyes turned inward, communing with the L'Hur. They, too, had learned and grown, so whatever the fate of the initiate, the L'Hur would lose nothing. It was the way. It worked.

If DonEel woke whole, he would be one of them; they would know him always, as he them. They were one, and Ridl had gained a son. Yet they were aware, more now than before, that this one was different, of other than L'Hur blood, and his becoming them would change what they had been. It was this chance Ridl had asked them to take, and their assent had come from the store of ageless wisdom that was their heritage. They had changed before, and still were, and would remain, L'Hur.

DonEel woke, feeling vast distance between then and now, though only a few hours had passed, and two of the moons still rode above the mountains.

There was water for his parched throat, and warm broth made of the Delphan rations, and he was grateful. He felt fragile and weak, and his head ached. Tending him, Ridl assured him it was the same with the L'Hur, the mind and body protesting a new activity.

He sat robed and thoughtful, feeling himself come awake slowly. He seemed to remember a strange conversation with Ridl during the forgotten time, and now he thought perhaps it had happened.

"Ridl." He said the word in his head, silent.

"I am here." The voice was Ridl's, but no sound touched his ear. *"It is the knowing, the L'Hur way. I hear-know you as you are."* It was thought, but textured of hard, spice-scented warmth and enclosing wings. Ridl. He had the peculiar sensation of seeing-hearing-feeling better than before, when he had seen and heard and felt. He could feel the flame of Ridl near, like a banked furnace, the shape and essence of him. And thinking of it now, he traced the links between them, down to the basic patterns transmitted in the moment of conception. That shook him, for he was suddenly, in his own senses, the culmination of that outrush of seed, formed in the incandescent pleasure of that joining, molded of the terrible beauty of lust and gentleness and fear that Ridl knew as love for the human woman. Now and evermore he would know himself a part of that superb maleness, however modified and transformed by the human female flesh that had nurtured him.

Dealing with it somehow, he looked up to the being he was beginning to know, and was almost shamed by this new knowledge he had not anticipated, this revelation of secrets he would never have dared to share.

Following the thought, the L'Hur's lips curved slightly, saying recognition and rightness. "It is so with us all, my son. A memory of the blood only." He chose to speak aloud, binding the texture of his voice with the tapestry of meaning that thought rippled between them.

"And the visions are reality also?"

"Of the soul, the true being." His head turned away a moment, as his attention focused on something more distant. "Listen." It was command and direction and guide, and somehow the newborn ability in the man caught the strands of that attention and opened to a rushing, spontaneous joy that wrapped him like strong drink: a song, filling him, mind and flesh, with pleasure.

"The L'Hur, DonEel. They rejoice with me and welcome a son."

Drawing back, warmed, not knowing if Ridl thought or spoke, he tried to sort the myriad knowings that flooded him.

"It will come more quickly when you are rested." Ridl soothed him, touched his head lightly. "You will sleep for a time."

It was sunset when he woke, and it seemed for a moment the night and day had not been. Simply a dream conjured up from a confused and troubled mind. He went to the creek and washed in the cold water, shocking the last of sleep's heaviness from himself, knowing as he did so that Ridl was once more in the mines, reminding him of the black gate. And knowing that, he knew it was all true, wonderfully, terribly true. Distance was no barrier to them anymore. He was L'Hur.

"*And more.*" Ridl's voice spoke soundlessly in his mind as he entered the caves, striking cleanly against the tangle of personal thought. "*The L'Hur marked it. You are not like the other young who have joined us. L'Hur, yes. But also man. You can know our history and being, but that in you that is not of us is yet hidden in a way we do not understand.*"

History? Wondering, he suddenly understood what Ridl meant. Each of the L'Hur was not only an individual, but the result of his race. The strengths and weaknesses of the whole worked in the one, either by acceptance or habit, or as a thorn in the spirit, urging action.

"For those who would change what they are, yes." Ridl smiled in torchlight as DonEel joined him before the black opening. "When it does, heroes or demons are born."

"And fools?"

A superbly complex and subtle shrug was his only reply as Ridl studied the featureless black.

"You wish me not to go." He did not know this from the L'Hur way of touching, but from the manner of him. The sharing of selves was not complete, after all.

"You have gained much, DonEel, but there has not been time for learning how to use it. Like any power, it is two-edged, and if you do not understand it, it will benefit neither you nor the Delphan."

"I cannot wait longer, Ridl." Not while Sa'alm had Pollo, might even now be doing whatever was done to kill those who were found returned and dead. "If it is with me now as it is with you, then I can know the purposes of those who have him. Their thoughts will be mine, and I can know where they are."

"If you listen correctly. They are many, and not in accord as the L'Hur. It is not so simple a thing as you now think, but if you listen for them, there are differences that you come to know, feelings and angers and loves and pleasures. Heed them. You can become lost in their images." The great silver eyes held to him, brooding silently a moment, but he did not say to take care. "Your Gods willing, we shall be with you. As we are now."

There was no reason to wait longer. Hand ready on hilt, DonEel moved to the square of black, looked once to the winged man, and, clasping him firmly in his mind, stepped through nothingness.

NINE

I T was the same: three wide steps; silent, blinking colors; cold white light. Empty as the first time. Behind him, the flat silver surface shimmered with a depth and emptiness that brought a shiver to his skin, remembering. Breathing deep, listening, tasting the alienness of this place, he found no trace of those deadly fumes, only a difference from the air in the mine. For a moment, before daring to reach out, he reached inward, found the hushed melody of the L'Hur with him—and realer, closer and knowing, Ridl. He had the momentary thought that his head had become an immense area where all lived, pursuing their own thoughts and actions, all within his view, seen by him and seeing him.

As quickly as he became aware of Ridl waiting there beyond the silver nothingness, Ridl was aware of him. "*It is well, DonEel.*" The word-meaning sounded in his head, but anything beyond that was screened behind a wall of Ridlness too solid to penetrate. Still, the communication was a path to follow, showing not only the way back but ways of knowing, of hearing and seeing, that were not his, but L'Hur.

There were others here; he could feel them like movement and tension of purpose on the edges of awareness. He reached, having the clue from Ridl, touched an anger that clenched his fists until he realized it should not; it was, after all, not his anger. And, understanding that, he began to listen beyond feeling, to understand new word-sound-meanings, not easily, not as he had expected after the superb clarity of Ridl and the L'Hur, but it was happening. Two men, arguing.

"He was here. He done it to Pojon. Jayt seen him. We chased him to the terminal and Jayt burned him. But he got out." A wave-chorus of sympathy-agreement wove about the anger-sharp word-meanings.

Then a feeling-meaning-voice that held menace in its total lack of emotion, colorless as ice on stone. "Inside, with the door autolocked, the gas pumped in, and the Portal set for income. And he escaped." Something bright and quick flashing through the thoughts.

"Pojon's murdered, Muset."

"Yes." The word was implication and indictment.

"Wait, now. The unknowner did it. We wouldn't, couldn't —not to a friend." The communication fell apart in fear, collected about the frozen stone of the one called Muset. "Friends die on Jimo. Men see to that." The response to those words, anger tinged with fear and frustration, brought sympathetic heat to DonEel's face; yet he was intrigued as well as repelled by the alien aloofness of this one. Following intent as well as word, he sensed that this was a situation to Muset's liking, that he hoped somehow to profit from it, and he gained from the fear and anger of those in his power.

"Muset." Another, less timid, thread of word-meaning wove through the web of DonEel's attention. "The caught Prime was not alone in the cave. I was with Sa'alm and saw him, as she did. It flashed her that our catch team missed him. Maybe he—"

"There was no body in the terminal." Cold logic interrupted the bravery of the speaker, battering down his confidence, leaving only feverish frustration and rage. But the mention of Sa'alm and the catch team had captured DonEel's attention, brought it away from his own position and mission. It was him they argued about. Muset, the one ruling here, did not believe he had been here and escaped, though others knew it.

Sharpened by his own place in the activity about him, he followed traces of the brave one, touching red-hot anger as it collected and moved away from the hard chill of Muset.

"I'm going to get away from him." The thought-words came so clearly DonEel thought they had been spoken, then realized they were only thoughts, safe from the hearing of all save himself and the L'Hur. The idea grew, solidified, became the sole focus of the mind he touched. He felt hard-lit and brittle word-images form. "It can be done, I can work the porter like anyone else. . . . I'll kill me that gorgon-snake before— No. Oso'd know. He knows everything that goes here. Too small to try . . . I can get away, back to Syrcase. . . ." Memory-images, fantasies vivid with desire and anger and need, filled DonEel's head, confused and compelling, until he forgot he stood alone in the middle of the white-lit room at the foot of the three steps. He followed the hopes and plans and dreamed-of victories of Jayt. He would go to the terminal, through the porter, not back to the caves like last time, but to the citadel. Sa'alm would be busy with her new catch already, or with Oso, and the relief teams would be taking time off with Muset here on Jimo. He could do it now. He had to do it now, before he and Kam were blamed for Pojon's death. Either that, or they'd have to try to kill Muset, and he didn't think they could do that. The Zniss had a reputation for being almost un-killable. And Muset would see they paid for a murder he knew they hadn't done. He had been out to get them since he'd caught them with Sa'alm two shifts ago. Black, but it had been worth it with her. She was wilder than tripdust and hotter than a Christian hell when it came to playing games for fun. No mother, her, demanding things of him and Kam, with Kam. . . .

The thought-images flowed from rage to swift male heat smoothly, compelling memory-feelings, detailed, shaming, exciting, glorious. . . .

"DonEel!" Cold and clean, the command severed

the connection, jerking him from the breathless waking dream of Jayt's fantasy. *"You have the way. Do not yield to what is not yours."*

"Yes." He thought the word gratefully. The way to Sa'alm and Pollo was his, taken from Jayt's thought. But he remembered other things. *"You never said Sa'alm was female."*

"I did not find it important." There was bite to the thought, and humor flashed between them before the worry Ridl held came forth. *"DonEel, the door carries you far. The danger is greater for you where Sa'alm is."*

"Perhaps. But with you and the L'Hur to—"

"If we can." Controlled doubt shadowed the Ridl-flame, doubt built of distance and time and lack of knowledge.

"If you can, then. I must go before Jayt or Muset comes here." Knowing they would, not remembering how he knew it, he turned to the silver shimmer, noting knobs and dials to the right, easily reachable from where he stood on the top step. And now he knew the symbols; directions and settings, not only from Jayt's mind, but so familiar from— He shook off the feeling, reaching to touch the smooth knob, to feel it turn easily, catch, then turn farther and stop with a faint snap.

The silver wall dissolved into eye-aching complexity and was gone to black.

Ridl's voice sounded clearly against his own thoughts: *"Remember, DonEel, it is Jayt who remembers Sa'alm, not you."* Jest or warning, DonEel could not tell for sure. He faced the blackness, knowing beyond it lay, not Ridl and the other darkness of underground, but Sa'alm and Pollo, and a place he knew from Jayt. Pressed by a knowledge of time, and Muset here, and a fear that wanted to grow on him, heart bumping slightly, he reached to the steady flame of Ridl above the mindsong of the L'Hur and stepped into blackness, wrenched breathless, dissolved, as his balance changed and his foot touched—solidity.

Yellow light struck him, gentle after the cold white of the other place, and he knew suddenly: I have been here before. Remembering the feel of soft high boots clasping his calves, tight dark fabric about thighs and chest . . . He leaped away from the feelings and clung to now, reaching fearfully until he held again the clear muted song behind his thoughts. It had worked; they were yet with him. The knowledge gave him strength and confidence.

The air felt odd against his throat, full of strange movement, heavy, and tainted with alien scents that set his teeth on edge. Reacting to instinct, he did not need Ridl's warning to seek about him for trouble. And he found it. Somehow, in the multitude about him pressing on his brain, he found multi-images of the place where he now stood, and mounting alarm both distant and near to him. They knew he had come here, and they were coming to find him. Instinct worked beyond the strangeness and confusion of his thoughts. He moved, running, soft leather striking whispers on the hard floor. He choose a corridor at random; yet it seemed he knew it. There were doors and feelings of emptiness and age, and the taste of dust here, and behind and above him the alarm grew, and orders went out. . . . Fighting panic, his eye caught a strip of dark where one door stood ajar in the long emptiness. He took the chance. Knife ready, he slipped into a narrow passage, felt rather than saw the downward slope of stairs.

Safe for a moment, he stopped moving. There was a chance he would be passed by here, but if he had to make a fight of it, a narrow door and stairway would be more easily defended than open corridor.

In time the searchers came down his corridor, not hurrying, coming close enough so that he could hear their voices.

"Don't know why they keep sending us down. Oso knows they can't go anyplace but up." Grumbling at

an unwanted task, and though DonEel felt nothing of
the excitement of the chase in them, he tensed, unable to believe they were less aware of him than he
was of them.

"Being on Jimo with that snake comin' all the time—
I'd risk running and facing Oso myself, man." They
stopped near the door and DonEel's throat went dry.
He braced for the moment the hand would reach—

"Not when Oso's Sa'alm takes the team," one of the
searchers answered, and the sound of shared laughter
moved away, back the way they'd come.

"He must've got past us, headin' outside."

Heart pounding, DonEel strained to hear, to know,
touching minds concerned briefly with vivid male
fantasies of the female Sa'alm, triggering a familiar
itch in his mind. He shook his head, struggling with
fear and confusion, trying to think his own thoughts.
Where was Sa'alm now? Where had she taken Pollo?

Then the searchers were gone, turned back to re-
sume their various occupations and games and talks
and leisure things he could not attempt to understand.
One clear image appeared in the thoughts of one of
them: a large and beautiful room, round and domed,
with statues and tapestries, unearthly in its beauty.
Yet he held it clear and close in his mind as he
waited, and as he thought on it, a name came: the
Rotunda. I saw it, he thought, when it had been seen
by so few, when the miracle of those colors was our
special joy, and the perfection of that sculpture. . . .

Impossible. But he had been here before. He knew
that. He had been here when it was different, still
locked and secret. He would go out of this corridor
and to the core, take the ramp that wound about
that featureless black cone that was the center of the
citadel, the one part of the structure they had been
unable to breach.

The strangeness of his knowledge swept him, over-
whelmed him. Because he did know, and it was not
possible. *"Ridl! What is happening to me?"* The ques-

tion rang in his head as he reached for that calm and strength, felt it surround him.

"It is not L'Hur, DonEel. It is your memory, from the human part of you. We cannot deal with it. You are too far, too different. We did not think it would come so quickly. You must come back. Perhaps—" . .

"No. Sa'alm is here, and Pollo." He clung to the familiarity of the L'Hur as he stepped from his hiding place; yet he knew where he was going, knew that central point, the spiral ramp that would lead to anyplace in the citadel.

The gentle purr of the alarm nearly sent him back to the stairway before he caught the direction and intent of those about him. Someone else had used the transporter. And as quickly, he reached out and touched a familiar mind. Jayt, made narrow with fear and excitement, running, knowing where he was going and how to get there. There was a good chance he would make it, and eased somewhat by the transfer of attention, DonEel wished him luck.

Waiting near the end of the corridor for the pursuit to move away, DonEel stepped back into the golden light that marked the transporter terminal. Above it, from where he stood, he could see the immense black base of the citadel's core. And he remembered that someone called Harmond had said this central part of the building was a power source, an impenetrable cone thrust clear through the vast and mountainous structure they called the citadel. This was the thing that powered the Portal. But he didn't know, or want to know, now, what that meant. He didn't pursue the thought. Instead, he disciplined his attention to the life around him, hearing it, feeling it—in some indefinable way, sharing it. Jayt and those pursuing him had moved upward, away from him, and the flavor of the chase was of a game, something they had done before, not serious. Good; let them play their games.

Across from him, past the ornate frame of the Portal, a wide arch showed the dimmer entry of the

137

main corridor, the ramp that curled around the cone of the power source, leading up through the many levels to the top of the structure. It would take him where he needed to go, to the level of the living quarters. Yet could he trust this knowing? A subtle reassurance from the one constant in his mind let him move forward, running lightly across the broad bare floor.

Accept your knowing, Ridl seemed to say, wordless, but there in his thoughts like a song he could not forget. Yet his knowing was confusion, vital nonsense. What did it mean? If he could just stop and be still, he could know, could understand. No matter. First he had to get Pollo.

Jayt's chase had moved up into the center of the citadel too fast for the ramp. Another mystery he almost understood, and he was alone here on the lowest level. His feet found the ramp an easy incline, and errant thoughts flashed pictures behind his eyes: of another level he almost knew, the living quarters that were—had been?—lavish in decoration, like the great meeting room.

Three levels, and there was growing confusion and impressions from outside. People here, a lot of people, so he felt naked and exposed in the wide corridor, and the rattle of memory churned in his head, pressed down by more immediate concerns, but annoying, like a steady ringing in his ears, interfering. Accept it, the steady presence of Ridl seemed to advise. If only he could.

The clamor of thought-activity was a growing threat, calling for attention he couldn't afford to spare. There were doors, widely spaced along one side of the corridor, and at any moment one could open. He realized he had his knife in his hand, and stopped suddenly, fighting the noisy confusion in his head. He knew he could shut it out, create silence for himself. But that would leave him blind. Instinct took over, and he moved to the nearest door, actually touched it, seeking the pressure plate that would slide it open. Then he sensed the activity on the other side, and sweat started out on his face. Beyond the door, a dozen or so people were relaxing, waiting for someone or something.

Back the way he'd come, quickly, to another door. More cautious now. And there was nothing behind it he could sense. It opened to his touch, and he slipped inside, into a short corridor. Again the sense of having done this before washed through him, swinging him toward the left-hand door, a dark room that brightened as he stepped inside. He knew that swift lighting should frighten him, but he had expected it. It was a furnished room of soft, muted colors and rich-pillowed couches, with tables and chairs and rugs. Beautiful. And empty. He leaned against the door breathing hard, forcing calm. Safe for the moment.

Gods, he was thirsty. And thinking that, he knew there was water through the curtained door opposite. Accept it. Later, when Pollo was safe, he could study it. He let his thirst push him across the thick rug, skirting tables and unfamiliar things, through the other door. Here was a bed and clothing hung beside it, and a small, austere alcove behind a screen, obviously functional. As he had known.

Thirst quenched, he sat on the bed trying to think. There were too many of them, more than his mind said there should be. He had been insane to think he could storm the citadel alone and free Pollo. He had to think, to plan. He would have to go where the people were, sooner or later, somehow. The internal confusion of too many thoughts, the constant almost-memory of being here, distracted him, leading his thoughts astray again and again. He took the chance, knowing he would have to do it sooner or later. He stopped listening. Silence, and relief, like setting down a heavy burden, swept him; relief so great it left him weak.

So. What to do? He knew (as he knew too many

things) that Pollo was here on this level of greatest activity. But how to get to him through the constant comings and goings he could feel around him? Finally his eyes focused on what he was looking at, the clothing hung neatly near the foot of the bed. Why not? It was something to try, something other than waiting here, enjoying the beautiful silence.

He stripped quickly, pulling on the fog-gray tunic and pants, concern over possible fit fading as the peculiar fabric seemed to mold itself to his body, oddly comfortable, clinging to calf and thigh and chest and arm, but without restraining him. He left his own clothing folded beneath the cloud-soft covering on the bed, strapping his knife about his hips.

He paused at the door, letting his mind open to the mental activity, once again aware of the L'Hur and Ridl focused on him, and the closer noise of unstructured confusion that had nothing to do with him. There was no more activity concerning Jayt—he must have made it. But now, for the first time, a more subtle flavor overspread the confusion, familiar from Jayt and others: thoughts of Sa'alm. She was somewhere near, and many of those around him were aware of her. The tenor of their feeling and thought was a peculiar combination of fear and distrust and challenge and excitement and the desire to please. His own blood quickened, touching the uncensored private fantasies, but Ridl's warning yet sounded in him. Sa'alm was unimportant, except that where she was, Pollo must be. Some inner warning kept him from seeking the female's thoughts. He avoided her, searching instead through the area near him that was the focus of many thoughts. He moved into the central corridor again, knowing it was empty, and followed the pervasive currents of activity.

At the center of the level, the corridor branched, another wide, level passage running out at an abrupt angle away from the core. Brighter lit, it was (he knew before rounding the corner) occupied.

The being—he could not quite call it a man—who sat at the desk in the center of the corridor saw him coming, but there was no alarm in the sluggish mind, only mild curiosity and stubborn officiousness. The thick head, hairless and vaguely off-shape, nodded a greeting.

"Yo, travel-tech. Out of your sector." The voice reminded him of the spring song of the great frogs in the waters of Blackwood, but muted. There was no threat to him for the moment, so he moved closer.

"If you be outbound, I don't see you, but be gone before the med-techs get back to duty." Flowing thoughts underscored the words, giving meanings. He knew now he was wearing a uniform, the wrong one for this area, and the being that spoke to him was a guard who thought he was leaving his post but didn't care unless it meant trouble for him. More important was the information about the med-techs. The guard's ill-feelings about this group came through easily. He envied them their easy and interesting duty.

"Med-techs on duty here your shift?" he asked, trying to appear casual, even bored.

"Coming. To follow up your last catch from Jimo."

"This soon?" It was hard to keep the emotion from his voice, to hold still long enough to grab self-control, for the image accompanying the guard's words were of a man, not clearly seen, but there was no way he could mistake that sun-bright hair. "Is it in there?" He nodded toward the door behind the guard, picking up the neuter pronoun from the other's thoughts, not questioning it. "I'd like to see it."

The guard stared for a minute, deciding, then got up, not gaining anything in height. He kept silent, but DonEel felt the flash of hate for him, for anyone in the smoke-gray color of the travel-techs, the ones who got to go out, to do the exciting things and see action. And hate for the one who stood with him now, the renegade Andro so much like the Prime Perfect, and lording it over everyone.

141

"Not a real view," the hornlike voice informed him. "Looks like a male Andro, but Sa'alm calls it Prime." He pulled a short metal rod from his tunic, applying the tip to the door, leathery head bent in concentration. The door moved, and so did DonEel. Knife ready, he struck with the hard hilt above what he thought was an ear. It had a sound like hitting wood. The guard squeaked and went down, broad rump blocking the doorway. DonEel vaulted the heap, found the room beyond white and dim-lit, and full of strange shapes and combinations of glass and metal. Silent. He pulled the limp guard aside and felt a flash of panic as the door slid shut.

"Pollo?" Calling quietly, scared now of what he might find in these alien surroundings, he sidestepped a bulky cabinet agleam with glass dials. And saw him, seated, bright hair alive above his still-white face. He was dressed yet as he had been on the trail, sprawled in the dark chair, head back, neck and chest exposed and vulnerable, eyes closed.

"Pollo." At his touch, the eyes opened, opaque and unseeing. Yet to that other touch ringing behind his eyes, DonEel felt confusion, images and phrases tangled like snakes, whipped by fear, gone to silliness and unable to help it. Giving up.

"Pollo. Wake up." There was more sting to his voice than he planned, and the eyes wavered into focus. For a moment then, the internal confusion drew into a brilliant point of pain.

"You, too, then. Or do I dream again?"

"We've got to get out, Pollo. Now."

"I tried—" Thoughts tumbled back to the fact of DonEel, clinging to that.

He might have argued further, but the figure lying near the door stirred, sighing. Acting on impulse, DonEel grasped the nerveless hands, drew the Delphan up. Out of the chaos of noise-feeling-hearing, Pollo laughed suddenly, and a chill roughened DonEel's skin. What was wrong with him?

There was no time to worry about it now. He shook the man once, hard. "Listen to me. We have to leave here or we will die. Come."

"If you wish it, then I must. As I have always. Do not be angry." The green-gold eyes were those of a child in the beard-shadowed man's face.

Swallowing a sickness there was no time for, DonEel led the unresisting man toward the door. It opened at a touch of the rod he had taken from the guard, and they were out in the brilliantly lit corridor. He paused, supporting Pollo with one arm. There was no alarm yet, no one coming into the area. But there soon would be. Touching his own fragmentary knowledge of this place, he decided suddenly, turning back the way he had come, toward the central corridor. Jayl had not taken it, nor his pursuers. Perhaps it was not used. And nothing would be served by getting lost.

His urging of Pollo was gentle, at odds with a growing sense of insanity, of being here in this impossible place. He wanted nothing more than to sink into the security and wholeness of the L'Hur singing behind his thoughts, and he was very afraid of seeing too deeply into Pollo.

Totally committed to his purpose, he turned downward, toward the Portal room. He very nearly ignored the warning, the sudden brightening of the mental noise around him. Then the cold ice he knew as Muset touched him, and he stopped short, looking around wildly, half expecting to see the known-unknown Zniss. He wanted desperately to step through the black nothingness, to get back. The thick, syrupy tangle of Pollo's thoughts spilled into his mind as he strained to know, tripping his own thoughts and impressions. He saw-felt Muset ahead-below them, in the room of the Portal. They were so close, another few minutes. . . .

When they stopped moving, Pollo sagged toward the floor. Hauling him erect with an arm already

143

trembling with the strain of his weight, DonEel struggled to listen beyond his confusion, to think. He would fight. There couldn't be more than two of them in the room, the two he could hear. . . .

But already his body was moving him away, up the ramp, obeying some deeper command, some memory of something else. It felt—right. And he didn't have time to sort it out. Pollo half-walked beside him, a constant drag on arm and shoulder. Up, he thought, five levels to the wide entrance, the beautiful museum-like gathering place that opened into the gardens— No. Wait. That wasn't his thought, but one he had picked up here. Wasn't it? He couldn't remember, couldn't be sure. He fought the confusion as he fought the physical strain of climbing until he reached inward for himself and found the calm harmony of the L'Hur and submerged himself in that healing touch that was his lifeline to home, to Ridl and sanity. And the fact that he struggled to move away from that was one more insanity.

Pollo's increasing desire to stop, to lie down and rest, flooded him, stumbling his feet, turning his legs to stone with a weariness that wasn't his. He moved through a series of fever dreams, balanced precariously between a memory of safety that moved him forward and the untroubled mindsong of the L'Hur calling him back.

The great carved doors leading to the gathering room were so familiar he scarcely looked at them. He couldn't remember getting here, but that didn't matter now. Panting with the exertion of half-carrying the Delphan, he forced some semblance of awareness, striving to reach beyond the heavy doors, to know if the room was occupied. It seemed empty in spite of the tumult of thought around him. He would have to chance it. Weariness, and the need to move both himself and Pollo through this nightmare, was becoming impossible. He had nearly reached his limit, and he knew it. Out, then, believing there was a chance for peace and quiet.

The doors separated as silently as always, and whispered shut behind them. A miracle of technology from— He forced the thought away, stood still, surveying the expanse of the mosaic floor, the delightfully random spacing of the statues. Even Pollo seemed partly drawn out of the fog of dreams and nonsense to know wonder.

Straight ahead, lost in shadow, was the great entrance, the wide stairs leading up to the exit from the citadel. But something turned him right. Their footsteps whispered on the marvelous floor, swallowed up in the immensity of that room as they moved along the wall for what seemed hours. It hadn't changed.

"DonEcl—" The soft voice shocked him from the waking dream as Pollo stumbled on the top step, pulling him off balance. For a moment the bright eyes were clear and hurting and frightened. "I cannot. Please—"

"You must." Feeling the lucidity fade, slip back into confusion, DonEel ground his teeth together until his jaw ached, and his voice, though scarcely more than a whisper, was hard, driving, and not his own. "Get up! Dammit! We haven't time!" He helped, sweating, aware again now of the waves of thought-feeling-being radiating from this place. There was a narrow alcove, and finally the door, high and narrow. Relief gave him strength to approach, to key with his palm. She had said there were twenty different woods from as many worlds in the carving of this one door. . . .

He shook his head savagely against the intruding memory, and then it was gone in a burst of alarm. Below them. Rage and fear—a ring growing from one sharp, slashing thought: *The Prime has escaped!*

Adrenaline whipped him. They knew Pollo was gone. There was no time for caution. As the door opened, he thrust Pollo through, tasting cool, moist air, and space. Stumbling in darkness, he needed no

145

vision to tell him they were outside the citadel. He half-carried his charge straight away from the door, pursued by the growing alarm as more and more of the citadel's occupants became aware of Pollo's absence. Moving as fast as he could force Pollo, he had a vivid mental image of the interior of the citadel, the uniformed guards spreading out, running through corridors, searching rooms, communicating, calculating....

The surface changed beneath his feet, and he tripped, fell heavily, twisting to protect Pollo, who was not even aware of the fall. Forearm bruised against a rock, he cursed, scrambled up, and tangled with a shrub. Panic kicked him, but he mastered the fear, shivering. He knew this place—he had to believe that, depend on it, however impossible it was. They were in the garden—he knew that. He tried to force an image of it but found nothing but confusion and mounting fear and anger beating against his thoughts. His head ached savagely, and he could not remember. Frustration brought a quick, absurd stinging to his eyes, a desire to weep, and this weakness shocked him. They were out and still free. That was all that mattered. He began to move away from the citadel, feeling the ground drop slightly beneath his feet, smelling water near, and the alien pungency of a vegetation he had never seen. Without his realizing it, his night vision had returned and he was avoiding the dark blotches that were shrubs and tangles of greenery.

It was important to get away. He had planned for it, wanted it, but— The thought slipped away as he reached for it.

A light flashed red and startling behind him, and his head snapped around, heart thumping— Nothing. But dark and—

A strangled sound broke from his throat as his eyes lifted up and up and up, seeing the citadel for—was it the first time? The bulk of it reached into the stars, blotting out the pale-green glimmer of the sky. Sharper than a mountain, it loomed like West Range.

For one paralyzing instant he knew the vast bulk of it was falling slowly to crush them— He found himself trembling, one arm thrown up to ward off the blow. The fear ebbed slowly as he saw what had caused the illusion: a faint string of lights moving over the enormous shadow. Familiar, one part of his mind said; the Belt, the seventy moons of Syrcase. The other half of him, the real him, son of Ridl, child of Scarsen in Blackwood, shivered in this alien place, seeing now not only the moons but the sky, the green and shimmering star-choked vault— His lips skinned back, snarling, as his hackles stirred. *No! No-no-no—* rang through a mind divided against itself. He wanted to run, rooted to the spot, seeking escape from the alien place. Eyes shut tight, all thought blocked out, he fought for stability and calm and comfort. *Where am I?*

"*DonEel,*" the sweet song whispered. "*DonEel, son of Ridl, of the L'Hur. We are here with you. Be at peace.*" Their presence, the greatest mystery, washed over his mind, stilling him, as the dark and noble face of Ridl built against the blackness behind his eyes. This was reality. Calmer, keeping his eyes from the terrible sky, he looked for Pollo, found him asleep, protesting as he woke, trying clumsily to get to his feet.

"Nothing works," the Delphan said cryptically. And at that moment DonEel walked face-first into an invisible barrier.

He was too strung out for fear; nothing remained but rage. His fingers felt a glassy web. A fence. He should have known. All right. That meant a gate somewhere. Ignoring the tumult of images and mental racket outside his own head, he turned left, down a gentle slope, then up, more steeply. His gate was a broken section of the web, overgrown with branches. Forcing Pollo to climb, half-pulling him, they tumbled into limbs and weeds and rolled free. Here the shadows were thick, and the air full of the scent of growing things, smells that, however alien, were reassuringly familiar to the woods-trained Souther.

A leg-aching eternity later, he found a place to hide. A ravine cut into a side hill, deep and narrow and overhung with branches. They literally fell into it, and feeling the closeness, the security, DonEel simply lay still, knowing by the images and half-formed thoughts from his companion that he was all right, not even aware of the fall.

After a while he stirred himself enough to get them back into the security of an undercut, and with immeasurable gratitude for stillness, he embraced the Delphan lightly and drifted toward sleep and dreams of Ridl and Muset and a female creature known as Sa'alm.

TEN

LIGHT woke him to heat and thirst and a protesting bladder—a sanity of ordinary physical needs. The noise in his mind was there, but not so overwhelmingly important, and he felt, as he relieved one need, that the long flight in darkness had been more nightmare than reality.

Pollo slept deeply, only vague dream-images disturbing the surface of his mind. Kneeling beside him, DonEel studied the pale, unconscious face. The faint glisten of moisture on brow and upper lip could be marks of some pain he could not touch. He knew that this was no ordinary sleep, but he feared waking him, so he sat and watched as the heat grew worse and the light brighter, and Pollo's hair darkened with sweat.

This would accomplish nothing. Licking dry lips with an equally dry tongue, he finally got to his feet and began to explore their hiding place. They had been lucky. They were screened from all but a direct search up the gully. But there was no water here—wherever here was. He knew suddenly that the step through the Portal had been one of incredible distance. Fear scattered his thoughts—fear of the sky, the air, the distance. Where were they? How had it happened? He should be even more afraid—he knew that—but something, some shadow of something, held panic at bay, as if he knew—

Ridl touched his mind gently, curious, but was unable to do more than ease the mounting tension. It helped. DanEel began to think of immediate problems. He had to find water. He debated a long time on leaving Pollo, but there was no choice. In the end he took the precaution of finding pliable vines and carefully but securely binding the man so he could not leave this place on his own.

"Pollo," he said softly against the sleeping ear. "If you wake, lie still. I will be back as soon as possible, but I must go." There was a flicker of awareness on the flowing mental pattern, but he could not know if the message had penetrated to the sleeping mind.

The wilderness they had come to was only a knoll. He climbed through tangled shrubbery unfamiliar to him and looked out over the slope to a sprawling city. The clamor of thought was like Long Sea breaking against the shore, and he tuned it down, surprised at that growing ability. His own dual feeling of familiar-unfamiliar was easier now in the light, also. He turned once to look at the citadel and felt momentary awe. Memory said it was a building, but his experience would not allow him to believe it. It was simply too big to mean anything to him. Besides, his needs were too imperative and he could not go there. He turned down the hill, toward the sea of buildings and people below.

He had thought himself prepared for anything after the citadel, but the reality was so far from his imaginings that it was unreal. There were people here, swarms of them. But they were like no people he had ever imagined. They were all Nomen, fantasy creatures, more of the impossible dream he was caught in. Only his needs were real, so he went down to them.

He lost the urge to hide himself because no one noticed. There was constant motion, and ignoring the ones he passed, he followed the mainstream. There were no shops here that he could tell, no fountains, only featureless buildings and hard paved walks. He didn't know what he was looking for, or if he would know it when he found it, and it was some time before he had the presence of mind to listen to the thoughts around him, beneath the constant rumble of sound.

Time was the greatest concern in those he touched. And things. Everything. Moving things. Nonsense until he made the effort to translate. Warehouses, then, and buying and selling and— Ships?

He had walked far with his eyes on his toes, trying to make sense of the muddled information. Now he saw that the buildings had thinned, and between them, ahead, were a high fence and gates, open for the streams of beings moving in and out. Beyond was emptiness and a wide paved area. Across this flatness were rows of odd-shaped— Buildings? *Craft*, his mind said, reminding, meaning nothing and everything. Excitement drew him forward. This was important, somehow—information that would fill a void he hadn't known existed until now.

Immersed in curiosity and excitement, he jostled someone, heard a sound midway between a bark and a three-note whistle that his mind interpreted as a cursed warning. Wisely, he kept the automatic apology to himself, staring at the furred and fanged creature dressed in what appeared to be wide bands of metal. Now that he looked directly at it, meeting its peculiar eyes, he could feel its unease, a sudden almost-fear it felt of him. *Because of the uniform. Oso's colors.* It was unexpected luck, giving him enough confidence

150

to approach the gate, to walk through unmolested, following a growing excitement.

So intent was he on what stood across the paved field, he did not at first notice the sudden press of the crowd about him, trying to push him back. Then he was annoyed, looked around for the cause of the sudden change in direction, found it in the attention of those around him. Coming in his direction through the crowd that parted like water before it was a creature more bird than man, towering above the other odd-shaped creatures. The proud posture, as much as the curve of furled wings over the back, reminded him irresistibly of Ridl. Touching the thoughts of those around him, DonEel sought a reason for the mass behavior. *Duratheen.* The identification flashed from a dozen directions, colored with automatic caution, even fear.

He stared at the Duratheen, not giving ground as the creature approached, reaching out to sample the thoughts of that massive head almost automatically. He knew strength and pride and a particularly predatory eagerness. It was a swift, clean knowing, and savoring it after the muddied conglomeration around him, DonEel stared as the cruel face turned suddenly toward him, black eyes meeting his. The stab of understanding and recognition was too swift for reaction.

"*Man DonEel?*" The thought-question was as subtle as thunder, jarring him, comprising unfamiliar concepts and referents, but there, in his mind, and not of his mind.

"*Yes, Duratheen,*" he thought strongly, meeting that motionless look, feeling his heart pound and knowing something of the effort exerted by the other.

"*Too difficult here, and danger.*" Curiosity, suspicion, excitement colored the thought. "*Not hurting you. Go. I follow.*" The head moved slightly, and, off-balanced by the encounter, DonEel turned and began to retrace his steps, guided toward the knoll by the tower-

151

ing mass of the citadel. Thoughts swirling, he wondered if Ridl knew what had happened.

Yes, the answer came, Ridl-flavored and warning. Where there is one, there can be others.

A possibility, certainly. But he had felt the shock of the Duratheen's recognition, and that one wouldn't shock easily. Moving away from the buildings, back up the steep little hill, he sought the mind of Pollo and knew that he slept, restless and dreaming and uncomfortable.

The brush grew thicker, trapping the heat, and he began to perspire freely. He was so thirsty he felt ill.

"Man DonEel, are you Oso's?" The rough voice caught him off-guard, pulling his attention away from Pollo, and he felt the hard touch of the Duratheen like a thorn in his brain.

"Not if I can help it," he said carefully, turning. The thorn was removed, and the Duratheen stepped through the thick green growth, taller than DonEel had expected, and at this distance, even more predatory. It was all too easy to imagine what could have happened if he had given the wrong answer.

"I am called Eg'l by man-types. A joke." The beaked face was not constructed for humor, but there was a feel of it in the brilliant thought, and the dark eyes blinked slowly. "To the Duratheen I am Galen, Master and Free Agent for Durath. You have silent speech." Not a question, the point to this meeting.

"Yes. I thought no one else here did."

"One other, now. Your unwell travel-mate has not?"

"No, I don't think so. Your people—"

"No." Galen anticipated his question. "It is a lone thing, secret and uncommon. Those who do not, fear, so is danger. All who have, know."

In spite of the mental contact, the Duratheen's speech was difficult to follow. It seemed he could stand unmoving forever to satisfy his curiosity, but the heat and thirst were punishing DonEel. He felt lightheaded and frustrated. "Galen, I have been without water a long time. Is there someplace—"

"To drink. Yes. I touch your suffering; forgive me. You are watering all outside and we do not lose fluids so. But to drink here on Syrcase, yes. First I would know how you got here."

"From the mines of West Range. Near Loos."

"Your ship?" The great head cocked slightly, and DonEel felt the rapid, questing curiosity struggle for understanding in his mind.

"I have no ship, Galen. One called Sa'alm came—" He could not find easy words to explain all that had happened to bring him here. Too much of it did not make sense even to him. But Galen's sharp-edged curiosity pressed, and he yielded memory tiredly, hoping for some understanding.

"You are not Andro-Alpha." One hand leaped out, closing on DonEel's shoulder. "Man DonEel, is true Oso sent to capture?" He must have seen it in the startled mind, for the eyes shifted to the towering citadel, visible over the trees. "Is not being. Our thought was Lord Oso being fool. But if old tales are history. . . ." The cruel hand fell away from DonEel's bruised shoulder, and his alarm faded, but he could not translate the unfamiliar emotion radiating from the Duratheen. He did not know how much Galen had learned from his mind, or what it meant to him.

Finally Galen spoke again. "Man DonEel, you do not know here. Is danger for both, and your mate is not helping to you. Go to him. Do not fear me, but others. I will bring meat and drink and find you for talking to about this."

Pollo lay where he had left him, eyes closed, but he was not asleep. "DonEel," he whispered as the other knelt to cut his bonds. "Where are we?"

Where were they? The question brought memory of the alien night sky and his own surrender to panic.

Another world, he thought, knowing it, but unable to understand. Worlds. Not one world. Syrcase, Galen had said. He didn't know. "A long way from home," he said at last, quietly. "Sa'alm—"

The eyes flashed open, bright with fear. "Sa'alm. I dreamed she had taken you, that you were, that you saw—" He broke off suddenly, and his too-pale face darkened. Unmercifully, his mind did not halt its recital, pouring a torrent of shame and sick humiliation into DonEel's unsuspecting mind. Before he could stop it, he knew how the female had used the Delphan, the sick, helpless rage of having his will destroyed by some magic stinging his shoulder that could not dull his knowing. They had gamed with him, made sport of his manhood for Sa'alm's pleasure. Kam, and some other—not Jayt, but some other like him—their near-human type belittled by Pollo's perfection. So they had done to him in hate and pleasure at his helplessness.

So real and immediate was the transfer of knowing that for a moment DonEel felt his own being violated, publicly shamed. He saw tears jewel copper lashes, slide across the sun-struck temple. "It was a dream, Pollo. Sa'alm did not capture me. I came after, with Ridl's help. A dream." He touched the wet face, allowing neither touch nor voice to hint at the rage swelling, bursting white-hot until he crouched, blind and hurting with it.

"*DonEel.*" The whisper sang behind his brain, sang against that heat, touched and disturbed by it, so the full attention of the L'Hur for a moment focused through Ridl stronger than he had yet felt it, saying nothing he cared to hear, but calming, cooling, pouring harmony over the ecstatic solo of his emotion. Grateful, after a moment, he knew from Ridl's compassionate thought that there was danger in his yielding to that kind of anger.

He agreed silently, feeling heart and breath more nearly normal. "*But they will pay for their game,*

Ridl," he swore. *"By my hand."* The thought was cold and hard and certain beyond any thought he could hold here.

There was a stillness from Ridl, a considering screened from him, and then a knowledge came to him, not in word-patterns but a knowing total and inarguable: his first duty was to his people, not his personal considerations. Yes. First, duty. And Pollo was part of that. But there would be a time for Kam and the other, and the female, Sa'alm. A time.

ELEVEN

"MAN DonEel." Galen stood on the bank above them. "Am alone me. Not followed."

DonEel had told Pollo of the Duratheen, making no mention of the silent speech; now he warned Galen silently not to mention it. Pollo's reaction to the big Duratheen puzzled him. There was interest and curiosity, but none of the instinctive reaction he should have felt at being confronted by a Nomen of such proportions. Instead, they both caught a surprised memory-comparison to the great gray-white bird of prey that ranged the high country of West Range.

"Eg'l." Galen's thought was bright with the laughter he could not voice.

"Eg'l," DonEel agreed, smiling in spite of himself. *"He does not fear you."*

"Is drug-happy. Put inside by med-techs. Taking fear away and will of self. Slave-maker." The information flashed full of images of sharp instruments and a hot stinging against his own shoulder as Galen came down to them, speaking aloud. "Is meat and drink, and news from Port City. All is search for Alpha mantypes from citadel. Even inside ships. Makes bad feeling for all berthing there."

Thirst eased, Pollo struggled with the Duratheen's speech and his own heavy lethargy. "But why do they want me? Or any of us? This is like a dream to me."

"No dream, man Pollo. I can speak what I have heard, and guess some things, but not fit. Oso is Syrcase holder after sire by strength and fear of him. Also shiplane controller. But there are being others like him, all with power-wish to control sector and keep out others. Saying was when Oso came here, housing in the Ancients' citadel, he was making search for a thing to give him biggest power from what is called Prime Terrans. What power is to do with is unknown, and all tales say such as he seeks were killed or flashed out to Big Black from sectors. But you are like them to see."

The referents Galen used meant nothing to the men. He was from a different world, a different order of things. Pollo turned it over in his mind, frowning, drawing parallels with the Beachers. "This Oso thinks we have something that will make him stronger than the others." That much he could understand. "But if we are important to him, why does he kill us?" He turned questioning eyes to his companion as another thought struck him. "How did he bring us here?"

Neither Galen nor DonEel could answer him.

"There are mysteries here we don't understand yet," DonEel said finally. "But they did bring you, and they want you back. Can you run if need be?"

"If I must." He smiled and touched his friend's arm. "Don't worry about me." But his mind was worrying questions DonEel could not answer. He could sense the fragility of the Delphan's calm and the chaos behind it, trying to identify this place, and he was afraid for him.

"*Man DonEel,*" Galen's thought ranged his mind. "*Is drug hides knowing of suffering from him. But is ending soon. Let me help.*"

There was no one else. This was a strange land, and there were dangers he could only dimly imagine. Ridl and safety lay beyond the Portal, and that was hidden in the base of the citadel. For a moment he cursed the madness and fear of Muset that had sent him out of the place.

The Duratheen's pacing thoughts were bright with curiosity, and beyond were reasons and excitement for wanting to help them, touching a real and impersonal hatred of this one called Muset. It surprised DonEel, but he didn't ask. Galen's reasons for wanting to help would have to be his own business. They needed someone to trust, and he did not wish them harm. That had to be enough.

Galen's pleasure at his decision was as uncomplicated as his hatred of Muset—just there, mingled with a sense of belonging known from the first realization that the man, like himself, had the ability to communicate thought. "Being good, man friend. Seekers will be done in port soon from bad feeling there. Then it is more safe away from here, on my ship. Walking there. With me, any will see only Andros and not trouble."

It was as he said. Walking with Galen through the crowds in Port City, they were accorded the same half-resentful awe as the Duratheen. Twice on the long walk DonEel was startled by a rush of thunder close overhead, though the blue-green sky was cloudless. Galen seemed not to notice, and Pollo was touched by nothing outside himself, walking silently.

They did not cross the great field as DonEel had thought to do earlier, but kept close to the fence, paralleling it until they were among the great machines. Personal vessels, Galen's thought told him. Impossible, his own experience said. Yet he knew they were as Galen said, and his unvoiced questions brought a running commentary from the Duratheen until he finally cautioned the man not to show such obvious interest in what should be familiar to him.

Galen's ship was not as large as most there, but she was sleek and almost delicate, as perfectly balanced as a thrown spear or the blade of DonEel's knife. And seeing her brought a thrust of quick pleasure, like seeing a onetime lover.

"You know her like?" There was pride in Galen's question. "Is speed craft rebuilt on Formout."

Pollo was beyond caring. The drugs in his system had outlasted his will, and he was unsure of any reality. It was Galen's strength that lifted him into the ship.

The interior, rather than merely functional, was constructed for pleasure and comfort, richly decorated, and DonEel knew, without knowing how he knew, that this was important for an individual who spent long periods in the solitude of the Big Black. Seeing it, coming into it, he felt like a man coming home after a long absence and finding little changed.

"Man Pollo suffers deep." Galen's rough voice was muted to a rumble as he bent over the Delphan. "Is not right way for drug, not being done now. In his head is like wars. Is bad."

Bad, yes. Following the Duratheen's attention, Don-Eel could feel the confused and hidden ambivalence, something like terror moving in the disjointed imagery. It was not only the drugs working in him; it was being here, in this impossible place, knowing everything he understood of life was incredibly far away.

"I've got to get him back, Galen." Somehow. It was a debt owed. Pollo had come for him once; now it was his turn.

"Where is your world?" The answer was simple to the Duratheen. His ship could take them anywhere. His mind touched on worlds and the distances between them, and, following it, DonEel felt a peculiar reassurance outside his burgeoning sense of wonder. But there were no distances he could explain.

"I don't know. Back through the Portal." Back into the citadel, to that golden room. And if that could be done, back to the place called Jimo that had nearly killed him once. Common sense said it was impossible. Being here was impossible. Everything was impossible.

"Only more hard, DonEel. You are resting here now." He touched his shoulder, pressing him toward a soft chair more suited to the Duratheen's size, and stepped through a doorway, to reappear with a white flask and a small porcelain cup nearly hidden in one hand. For the first time DonEel noticed that hand, seeing it as it was. There were too many fingers, five, oddly jointed and flexible against the opposing thumb.

"Still are hands for touching and doing, like yours." The reasonable observation told him he was overreacting, broadcasting thoughts too freely. He apologized, humbled by the alien's understanding and humor. "Likenesses are more real, friend DonEel. Inside knowings between is closer than blood things even. Yes?"

Yes. For the thoughts, however clear-cut and focused, contained every texture of feeling and meaning. Ultimate sharing and truth. It came to him that he was accepting this thing too easily, without examination. But the thought dissolved as Galen held the cup out to him. "Drink. Is peace-giver like wine, but more fire for gladness and know untying. Is safe for man-types."

The sweet fire of the liquor was a gentle explosion against his throat, spreading quickly through his belly, pleasant and relaxing. He looked down at the cup, one dark brow slightly raised. It was good, but a man could get lost in a few tiny cups like this.

"So, if Portal thing is being the way back, we go," Galen said. "But not alone you. Needing weapons against Oso's guards. Together we go after dark. I maybe can help Pollo for that now; maybe not so much later." He was familiar with DonEel's experience of the Portal, curious, but hesitant to believe all the subjective information in the man's head. He questioned him closely, discussed possibilities. Finally the one thing that held his attention was the Zniss,

159

Muset. "If it waits after second, in the white place, danger will happen."

Waiting for the stimulant to work on Pollo, he told what he knew of the Zniss. They were one of the few humanoid races from the cluster worlds that held aloof from all others. Classified mammalian, they lacked the psychophysiological responses generally known as excitement, joy, even anger—feelings that were present to one degree or another in other species in their classification. "If one belongs to Oso," he told DonEel, "it is criminal, or after something for increase of power to self. In mind, Zniss are like cold-meat life."

Night on Syrcase was as cold as the day was hot, and Galen provided cloaks for the men, warm and soft as down. They were the product of his world and would serve as a sort of disguise, indicating they were in his employ.

Pollo was awake, after a fashion, but to DonEel's worried investigation his thoughts had a fever-dream quality, composed more of imagery than thought-sense.

"Is good for now. He will not leave you. As you say, he does. It is enough."

DonEel hoped so.

He wouldn't have made it without Galen. The Duratheen's care of Pollo, his knowledge and ability to communicate silently, were a handle he held to desperately until they were inside the citadel. Then Galen's cool excitement at being in Oso's stronghold was bracing, washing the confusion from his own thoughts. Their success was due in part to the attitude of the citadel's personnel; alerted by the escape, first of Jayt, then the Prime, they were not expecting anyone to try to get in, only out. The three surprised witnesses to their entrance were silenced by quick flashes from Galen's weapon, faces gone to cinder. The Duratheen's reaction was cold and fast, devoid of any feeling other than satisfaction at having been fast enough.

The interminable walk down the spiral ramp was

too much for Pollo—the stimulant administered in Galen's ship was not effective enough. He sagged, helpless, unable to respond to DonEel's urging. So Galen carried him.

This was a lark for the Duratheen, this intrusion, following the man who had silent speech and mysteries about his being that Galen could touch but not understand. Until they reached the arched opening into the golden room and the expanse of empty floor between them and the Portal. Here, for the first time, belief and knowledge came to battle for him. The black gate was too empty, totally outside his experience, and therefore not easily trusted. He paused, and DonEel, already moving across the open, turned back to him. *"We must hurry."* Anything could happen here. Someone could come through from the other side, or down from the occupied level. Then, suddenly, he shared Galen's realization of absurdity. How could he believe that by stepping through that golden trap they could walk from here to their homeworld? Yet when he resumed his advance, having nothing else, Galen followed, and they came to the Portal together. They stepped through side by side, Galen recoiling from the shock of dissolution, of being elsewhere, of white light and three steps—Jimo.

"Is far out," he said, thinking distance. "Is"—he went silent, but his thought cracked sharp—*"not real place, but made. And Zniss being here."*

Muset. Reaching out, DonEel, too, felt the cool presence of the Zniss, made doubly unpleasant by Galen's reactive anger. Never mind. They couldn't stay here, must not be caught. He reached to the panel to the right of the portal and his stolen knowledge told him that if he chose the wrong setting they could step right back into the golden room of the citadel. The knob turned, clicked, and the silver wall shimmered itself to black. He looked at Galen. They stepped through together. Going.

Stumbling on the rough cave floor, DonEel's first

thought was that Muset or some other from Jimo would notice the Portal had been used. Ridl was there, waiting, as DonEel had known he would be, standing silent in shadow, as impassive as the stone around him. But the touch mind-to-mind was realer than any distance.

He was home, freed by Ridl's presence to realize a fatigue so complete he felt disjointed. Nothing registered but being back, and Ridl, until Galen stirred beside him, reminding. . . .

Galen had seen Ridl, still shadow-cloaked, and the great Duratheen was absolutely motionless, black eyes staring, mind gone still, Pollo lying across his arms like a forgotten sacrifice. "Galen." DonEel broke the silence, watching the eyes move to him slowly.

"I heard but did not know the First One was sire to you. But you are different."

It made no sense at all to DonEel until the subtle message from Ridl. Galen was surprised because Ridl reminded him of something from his people's legends —not a memory exactly, but a belief, a faith. Aloud, the L'Hur's voice rippled the shadows: "DonEel, Muset may well follow. We must take Pollo from the mines. Come." The soft speech-sound touched the Duratheen's shock and DonEel's fatigue, was a leash drawing them away from the square of black along the tunnel behind the flickering torch Ridl carried.

DonEel was sleepwalking, not even aware of being outside until he saw Ridl beside him, offering him a skin of water, silver eyes watchful.

"I'm all right. Really."

Ridl smiled and nodded. And he was all right. The late sun, the trees and rocks, were, like the cold, sweet water against his tongue, familiar and right. He even recognized the place they had come to: the place he and Pollo had chosen for their camp. It seemed like a long time ago now, like childhood before learning that reality was something other than you dreamed. Now Pollo lay quiet on the sleep robes, and Galen and Ridl stood to one side of him, talking together. How strange they looked. Ridl seemed fine and slender, a dark flame beside the white bulk of the Duratheen.

Resting in silence, making no effort to know more than he could see and hear, he watched, thinking how strange it all was, and how wrong. Everything was twisted out of focus, and thinking was like walking in sand, every thought a foot pulled free and reburied. One thing stuck in his bemusement: it should not be Pollo there. Pollo was the one with the answer, the one who had cared for him. . . .

Ridl bent down to the unconscious man, and the action was a spur waking DonEel from his lethargy. He went to kneel beside the L'Hur, watching the strong dark hands move over the still form, pausing at belly, chest, and forehead. But it was the touch of the attention, probing, moving cautiously through patterns and feelings that were Pollo that DonEel followed most closely, learning a way of knowing he had not thought to try. Closing his eyes to better understand this that he was beginning to know, he found it familiar, confused, but still the Pollo he knew, had always known. Having the way from Ridl, he quested deeper into the unconscious mind, seeking causes and reasons, until Ridl stopped him, forcing him back with the closest he had come to sharpness.

"What is it?" he asked aloud, startled by the interruption.

"If he wakes, he dies, DonEel." Calm regained, the dark face brooded down at the flame-gold head, and his winged brows drew together. "There is a done thing here. An intent I do not understand. A manipulation of the flesh itself." He stroked the pale brow lightly, then rose. "Let him sleep. This thing must be studied."

Leaving Pollo in Galen's care, they moved high enough out of the hollow to be able to see the mines below. "There is a part of him that is not natural.

But it is a part of him. It makes him a danger to himself from his mind's ability."

"How could Oso have—"

"Not Oso. It is a pattern of Pollo himself, of the flesh, half given by his father, half by his mother. So it is not—" His eyes flashed silver to meet Don-Eel's. "Look at me." The command held him still, and he felt the subtle invasion, somehow good because it was Ridl. "You also," Ridl said after a time. "It is in you. The thing that encases your other memory. Yet you did not die of it. The half given you by Chiral is there. But I am not of your people."

"But Pollo?"

"If his mind opens, becomes as it can be, as it was meant to be, he will die of it. And the others. This thing was done to them for a purpose. If we knew the purpose and way of it, it could be undone." The L'Hur turned away, back down into the hollow, and DonEel followed.

"Perhaps Oso knows what was done," he suggested. "He thinks we have a power to give him."

"This was not done only to Pollo and yourself, but, I think, to all Truemen. And you alone are other than they—of them, yet not of them. You remembered. First in the Portal—"

"A dream."

Ridl ignored the interruption, watching the worried face closely. "Then again in the citadel, the passages and gardens."

"It was not my memory, Ridl. The ones I touched, I had their knowing." It couldn't have been memory. He knew he had never seen the unbelievable structure, that alien sky. Even thinking Ridl might be right brought a slow fear that pulled at his muscles.

"Perhaps you remembered as you remembered the L'Hur."

"Not wanting to know." Galen spoke from where he stood by Pollo. He had followed the conversation on both levels, knowing DonEel's unease. Now he drew their thoughts to the whole of the situation away from the man. "If old-telling Oso followed was fact, Prime Terrans did flash out, not to Big Black, but here. Then it forgot them why and how to be."

"Partly right, my friend." Ridl smiled briefly. "But the forgetting was done to them. DonEel remembered they were fleeing."

DonEel shook his head. Fleeing what? And what were Primes?

"Being like First Ones, with silent speech," Galen answered. "Maybe long-ago warring of sectors gave flight." Galen's thoughts were easy to follow, putting together what he knew of history and legend with what he knew now of DonEel and Pollo and Oso with quick, uncluttered logic. "Was done to them, yes. And brought them here with the Portal. Unlike us, without silent speech, are afraid, so would make for killing even now."

For a moment the Duratheen's loneliness and constant vigil against mistakes was in his thoughts, and DonEel was touched by it. Then suddenly he was tired of it, of the speculation. "If they could be made to not be what they were, why bring them here? What was the threat?"

"Think, DonEel. The not-being is a thing of the flesh; it is in all, and passed to the children through the parents. You alone are not so caged, because I am not. The half of the done thing in you is making you not want to be what you are. But you are L'Hur also, so the being will not kill you. Your own memory told you there would be a time for undoing this. So they all came together to a place where they could wait in safety."

He almost searched his memory for that, feeling it close; then the weariness of it swept him. It was too much effort, too much confusion of Primes and other worlds and. . . . He closed his eyes, rubbing his face, indulging himself in the deliciousness of it. "Can't you just undo whatever Oso has done to him?"

"Oso did nothing to cause this trouble for Pollo."

DonEel's eyes opened. "Until Sa'alm took him, he was well."

"Only the taking him. It was the Portal and citadel. They were familiar, and the drugs merely kept him prisoner without the will to fight even himself. Now his will to live keeps him from waking." Ridl frowned slightly, and DonEel caught a trace of guilt in his flowing thought. Knowing his curiosity, Ridl turned to him. "Perhaps I am a part of it. The L'Hur are like what the Primes hid away from themselves. It had to be familiar, to make some strain in him. It was because they never really forgot that they placed bans on certain gifts."

"But maybe we aren't the Primes," DonEel said, wanting to believe it, wanting the security of the old life to remain, at least in memory. But he knew Ridl was right. The people had come here, had given up their special gifts. But not forever. The half of him that was of them fought the knowledge with fatigue and fear, but the other, the Ridlness of him, knew.

"My son, you are not letting yourself know." Ridl's hand touched his head, bringing his eyes open once again.

"Know what?"

"That Pollo is like you. That the sharing between us could be with Pollo. Do you not want that?"

Want it? The barriers he had erected against that desire dissolved. To be with Pollo as he was with Ridl and, to a lesser degree, with Galen. . . . Want it? Wanting was a bitter flame consuming him, a disproportionate desire for some universe lost he dare not reach for with hope.

"Now that those of other worlds have found you, you must find the way of return for the people, to what they are." Ridl's thoughts were far beyond the personal concerns of DonEel's desire, reaching a point Galen had already considered. "Only you could know what it is that will return them. If you do not find it, the Portal will have to be destroyed."

"No!" Instinct alone prompted that negative. The Portal must remain, it was— He did not know what it was, only that it must not be destroyed.

"Oso has found the people. He is the only one now, but where one can do a thing, there will be others. He has too many people with him; some of them will speak of his doing with others—if not all of it, enough to make them think."

Galen came to support DonEel's defense of the Portal, pointing out that the place they were now was unknown. "Portal got ones here. They could have destroyed for safe being, but did not. So is reason to remember. And is only way of getting to other worlds, through Jimo to Syrcase."

Other L'Hur, summoned sometime by Ridl, were coming to the hollow; DonEel could feel them near in the growing dusk, appearing silent as shadows, holding back until Ridl went to meet them. What passed between them was screened from DonEel as well as Galen, coming into DonEel's mind as music and beauty remembered from a time that had never been. Once the silence was broken by ritual, greeting extended to the son of Ridl—formal, yet rich with understanding and acceptance of him. These were no adventurous youths, but the wise and experienced, and they knew their strength. He would have nothing to fear for Pollo. But time. They could protect him; they could not heal him, and he could not forever remain as he was.

TWELVE_____

A night's sleep, even with the urgency and pain of dreams he would not remember, did much to restore DonEel. In the familiar morning forest it was somehow easier to think of his strange journey after Pollo, and of Galen, the alien friend yet asleep against the rock. And to wonder again at his acceptance of it all.

Lying in the warmth of the robe, he recalled the arguments and confusion of the night before and knew a decision had been made. The answer to the strange seal he had felt in Pollo's mind lay behind the Portal. Perhaps Oso, who knew of the Primes, knew that answer. And he, DonEel, was the only one who could tell what it was.

"DonEel." Ridl's thought ran silently into his head. *"There were other times of memory for you. Before we met. They show you know more than you realize."*

Memory of this? He sought them and found nothing but the skittish gift of his youth, of knowing sometimes what would happen before the fact.

"No." Ridl led him away from that thought. *"The gift knife from Tarhel, the jewel-stone taken from the Zona at Beauty. They meant something to you."*

But what? He remembered the stone, still hung about his neck on its golden chain. It was just a stone, beautiful with its deep fires, warm from his own chest. He could remember first holding it, the sudden vertigo, the fear he had felt then, but holding the stone fisted beneath the robe, it was another memory from that night that surprised him with hurt. How easy it was to imagine Pollo dead, cold and unmoving, that beautiful face saying nothing, those golden eyes. . . . He threw off the robe and got up quickly, taking refuge from thought in action. Ridl watched him silently from across the fire.

"I will go to Syrcase. Beyond if need be. If there is any answer to this, more than hope, I will find it." DonEel spoke aloud from the edge of the creek, shivering as icy water trickled down inside his shirt.

"Useless without outside knowing and help, DonEel," Galen said, surprising him. "Self-thinking for helping," the Duratheen said obliquely. "For us of like being in silent speech, this Prime Terrans could make a place of no-hiding, and free to learn."

168

Remembering the glimpse of loneliness inside the sharp-edged mind, DonEel nodded, letting his understanding speak between them silently.

Galen did not like the Portal. It was too good a trap. If anyone on the other side knew they had come through, they could seal it up, prevent them from leaving. But the gate in the cave was empty blackness, indicating openness.

"Maybe this one is always open," DonEel suggested, pushing his smoking torch into a crack in the wall.

"Possible." Galen checked his weapon casually. "Too possible Muset waits just there. We gamble."

So they gambled. There was not even any assurance they would step back into the white room on Jimo. But it had to be done. Wishing they had some way of knowing what was waiting for them, DonEel was the one who hesitated.

"My coming is not known," Galen reminded, looking at him. "We go."

They went. And the white room was there, and empty, though there were invisible traces of activity near. Without pausing, they stepped through again, into the golden silence of the citadel, confronting a very surprised individual in the colors of Oso. Stunned by having his fears so abruptly realized, DonEel froze, feeling the mental cry of recognition like a scream in his head. *"Duratheen!"* It was the last thought the mind held. Galen's weapon flashed.

"Send it to Jimo!" Galen's thought moved him, and they lifted the body together, swung it easily into the blackness of the Portal, and it was gone. They didn't linger. Both were aware of the alert that had gone out as they came through.

It was easier now, a familiar road to DonEel. Instead of the spiral corridor, he moved left, toward the dusty hall that had offered him sanctuary the first time. The narrow stair didn't tempt him this time. He knew the passage led to something memory called the warrens, a senseless maze of rooms and passages whose initial purpose had never been defined.

Galen said nothing, only moved at his side, quick and silent for all his bulk.

Rooms and passages melted into each other in random sizes and shapes; stairs and ramps of varying incline forced them to take care in their hurry. Only two floors were connected at any one place, so there was as much horizontal as vertical travel, with no apparent pattern. Each stair or ramp became the object of a search. But there was no pursuit. All activity remained below them and to one side, and finally ceased as the search was called off.

Galen showed no signs of fatigue, but he was acutely conscious of DonEel's cramping legs and pounding heart, and suggested a halt. "You know this place. You were here again?" He moved about, examining the smooth white walls.

"I know it, but I could never have been here." It was as true as any truth he knew. He didn't try to force his knowing to match his memory, or to reach beyond the moment for knowledge that would only confuse him.

Here in the featureless rooms it was impossible to tell where in the citadel they were; there were no trustworthy referents. But it felt near the third level, the area of the living quarters. No more stairs, then. He was glad. The fatigue that wanted to claim him in this place was a constant pull on his muscles. Maybe Ridl was right and some part of him didn't want to do this, wanted the questions unanswered.

No longer climbing, they made their way inward toward the core of the citadel, and the monotonous white gave way to soft pastels, and the rooms became more nearly uniform, relaxing an almost subliminal tension both had felt in the random surroundings. The continuous silent activity of the citadel's occupants, while not directional in any real sense, seemed closer, and they came finally to the last door-opening, leading out into the familiar sloping corridor. Caution held them behind it, and they sat silent, each reaching out into the activity that seemed to originate in their own skulls, but did not. It was difficult at first—there was too much imagery and word-sense, all irrelevant. Then, remembering how Ridl had followed an idea into the depths of Pollo's mind, DonEel forced himself to selectivity. Terran Primes. That was his goal. Nothing else happening here was of importance. He felt Galen pick up on it, reinforcing and expanding his own sensitivity, and that helped.

Even with a selective goal, there was a surprisingly complex selection of thought and feeling on the subject of the Primes, most of it a combination of fear-hate and envy. Slipping into the attitude of the watcher, DonEel sat on the smooth floor, arms clasped about his knees, head bowed, losing all sense of self as he drifted in the imagery of othernesses. Some of the images were familiar, of Pollo and others; some were obscene fantasies from which he shied quickly, seeking, seeking. . . .

"*. . . no proof that these ones are anything but what they seem.*" The clarity of the thought caught their attention, and they tracked it. "*They don't know why they are brought here, or even where here is. A simple with no knowledge of the most basic things. What is there in them that makes that son of a Zniss Oso think they could be his long-lost supermen?*"

The concise verbalization of the thought was so clear both watchers thought at first the being was speaking aloud to someone. But it was only private thought, lucid and disciplined. There was a distant anger in it, and awareness of superiority.

Galen's hand touched his arm, startling him. "Is Andro-type, like Truemen. Thinking like from Stilks, study and teaching world of all knowledge. None of its types form loyalty bond as are mind-bound to Stilks for all living time." The Duratheen was puzzled by the Stilkser presence, giving beyond speech a brief

171

sketch of a people devoted to study in all areas, disdaining all emotional motivation in purpose, embracing intellectual superiority.

"He hates Oso," DonEel pointed out.

"Is mind hate, not blood heat of wanting battle, win or lose. Maybe caught. Oso might need scholar aid, so is forcing or buying it. But it wants to know, too."

DonEel agreed. The curiosity in the mind had been as important as the feelings toward Oso. He frowned in annoyance, frustrated by the long period of motionlessness. As useful as the gift of knowing was, it was difficult only to sit and follow, never knowing when the thoughts would wander or turn to something they needed to know. If only he could talk to the man . . .

Galen vetoed the idea. There was no reason to let Oso know they were in the citadel.

"Knowing nothing but possibles makes it curious," Galen said after a time. "Records of times with Truemen like Pollo in thinking."

"Records?"

The silent answer was a quick description of what the Stilkser had been doing, a picture of a device, tapes, words and pictures. A miracle he accepted. And the man was nervous, watchful.

"Possible not for Oso; maybe spy for others."

Both were up now, touched by the unpleasantness of the information developing in the mind they watched, the history of the actions performed on the people brought here, from the first drugging to the inevitable death.

Death. Of all but one. DonEel felt the mind change from attention to speculation. What had happened to the last one? Why was there no report?

Because the med team had been delayed by a report about some trouble on Jimo. No tests, no situation setups, nothing. Thoughtfully, the watched mind reexamined the circumstances of the last capture, the first escape. They were still looking, but the consensus was that the man had gotten into Port City. A quick personal bitterness colored the thoughts, and flashes of personal memory were enough to indicate what must certainly happen to an Andro-type who was helpless to defend himself. Slavery was the nicest of the possibilities.

"Is that true?"

"True, yes. Hate is for being good without caution. Fear beginnings are in Primes who knew everything. Not knowing, other types had bad feelings wanting also, but man said no, so was fighting to start Sector Wars. Then even types not knowing Primes was turned to hating them."

For being too good? That made no sense. He thought of Galen's image of the Primes, and Oso's desire to find them, and wondered if maybe they were the L'Hur. Their understanding would mean nothing to races without it. They would be much like Gods, lacking immortality.

"They, like your sire, are being First Ones, not man-types like Primes. Not easy for killing, too," he added. "Knowing let them escape. Old legends say Primes would die easy and happy if trapped. No force bought loyalty from them. On some worlds is telling like Gods. Yet other knowings of them is bleeding and hurts and sadness for all loved. If they knew all, like saying is, it wasn't help for them."

They didn't know all, DonEel thought suddenly. They only saw a little better, and they knew themselves, their own mistakes in all the long ages of becoming. And they wanted to, really thought they could, help. But there were too many who wanted what they had, like a gift, without paying the price. Or wanted to use them for their own gain. Yawning hugely, he moved, stretching the stiffness from his muscles. This was neither the time nor the place for a philosophical discussion.

"Oso isn't here," he remembered.

"Or the Zniss. Not knowing, either, or the Stilkser would. Maybe the records say more to us. Shall we get them?" The Duratheen had patience and curiosity. But he was by nature a creature of action. And behind his suggestion was the thought that this place had neither food nor water. He was worried for the man, not knowing his limits.

Once in the central corridor, they suffered a momentary confusion about direction; then DonEel noted the markings above the doors and realized they were yet below the level where he had found Pollo. Galen, too obviously alien in this place, would have to remain out of sight unless it came to open battle. So he offered DonEel his weapon, a stubby, bulbous rod, but he refused it, more at home with his knife. Galen would know the instant he needed help.

With no subjects to work on, the area was quiet. Maybe in Oso's absence, vigilance was relaxed. There was a uniformed guard at the station—not the one he had attacked, thank the Gods, but close enough in type to accelerate his pulse. The door behind the station was open.

"Port team's not allowed up here," the guard growled, seeing him finally, thinking, *"Another Andro, the stiff-necked sons of Zniss are taking over."*

"No harm." He let the other's expectations lead him, seeking a lever into this place. "I'm opting for close-in duty off Jimo. Too much trouble in it. Like to see what goes here."

"Chart your own course." Rather than push it, the guard chose withdrawal. What was it to him, anyway? There was nothing around.

Trying to ignore him, DonEel entered the room. The records must be somewhere near. How would he know them?

"Compdeck," Galen's quick reply whispered. *"Not there, but close."*

Not here. There was only one exit, back to the

174

guard station. Feigning idle curiosity, he left the room, started down the corridor feeling eyes on his back. But it was only the automatic dislike of a nearly man-type for one closer to the physical ideal. There was no personal threat in it. There was another door, closed, but opening easily to his touch, and a large room that felt of seriousness and study. The walls were lined with banks of instruments and machines, and it was occupied. He was inside, the door whispering shut behind him, before he saw them, and it was too late to hide. They stood close together in a far corner, and in the instant before they became aware of him, he understood the nature of their preoccupation. The texture and content of their minds brought a quick heat to his face.

Aware of him finally, they drew apart. The man—and Trueman—obviously surprised and embarrassed; the woman—DonEel looked at her, and for a time saw nothing else. She was impossibly beautiful, a wild animal all tawny and bronze, and the two-piece garment she wore molded every curve and depression of her, leaving no questions, only an unbelievable statement of femaleness. She laughed, a low near-purr, and the feline identification was complete.

"I think he's lost, Rarde. Relax." She left the man and came toward DonEel, bold eyes measuring him, making it plain she liked what she saw. And his dread of being caught faded to a more familiar challenge, so he stared back at her, a half-smile on his lips.

"You're new here," she purred, stopping just out of reach, legs wide, hands fisted on hips.

"Up here, yes." The intensity of her interest, her obvious attraction to him, was a pleasant excitement, something he knew. He felt Galen's sharp warning but shrugged it off irritably. In this encounter he was already master. The woman preened beneath his stare, shaking back hair that danced like flames about her neck and shoulders.

"Is there something you want here, Andro?"

175

"Maybe." The old game, until he reached out, curious, almost instinctively, to touch what lay behind her mocking eyes. What he found was so female, so explicit, his own immediate reaction shocked him awake. And she was aware of it. Gods, she knew her power over men, reveled in it. But what she promised— He almost reached for her, then realized the man had come to stand beside her, his embarrassment grown into jealousy and anger.

"Would you care to join us?" She laughed at her intended double meaning. "Rarde won't mind."

"*DonEel!*" The warning stung, sobering him. He forced a laugh through a dry throat, moving his eyes from hers. "Another time. I don't like mixed company." He felt her fury, sudden and surprising, and mixed with challenge and some decision made as she let the other take her hand.

"Another time, no-name. Most definitely another time," she purred as they moved to the door.

When they were gone, he found himself shaking inside as from a narrow escape. Part of it, he knew, was frustration. She was the female fantasy conjured up in the long nights of early manhood, the impossible perfect playmate. And she had offered him. . . .

"*Is time for dreaming later, man,*" Galen prompted impatiently. "*Time goes.*"

Annoyed with himself as the woman's impact faded, he sought quickly for the small metal packets Galen pictured for him. There were four of them on the table, and he found another in what the Duratheen recognized as a standard reader.

The uniform he still wore was without pockets, too tight for him to slip the cassettes inside the tunic. He had no choice but to carry them. The guard was visiting with something that appeared to be a vaguely female stump, but he kept his eyes to himself and managed to pass by them without comment.

Galen was relieved to see him, but still upset. "Female is not man-type, DonEel. Cruel like your forest cat. She would have had you." He missed the humor of the phrase and was impatient with the man's amusement. "Hearing between is to be an always thing when we are apart from each. Yet you did not hear that the Zniss is back in citadel, and messenger is coming into Portal room below with trouble. We go to ship now."

It was a long way from the Portal, but safe. With luck, no one would know they had been in the citadel, and the ship had the equipment to play the tapes.

Galen left DonEel in the ship after showing him how to use the reader. He had business to take care of in the city.

There were no answers on the tapes. The softly accented female voice explaining the lifelike scenes in the viewing window gave him nothing but anger. He recognized none of the dozen or so subjects, but their fear and shock were apparent. So was the subtle cruelty of the green-clad techs working with them. His interest was so intense he forgot his confusion with the machine he was using, accepting it as normal and familiar.

When it was done, he paced his anger through the close room, reaching into the depths behind his eyes for Ridl, knowing the L'Hur would be there, observing but not disturbing. His anger was touched and understood, but the calm presence had no answers.

"They are curious. Truemen are unlike them, and so they do not see them as equals. And there is some fear."

He could understand it, to a degree; the same reaction was present on his world in the reaction to the Nomen. But understanding didn't cool his anger. Throughout the taped episodes it was obvious the subjects would die. Some of them, the ones DonEel thought to be Delphan, died quickly. It was an annoyance to the captors, but the reason for the deaths was as much a puzzle to them as to him. It seemed they knew even less than he.

To his concern about Pollo, Ridl said only, *"He*

177

sleeps." Then added, *"Alchia knows now Pollo did not meet with Kylee in Loos. There is anger in Delpha, and questions, and thought turns to the mines. There is one in Delpha who can find the Portal. If that happens, all will face Pollo's danger."*

It was the last thing he had expected or even considered. He had been so involved in his own happenings and Pollo's danger, he had nearly forgotten anything else existed. Now, thinking of it, he knew Ridl was right. Dioda would know, as he had known Pollo would come to Scarsen to find him. Maybe he wouldn't know it all, but he would know enough to begin the danger. He slept more lightly than the others. And Alchia also. The mystics, the seekers after truth, the ones who knew it was not all as it appeared —they would need to know it all, and it would destroy them. He touched the black-and-gold band on his finger and felt close to panic. There was very little time. And there were no answers. He knew little more than Oso, who knew nothing.

"You do know, DonEel." Ridl's calm statement irritated him. If he knew, would he withold that knowing at the cost of Pollo's life? With an effort he restrained himself, feeling Ridl's close attention.

He was glowering at the silent reader when Galen returned; the tapes had provided no clues. The Duratheen took this first failure philosophically. He hadn't expected it to be so easy. Now, certain activities at the citadel had given him another idea. The native of Stilks they had "read" to learn of the records was dead, accused of spying for the world of Stilks, with as yet unnamed help from inside the citadel.

"Zniss thinking of cat-type female. They will war together sometime. He hopes to kill her," Galen observed casually, stowing the supplies brought from Port City. "If Zniss fears tapes will make sense on Stilks, maybe learning comes from there."

"Can we go to Stilks?"

"For study, yes. Is all doing. Even Oso."

178

It was better than nothing. Further, he knew from Galen's unspoken sharing that the Duratheen vessel was drawing attention in the port. As a mercenary with no overt loyalties, a Duratheen's unexplained lingering at a vulnerable port gave rise to speculation and eventual trouble.

Moving from planet to planet was a large part of Galen's life; he thought little about it, or the distances traveled, thinking more of time spent than distance. But DonEel, gathering his information from the other's few words and brilliant thoughts, was ill at ease. He followed the preparations closely, finding some security in the Duratheen's explanations and casual attitude. But when they were ready to leave at dawn, he didn't know what to expect. He had traveled between worlds, from his home to Jimo to Syrcase—his head knew it, believed it, after a fashion—but there had been no sensation of travel, only stepping through the Portal, leaving one room, entering another. This time it was different.

The Duratheen craft was comfortable, but the sensation of movement was extreme, lifting, thrusting away the chains that bound it and him to the surface of Syrcase. It was the first freedom, the pure feel of power he had felt in another way on the mind-flight with Ridl. He gloried in it, staring into the large panel that was not a window but some other miracle of seeing outside. Ignoring the fact of metal and machine and being inside, safe in the mystery of inverted gravity, he leaned back, tense and silent, feeling-seeing the dawn-shimmered air split around his thrusting body. But the release into soaring, swinging flight did not come, only the knowledge of leaping up and up. . . .

The screen changed; no longer useful for upward vision, it showed the planet below, and DonEel lurched from his power-dream into another reality. He was not moving; he hung stranded in nothingness, caught in the void he could feel surrounding him, a place of nightmare, deadly; and the beautiful solid planet slipped and fell swiftly down and away out of reach, leaving him— The sound of protest was purely reflexive, pushing against his throat.

"Look at the floor."

The conversational request hit his ears like a blow, and the roar of flight became nothing more than the blood pounding in his ears. The spell was broken, and he went limp, shaken by his own heartbeat.

"The eyes lie to us, dreaming it inside out for real." Galen's black eyes blinked humor and understanding. "The ship sings her own power-song, and you thought it yours. This is the beginning, friend DonEel. It will not be new again, or afraid, or beautiful. Only a way of doing. But it remembers me that it came so the first time."

This sharing of a private and good thing, mixed with the wonder of this happening at all, made DonEel doubly glad for Galen, the honest.

"I felt how empty it is out there for a minute," he said, knowing Galen already knew his thought, and speaking, anyway.

"It accepts us. Dangers are from not knowing or forgetting self. In time we commence flasher. For now, drink and resting."

The fiery Duratheen wine put distance between him and the strangeness outside the ship, and when he thought of that emptiness, he was tempted to increase that distance, to drink himself silly and sleepy. But Galen refused, knowing it was a passing thing. He directed their thoughts to the reason for the journey.

"Silent speech with father comes with you. It was so on Syrcase at the first. Not to my hearing, but knowing it is in your thinking, so I can know, too. Is it still being so with you?"

"Yes." Caught up again in a situation, he had not thought to wonder about it, but now that Galen directed his thoughts to it, he was aware of the constant

L'Hur song, a presence in him, perhaps now an always thing, binding him forever. He was relieved.

"Ridl is wise, DonEel, and knowing more things of inside than is able to us yet. Still you do not believe the truth he says to you, that all answers are in you and not for outside finding."

"It makes as much sense to say the answers are in Pollo's head. What good does it do him? Or any of them. There is something in us, maybe not so much in me, but the answers are hidden. Even Ridl does not know how or why."

"Knowing is not changed. The clues in his telling on your world—you did not want to know of them. Making anger for not thinking is perhaps a danger, to you as well as man Pollo. And, if Ridl spoke true, to all others of Truemen on your world."

Irritated by Galen's insistence and stubborn effort to make him share what could be of no importance on this quest, DonEel showed the Duratheen his knife and the stone he had taken. He didn't need words to share his experience; his own sudden memory of the stone was enough. Galen looked at him, his thoughts too obscure for following. Then he took up the knife and stone and looked at them closely.

"The blade is your belonging."

"Yes. A gift—" He would have explained again, but a chime sounded, and Galen moved from the table to the control room. It was time to set the coordinates for the flasher to carry them to Stilks.

"Before trading for music," he said, reappearing. "The blade is yours from its making."

"How could that be?"

"I am not knowing that for now. But it is Weirdling make. The patterning folk. Is gift of private meaning. In the hilt, see. Pattern of markings says you. Not naming, but picture of being you told in the lines." He showed the delicate repetitive pattern.

"That's not possible. I don't know these Weirdlings.

181

The knife came from the Afs—they got it in trade or something. . . ."

Galen watched him, unconvinced. "Not knowing Afs, but picture being is you." The feel of the design was somehow the identity by which Galen knew him. Following that information, which went beyond the simplicity of speech, DonEel knew what his companion was saying. But it was not possible. "And the stone?"

"Is pattern of telling strength and proud being of Weirdlil. A price making thing for trade."

Then it wasn't his. Yet he had felt a peculiar something when he first saw the stone, more than when the knife came to him. . . . It was too complicated. Galen must be wrong about the knife.

He made an effort to change the subject, caught on the strange name of the people who carved the designs. "Why are they called Weirdlings?"

"Andro-type-named, and it stuck for being right. They are Weird. Not people sort of being, but like little-life on warm worlds. No talking at all, and all feels between selves is nothing to warm-meat-types. All are one but female-priest-chiefs, and is warring every year in living places by warriors to win breeding rights with holy one."

Their culture sounded like that of insects, and picking up his mental identification, Galen agreed.

A sudden warmth and tension struck through the ship. The flasher. The muted viewport exploded into a kaleidoscope of unnamable colors, then faded into silver. A normal thing to Galen. He turned the conversation back to its beginning.

"DonEel, knife is old. Like before Sector Wars." Again his thoughts were complicated and obscure. DonEel pushed down frustration.

"I felt it was old, yes. So—"

"Attend. There is a not-wanting-to-know in you. The Pollo thing. Knife is old, and the citadel knowing in you is before Oso's time. A thing of the Primes."

The black eyes pinned him, forcing him back, toward something—

"No. Galen, there's no sense to this. I don't know these Primes!"

"The not-wanting is clue. The two cannot-be's are, and means something. Like message to self, maybe."

"That's impossible. What about the stone?"

"Weirdling make. Is not old, sure, but the same is true. Is making Weirdlil mean something to you. Clue again."

"So what are you trying to say?" It was impossible to keep the sharpness from his voice. Galen's logic was too difficult at times. Edging away from anger, he took refuge in wine.

"Is not understanding, DonEel. Not impossible. Like impossible of silent speech. See?"

For a moment he saw nothing; the oddness of the Duratheen's spoken communication confused all sense, left nothing but a blank.

Galen shook his head once, patiently. "Thinking is you want to say once and forgot. If right thinking, your meaning was go to Weirdlil."

But that was ridiculous. He had never heard of Weirdlil and its insect people until now. He knew that. So why did the simple statement affect him so? Fear and excitement burned together in his belly, and he swallowed wine quickly, seeking something to say.

Galen nodded and got up. "Your thinking is tangled up, but clue is in that, too, now, friend. We go." He moved to the control room to set course for Weirdlil.

Once the decision was made, Galen did not return to the subject; nor would he be drawn into an argument about it. He knew, as only a telepath could, the games DonEel's mind played to deal with its confusion. Something in the man feared the trip; yet with the information they had, it was their only possible destination.

For DonEel, the journey was paradox. He could

feel the swift passage of time, the worry about Pollo, but all things outside this traveling were held apart, having no place in the vast emptiness of the Big Black.

There were information tapes aboard the ship, and at Galen's suggestion, hoping for some clues to the link between himself and the unknown planet, he studied them.

Weirdlil, he learned, was one of the few inhabited worlds that took no part in galactic affairs. Its only claim to importance was its position, offering the current Lane Lord of the sector a way to patrol not one but three separate lanes of traffic to and from the central cluster worlds. Thus the small world had become an armed camp, boasting a military garrison housing troops at all times. Galen's Duratheen forces had spent a tour there just after he took command, and because of it, Galen had an abiding interest in the natives, a race given little attention because they had nothing of value, and also had no dealings with the garrison.

In spite of Galen's help, the information meant nothing. There were no surfacing memories, nothing.

There was no port city on Weirdlil—the natives had no use for one, and the paramilitary base was generally closed to visitors outside of an occasional emergency. However, identification of their vessel as Duratheen brought them permission to land. Galen was known here as a onetime commander, and the Duratheen autonomy was recognized by other mercenary people.

During the three-day journey, Galen had formulated as much of a plan as was possible to give them the freedom of the planet. As Duratheen, that right was his, but DonEel, a Trueman in fact as well as appearance, would be suspect, and his lack of credentials could involve him in serious problems.

"Being Andro-type has safety only in being Stilkser-

184

born. So student acting," he suggested. The Stilkser student was suffered on all but militarily oriented worlds simply because the vast repository of knowledge and research equipment on their world was important. No one wanted to make Stilks mad enough to withhold information or study rights, so they were allowed to parade their humanity. And they took advantage, proud and aloof and notoriously touchy about the slightest affront.

"Believing you have bought me, they know your safe-being is my work here." Galen blinked amusement.

DonEel was more worried about his real purpose here. He had no idea what he might find, or even what to look for. He constantly had to push aside a fear that he would find it and discard it, whatever it might be, because he wouldn't understand it. The situation was too ridiculous and too important. Yet Galen argued otherwise. The knife and stone were clues.

"Is not finding you need," he pointed out. "The memory has you, but you are shutting it away inside. Maybe nothing waits, but Weirdlil things touching inside makes patterns start alive. Everything Weirdling gives biggest weight to hidden knowings."

He could not argue against Galen. Even his wanting to do so was a point on the Duratheen's side. His desire not to do this thing meant he must.

THIRTEEN_____

EVEN without the unforgettable experience of planetfall, DonEel would have known Weirdlil was alien. His skin tightened, though Galen's memory said the planet was not unlike Syrcase or his own home world. Senses trained from childhood to test every nuance of his environment in Blackwood brought warnings and strange messages to him, though the port itself was very like the one on Syrcase. The air was richer, heavier, with alien scents and flavors. A few moments of breathing brought a rush of pleasure and optimism, gaiety, then dizziness. Suddenly he could not breathe at all.

"Too much," Galen warned, supporting him, banishing panic. "Breathe short."

"What is it?" He thought of the gas in the Portal room of Jimo and was suddenly afraid to breathe at all.

"Air will not be killing you. Only too much for needs and not being used to parts in it." Galen's body had adjusted automatically, a talent he recognized and accepted as normal to him, product of a long evolution based on survival under extreme conditions. But he was not unaware of the problems Andros had with things like air pressure and density. The important thing now was that natives of Stilks excelled in self-discipline, both mental and physical. Their masquerade would fall flat if DonEel continually hyperventilated.

Forcing himself to follow Galen's silent instruction, wondering why a surplus of air should make him feel suffocated, DonEel stopped breathing against it, trusting the other's experience and confidence. In a little, the pressure on his chest eased and he began to relax, though his ears rang disconcertingly.

Galen gave him time, silently reminding him of what he had to know about the Stilksers. He must not become angry or overly amused. He must take his time. . . .

He listened, but other things claimed his attention. Beyond the dull square buildings of the garrison, the land of Weirdlil ran in billows and humps of green away to the horizon. Green in as many hues as the eye could separate, but only green, fading into the turquoise sky.

In minutes he had adjusted to the breathing difficulties, no longer concerned, reaching out to touch the somehow regimented emanations from the building across the field. The Pkal were serving now, Galen said. Fighters and rigid rule-followers. Good troops for duty like this, but too dependent on central authority. He had little respect for their individual ability as warriors.

The commander met them in his office, and DonEel was glad Galen was to do the talking for them. He couldn't have managed. The irrational and seemingly universal enmity of the hominid for the apparently true human type was exaggerated in the Pkal to an active hatred, though the Pkal were most deviant from the type. But this time DonEel had his own feelings to contend with.

The Pkal was not large; nor was it, from the waist up, even vaguely humanoid. There was no visible head to its body, unless it could be the slightly more bulbous of the several arms, fronds, whatever, that seemed to sprout at random from the tapered torso. The vocal sounds, distantly resembling speech, came from an organ extruded from beneath the limp mass of appendages, withdrawing between speeches. It was impossible for DonEel not to reach for analogies, and obvious that the alien communication should seem suddenly a parody of obscene exhibitionism. It didn't help that the overall color was a mottled grayish-pink. Helpless to banish the vision, he turned to stare out the open door, fighting an impulse to hysterical laughter, struggling to listen as Galen outlined their request.

As a student of Stilks, and native-born on that world, Galen pointed out, the Andro was planning to establish study teams on Weirdlil. This was an initial expedition to determine feasibility.

It was not an unreasonable request. During the Duratheen occupation here, a team of researchers had come to examine Weirdling life, and even presented a formal study of their art to the University of Stilks. It was this study that had created a small and exclusive market for such objects as the natives would make. Of course no Weirdling ever profited from that market, but then they never felt bound to meet any particular quota, either, as far as could be determined.

Technically, the garrison force had no authority outside the area of the base itself, and no connection with the natives, who were classed as functionally nonintelligent and expressed no curiosity or desire to contact any other civilizations. However, courtesy to the military and the ownership of the only docking area made the request routine.

The Pkal heard Galen out, and then its rubbery, bubbly voice began formulating questions. How big a party would be in the study group? How long would they need docking space? Would they all be natives of Stilks, or would there be Duratheen mercenaries attached? Interminable questions, only partially masking the desire to discomfit the Andro.

Now that he wasn't distracted by looks, DonEel could follow the subliminal flow of thought behind the questions, knowing the idiot would give permission simply because he could not refuse, however badly he might want to. He let the questions continue for a time; then he turned, refusing to look at the alien commander.

"He cannot refuse, Galen. Tell him we will treat with the Weirdling priest-ruler, if possible. No other authority is involved. We will return to our ship when we have done."

Galen looked at him silently, but his slow blinking eyes and the flash of humor shared between them nearly brought a laugh from the man.

The Pkal added insult to the list of imagined grievances against Andros, but he heard Galen's rumbling message and agreed to furnish rations from the garrison stores for the two of them.

They were escorted from the fence-enclosed base, moving from the paved surface into a wall of green-

188

ery that was like nothing DonEel had imagined. Soft and dry, light as down, the limbs or leaves made seeing impossible but did not impede progress. Galen took the lead, following what he seemed to think was a trail, and his mind was still sparkling with humor, partially directed at his companion.

"Now what did I do that was so funny?"

"Not doing," Galen answered quietly. "Is picture thinking of Pkal. It was a female being. Duratheen is not Andro-type, so body functions otherlike. But now understanding what first seeing said to you."

But beneath the humor was a more sober thought. The Pkal might not know what DonEel thought of it, but the treatment and imagined insult offered by the supposed Stilkser had roused an easy anger. This was an out-of-the-way world with no law but that of the base commander. It would not be wise for DonEel to be alone with the Pkal. "Stronger than seeming to you," he advised. "And never being alone in deeds."

The silence of the forest, if forest it was, was total. The thistledown vegetation made no sound as they moved through it, and the soft soil beneath their feet, invisible in the green growth, swallowed the sound of their steps. The trail seemed nothing more than a fortuitous thinning of the greenery that closed behind them, but Galen walked on unconcerned, silent now. His attention was focused on his companion. DonEel could feel it, and after a little the silent watch began to irritate.

"I don't know what you wish from me, Galen."

"It doesn't wish me. Seeing you is all, and knowing what you will not. You have been here before."

"Galen—"

A quick gesture cut off his protest, and he was forced by the silence between them to follow the flashing thoughts of the Duratheen. This world, he was thinking, demanded adjustments, as with breathing and the lack of visual orientation. And DonEel was making them automatically. He was comfortable here, though the planet was alien enough to all his senses to be disturbing.

It meant nothing, DonEel told himself. He had the advantage of Galen's familiarity with the place.

The Weirdlings came to them as silent as the surreal forest. There was no warning, not even the silent speech that would give them away. They were just there. Galen saw them first and halted DonEel with a touch, indicating the company with a slight nod.

To DonEel they appeared made of the same stuff as the vegetation around them. Green, ranging from emerald to jade to dusty gray-green. Fluffy nothingness. Yet alive, moving as he watched, to surround them. They were tall, and once he could see them apart from their surroundings, beautiful. Fairies came to mind, willowy and graceful.

"*What do they want?*" he asked silently.

"*Seeing us,*" came the immediate reply. "*Knowing me from last duty time, maybe. But you question them.*"

It could be that. The five or six he could see, though there may have been dozens, had moved from the trail back into the brush, and their great, multifaceted eyes were turned toward him. They had faces, or the appearance of faces, with nose and mouth set in the narrow wedge below the eyes. But they gave nothing, rigid as glass. And there was nothing he could touch in their presence, not thought or feeling. When they stopped moving, he had to search carefully to be sure he was seeing them.

"*Follow close,*" Galen thought, calm but wary. "*There is a place of growing near. Many being there before; maybe is now.*"

They moved. The Weirdlings moved. Visible only in motion, pacing them.

The feathery brush parted suddenly, forming a clearing that could have been natural. A circular patch of moist black soil spotted with ordinary rock, like earth and rock anywhere. And their escort moved into view for the first time. The fluffy green about them became cloaks, fastened over one sloping shoulder. Some had coils of woven rope or vines hung at their waists, and all had knives that could have been great green thorns. They were standard-form bipeds, but how delightfully delicate and magical they seemed, moving in dance rather than walking. And silent. Perfectly silent, in motion as well as behind the great eyes. They stopped equally distant from the two and waited. For what?

"I am not knowing," Galen said aloud, and there was no reaction to the rumbling voice. He stood at ease, but close-linked to his inner thoughts, DonEel could feel the tension coiling, a readiness. "There is saying they have killed before, here. But off-worlders are not knowing why they do or not."

"Do they also hate Truemen?" It was a possible explanation, but he felt no personal enmity, only the waiting. Galen moved once, stepped toward what could have been a continuation of the trail across the clearing. One of the Weirdlings shifted slightly, blocking the move.

"We wait." Ready to do battle, the Duratheen saw no need to precipitate it.

They stood long enough to get bored, to exhaust all sensible reasons for their detention; then, with no prior warning, the Weirdlings moved, placing themselves to block the back trail and the one Galen had attempted. The meaning was clear: they were to move on, and the only route was a nearly invisible trail they had not noticed.

The feathery vegetation gave way to a coarser growth, and the pull in leg muscles said they were descending. Uneasy, but not yet disturbed, DonEel kept close touch on Galen's thoughts, welcomed them in the uncanny silence. The Duratheen had been here in the Weirdling forest before, satisfying his curiosity while commanding the garrison for Lord Lindig. He had never had such an escort, but his mental commentary was some frame of reference.

There were periodic clearings now, considered by some, Galen's thought told him, to be the arenas for the seasonal prenuptial combat. The Weirdlings gave no sign. There were no cities or towns as such on the planet, as far as Galen knew, but there were structures, mostly underground and well guarded, about which non-Weirdlings knew little more than their existence.

The descent grew steeper, and the foliage, now more like trees than brush, closed over their heads, making a canopy, a tunnel of dull green that reminded him of something—someplace he had been, perhaps. But the memory eluded him.

Then there was no more time for wondering. The forest ended abruptly and artificially, and the Weirdlings surrounded them again, half their number facing Galen, the rest facing DonEel. Somehow the great jewel eyes separated him from his companion. When those facing him began to move, Galen's thought underscored their silent command: *"Do not resist, DonEel. We will not be parted for real, and they are not knowing it. This place ahead is maybe house or temple for them."*

Intent on the immobile facets of the great eyes, DonEel had not seen the opening ahead, thinking it no more than a natural rock formation. Now, as he walked toward it, surrounded by Weirdlings, he saw the narrow opening. *"Galen—"* He was scared. Not of the Weirdlings or what they could do, not of anything he could name, but even the hard, bright presence of the Duratheen touching his mind was no comfort. He stopped. Immediately, the escort began to close in on him, slowly, but with an inevitability that sent shock waves through his chest.

"Obey them, DonEel. They have meanings we do not know."

The voice sent him forward and into the shadowed opening, out of light into—

Light, pale and green. Alone. Dry and comfortable. The Weirdlings did not follow. He looked about him, seeing this was no cave but— But what? Swallowing against a dry throat, as his eyes began to adjust to the light, he saw the large passage, the walls, the carved panels that—

Vertigo shook him, and he shut his eyes, hard, holding an after-image of design like that on the stone about his neck, alive and glowing in the dusk light. In the self-imposed dark he felt more afraid, threatened and out of touch. No. Reaching, he felt Galen's hard attention, waiting, curious. And inward, deep down beneath the fear, the L'Hur and Ridl.

I don't want to do this, he thought distinctly. It was a dream, all of it, Ridl and the L'Hur and Galen and the Portal. . . . He wanted to wake up, to have it back the way he remembered it, in Scarsen and Blackwood. Who was he after all? Certainly not one of the old heroes stepping from world to world, not a mythmaker.

Struggling with disbelief, hoping it would pass, as before, he opened his eyes. But the vision was there. Worse. The walls crawled with their lines and forms. The stone burned his chest, forcing his attention on it. He wanted to run—somewhere.

"I don't understand it," he said aloud, too loud. And the walls whispered back, "—understand it."

The lines drew his eyes open, to the wall, remembering. . . .

No, not memory, but . . .

His heart beat, making breathing difficult, and his hands were wet.

Wait. She had drawn a picture like this once. . . .

It was so hard to get into the pattern. How was it, now? The lines? Yes. The beginning, always in the center. He must look for—metaphor. Exactly. Feeling, translated to meaning, to word, to line.

193

I don't know how they communicate, maybe never will. Had he said that? He had. He remembered, once. . . . She found a way to make me understand. This is the Hall of Record for her people. Gene lines and heredity. So. Who is who. Lines are design are metaphor. . . . Words—alphabet, maybe, but certainly emotional content also. Angular yet fluid wording, joyous . . . Total design (like voiceprint?), and . . . *Oh God, they are so loud when you can finally hear them!*

Shaking, he moved, and forward was his only direction. Anything was better than standing still, drowning in vision.

She had known his fear, drawn it in the green clay with a twig-like finger. Yes, I am afraid (but not this fear, then). Did she hear him, or did she know another way? He had felt her listening. . . .

Drawing . . .

A fear of ending; lines terminated shockingly or, delicately changed, wandering . . .

Yes.

"How will it happen, this changing?"

How did he know her question?

Later he would know how his being had told her—auric changes, colors of meaning she knew from seeing him, and the minute muscular changes and odors. . . . Complex sensory intake, unbelievably detailed and catalogued.

When he began to know the truth, he had known these, with their soundless, wordless speech, were the race they had always known they would meet: wise and intelligent, a race with no things in common with which to measure and define, so far apart as to be virtually unknowable. Yet they were reaching out now, making the first moves, offering, asking. . . .

"It's got to be visually oriented. Only their eyes are specialized. Visual." He had said that to—

Back and back, beyond the work in galactic communication, beyond the translators and agreements

194

on common language. Back to the Earth sciences un-used for ages, worthless in the wider area of the galaxy. What have we in common? Kinesics. Body language. Basic chemical reactions to stimuli.

Did they feel or react to the basic situations, like sexual impulse and threat of death?

They did. It was a place to start. And so little time. He had learned.

Their language had once been intentional, rather like charades in that it involved gestures and move-ments. Now it was intuitional, subtle. Only the dances and formal stories that were the introduction to the seasonal matings were yet stylized with the old broad gestures and actions.

But they had learned quickly to understand others, somehow linking the diverse physiologies and situa-tions with intent and reason, making observation an exact science. And they had come to him unexpect-edly, on one of his planetfalls, when he was gathering information for Timaret, back on Stilks. They had come to him silent and taken him to the female. She had shown him patiently. He had to understand, not in words but in feeling, and just knowing. It was not a way of thinking, so much as a different place from which to understand. Not a difficult place to get to, so much as surprising. The only way he had been able to get there at all was not to try. . . .

But he did learn, or dreamed he learned, and Happy Dancer, the queen-priestess, had brought him here, finally, to see their past, a drawing and singing and dancing of history. . . .

Pain, hot and annoying from eyes too long open, interrupted the dream, and he found darkness behind his hands, wiping the sudden tears that washed the pain away. What was happening to him?

"Galen, what is this?" he whispered aloud, and felt the ready response.

"Trust your feelings. The way is making for you, I think."

195

Feelings? What did he feel? Scared, but not all of him scared now, and somewhere in him was a reverence and hope, not for now but. . . .

He opened his eyes and remembered the dance. . . . She had wanted to talk, to remember, to dream. . . .

He dreamed, and she was a fairy creature, elfin in shape and sound, singing to him, loving him innocently, swamping him with her until he saw as she saw the fairyland that to her was Areen'im.

This was not telepathy; it was transfer. He was she, seeing him, the grotesque Terran, seated, watching intensely. He was she, tasting the delicately flavored spore—drug—whatever. He was she, and the fear he felt of that was somehow soothed by knowing she was he, not caught, but seeking, seeing, knowing. . . .

And being she, he could see the glyphs. The eyes that had once terrified him, bulging bright-faceted from the tight facial planes, rendered them readable, each not seen as before, but fractured into planes of focus, superimposed. . . . He/she saw and read and heard, and caught here, forgot, and let her be himself for as long as it was possible.

It was the drug, of course, his Earth-bred logic told him after it, when he was sick and bent over with pain and sweating before the continual tracery of the young queen.

She was, he felt, curious as to whether or not he would survive. Not worried, only curious and watchful. And he hadn't died, quite. Thanks to Zhan. He was too shattered to help himself.

Getting himself back was painful. He had accepted the translocation too completely; now everything was alien. But he knew the glyphs. He couldn't see them, of course, not like he-being-she had seen, but he knew how to look and make them speak. So she talked to him with her hands, making quick, subtle strokes in the clay. Simple patterns because he could no longer see the design-with-sound. And he talked—told her, anyway—of his people, and how the dance-talkers had chosen the wrong ones to bridge this gap.

"We are not leaders," he said, and told of the killings and the coming proscription against them as Primes, and the pressure now to make them leave even neutral Stilks.

She was he; she already knew his thinking-ahead-of-doing—his future plans. She drew him thought-lines of voice and meaning and him-being-himself, frozen in the tight clay of the floor. The design poured out of her hand too fast to follow, and then she changed it.

This, the queen drew, is you (present being), fearing to become this (future being probable). The lines changed, only the base pattern remaining in the center, well-defined, with a boundary, a moat between subtle complexities of design. Perfectly put. She knew Timaret's plan, if not the procedure, and he barely understood that; but, like him, now she knew the purpose and effect on the Primes and his reaction to it.

As he watched, the clay glyph exploded. She, subtle design he knew from being she, became a bridge over the moat between him present and himself—reweaving, joining, making a thing that was both, yet the same as the central pattern.

"Can you do this?"

For the first time, she touched him, a dry twig brushing his knee. Affirmative.

Giving all of himself back to him, she took damp clay and drew all she was of him, which was by far more than he knew of himself on the top of his mind, and his eyes followed, rapt, knowing it was a simple design made for the limits of his near-blindness. Yet it was all there, a key and lock, the song of him frozen in the drying clay.

"DonEel!" The bright summons held danger, alertness, and plea, shattering his syrupy reverie, jerking him awake. Confused, he looked about him at cool green walls covered with murals of design that seemed to waver and crawl—where?"

"DonEel, danger is here. The Pkal followed."

Galen, of course. Where had he got to? There was no direction here, and he had to keep his eyes on the tight-packed floor to avoid the crawling walls. *"Galen, I think I'm lost. This is a warren of some sort—"* The light brightened suddenly, pulling his eyes up, startled, to see huge, faceted eyes glowing with cool fire, beckoning. . . .

No!

Heart kicking, he almost ran, but the stillness bound him to the spot long enough to realize it was not real —a carving in the wall opposite, polished stone, only that. He looked away then, able to see the chamber, vaguely familiar, tugging at a mind that, awake, refused memory.

There was no exit save where he stood. The room was roughly round, higher than it was wide, the ceiling glowing with what must be some phosphorescent fungal growth. There were niches, like shrines, carved into the wall at intervals on either side of the great carved queen's head, and each oval niche held a figure, delicate and exquisitely worked in what might have been porcelain. Behind each figurine was a complex carved design of lines so fine the eye had difficulty focusing, making the pattern seem to dance and move.

He moved about the circle, wondering, and came finally to the one empty niche. Puzzled, he stopped. The pedestal was there, but nothing resembling a statue or the background design. Only a flat object, like a small plate. It lay at an angle, and he bent closer to see it. Lines traced on the shiny surface leaped into focus. . . .

Pain exploded through his head, a green-white flash that speared his eyes open, pouring him out between stretched lids. . . . He fought, lost, and fell through green light, falling. . . . Pain whined along his nerves, high-pitched and jarring, banded his chest, squeezed tight, tight. . . . Became pleasure, shattering spine and head, plunging ecstatic into the vast dimensionless pool of space inside his head. . . . Yes, and yes, and yes. Being flight and song and singer, greedy now for the pain-turned-pleasure, stripping away here and now for. . . .

"Deon, the word has gone out. There isn't as much time as planned. Especially in the cluster worlds. Maybe more on the Rim. The safe-conduct for you and Zhan has been arranged, as far as possible. It's time to start bringing them in." Harmond's dark eyes were as calm as his words. Any panic or nervousness was locked behind a screen even he would not break.

"The 'forming'?"

"Well enough along to be self-sustaining in as much area as we will need. Better than we could have hoped for in just five years."

"Harm, I still think a hundred percent's a bad—"

One slight gesture silenced him. "We've been over it, Deon. We're losing people too fast now. The young, the breeders. Every one dead is weakening us. Some genes may already be irretrievably lost. The propaganda drive has been too successful; already more than a hundred worlds have outlawed Primes, and we have projected the trend here on Stilks far enough to know that in less than half a standard year we will be openly challenged by the University."

"After all we've accomplished for them."

"Because of it, perhaps. We know only what they think, not why. Simple fear, maybe. It doesn't matter. We've known since my childhood it would come to this."

Known, prepared, and hoped somehow it wouldn't happen. It was so unfair, now, when every hominid world had used them to gain its own ends. Jaws locked, he knew Harmond followed his frustration and anger, and he let it grow, not hiding.

199

"Deon, it's late for that."

"But their reasons are madness. We all know it."

"Knowing does not keep us alive."

He knew that. But running—

"Means survival. Not just us, Deon. The whole of what we are, our genetic heritage. The young must survive." He dismissed the old arguments. "Your itinerary was worked out by Tim on the subject comps. You and Zhan will leave at the end of the next period. Phoenix is refitted and ready."

"Timaret?"

"On Syrcase a month already. The team left at the end of their teaching schedule."

"And you?"

"Go with Mirad and the rest before you leave. They are already on board. I only wanted to see you, to tell you—"

No seeing was so important, no telling so vital it transcended the perfect communication of the Primes. But the physical presence spoke too, of caring. And he knew.

"I will not see you again."

"You may, Deon. I will not know of it."

The other teams had not so far to go, so he and Zhan would be last. Their jobs, beyond ferrying their people to Syrcase, would. . . .

The blow exploding across his cheek was nothing like the shock of visual silence as the whiteness spun him out and away and away, soaring into the cool green glow.

"DonEel!" Unmodulated, Galen's voice rang like hunting horns through the round chamber, shattering the delicious existence.

"Do you see?" The voice challenged, and for one awful moment the Duratheen seemed an ancient bird of prey swooping down on the helpless man. . . .

Only bending close over the prostrate figure, taloned

hands hard on the surprised shoulders. "They hold Pkal distant for saving you here. Fighting. Sending me to you."

"Who?" Stupidly, as his thoughts began to hurry. The Weirdlings, of course. The Pkal had followed them here. He struggled against the grip, and it eased as Galen touched his mind.

"You were not hearing me down here from noise of Weirdling songs in stone."

"You hear them?"

As noise and bits of knowing. The information flashed as Galen stood, helping him to his feet. Don-Eel glanced toward the niche, mind already reaching, but Galen anticipated him and the great hand flashed out, taking the disk.

"Is what wanting for Weirdlil was telling you, but better not staying here for danger."

Danger. The final veils parted, and he realized that he had been helpless here, entranced. Seeing more clearly now, he noticed the wet crimson stain on the bulky shoulder. Concern and guilt moved in him, but Galen shrugged it off. It was unimportant for now, and there wasn't time. "Happenings so are expected; care is in ship. But trouble is from Pkal between."

They hurried along the dim tunnel, Galen slightly bowed to avoid the rough ceiling. Following him through the disguised opening, DonEel squinted in the brighter light, seeing the motionless green figures surrounding the clearing. Once he was out, the Weirdlings melted into the undergrowth, leaving a handful that could have been their original escort. A short, bubbly sound broke the silence, and he didn't need Galen's quick thought to know it had been made by a Pkal, dying. There would, he thought, be hell to pay when the Federation found out about this.

"No Federation now, friend DonEel. Only sector rules by Lane Lords. Lindig not caring if Weirdlings war here."

Their escort moved quickly, pressing them to hurry through the thick vegetation, and it was a moment before either of them realized it was no longer silent. A sound like wind-distant storm came muted through the thick growth, directionless. On this silent planet it was wrong, out of place. The Weirdlings stopped in the first clearing, motionless, waiting, and the sound grew, rising in air as still as stone.

"Lindig's garrison!" Galen's sharpness made him jump nervously. "Sound is battling—" He started forward, but two of the Weirdlings turned to face him, and he stopped.

"What's happening?" But he knew already from the rushing mind. There was fighting on the base. But between whom?

Galen fumed inwardly, and his arm had begun to hurt. DonEel was aware of it as a distant ache in his own shoulder, and he was worried about it, but they were held to the clearing by the pairs of eyes, motionless, waiting. . . .

It seemed hours before the Weirdlings turned, began to move forward along the faint trail. "Take care," Galen warned, unnecessarily. "Thinking to me is they work protection for us, but not knowing that." The quick mind was familiar with crisis, searching possibilities. He did not want to move against this delicate green people, but his ship was on the garrison field, and they had to reach it to get off-world.

Battle sounds came clearly as they neared the base perimeter, and as they came out of the brush, Galen halted on his own, holding DonEel back with one extended arm. The fence was broken beyond—

"Weirdling!" The open ground about the base swarmed with them. Expecting anything but this, Galen held back, though their escort plainly wanted them to move. This was wrong. Never, since he had first known of the Weirdlings, had there been evidence of hostility toward the Lindig garrison. These were an unknown people, timid and secretive, with no warriorlike tendencies beyond the ritual mating battles. The occasional personnel losses from the base had been written off as individual accidents or possible interference in native ritual. Yet here, to the knowledgeable eye of the Duratheen, these simple natives were in control of the most sophisticated weapons, and were methodically destroying buildings, ships, and Pkal.

The garrison personnel were putting up resistance, but dying by their own weapons and not knowing why. Somehow the natives had gained a knowledge of tactics. They were everywhere, swarming over buildings and ships, surrounding the base. Only the slender shape of the Duratheen vessel stood clear. It should not be.

Their escort had been joined by dozens of the green people, watching them, huge eyes catching the cool light, green on green, moving toward them.

"We go." Galen could no longer avoid the obvious intent.

They went, keeping close together, surrounded by Weirdlings, moving through bedlam as the commander's office and two near ships were attacked and destroyed in quick succession.

The silence in the ship was beautiful after the battle noise, but Galen allowed no time for appreciating it, and soon they hung in the vast silence of nothingness far above the surface of Weirdlil. But they did not leave, yet. Galen halted the ship while Weirdlil still filled the screen. He spent silent moments at the controls, and soon a clear picture of the base appeared in place of the globe. Even from this distance it looked a shambles.

"Maybe ships not crippled will follow. Or help comes fast if Pkal is patrolling near," the Duratheen said aloud, and his thoughts were alert with possibilities, as well as puzzlement.

"To attack the Weirdlings?" DonEel did not yet

comprehend what had happened on the planet, only touching Galen's confusion.

"Understanding of Weirdlings is they are not fighting, so looking for reasons will show record of Duratheen ship coming and going if records remain."

"Then they'll think we—"

"Knowing for sure Duratheen ship came. Maybe not knowing us being here, but if ship is named, record from Syrcase says there is time for coming from there."

A flash lit the screen, and when it faded, the last of the buildings on the base was gone.

"Why are they doing this now?" He knew from Galen's knowing that the base had been built during the reconstruction period after the Sector Wars, nearly seven hundred years before. And that it had been occupied by many forces since that time, with no trouble from the natives.

"It questions me also," Galen admitted, but there was speculation in his mind, clouded now by a growing awareness of pain from the shoulder wound.

"You better let me see to it."

Agreeing, Galen set out the medical equipment, instructing the man in their uses. The Pkal preferred a peculiar weapon for close combat, one that fired a projectile rather than the more common laser or microwave that burned or destroyed tissue. "Hitting knocks down opponent, making time for action," he explained, commenting silently that he thought it cowardice.

Whatever the projectile, it had cut none too neatly through the muscle over the top of the shoulder, missing the complex joint of near wing and shoulder. It wasn't a serious wound, but ugly and painful. Don-Eel felt responsible again. He should not have left Galen alone to wait for him.

He had never looked at the great body closely before, but now the power and complexity of it struck him. There were many scars beneath the white down that was neither feather nor fur, but felt beneath his fingers like the finest sueded leather over muscles that swelled hard and warmly alive.

Galen's self-conscious amusement at the man's wandering thoughts brought him up short, but it was a sharing more honest than speech and he wasn't sorry. Galen was a wonder to him, though they had come so close in mind he scarcely saw the alienness of him.

"Goodness of silent speech understands between kinds, DonEel. No wars would be."

"Maybe." He was depressed suddenly by the hope he touched in the Duratheen. "I'm sorry I was out of touch again. This shouldn't have happened. I forgot everything, even how to breathe down there." It was the only excuse he could find for the dizziness, the peculiar sensations and loss of time.

"Backward thinking again. Forgetting nothing. I was hearing it. It was remembering. It got between; yet now you are not knowing about words of Weirdlil." The black eyes studied him no less intently than the mind behind them.

"Galen, I—"

"Weirdlings gave rememberings to you on disk. When we are safe, with time it comes back. I know this. Fitting to Weirdling attack must be there, too."

His head began to pound abominably as he finished dressing Galen's wound. He wanted to ask what Galen meant, but the Duratheen's thoughts had turned to their safety. Through no fault of their own, they were now in a complicated and dangerous situation.

"Lanes are open places, but watched. Wisest thing to flash out to open Black between."

As the flasher sent them farther out, away from inhabited worlds and the shimmering jewel-clusters of stars, they rested and ate and rested again. DonEel was glad for silence and emptiness, wanting nothing more than to sleep and dream unrecalled and confused dreams. . . .

He woke from a doze to find Galen before him, the screen behind him showing deep black lightly sprinkled with diamond dust.

"Where are we?"

"Here." There was purpose in the mind behind the single word. "Sleep is running, too. Fear brings. Safe being here and time is for you to take back what you got from Weirdlings. You do not even think of Ridl now. Sleeping is only to hide."

Galen's attitude annoyed him. What good would it do to think of Ridl now, or Pollo. They had gambled on Weirdlil and lost. Not only time and hope, but their own safety and the chance to return quickly to Syrcase. Why not sleep here in the ultimate quiet of the Big Black?

Galen only looked at him, the eagle watching, forcing. . . .

The disk lay on the table near the couch where Pollo had once lain, beginning the sleep from which he must not waken. He could feel it there through Galen, waiting. It took effort not to glance at it because, as frightened as he was, curiosity sparked, began to burn.

"Galen." He heard the plea in his voice and was ashamed. "Galen, it caught me there once." The fear was of losing himself, or. . . .

"So, remembering still has you."

No, he wanted to stay. But he did remember—parts. The rush of pain become pleasure, spreading into desire to get where he was going to have. . . .

He got up, stiff from too much sitting, knowing it was all they had, that Galen would be here with him, knowing nothing. And everything.

"Thinking right, DonEel. Time for it is here, and I will not be letting you get too far."

Light struck the pale disk at an angle, bringing the design into relief as when he had first seen it. It was a strange pattern, finely drawn and incredibly com-

206

plex. Curious, waiting for something terrible to happen, watching himself closer than the disk, he studied the pattern, discovered it was one unbroken line, beginning in the center of the disk, moving outward, curving back, but never completely back to the beginning, repeating a basic theme with variations, ending—where? There must be an end to the line. He bent over it, chin on fist, frowning slightly. He found the beginning, followed it slowly, lost direction. Odd, the line seemed to anticipate logic and confound it, losing him. At any rate, there was no danger here, none of what he had felt on Weirdlil. It must have been the air.

His attention narrowed on the design, eyes moving continuously through the intricate pattern as he relaxed, breathing slowed, deepened. . . .

Motionless across the cabin, Galen kept close touch on the man's mind, felt the sweet, expanding lethargy as the consciousness sank deeper and deeper into the unknown.

It was sleep of a sort. A delicious drifting, letting go of every real thing, accepting the dreams, reaching down and down. . . .

FOURTEEN

THE call tugged at him, insistent, pulling him up until he no longer dreamed easy. He felt heavy with time he could not answer. Because he knew, and—

He knew. He became memory, bridging, and a beginning of knowledge, and it was—*"DonEel!"*—all fantasy. All of it. Delpha, Scarsen, all of Eden. Unreal. It had never been and could never be anything but the creation of minds steeped in the beauty of the ancient times of manhood, times new again in the forever-reaching memories seeking a truer beginning. The time of the transcendent philosophers in the time-place called Greece. They all knew it. Yet they had to play the same game because they had agreed on the rules and all who did not play died. It had to be that way, Harmond said, because the dying did not matter anymore with their extended memories, and. ...

Other than the occasional call, the prodding, seeking responses that would tell him the man was not lost to him entirely, Galen kept silent, following the narrow thread of surface activity in the man's mind, feeling walls crumbling, locks melting away, awarenesses crossing the bridge of the design into the real world of what once was and still was, and if hope could exist in the world he knew, would be again.

"DonEel." It had been a long time, however right it might be, and there was a limit to the man's ability to stand the strain.

He woke, or maybe just became aware again of what was not entirely inside his own head, pouring from his own strange new memory.

"It did not exist, of course. We had to make it." He said it, wondering, yet as though he had been asked to explain. "We built the world into a new home. It isn't any of it real, the plants and animals. . . . We brought all that was good and useful, and nothing that was harmful or bad for us. Another Eden. Or maybe the only one." He spoke to himself, but that self was Deon, classification Sol-Terran Prime, knowing DonEel, not really speaking to—Galen, of course —because the vast space in his own head was exploding with knowledge and so much—

A taloned hand fell over the disk, breaking the fascination, and his eyes moved up, seeing finally.

"Done now, DonEel. Is like drink. Better and better is worse and worse."

"Yes." It was something to say to the black eyes watching him. Then, forcing union: "Galen, I know so much. Eden. It's our exile." Terra-formed, he remembered, in an impossible five years when there should have been twice or three times that. And he

208

recalled the quick, secret journeys to Syrcase, bringing the seed of Terra, the livestock. The reason hadn't been real to them then, even knowing the trends and probabilities, and the dying someday. They could not believe that insanity would triumph over—

He shook his head. There was so much, so much detail, so much right-wrong confusion twisting him up, leading every thought into others and more and more relatednesses. . . .

"You are being Terran Prime." Galen focused his mind again, and he was grateful.

"Yes."

"Is knowing in you, then, the answer to the trouble with bright-head?"

"Bright—" Pollo. No, wait, he knew— Not Pollo. Zhan Llir was— Yes. It had to be. He had known it in the DonEel time, and not known he knew it. Zhan Llir. Now, suddenly, he knew it all together. The special connection, the importance, because of being together. Not just now, but again and again, and all the togethernesses remembered. And yes, they had loved, by the Gods they had loved, sharing pleasures and selves and every dark and twisting alley of mind and experience as they sailed the Big Empty. It was part of them, superimposed on all the experiences of love possible to them. Zhan Llir, friend, confidant in a way that word was never meant to tell, and, finally, comrade in arms as they raced time and insanity, seeking the last children of Earth, bringing them from worlds and dangers, ferrying them to Syrcase and the loss of all they were for a time, until the madness against them would have passed, leaving them with a forgotten hope of some future when they could be forever themselves.

For a shattering moment the wonder was not that he remembered after the time that had passed, but that he could have forgotten. Timaret had done his work well. Timaret, the wise and warm one, loved and trusted by them all. Behind closed eyes he called up the memory, and in sudden dislocation knew the vision to be as familiar as DonEel's yesterday. Alchia.

"We didn't forget what we were," he said aloud, remembering Alchia and how much he was himself, feeling idiot laughter in his throat. "We only forgot to know what we were. Are."

Washed with the man's continuing confusion, Galen let it be. It was too sudden and too much to be useful. But the disk had fulfilled its purpose, and time would do the rest. He held to isolate importances. "Man Pollo yet sleeps," he reminded, watching the mind.

"Aye. He sleeps." DonEel looked up and felt the energy run out of him. Pollo/Zhan Llir, still condemned. Ah God, it should not be, was never meant to be like this, one of them, alone. Something had gone wrong. Pollo could not just die. Not now, after so long. It was not even the idea of his death, but the separation, the thing he had last feared, prompting that impossible suggestion of not returning to Syrcase. That, too, Zhan had known of him, and shared, but he had accepted the Portal, hoping there would be time and place, sometime, someplace. . . . A fear ran through him, and a need to be back before—

He was so tired from the weight of so much time.

"Sleeping heals," Galen said quietly, feeling the breakdown of coherence. He picked up the disk. "We return now. You are having the way to help him."

"Maybe. I don't know." He tried to think, but the unplumbed depths of his own memory pulled him away from the thought and he was too tired to resist. This was him, all the memory, all the self-awareness, were real and familiar in some impossible way. Only one thing was different. The constant shifting flow of other awarenesses, the subliminal taken-for-granted contact with his own kind that every Prime was born into, was gone. Only Galen touched the fringe of his mind, and below that, dimly, in a place never known to Deon, something else, something— He felt suddenly exposed, vulnerable.

"Not only being Deon," Galen said into his long silence, feeling the insecurity. "DonEel of Erl is remembering Deon. Your now being questions me without answers, but the realness is Ridl siring you on the female Prime, making you."

Ridl. The L'Hur— And now, beyond the innocence of DonEel, he thought of that, understanding the physical truth of his conception, and it shook him. His flesh and bone and being sculpted from that transcendent ecstasy, shared during the Awakening to become him in a way the Primes had never known. That was him too.

He leaned forward and darkened the port with a quick hand, staring at his sudden reflection in the mirror surface. He did not look a stranger to himself, but Deon had not looked like this. How strange it was to know this and something else, and be both. Yet now that he looked, there were the physical signs of Ridl's legacy, the high cheekbones, the tilt of dark eyes and brows. Ridl's son.

Staring into his own dark eyes, he remembered Harmond's argument for genetic survival. The memory, like the mental talents, were locked in the genetic structure of the Primes, developed in the centuries they had stayed on Earth after the general exodus into space. They had stayed and grown inward, brooding and interbreeding, and becoming Primes. Until the children born to them took their talents for granted, and grew and began to remember being before, and they were never sure if they had discovered a truth or created immortality. But death became something else because they remembered. He knew that was true. He remembered being before Deon, and before that— And that was the reason for Eden, for the exile. The lines of descent were complex and tightly woven in the group, and each of them mated and produced a child within the group, not only for the sake of individual survival, but for the whole of the Primes. But they were being killed, the young were being lost before they bred. And so the exile, the one way the Primes could survive, remembering or not.

He opened his eyes and looked at his reflection. But how could that apply to him? He was not wholly Terran. He was—

"L'Hur are not being Primes, yet a sameness is to you." Galen again, listening to his ponderings, making points he missed in his inner searchings. And he remembered a speculation, not his and not generally accepted, but born out of the always reaching back in memory. Now, tracing memories given by another blood, braided somehow with the Prime memory, it was more than speculation.

"*Ridl*," he thought, cool fingers pressing darkness into his eyes, ignoring the vision of vaster patterns and repetitions beyond coincidence. "*We knew you once, in the time that we have not yet remembered. Long and long ago. Before we became us.*" The clues were there in Harmond's research into their own genetic structure, that unfound but necessary common factor in the ones that had remained longest with Earth and become Primes. Evidence of ancient contact? Could it be?

And from his own otherness, as DonEel beyond Deon, and from the massed and aware L'Hur, the answer shaped—

Yes and yes and yes. Affirmation and revelation pouring through flesh and mind alike. "*We are one.*"

"Is God-speak," Galen said into the silent chorus, pulling him back to himself. "The Old Ones all know."

"You heard?"

"Felt yeses and joy to you, and shared me." For a moment a deeper, more subtle bond united the two, a good thing, kinship. "Now is time for real sleeping, DonEel."

Memories woke with him, without the urgency of the disks's recall, like memories of childhood with some of the wonder yet there. The healing function of sleep, he knew. Most of that last journey with Zhan Llir was clear in him now, the race to call together the last of the embattled Primes, to participate in the retreat to Syrcase, the enigmatic planet, and yield to Timaret's processing. How easily information had passed between them. There was no need for messages, only the enfoldment of recognition, the twining of knowledges. How much there had been to that time, the time of battle and fear, and feeling the deaths they could not prevent. And there were the children and loved ones, who were, to the eye, completely alien, yet who gave a depth and warmth and wealth of otherness to the whole. Loved and lovers, and mates, all feared and under the sentence of death. They had been so few against so many.

He remembered the exile, and the reason for it, and he woke with Deon's old anger, closed and hot with it.

"Yesterday's anger," Galen pointed out. "All is changed. People and worlds are different." During DonEel's sleep he had set the ship for Syrcase. It would take time, even with the flasher, for they had run far for safety, not sure of the threat. And in spite of the man's impatience, the time would be a good thing, letting him become familiar with what he was, and had been.

Perhaps the greatest mystery to the Duratheen, or the one he could relate to immediately, was the man's long-ago involvement with the Weirdlings. "How was it knowing you about them?" he asked as they ate together. "And making the way for you to remember."

The Weirdlings, the dance-talkers. He wasn't sure how they knew. But they had. By watching, perhaps. For all their patience with him, he had not begun to truly understand them. One, the priestess-queen he had named Happy Dancer, had taken a special interest in him, being with him, showing, repeating, until he knew there was something he should know and do. It was, he began to think, in the eyes. And he thought she agreed. It was a frustrating problem for one to whom communication on even the most intimate level was a fact of everyday life. But he had persisted, intrigued, trying and failing and leaving and returning, until he could understand what she wrote, or drew, to him, and believe that she, without knowing sound, saw what he said-meant. It seemed a short time ago now that she had helped him to understand their need and fear. They were not, as other races thought, a hive mentality without individual communication and thought. They were just incredibly different, and more aware in their way than any of the races that had contacted them. They were afraid now of being overrun, classified as nonintelligent. They needed a way to communicate, so they had chosen from a people whose total life was communication. They had not begged. There was a bargain. They knew what he wanted even more than he did, and after he had taken the theory of visual sound-design to Stilks, and with Zhan's help hidden it in the language comps, she had drawn the disk, putting him down for safekeeping. The knife had been a parting gift, to remember her by.

"The gift knife." He laughed suddenly, remembering it. "I took it to Eden and lost it. I was hedging the bet. It's a wonder Tim missed that." And the flute—he remembered now also. How strangely it had turned out after all this time. For the flute had belonged to one of the Primes rescued from the Central Sector, a youth of exceptional musical ability and grace. He had left the flute behind on Syrcase without complaint, but Deon, knowing its importance, had fallen prey to a romantic notion and taken the instrument to the new world, leaving it where it would be found. How strange if that youth happened to be—

"So, you bringing it to Eden." Galen blinked humor. "And it found you instead of knife, then brought knife to you."

"Yes. Exactly so." Did concidence actually exist? Or cliché?

Later, as they neared Syrcase, Galen wondered about the exile itself, and the manner of it. How could the Primes be not-Primes?

"It was Timaret's work on Stilks, with Harmond. They were trying to find out what Primes were, why they were different from other Terrans. They found out that being a Prime isn't just in the head, it's everything, down to the individual cells. It was Tim that found a sort of awareness in the cells, not mind exactly, but a sort of self-realization that's tied in with how it remembers what it is. And that awareness can be controlled and commanded within certain narrow limits."

"With silent speech?"

"Like it, yes. A sort of hypnotic command to the memory of the cell itself. I don't how it works, but it does." He had seen the results in the perfection of the children born to those who had learned to move in the dim and misty world of that basic existence.

It was this manipulation on the cellular level that now affected the Primes. Each Prime that stepped through the Portal to Eden voluntarily accepted the amnesiac suggestion on the mental level, and genetically each carried the command to retard awareness of psychic abilities until the posthypnotic stimulus was received. If something went wrong, if the memory was triggered (and it could happen), there were factors that would cause minute physical changes, so the body would cease to function. Most important now, the command was intended to be reversible. The how hadn't been secret, but he had been concerned with things outside Tim's technique and discipline. Maybe somewhere in the impossible collection of knowledge he had begun to touch in himself there was an answer. If so, he could not yet bring it to the surface.

"Yet you are being remembered," Galen pointed out.

True, but not his doing. Happy Dancer had known his fear of losing himself, and somehow she had found a way to speak directly to the body-mind on a level that could not be stopped or confused. The disk was him in symbol.

"Weirdling drawing may answer for friend," Galen suggested, but it was more hope than anything to depend on. They had been so close, so much a part of what each was, a gestalt in miniature of the whole Prime society. It could. Maybe.

Since the first waking after exposure to the disk, DonEel had found the psychic abilities somewhat easier, more familiar, as though he had finally learned to focus and use the talents he had always had. Galen didn't seem to notice any difference, but it was easier now to be aware of Ridl and the L'Hur, and, through them, Pollo. He knew the Delphan yet slept, unconscious. Alive, but not living. How long could he remain suspended like that before the flesh simply refused the burden? Ridl did not know.

FIFTEEN

THEY could not approach Syrcase directly; word of the attack on Lindig's base on Weirdlil, and possibly the identification of Galen's ship, would have reached Oso by now. If the connection was made, they would be taken for criminals, if they were allowed to land at all. So they came in through the Belt, the band of moons circling the equator.

Away from the oasis of Port City, the planet had a bombed-out look, scarred and dusty, with only occasional patches of gray lichen dotting the rolling hills where an assortment of secretive insects warred incessantly for survival.

They waited until the mantle of darkness slipped over the citadel, then came in low and fast onto the desert behind the low hills north of the great building. Galen was an exceptional pilot, and, remembering now another craft in another time, watching the Duratheen at ease with the controls, automatically adjusting, correcting, aware of every option and enjoying it, DonEel felt both envy and admiration.

They came out of the ship into darkness, and it was cold. Their breath frosted in the pale necklace glow of the moons that turned Galen's whiteness ghostly. Again the I-have-been-hereness sliced through DonEel, but now there were conscious memories of it, of the times before Port City when the citadel had been new to them, and dust-shrouded, and he and his companions had traded speculation on the mystery of Syrcase.

Could yesterday have been so long ago?

Walking through darkness, shivering in spite of the Duratheen cloak, he pondered his own mind. He held now a wealth of memory so rich even the memory of its loss was overshadowed. Was DonEel real? Or those memories? He half-expected to find emptiness and dust where DonEel had found life, and through the Portal—

No. The newer, younger DonEel fought to retain home and Delpha and loves that meant—something. Maybe everything. Same loves? New loves? Could they be loves at all, now?

Eyes on the white blur of his companion, he reached into himself with momentary desperation and half-formed fear. But it was there, muted and aware of him, with a power of self beyond him. L'Hur, Ridl, Father. The contact was wordless, but it was enough. This was real. More, it was all there was for him. The other time no longer existed. All that had meant reality for him as Deon lay beyond the Portal, and further, beyond a wall of their own building. It might never have been, or be again.

He did not want to examine that. Moving away from his night fears, he caught up with Galen, glad for the steady force of that mind touching his thoughts. Reaching for that silent companionship, he touched a loneliness in the Duratheen he had never known as DonEel. It flashed him out of self-pity, making him break the silence quietly.

"Before, in Deon's real time, there were always so many of us, knowing each other, being there, part of us. It was what we were. The silence now— It was the first thing I really felt when I woke, remembering." It had frightened him.

"Differentness from before," Galen replied logically. "For me and others with mind knowings, silence is always. Unless Primes return."

A question of numbers came to DonEel, and Galen responded automatically. Seven telepaths he had known. Seven, in a lifetime of natural ability. And he was by nature and birth a traveler, moving at will through the galaxy. Others had known one; two if they were lucky. Seven he had found. And no other Duratheen.

"Did you look?"

"Always." In his youth, searching was all he had, and desperation. Deep now, in the concerns of a past he had come beyond, was a memory, buried, of the bad time, a time of shadowed self-doubt and huddling near the abyss of insanity. It had passed. He had found first one, then another. And the finding had not been a casual thing for any of them. They were joined and supported by knowing that even now, going about their ways, they could find one another if necessary. "Traveling is our doing. Danger waits in one place." Discovery through some unconscious error, or impossible knowledge, or the impulse to trust, to confess . . .

"Yet you survive." It was a Deon-thought, remembering they could not, except by running. Perhaps there was something these new ones—not Primes, but like them—had, a sort of power. And I, he thought, could not have survived with it, after the awakening, except for the L'Hur, nor after the disk, had not Galen been there, close and strong.

The Duratheen heard, and was moved, sharing in turn a warmth and private pleasure in shadowed honesty. But logic still worked for the warrior. "Deon is perhaps not seeing aloneness. But now being DonEel is also you, and not having silent speech. You are all you are, not returned to before now."

DonEel's eyes flashed faintly as he glanced up at the cruel face, feeling Galen's silent humor. He was right, of course. It was his own fault for falling into confusion, for seeing Deon (himself in the past) as different and superior to DonEel (himself—where?). He was not only all that Deon had captured of his pasts, but all that had gone on after coming through the Portal that last time with Zhan. He wondered if they had lost all that time, or if the exile time would also come to them, become part of them.

Galen's sudden stillness halted his reverie. Somehow the barren night had been crossed, and now the Duratheen's thoughts quested out toward where the citadel rose dark and solid against the jade sky, its base still obscured by the swell of the hill before them. Reaching out away from his own thoughts, DonEel felt, with Galen, the tension of trouble and excitement. War-thought, Galen's mind said. They did know of the attack on Lindig's garrison. But not the truth. The citadel was preparing for defense against an unknown enemy.

They had to get into that busy place. Galen thought there were probably no guards watching against an approach from the desert, certainly not for two individuals. DonEel remembered the explorations, when they were trying to discover who had built the titanic structure and why. The strange alien side of the citadel had entrances; if they could reach them, they could return to the Portal room the way they had left.

Galen accepted his knowledge without question and moved forward, hurrying now to beat the dawn. Already the sky was paling, showing streaks and flares of topaz and emerald as they descended into the unkempt gardens surrounding the base of the citadel and moved to the left away from the ornate grand entrance. It was like circling a mountain—impossible at this range to think of it as a building.

The way of entering was screened behind thick shrubs, more tunnel than door, so Galen had to bend and move sideways to fit his broad shoulders through. Inside, the glareless white light stung DonEel's nightwide eyes. The place was empty, but there were signs of occupation: litter and what could have been a blanket or robe tossed against one wall. Not surprising this close to the outside—someone was sure to have found it, used it as a refuge or a place for solitude. But it meant someone knew of the passage, so they were not safe until they moved into the maze, in toward the center where the walls and light took on color.

The featureless white gave nothing to hold the eye, leaving the mind free to explore the not-too-distant activity of the citadel's occupants, but with so much activity and no single focus it was impossible even to tell if Oso were present, though the quick discipline and tension made it seem likely.

They moved down, finding stairs and ramps, though it would be easy to get lost here. They were silent, but Galen's tense preparation for attack was eloquent, keeping DonEel alert. It was not personal fear in the Duratheen; rather, knowledge that they were pushing their luck. Twice now they had negotiated the Portal, the secret of secrets, undiscovered. Once leaving death as witness. It was too much luck, and he was a warrior who did not believe in it. His racing thoughts were concentrated on possibilities as they descended. There could be a trap. The other side of the Portal was blind to them; they had to go through with nothing but faith and readiness.

Caught up in the worry now, DonEel remembered

the gas in the white room. It could be waiting again. But then no one, even those authorized, could use the Portal. More than likely there would be a watch set. He wished he knew more about Jimo, but it was a blank spot, with none of the familiarity he felt about Syrcase and the citadel. All he knew of it was the corridor he had entered in search of Pollo.

"Getting back matters only for now." Galen's voice stirred his thoughts. "Once through, Portal door is easiest for our defending. Fearing skyside attack might think them less of using Portal and more to defending it from here."

That was true, but something about choosing the Portal itself as a battle station troubled him. The Portal must be protected at all costs.

Galen glanced at him but said nothing.

They came through the maze to the Portal room undetected, but the room was occupied. The constant activity throughout the citadel had made it impossible to determine accurately which areas were occupied. There was something fantastic about Galen's attitude. He had expected trouble here.

Through the narrow door, DonEel could see a small group near the silver shimmer of the Portal, and all of them were wearing the fog-gray he had come to associate with Jimo. In the confusion of voice-thought-intent, it was difficult to unweave meaning from the overall mental chaos. There was anger and suspicion here, as well as caution and uncertainty. Needing to understand, he moved out of the shadows, hoping to improve understanding with vision. The wall cut off part of the activity, but he recognized the tawny mane, though the woman was facing away from him. The one he had met in the upper level. Even in this uncertain position he felt a flash of interest, wishing she would turn so he could see her clearly again, and knowing the wish was insanity. The men with her were silent while she appeared to be arguing with someone he could not see. She was angry—he could

221

tell that from her posture and gestures—and watching her, remembering her, he began to pick up the feel and intent of her thoughts. There was, he found, caution riding the fury in her.

Relinquishing his hold on the multitudinous referents about him, he concentrated on her, following her attention closely. And suddenly he knew her adversary. The undercurrent had been with them throughout the citadel. It was Muset. The icy texture of that mind was unmistakable. Recognition, shared with Galen, brought a quick thrust of hate. A hate that was Duratheen and predatory, as natural as breath, quickly repressed but not forgotten.

Moved by a stronger curiosity now, DonEel did not draw back, as Galen would have had him do, but watched as the slender figure of the Zniss moved into his view. Incredible. The form and size were slighter than he had imagined, almost boyish in the fitted uniform. But something in the proportions said it even before he turned. That this one was alien. Then he saw the face and went cold. No man's face this, though the structure was more manlike than many he had seen at the citadel and elsewhere. There were the standard number of eyes, a nose and mouth in the right places, but subtly wrong. The brow was too broad, the chin too narrow below the wide, straight slash of mouth, the eyes set deep in bone-ridged wells. Jayt had thought snake, and so it was, the serpent of the ancient tales become almost man, beautiful, evil, and alien, and DonEel's hate came from the old depths of himself. This was the enemy.

He forgot even the woman, reaching out in his fascination, using secret senses to know the Zniss. The lack of feeling in what he touched was absolute. "Jimo is unmanned by my order." The thought-voice came as one impulse, so DonEel was unsure if he heard with ears or mind. "Your plans are meaningless."

"If we are invaded and this transporter comes under

222

attack?" She knew her plan made the only sense; the Portal on Jimo was perfectly defensible.

"It will not. Now, take your warm games up to Oso where they may serve you better. They do not touch me." Coiled and fluid the Zniss moved, reached to touch the woman's hair. "And you will not see me dead."

White with fury around her fear, the woman pulled back, and, seeing the gesture, feeling the feelings, DonEel tensed, ready to move, controlled more by confusion over his own impulses than true caution.

"DonEel, Zniss plans." The powerful hand pulling him back broke his fascination with what was happening in the golden room, and he thought that Galen must have been trying to get his attention for some time. He had picked up nothing of a plan Muset might have for them.

"Preparation against us is not yet," Galen reassured him. "Self thinking now is about Oso. Not wanting on Jimo in battle time, so is clear for us going in."

That didn't make sense. Jimo was the central Portal, pathway to Eden and Syrcase. As the woman had said, it only made good sense to have a small force there where it could protect the Portal without risk.

They were aware of the woman leaving the room with her crew, and of Muset staying, watching them go. The Zniss mind was all but unreadable for DonEel, lacking the emotional keys that gave structure and meaning to concepts. He could only tell that there was activity and concern dealing with time and security as the Zniss worked quietly, alone.

"Trapping device," Galen rumbled after a moment, and his identification gave sudden meaning to the thing seen only by Muset's definition of his own activity. The device was totally unfamiliar to the memories DonEel could reach in himself, something new, and from Galen's reaction, deadly. It took a while to learn that the Zniss was not rigging the Portal, but the entrance to the room. That made no sense, either.

And there was no explanation to be had from Muset. The reptilian thoughts ran subtly discordant, disturbing, and the core of those thoughts was Muset, no other loyalties or importances.

"This makes it sure of being topmost, but why is not knowing me yet. Only sure is making trouble for Primes."

They waited until Muset moved up into the citadel and his thoughts became vague and general; then they crossed the room quickly, not entirely trusting its emptiness. There was no way to anticipate Jimo; they went through fast and ready, and found nothing, not even a thought-trace. As quickly, they set the Portal and stepped through into the torch-disturbed caves of Eden, knowing even before their eyes adjusted to the moving shadow that Ridl was not there, but waiting for them above the entrance to the mines.

Touching that mind, welcomed and welcoming, they knew before they came out into daylight and the scent of pines that there had been many visitors through the Portal in the past few days, making it dangerous even for the L'Hur. They knew, too, that Ridl was glad for their return, that he had been concerned for them, knowing something of the confusion that had touched his son, but not fully having the reason for it.

And Pollo yet slept.

There was a sense of urgency here, though none of it showed in the dark L'Hur face; it pressed about them, leaving no time for thinking and planning options. Galen took the Weirdlil disk from his pouch and handed it, still wrapped, to Ridl.

"This is knowing to you, Lord Ridl," and the statement was colored by the wonder he felt at the always contact between the man DonEel and the L'Hur.

"It may not work for him, Ridl."

"There is nothing else now." The quiet voice gave nothing, but the silver-dark eyes held to him, knowing his fear and hope, and unable to answer it. "Lord

Alchia is in Loos, with the seer Dioda and the dark warriors."

"So soon?" Or had so much time passed while he indulged himself?

"He fears for his son, DonEel. If no word comes soon, they will surely seek for him. First at the mines." Dioda was the trouble Ridl saw. If he should come to the mines, he would soon begin to know everything he must not.

"He will die of it." Deon-memory spoke the words, but it was DonEel who knew Dioda.

"If he does not, others will." And Ridl's thought was of Alchia and Argath, and after them, others. And he was right. Dioda trod the edge of the false sleep and lived, somehow. But he had the faith and trust of all Delpha, and through them he touched nearly the whole of the Primes. "Come." Ridl halted his thoughts. "You must rest and eat before we begin." He turned up the mountain, but Galen halted him.

"Resting here for DonEel, and helping, as I cannot. But the doing on Syrcase and the plans of the Zniss are for my watching. To keep knowing on both sides."

It was the wisest thing, and DonEel knew it; yet he was reluctant to part with the Duratheen.

"Safety on Jimo. None is coming through trap of Muset." And more important than the safety was the fact that the Portal was set for a journey to Eden, telling anyone who looked that the Portal had been used after Muset ordered Jimo evacuated. They could not hope for it to go unnoticed. Galen's plan was to return to Syrcase. If necessary he would get to his ship from the citadel and out beyond the planet, where he could contact allies. One in particular came to mind, neither man nor Duratheen, but friend, and telepath. He would come if there was need for him.

They parted above the mines, Galen turning back down, DonEel climbing beside Ridl, following in his mind the brightness that was Galen into the darkness of the mine, to the Portal, to—

Nothing.

"Ridl!"

"It is the Portal only. He is about his task."

"But you and I—"

"A thing of the blood. Our kinship."

They surmounted the broken rocks above the mines to where great trees crowded close to the creek bank, and grass and flowers waged gentle war for the patches of sun-warmed earth. The protected hollow they came into had the feel of long occupation, and he knew Pollo was here. He was divided suddenly between needing to see him and fear of it. Ridl took the decision from him, halting him.

"It is best for you to rest and bathe now, until day's end. He lives yet, and the L'Hur are gathering."

He knew it was not a physical gathering, but a coming together more basic, if distant. He went to the pool at the bottom of the park reluctantly, but the cool water refreshed him, brought him back, and he lay on a sun-hot rock to dry, feeling the L'Hur focusing on Ridl and the hollow, a slow-pooling, harmony-building tension that somehow comforted him. He dozed, and dreamed of Scarsen and Blackwood, and woke wishing he had his flute, before remembering where he was, and why. And who.

The sun was well toward the western peaks, and he dressed quickly, not in the off-world clothing, but the leather and linen sometime provided by Ridl. His mind was suddenly full of one question: How could it be done?

Straight and dark, great wings cloaking his back, Ridl stood near the fur-soft pallet where Pollo lay. His face, beautiful in stillness, seemed to sleep, but the power flowing to him from the distance pulsed through the westering light, weaving impossible webs, stirring the hair on DonEel's arms and neck as he approached.

There were no words, but answers were made of how. The L'Hur could not do this thing alone, even with Happy Dancer's gift. They knew Pollo of

226

Delpha, but it was not a kinship knowing. And only Deon knew the Prime Zhan Llir.

"You know the all of him, then and now shared." Ridl spoke finally, seeming to come from a deep place to make the words. "His mind is open, and we can give the dance-talker's gift to him, but we have no common link. If, beyond Pollo, he remembers you as well, only you can know and touch his other being."

If he remembered. They had been together until the last. Those weeks of flight and fighting and swinging through the vastness of distance between stars, under sentence of death on every world they touched. They had shared the foreverness of the Big Black and a fear of endings. "He will know, Ridl. If the pattern can reach his memory, he will know me."

But only Deon could know for sure, and so be able to guide the memory to waking. He looked down at the silent form. The face was still and perfect as death, but somewhere in the unmeasured halls of the sleeping mind, the memories of Zhan Llir lay caged. If he could wake, even deep inside, beyond the body's knowing . . .

How will I know? he wondered, and fear lay suddenly against his lower spine and belly like sickness. The question echoed back from Ridl.

"He will wake." That knowledge alone was sure. Sentence of death. He will wake. He must wake—or die, truly. And now there was no safety of time, no postponement hoping for some other miracle. He could not go back to being DonEel of Erl.

God help me, he thought, and wondered which god. Ridl glanced at him, aware of his private depths and saying nothing. It was time.

Silent, more out of fear than resignation, he nodded.

The hard part was getting beyond incongruity. Wanting the mystery, he became suddenly hooked into a now-time reality of sitting in dappled shade, hearing the sound of birds and breeze and water, the here-and-now all touching him, and seeing the sleeper's face utterly calm and unstirred.

"You would put it by you even now, DonEel." Ridl's words sang easy against his guilt, and he nodded, yielding to that powerful, sure mind, accepting its direction as his direction, letting his eyes show him the target as he reached, strung on the bow of L'Hur power. This was Pollo; keep that. Pollo, not yet Zhan— Ever? Don't ask. Commit.

Pollo, then, remembered. Alive and being and giving.

The mirror surface of the mind barely rippled, giving no evidence of awareness. DonEel's eyes closed, unneeded as he became texture and place and time of familiarity.

Pollo, locked tight and not caring.

Pollo . . .

Veils of being/not-being blew back, peeled away, metaphors that didn't matter much because they were DonEel's, or Deon's, and the path simply was. L'Hur paved.

He knew when Ridl opened the cloth about the disk, felt the cool porcelain shape against dark fingers. He saw with Ridl's eyes, and the design was Deon-familiar in the neverland of feeling like Pollo. He wavered with confusion—brief, but threatening in so many definitions of who, being where, doing what— and the L'Hur steadied him.

The design would follow him to Zhan, somehow, but there was noplace to go; he had to create his own Pollo-referents, moving along spring-familiar paths to the deep shadows where the Polloness reminded him of Zhan, waiting passively, dreaming eternally. Was it possible? No matter. If he said so, it was. The metaphor worked.

Down and down they moved in slow flight, touched by a hundred minds. And finally there was resistance as the flesh itself seemed to feel the threat of annihilation, will-bound to reality and afraid.

"Pollo," he thought-said silently, meaning Zhan, and feeling sluggish attention and surprise, slow-focusing. . . .

The L'Hur intent-design burst upon them both, flame-bright, bringing fear and realization that pain was a thing he had known before, shattering, scattering will and being and yearning and memory into fragments swept wild on the winds of yesterday's agreements. Desperately he held the bits together, clasped in his own will.

"Pollo—" Confusion.

"Zhan—"

And finally, *"Deon?"* The voice laugh and cry familiar. *"Did it fail, then?"*

"It did not fail." But for a moment, speaking, he wondered, juggling realities in the suddenly Zhan-structured universe. Was this reality or memory? Deon's intellect warred with DonEel's faith, and the only surety was the pattern held still and strong by Ridl.

"Deon—" Questions and disbelief sang in the picture game his mind played. Believe. He had no choice. This was Zhan Llir, before Pollo.

He told, somehow.

"It cannot be, Deon. I am not beyond what I am—"

"It is real. This is a dream, a memory of before. The danger is now, what Timaret set for us." He could not keep all the anger from it.

"Death is no danger to us."

"Zhan, do not game me with words."

But the remembered one doubted. He had imagined this time often in that last race. This was not as it should be, this solitude and emptiness filled only with Deon. It was too much like dreaming.

It took time, and time here was an ill-mannered guest. Often they were back beyond Syrcase in the last good time. Patience, never Deon's strong suit, was needed. And strength. It was too real here. He knew, though the knowing was outside this place, that Pollo must join Zhan before waking, must remember and believe and become all of himself. Yet here, where Zhan was safe and all there was, it was impossible to accept.

"You are not solely Deon." Distrust laced this unexpected thought, and the confusion of why with no answers.

"No . . ." Caught off-guard, unbidden answers and visions were yielded because he could hold nothing back from this one.

The construct wavered, pain-flashed, yielding. . . .

"Ridl—"

—was there, always.

"Zhan, Pollo, you know." He had forgotten now if it was faith or knowledge, but this union was a familiar place, and Zhan knew it as he did.

Shattered out of the memory of reality, unanchored, he agreed finally to be led, coming—without the useless stumbling of DonEel becoming Deon—to the what and how of memory, and it was suddenly easy because all there was for now was Zhan Llir, recalled. Accepting the truth of the unnoticed hiatus, believing finally that he could live with it simply because he did. Zhan was more than Pollo's dreams—was Pollo, rather, plus, and so master of his fate if he so chose. It was the truth he had.

Deon knew the conviction as his own, releasing him from the imagery of the other's curiosity, feeling a strength greater than his own yielded will drawing him irresistibly away. . . .

Ridl lay the disk down and looked at him, eyes clear in the soft dusk, and the glade shivered with the invisible presence of multitudes.

"He remembers." It was the only fact brought back, outside. Supported on borrowed strength, he looked down on the sleeper, afraid now to touch the mind he had filled. Would the knowing, remembering, be enough? Or would it serve only to occupy the living part of Zhan-Pollo while the flesh cooled and died?

Blue-shadowed lids trembled, bringing the face alive but not conscious. Ridl answered nothing. It was done.

"He may not be strong enough." He had to voice some part of his fear, knowing only this of all the responsibilities thrust on him was important, this one selfish personal need. He couldn't help it; it was what he was. He needed Zhan, the anchor for his renegade spirit, giving reality to his real self, as much as Zhan needed his freedom, his wings to fly—

"He wakes." Ridl's voice wrapped him as the sleeper stirred, one hand moving from the furs.

"DonEel—" Eyes opened, sleep-fogged, but seeing him. "I dreamed a strange dream—" The voice faltered as he woke, staring up, seeing beyond DonEel in the dark and waiting eyes, feeling back into his own being. The eyes closed. "It is too much," he said clearly, and the voice was not Pollo. "I know you are Deon, too." There were too many questions. All the preparation and speculation of that other time was worthless, but he remembered it all. Bits of knowledge from the waking time moved through his thoughts. "It was not supposed to be like this." And another. "Only us, Deon?"

"Only us."

"How long?" The golden eyes flashed open in the last light, knowing the unvoiced answer. Seven hundred Terran years. Disbelief tried itself against knowledge and a growing sense of loss. So much time. Yet only yesterday they had come to the golden Portal room to meet Timaret. Impulsively his hand moved to touch DonEel's, fingers lacing close.

DonEel looked at the linked hands, felt the texture and warmth, and thought against a strange, wild hurt that they had touched before, but not with these hands. Questions wanted phrasing, but now only the present mattered.

Catching the mood, the relief, Pollo's soft laugh flowed into the shadows. "I feel very distant from

Pollo of Delpha now; yet when I look at you, you are DonEel of Erl." Then his eyes leaped to the darker shadow beyond them, and his mind greeted what he could not see, knowing, and he added, "Son of Ridl. Ah, Deon, there's so much. It will take time. . . ."

Time. So much of it gone, and it was nothing; and now there was so little. Nothing had changed, except he was not alone. The reason and need beyond himself came back as the power ebbed from the darkening air and Ridl crouched to rekindle the fire.

Physical weakness rebuffed Pollo's attempt to rise, and Ridl came to them, assuring them it would pass, that it was the flesh, having the habit of sleep, protesting. He set DonEel to the task of preparing food for them while he tended, L'Hur-fashion, to Pollo's needs, taking him finally to the pool where DonEel had bathed earlier.

Watching them, DonEel smiled slightly, wishing again, wearily now, that it was done, or that they could postpone the future awhile yet. It was good to share again, to be part of completion. He wanted time to rest in it.

"Zhan, you are much the same," he said, mindtouching the moon-silvered slenderness, feeling the warm Zhan/Pollo response.

Time came back to them, pushing, as the reality of someplace other than this L'Hur-protected clearing intruded on their thoughts, bringing worry for Alchia and Dioda and the others who would be affected if they should fall to the Portal, or even suspect its existence.

For Pollo, the Portal and the danger it represented was close-linked to Zhan's yesterday, closer now than even the memories of Pollo, who knew little more than Delpha and her business. Sitting near the fire, he ate slowly, not yet awakened to true hunger, though that would come in its own time. His thoughts turned to Alchia. He was inclined to agree with DonEel. There was much of Timaret in the man he knew as father and leader of Delpha, though that knowing was not now so close as his memories of Tim. All that had passed after his rescue from Syrcase and Oso he knew from DonEel's mind, but it was hard to give everything proper perspective in the shadow of his own private happenings. He knew he loved Alchia, even as Zhan. Being loved was a talent Tim had had. Alchia had it now. And he could not bring harm to him. But there was more to his sense of urgency than that. As DonEel had done first, he felt the emptiness, where once had been the constant subliminal presence of the Primes, leaving a strange and absolute silence beyond what he shared of DonEel, and in a different way, Ridl. It threatened him, cutting off much he had always been a part of, an extension of this wonder between them. And he, as much as DonEel, wanted it restored. What they were alone would matter little if the Primes were forfeit, if too many died and the miracle was lost. It couldn't be allowed to happen. An eternity of this silence was something he could not contemplate.

"There was a way," DonEel said, following his thoughts. "Something that would reverse the command. If we could find the key Tim left . . ."

"Suppose it was time." Pollo sifted Zhan-memory, knowing there had been a plan in those last months, but he had not been a part of that planning, trusting to those whose business it was to prepare for the future. "Perhaps it was something based on a projection of the galactic society, a thing to be done in the future." He knew there had been a lot of emphasis on projection of trends during the months before the decision was made to come to Eden. Timaret had been the one to set up the analog in the computers on Stilks.

"If you're right, we have no hope."

"We could destroy the Portal." But even as he said it, he felt the instinctive need to protect it. The Portal must not be destroyed.

233

"We would be trapped here. Even Oso doesn't know where this world is. Maybe none of us does. I never heard." And he had asked, more used to traveling free through the unstructured wholeness of the Big Empty. He had not, even then, trusted the narrow gate of the Portal. But Harmond, the man who knew more nearly everything than any other, even the scholars, had not known.

"The Portal was here long before we found it. Probably it was the reason for the citadel," Pollo reminded. "We found Eden through it. And none of the Primes recorded this world."

They had no options. They had to find the key. If it existed, it had to be something automatic, something logical.

"First Loos." Ridl rejoined them. Burnished by the fire into seeming a creature more of precious metal than flesh, he brought back the wonder of this place. "This will be for nothing if Alchia or Dioda the Seer learns of the Portal."

Time again. Tomorrow, then, they would go down to Loos, set Alchia's mind at ease about his son, and convince him to return to the north, away from a threat he did not know existed.

SIXTEEN_____

POLLO seemed to suffer no ill effects from the long sleep, but he was still weak. Fortunately, Ridl had again provided horses for the journey.

"There is an otherness in you that Alchia may sense," the L'Hur warned as they prepared to leave.

It was a chance they would have to take. It was difficult enough now to think in Delphan limits, to remember that Alchia and Dioda and the Afs knew nothing of other worlds and races or travel between the stars. They did not even know of the L'Hur who shared their world. The beginning to this journey, the ancient highway and the battle with the Nomen, seemed a distant dream.

Not for the first time, Pollo thought it would make their task more simple if they could introduce the L'Hur. But Ridl knew better. The qualities the Primes had forbidden themselves were in his people; it would be a danger to them.

"I suppose we must have gotten lost," Pollo laughed as they rode down through the pines.

"Aye." DonEel mimicked the Delphan manner of speech, feeling it against his tongue. "They will know of the attack, or at least the possibility of it, and the old road is unknown. It could be longer than the map shows."

All the west land was unknown—many adventures could be claimed, and planning was easy as voices faded and thoughts merged faster and more complete. Once Pollo laughed aloud, breaking the silence, and the horses jumped. He hoped, he said, they remembered to speak aloud at the right times.

"Alchia will be blaming Kylee for your absence," DonEel remembered as they moved onto the road below the mines. He had brought the distrust to Alchia himself in what seemed another time.

"He has a Weirdling stone. Could he be involved with Oso?"

It was a possibility, but Kylee was, before anything, one of the Primes. The danger would be as great for him as the others. Perhaps he had taken sides without knowing the truth. Not that it mattered, really—all the business of Eden was fantasy, waiting and sleeping until they could again be what they were in truth.

How long would it take to convince Alchia to return north without his son? The longer they had to be with the Delphans, the more chance there was that Alchia or Dioda would notice the difference in them and become suspicious. And that was not the only pressure. DonEel thought of Galen, alone and in danger for a people he did not truly know. And he felt Pollo touch his thought and enlarge it.

"We owe that one," the Delphan said aloud.

Ahead now, through the thinning trees, the gold and green of Plains was visible, as indistinct as the sea, and the scent of sun-hot fields came up to them on the breeze. The white ship that was Loos beckoned in the wind-stirred waves, and they fell silent, sharing a growing tension.

The most westerly of the Plains towns was astir with too many people who should have been about the business of wheating or working in their shops. It was not like these people to put aside their work for casual holidays, and there were too many men and too few women and children. Pollo slowed his mount, frowning. He had hoped Delpha would keep its worries private. The less notice he and DonEel received, the easier their task would be.

"Plainers!" he called to a group talking near the corrals. "Do the Delphans meet here?"

"Aye. To school." The reply came on a burst of curiosity that they ignored, threading their way through a tangle of people and animals.

The school was an oasis of silence, its white walls shutting out the worst of the dust and noise. This one time they did not wish to be announced. Already they had picked up on the ebb and flow of thought from the audience building. Anger rose from it like smoke, dark with suspicion.

The wide door stood open in the heat, but all attention was on the tall, white-robed figure at the front of the room. Speaking from his position of authority on the dais, Kylee did not notice the two travel-stained men for a moment. "In seeking to place the blame, it is too easy to think first of the Beachers. It is true they may devise a way to gain from our misfortune, but this is not a way they have chosen before. And there were opportunities.

"We have heard of the attack made on the Afs south of here by Nomen and Zonas together. But there is no answer to why Nomen should choose to attack in the south when they have always stayed to the west, away from Truemen. And why now would Zonas, who claim the land to the south, appear and attack a Delphan at the pool Beauty? There is only one common factor. The man from the south. The unknown one. He came to us, and we opened our homes and hearts to him; yet it seems he is the one to draw these attacks. Who among us knows—"

The expression on the stern face would have been amusing, alone. The shock-paralyzed thoughts and immediate guilt were like a cry against their minds, too naked and painful. Together they walked to the front of the room, mounting the dais to stand beside Kylee. The hall was silent, but even before the expected faces were found in that multitude, the relief and joy of three minds wove warmth and love into the two hearing minds. Alchia, Dioda, and Argath. Seeing her, DonEel reached instinctively for that mutual sharing, so familiar and precious to the Primes. And found silence. Only will kept his face silent. To rechannel his thoughts, he turned to Kylee, standing still beside them.

"What you would know of me, ask, teacher." He let it be challenge, felt the waiting of the audience and closed his mind to it.

"We thought—"

"That I had stolen a prince of Delpha, brought him to hurt and perhaps death. To what purpose? It is known to Delpha that I am cast out by my own people. Indeed, I would be long dead but for your nephew."

"It matters not, DonEel." Pollo broke in, surprised by the tension growing between his uncle and the

Souther. "We are returned, and there is no blame to place."

"Returned from where?" Kylee asked it for all the people.

"In good time our tale shall be told. Now we wish only a chance to rest and meet in private with our father and lord, Alchia." As was his right by birth and earned position, Pollo dismissed the Council effectively, and they waited, sharing silent thoughts until the large room emptied of all but the delegation from Delpha and the dark Afs guarding the door. Alchia stood as silent, waiting. But his eyes and heart spoke gladness and relief, and the power of those feelings moved them both.

"My father." Pollo spoke the words proudly, glad for the feeling. And Alchia's embrace was no less warm when he turned to DonEel.

"None here who knows you heard Kylee, DonEel."

"I did not suppose you had, My Lord."

"He loves you, as I said." Pollo's thought laughflashed through his mind, and he remembered another time and felt heat in his face. He did not dare to embrace Argath, sister and daughter to these two, but her joy in seeing him promised a more private reunion.

"Come." Alchia took their hands, keeping them close to him as they moved to the door after a quieter but more silently intense greeting from Dioda. "You must rest. There is a room you may use, and it will serve us for talking when you wish."

Pollo was glad for the couch and cool wine. His strength had failed suddenly, and he was pale. Close-joined, DonEel knew it was as Ridl had said, and would pass quickly, but for now it would serve to keep Alchia from pressing for too many details of their journey. None of them had said more than greeting, but he felt Dioda's eyes on him yet, watchful and speculative beyond the joy of seeing them well.

For all the questions he wanted to ask, it was not

Alchia's way to rush. They were together, and already a message bird was winging from the dark hand of some Af, on the way to Delpha to reassure the Council and, more especially, Masila.

Sharing knowledge, keeping close watch on Alchia's mind, DonEel let Pollo tell of the journey and attack by Nomen, thinking that the threat of Nomen so far north was enough to keep Alchia close to Delpha. No mention was made of Ridl, only the retreat to the top of West Range, and the passage over into the west land, and being lost. As they hoped, Alchia's thoughts fixed on the Nomen.

"We thought Zonas had delayed you, perhaps even taken you. You are certain it was Nomen?"

"Certain. They range far into the mountains, perhaps even into the west land, though we saw no sign of them there."

"They knew of the journey." Alchia's face hardened, and he thought of Kylee. "Could they benefit from the Beachers' access to the mines and West Range?"

"More, I think, from war between Truemen, for whatever cause," DonEel put in.

Alchia nodded, accepting the thought. Dioda merely watched from his stool by the door. "But Jania, and you also, know of Nomen dealing with Zonas to the south."

"The Zonas may treat as Truemen"—Pollo picked up DonEel's thought and expanded it—"but I'd wager they'd be as glad to see us warring and leave them to their work and will. They are closer to Nomen than any." He yawned suddenly.

Alchia rose immediately. "Rest now. A student has been assigned the house. When you wish, you may send him to me and we will talk further."

In the silence after their leaving, Pollo was relieved. He had never hidden anything from Alchia, and now, knowing the warmth and strength of him, he had felt almost compelled to unburden himself completely and seek his advice.

"It is the weariness only. Sleep now awhile." DonEel took the wineglass from him.

"Will you wake me?"

"Aye, you know I shall." He was not sleepy. Argath's presence here tantalized, and he knew she would be waiting for him.

As sleep overtook the Delphan, one last clear thought was voiced: "He will insist on our return, DonEel. Back to Delpha."

Yes. And they must not return there. Galen waited beyond the Portal, and this was the second day. Somehow Alchia must be persuaded to return north and leave them in Loos.

It was more than pleasant to be with Argath again, to see her even more beautiful than he remembered. And his feelings for her told him he was more DonEel than he had thought in the breadth of the remembered Deon-time. Yet as he had known on first seeing her in the hall, it was difficult. She could have no secrets from him now, and he was vain enough to want her admiration and concern and desire; yet he felt guilty, forcing hard control on what had been instinct and accepted to Deon. He had not missed that dimension of relationship until he recalled it, and remembering, he felt oddly lonely. And she, he could not help knowing, felt uncertain and shy of him. She looked quickly at his hand when they met, and saw the ring.

"Aye, Lady. I have worn it since I left Delpha."

"As a remembrance?"

"And a hope, Argath." A hope larger now than she knew. She looked into his eyes, and he was helpless against wanting her. Womanwise, she knew, and touched his face lightly.

"When you were not here to meet Jania, there was a time we thought—"

"We?"

"I stayed the time with Masila. She, like our father, has great faith in you."

"How is it with her?"

"Well. Better when the news reaches her. She loves Pollo full but free. Dioda says the child is a son."

"And is he never wrong, then?" It was teasing, but she looked at him close, tempting him to pry.

"Never that I know, DonEel. If he does not know, he does not speak. He told us, even before you came north from Scarsen, that one not of Delpha who loved Pollo would work great changes. I wonder at times what he does not say of what he knows. He has been quiet of late, but he did not believe you dead." She flinched from her own mention of the possibility, and changed the subject, talking softly so the few students in the yard could not hear. "I would we were back in Delpha and all this behind us."

"In the garden?" Teasing again, troubled by her mood. Or was it the change in himself he felt, his desire for impossibles? He touched her cheek beneath the silver fall of her hair, like silk over his wrist. She laughed softly, and her eyes darkened.

"Yes. That, too. For you are not like other men. But there is the other here, even perhaps at home. A cloud. Some trouble hovering. I can feel it in the people like fear."

"Perhaps it is your own worry."

"Not only. There is some evil abroad." She leaned against a silver-leafed tree, unconscious of her beauty, and her eyes were brooding. "There is death with it. I heard talk here that the woodcutters found two bodies not far from the mine road. Young people. One was a girl I knew when I schooled here for a time with Kylee. She was so pretty, with a talent these people seldom breed. A singer. She was to have been married this harvest."

Her words chilled him, reminding him of the tapes taken from the citadel. Senseless deaths, repeated senselessly. "Was it known how they died?"

"Nothing could be learned." She looked toward West Range, darkening now against the westering sun, and the pleasure ran out of the man as he followed her gaze. Too much attention was being called to the area of the mines; pressures building, forcing the best minds inexorably toward the secret of the Portal. He wanted to warn her away from the place, tell her to think of other things, but the warning would serve only to push her closer to the danger.

"Argath." He called her eyes back to him, hoping someday the remembered would be again and she could know and see and be all that was possible. His face showed it, and her nearness to him let her know something of his feelings, if not his reasons. "Do not travel from Delpha alone. Not even into Greenwood. Promise me."

"If possible, yes. But I do not go far alone, except at times to Beauty."

Not even there, Argath. For a time, I must know you are safe."

"Do you love me so much?"

"More than you yet know."

"For one night's pleasure, man of Scarsen?" She laughed, teasing him now, but beneath it something leaped like fire and softness and fear.

"Perhaps for the hope of future pleasures." She did not hear his true meaning, only the challenge and promise as he embraced her. She answered his need, yet drew back reluctantly.

"Loos has no privacy for us, DonEel."

"Our love needs no hiding." How seldom in his pleasures had DonEel spoken of loving; yet he meant it now, learning again how much he could mean it.

They walked away from the school, talking, but knowing that they were seeking more than talk. He shared her feelings and desires but avoided seeing too clearly into her thoughts.

They were only another man and woman on the street, ignored in the larger movement. None cared where they wandered, and the barn they came to was fragrant with new, sun-bright hay, sweet and natural as her turning to him, eyes saying what he already knew.

For a time then, in the new urgency shared, and pleasure, he forgot the loneliness, substituting the knowledge of flesh and nerve for the other intimacy, and hoping it was enough, until the last explosive release and surrender. . . .

He held tight to her, caught between ecstasy and defeat, unable to master his own self. Not until he kissed her, gentled out of the first fever, did he know she wept. "Why, Lady?" he whispered.

"A woman's foolishness. It means nothing." But her eyes held him hard, and she shivered in his arms. "You are not returning to Delpha with us, are you."

"I cannot." He moved away from her, all pleasure gone from him. Turning away, covering himself, he spoke with none of what he was feeling. "Not for a while, until the trouble here is resolved. But you and Alchia must return, and soon."

She sat up, brushing bits of hay from her hair and clothing. "In Delpha the women are not sent away. We are part of all that happens that concerns us. And you—"

"It must be as I say, this once. I love you, and so you could come to be a danger to me."

Understanding her own meanings, she nodded. "Sometimes, DonEel, the best thing is not the easiest."

There was peace between them as they returned to the school. The crowds had thinned, but there was a glow of fires a little away from the town, where those who had come made their evening meal and prepared for sleep. And there was a restless tension in the air.

The schoolyard was empty, and only a few of the rooms showed light. Argath bade him goodnight and went to her room, and he crossed the tree-shadowed lawn to where Pollo waited. Midway, he felt a sudden stab of attention, colored violent with anger. He knew that mind, knew without looking, that Kylee stood in the corner of the buildings in dark shadow watching him. And not alone. The intent of the mind made clear what he might have missed without the sudden seeing: a planning and anticipation of victory. In the thought, Alchia and Pollo were somehow linked. He held quiet, holding the thought, letting it come together in his head. A trap. The one with Kylee, unclearly seen in Kylee's mind, knew. It was shared, and it would be soon. Enough. He knew what he had to know.

The light was lit in their room, and for a moment his new knowledge was buried in more private concern. It was oddly difficult to return to Pollo from being with Argath. Warm as he was with her love, he was struck with a purely DonEel sort of reluctance to have Pollo share his knowledge of the woman. She was, after all, Pollo's sister.

"How strange." Pollo lay on the lamplit couch watching him, not quite smiling. DonEel's concern had served only to focus his thoughts on the near memory. "I had forgotten the scope of our sharing. We have not truly become so different."

"I love her, Pollo."

"And she you. Even in Delpha. But I know your thoughts, and I see myself and Masila here also. It will be lonely for us being in a place they cannot reach."

"Yet."

"Yet," the Delphan agreed soberly, coming back to the here-and-now problem. "You have news of Kylee."

Silently he let Pollo know what he had learned. There was no doubting in them that Kylee had hoped they would not return, had taken action to place all blame on DonEel. Now he had to make other plans. Had, in fact, made them this night. Pollo's anger was hard.

"He is Delphan, and my father's brother." He moved from the couch to pace the floor restlessly. Whatever the truth of Alchia's being in Zhan Llir's time, the man was his father, and nothing outweighed

244

that fact. It was as much of the blood as DonEel's kinship with Ridl. "They must be convinced to leave at dawn, before the trap can be set."

But would they go? Alchia would not want to return without his son, and Pollo must not return.

On hearing his son was awake, Alchia came alone to their room, bringing word that Dioda would speak in private with DonEel. It was as well, perhaps. If he could convince the seer that he and Pollo must not return, Alchia would agree without argument.

He found him in the garden, waiting quietly. Without comment, Dioda handed him a long, cloth-wrapped bundle. His hands knew it even through the wrapping.

"My flute. You knew, then, you would find us safe." Alone with him, it was impossible to ignore the quick-reaching flame of that mind. Aware of it, DonEel dare not reach in turn to touch it and disturb the crystal balance and harmony he felt there. It was only more clear to him now why Dioda was loved as well as respected.

"One should hope for the best, always, and between you, you share a strength. I was not surprised to find you well." He touched DonEel's arm, and they began to walk aimlessly along the paths. "I feel you bring news to further trouble Alchia. Is it so?"

The need for preamble removed, DonEel came to the point. "Tonight in the garden I heard Kylee plotting against Alchia."

"First the son, now the father."

"He hopes for both now. And he would not let you free. You have too much influence."

"Not so much, DonEel." He spoke absently, his attention on the younger man, and his ageless face was still as he considered something brought to him beyond the words spoken. "There is much to this danger you have not said."

"Alchia must return to Delpha and stay the summer."

"Alchia?"

"And you." He kept his words as quiet, facing him, and was jolted suddenly into a time long past when he had stood just so with Harmond, the last time. Just so had the gentle attention seen into him. Harmond the wise, the one who had cared. He was. As Alchia was Tim. He felt the division between then and now, a fragile bridge he could almost reach across. How much he remained the same. Harmond, he thought, so much depends on your survival to help us back.

"Why should the thought of my death trouble you, DonEel?"

The question, so close to what he thought, shook him, and he could not answer quickly.

"And what of you and Pollo?" Dioda said into his silence.

"Our danger is not so close." A fine truth that, he thought. "Pollo is emissary of Delpha, and loved. But he is not the head. Together here, we can do more for the people, without the danger Alchia or you would face."

"The danger goes beyond Kylee, then."

"I do not know the scope of the trouble. I only know that Alchia here would bring added danger to Pollo and myself."

"You wish me to convince Alchia of this." Brief amusement touched the voice. "Very well. I feel, though the why of it is hidden, that you are to be allowed to follow your path with as little interference as possible. But I must say to you that I have been wrong often enough in my feelings so that I do not trust them wholly. So. No more questions. Let us join Alchia and Pollo."

Pollo had told Alchia of the danger to him, and their desire to remain in Plains, but it was apparent the Councilman wasn't convinced. He was as close to anger as DonEel had seen him, hazel eyes burning him in an attempt to see the truth. "Your danger will be all the greater with us in the north, both of you. Our greatest safety is in remaining together."

Pollo shook his head. "Kylee has already sent word to the Zonas that we will travel north. He could not expect DonEel and me to remain behind. He thinks to deliver us together after his first failure."

"You cannot prove Kylee's intentions or actions," Alchia reminded.

"Not now. For that reason alone, we should remain near Loos. He would not take such action unless there were some gain to be made."

"What gain? He cannot hope to lead the Council; the people would not have him."

"The Beachers and Zonas do not know that."

"I do not think Kylee's intent is evil in his own mind." DonEel spoke, trying to cool the anger. "Perhaps he feels his way could join the Zonas and all people in common with Delpha. Perhaps even the Nomen."

Dioda glanced at him, and there was a sound of silent laughter behind his eyes, though his voice was measured. "Kylee's ambition could be used against him, Alchia. It has blinded him before. I would say we should leave at dawn as Pollo suggests, and travel to Delpha with all speed. Perhaps we can outrun Kylee's plans, and our young warriors can learn the reasons for them."

"I am outvoted." Alchia spread his hands in a gesture of surrender, but he tried one last time. "And what shall I say to Masila?"

"That what I do is for love of her and the safety of our son." It was truer than Alchia could know.

"As you will, then. At first light we leave for Delpha."

The parting in the predawn gloom was brief but emotional. DonEel and Pollo rode north with the Delphans until Loos was only a shadow on the edge of the vast fields; then they turned west, to where the

247

sun pinked the white peaks, leaving Alchia and Dioda to speculate on unanswered questions.

SEVENTEEN_____

GALEN had returned through the Portal once, bringing word to Ridl that both Jimo and the terminal in the citadel had been deserted by Muset's order, and that the Zniss waited safe in the white side of the citadel. DonEel and Pollo felt better knowing there was no trap waiting as they stepped through, but they were glad finally to be with the big Duratheen, the Portals behind them.

"Man Pollo," he greeted the Delphan. "Seeing you well is pleasuring me, not only for friend DonEel. All is good being together." And he had news that might make things even easier for them. "Lords Lindig and Rulf are making blame on Oso for Weirdling base attack, not having truth to it. Law for Lords is demand Oso for trying by their court." The confusion of the Lane Lords amused him, and he blinked slowly, his silent laughter touching them.

They left the citadel in darkness, not trusting the place, and crossed the barrens to where the Duratheen ship waited.

"Doing what now?" Galen asked after they had made themselves comfortable. It was the obvious question. How could they accomplish their task: finding the key that would free the Primes from their self-imposed exile?

If there was anything to find, it would almost certainly be on Stilks, the knowledge planet, home to both Timaret and Harmond. Even before the Primes left Terra, Stilks had been the research and educational center for the emerging galactic society. Built by a humanoid race who considered intellectual development a religion, and philosophy a marketable commodity, it had become the nucleus of the loose-knit Prime community. The library and computer complex became the repository for many projects that were strictly Prime in nature and importance. It was here Harmond's work had been done, and the projections that had sent the Primes into exile. Here Timaret had developed the method of extraphysical coercion that had made the exile possible, guaranteeing that even if discovered they would be no more than a simple pastoral people. And it was here Oso had studied before beginning his search for the Primes. Perhaps something in the work done here was a clue to ending the exile.

Galen followed their thoughts as he guided his ship through the crowded moon belt, heading out from Syrcase. Stilks might be the place with the answers, but it was not so easy just to go there to get them.

"Differences are now from your time," he cautioned. "With Lords watching. Not coming from Syrcase as Primes. All Lords knowing who comes for keeping watches on learnings of worlds."

If Oso learned two men came from his world unauthorized to study on Stilks, he might soon learn of the Primes. Now he had only suspicion without proof. And he controlled the Portals, the only way on or off Eden.

"Being you from Alb F, craziness world," the Duratheen suggested. "All things doing is accepted from them."

Settled by Andros before the Sector Wars because of the valuable concentrations of minerals, Alb F had become wealthy through a judicious juggling of loyalties. A small world, only lightly populated, they preserved their position and wealth by an insane but effective move. The planet had been rigged for self-destruction. Should any Lord or combination of forces attack Alb F in the hope of controlling the mines, the world would be demolished. As far as the Albians were concerned, if they couldn't have it as they wanted it, no one could have it. All the near ruling Lords had been given tours of the engineering miracle that made the world a superbomb, and all agreed it was superbly efficient and workable. The mines were vital to the transport fleets that supported the Lords, and the Albians now traded with all equally, so they were left alone.

Free from fear, Alb F had become a paradise world. The mines were almost fully automatic, leaving the people free to pursue their individual ideals of culture and beauty in an anarchy possible only because of their small population. And of all the galactic peoples, the natives of Alb F were the most likely to pursue an interest to the point of absurdity. And the least likely to attract attention because of it.

They agreed with Galen's proposal, and the days in transit from Syrcase to Stilks were divided between learning all Galen and his tapes could tell them about Alb F, and speculation on what they might find on Stilks.

Stilks was—Stilks. Built by the creative talents of minds both manlike and completely alien, free to express every concept of beauty. Buildings, dream-delicate and impossible, spiraled and towered in crystal and stone, fluid and rigid, side by side or together, making a lucky combination that came together in breathtaking splendor, amidst the green and growing reality of the gardens, scenting the air with the perfumes of a hundred worlds. The price of knowledge had made Stilks a wealthy world.

It had changed, but not too much, not enough to be different, and the familiarity was disorienting to the men, taking them back to that other time.

Before landing, Galen reported their world of origin as Alb F and made the standard request for study privileges. They were asked to report for temporary registration immediately on landing to expedite their research. The fee would be charged to the account of

Alb F under the standard agreement. That bit of information bothered them, but Galen was certain Alb F would settle without asking questions. They didn't trouble too much about keeping track of individuals.

A small unmanned car drifted out to the ship for them. Galen blinked at the Stilksers' instinctive distrust. "Not Eden here," he observed unnecessarily.

Indeed, it was not Eden, and Eden-trained senses struggled to compare this reality with old memories of what should be and could be possible.

"*We are watched,*" Galen informed them silently. "*Being way here until we are known.*" Once warned, they could feel the curiosity and attention measuring them. This was not the way of Stilks before. Such security measures had not been necessary when Primes ran the schools.

The greeter waited for them at the head of the graceful stairs leading to the registration building, a tradition that had survived. It was a slender hominid form, and for a moment it was possible to see Harmond there, waiting. But this one was not a man, not even Andro. Tqulot, Galen supplied, as they responded to the formal greeting and followed the being through the entrance into the great hall. Here the sense of returning was overwhelming, and the men shared looks and thoughts, remembering Galen's warning that it was not the same.

It was natural now, in this place, to use those senses recalled to them, to be what they had been before. And they knew quickly that since planetfall they had been spy-watched. For a moment they became their own watchers, monitoring the data that was being fed into the computer to be matched with records to learn if they had ever been here at the receiving center or any other point of entry on the planet. The thoughts of the monitors were bored and casual; it was a common thing and meant nothing to them.

The enrollment center was a crisply functional booth where their identification and interests were stated vocally to the central computer system. A change. In Timaret's time as schoolmaster, the registration had been a time of personal contact and acquaintance, a welcoming. Now Tqulot stood silently near, patient and unaware of giving them clues and instructions as he passed the time thinking of going off duty to more rewarding activities.

DonEel gave the verbal request for permission to study the record of the Terran Primes. There was a moment of waiting; then the computer asked what area they wished to study. That had not occurred to them. Obviously they could not mention the exile or disappearance of the Primes, and they did not want to be restricted to irrelevant areas. His hesitation caught the attention of their guide.

"State your specific interest, scholar," Tqulot prompted.

"We have." There was no substitute for the truth. "We wish to read the records of the Primes."

"Which records?"

"No specifics, instructor."

"You do have an objective?" Suspicion that this might be a game was mixed with disbelief in the suddenly focusing mind.

"Yes." It didn't take telepathy to know the guide was at a loss. "Perhaps there is a professor we could speak with."

"A professor. About the Terran records. Yes. I will arrange a meeting. Follow." He swept them out into the wide hall, hiding uncertainty in action, glad to be able to turn this over to a higher authority at the request of the Albians. "It will take time. Most unusual, of course."

They were shown into a comfortable room, pillowed and couched for individual preferences of comfort. Without intending it, they had got more attention than they wanted. From several areas they were aware of increased surveillance and curiosity, but the

252

identification as Albians provided a measure of camouflage.

Two professors came into the room. One, which DonEel thought could have been a slightly lavender toad, but was not, introduced himself as Ale. The other was a centaur who put Pollo in mind of another, a professor of history when Zhan Llir was a student new to Stilks. Ale's unexpectedly beautiful voice, singing harmony with itself, said the centaur was Lzar, professor of history (what else?).

"Students of Alb F, it is customary to state the exact nature of your needs to the record keeper on arrival. It is not binding, of course, as information you gain will change the nature of your studies here. But it gives structure to your work and prevents confusion and overload. You have had difficulty with this?" The lavender biped was not sure he should take them seriously; they were, after all, Albians.

"Perhaps we are seeking blind, Professor," DonEel began. The thought-warning from his companions jarred him. Truth-sensors. Somehow the room itself could tell if he spoke the truth. Truth, then. "We are not sure that what we seek exists."

"Without questions, how can you be sure if you have the answers?" The centaur spoke for the first time, softly and rather sadly.

"Perhaps we can find the question here."

"About the Terran Primes?" Ale sang.

"About something the Primes might have found."

"They have been gone a long time."

"But their work was here on Stilks, and their records survive. Especially their study of the Ancient Ones, the Builders." He felt their attention at that.

"You believe they found something of the Ancient Ones that is not common knowledge?" Lzar's sad voice contrasted oddly with his quickened interest.

"There is a world. . . ." He left it hanging.

"Syrcase. Yes. The Primes were involved in the

study there. A structure called the citadel by some. This was reported and is well known."

"Perhaps not fully." He played on Lzar's curiosity, but Ale was more skeptical, watching them.

"This is not the best time to be interested in Syrcase. There is friction there now between the Lane Lords."

"We have heard this." Pollo ended his silence. "But there have been battles before. It does not concern Alb F or our study. If there is something remaining of the Builders, the clues could be here. Alb F would prefer to have the knowledge come from Stilks and our study if it is something the Lords may battle for."

That touched Ale. His thoughts became speculative, a thing worth fighting for could be sold. "This may be true, seeker, if there is anything to find. Your search of the records will be granted without restriction."

"Their suspicion was not directed at us," Pollo said, once they were quartered and alone. They had insisted Galen be allowed to share their rooms as bodyguard, a request that would have been laughable to the Stilks they remembered, but was accepted here now. The changes in Stilks were below the surface, a way of thought harnessed to ambition and greed. The urge for knowledge, the pure gratification of knowing, was still here, but the ruling body was politic.

They were not surprised that their first visitor the following morning was Lzar, the gentle centaur, come to acquaint them with procedure and act as guide. There was no preparation required of them for their study; they would receive whatever aid they needed.

They breakfasted in the student meal room. Galen was amused by the attention he drew. He knew his people's reputation—as warrior mercenaries they had earned it honestly, and they were expensive. Types of many worlds were represented here, but none of his kind, and he blinked slowly, watching, towering over them.

On Stilks the business was information and education, and they weren't giving away free time. Immediately after breakfast Lzar showed them to a general research facility and set about teaching them how to use it. The comp-system had grown in seven hundred years, but the basics were the same, and the language, spread through the galaxy with the Prime's influence, was their own. By unspoken agreement Pollo would obscure; too many people wanted to see the Primes before the exile and DonEel would examine records dealing with the citadel on Syrcase. These two areas were the most logical places to find information on how the exile could be ended.

It took a full day, even with Lzar's help, to locate the proper strata of information. And that was just the beginning. They expected the information to be obscure; too many people wanted to see the Primes destroyed. There would have been searches made even after the Sector Wars. They didn't expect to find nothing.

DonEel waved off the reader and rubbed his eyes. He was tired and hungry and Pollo had already gone back to the suite with Galen. Even the young Andro assigned to help (and probably spy on) him had been reassigned. Apparently the administration had decided they were wasting their time, and he was inclined to agree with them. All the information on Syrcase and the citadel in the records was already part of his memory. In fact, he knew more than the records because the discovery of the gold room and the great Portal had not been recorded.

When he returned to suite he found Pollo even more frustrated. "All I found were negatives, things that should have been on record and weren't, like the investigation into some kind of power source for the citadel. Tim must have taken it out of the records."

"So how is Oso knowing where to look?" Galen asked.

Pollo shrugged. "Luck, maybe. His father was Lord of Syrcase, so he's been around the citadel a long time."

"But only Oso is looking."

"And he was schooled here on Stilks," DonEel pointed out, watching the Duratheen. "He must have found something."

"And there are more than two hundred years of Prime records here," Pollo said, reminding them silently that they didn't have a lot of time. Sooner or later Stilks would submit a claim to Alb F for payment, and on Eden there was increasing danger from Syrcase.

But they could trace Oso's studies.

It took a session with Ale to get permission, but they got it. And it allowed them to find out that Oso had started out studying the ancient Builders of the citadel, then had gotten involved in research on Primes and studied their entire recorded history. Not unusual, as the Primes had been the first to do real research on the ancient Builders, had, in fact been the first to explore the citadel and identify it as a Builder artifact.

"So we're right back where we started."

"Oso not knowing all of Primes before," Galen said. "Records would be saying different to him."

"What d'you— Oh, wait—" DonEel turned to Pollo. What data did you pull for that last year?"

"The work on Syrcase. Toward the last that's about all there was."

"But there was a lot of outside work coming in—" He broke off frowning, and Pollo caught the intuitive flash across his own thoughts.

It took another day to be sure, to get a complete subject index of work submitted by Primes back fifty standard years from the beginning of the Sector Wars. And they knew what had sent Oso on his search for the Primes. The material was structured so that, while the volume remained fairly constant, the focus narrowed until during the last six months every entry dealt with Syrcase, and finally the citadel itself.

"It's not a coincidence," Pollo said. "There was work coming in in other areas. Tim must have done it."

"So the message says go to the citadel. Oso did that, and the exile continues."

"He must have missed something. Its the only direction given."

Hoping for more, DonEel had to agree. The answer had to be tied into the citadel somehow. And it had to be something someone could find.

There was another possibility, of course, one neither wanted to admit, though both knew it. Maybe Timaret had miscalculated, maybe the thing that was supposed to end the exile hadn't, couldn't.

"So. We go to the citadel."

Both Ale and Lzar responded to their decision to leave with questions and suspicion, but they couldn't detain them. On the eleventh day they lifted from Stilks and began the flash for Syrcase.

Three times as they entered the Osoan sector they flashed into areas occupied by other ships—not singles but convoys whose greater bulk alerted the Duratheen's automatic option selector, shunting them out of danger. They did not make visual contact, but the ship's sensors picked up information on deployment and possible identification of type. They were not transports. Galen's experience told them a Lane Lord seldom had this many of his own ships so close to home port. It was more logical to assume they were the ships of Lords Lindig and Rulf, controllers of the bordering sectors, keeping watch on Oso or establishing a blockade, cutting off the lifeblood of the Lord's power and influence in his own sector.

The question of what they might find, or should look for, when they got to Syrcase preyed on their minds, became finally part of the fabric of their dreams, weaving them around in circles. DonEel watched the kaleidoscope of the flasher in the viewport, tired of the question. He felt they were missing the obvious, that they had been given the answer they were looking for and just didn't recognize it. He made an effort to get away from it, to let his attention wander, drifting about the two flames sharing this island in the Big Empty, feeling the vast silence about their tiny metal cocoon, then finally reaching back inside himself to the steady harmony and Ridlness that was a part of him, soothing, being all that was necessary, taking him into it so that he slept loose and sweet, moving into dream.

Watching from across the cabin, Pollo envied him a little, wondering about that part of him that was neither Deon nor DonEel, but kin to the winged L'Hur.

"The power source." He was awake quickly, already forgetting the dream of darkness and bringing light and—something Harmond had said to him once. But the answer felt important. He swung the chair to face a startled Pollo. "We were going to turn out the lights. It was a joke Harmond made. I was dreaming, and— Never mind, that has to have something to do with it."

"The power source is necessary for the Portal to function," Pollo reminded. "Oso must have found a way to turn it back on."

"Or used an alternate power source." But it was a slender hope.

"All we can do is find out exactly what Oso did to the Portal and compare it with what happened before."

"Maybe this trouble between Oso and Lindig will help us." DonEel began thinking ahead. "There are almost certainly records of Oso's work in the citadel, and I'm the only one who can get to see them." Galen, as a Duratheen, would never be allowed into the citadel unless under contract to Oso, and Pollo had been a captive of Sa'alm. Not for the first time he wondered what, if anything, Pollo remembered of that time. There were things they didn't share.

"Coming from Stilks to Port City open," Galen recommended as the dusty-gold planet appeared in the screen. They had papers to prove they were from the school planet, and Oso must be aware of the ships in his sector, even if they weren't his. If they were his, they would already have reported the arrival of a ship from the area of Stilks. As far as Syrcase was concerned, they were Albians, interested in the citadel and the Builders.

EIGHTEEN

"DURATHEEN, identify."

The no-nonsense voice startled them. The request for identification was not standard procedure, but any port had the right to establish martial restrictions in a crisis. The price of refusal was immediate attack from ground-based weapons or patrolling warships. Galen flipped the toggle that automatically transmitted his ship's registration, name, and last planetfall, adding the standard request for clearance to land. All ships, from explorer class to the huge, nearly automatic transports, were required to have automatic transmitting codes built in, a tradition held over from the long-ago Sector Wars.

There was no further communication until Syrcase expanded to fill the screen, and they began to wonder if they would be refused landing.

"Request received, Duratheen." The voice came back without feeling. "Lock onto guides. Special pros will post you down. All personnel aboard will report to the field commander's office immediately on landing unless there are environmental factors involved. In that event, personnel from the field will come aboard."

"Telling them true of Stilks," Galen warned as the ship's sensors found the guides to a fast approach and touchdown. It was not impossible for Oso to have their stories checked with Stilks, though that sort of communication was rarely used except in emergencies.

The port field had a deserted look; the normal chaos of private and cargo vessels, the multiplicity of races milling about between ships and perimeter, was replaced by a sterile military order. Galen's thoughts were quick and alert, sampling the atmosphere. There was a war brewing here. They were alone on one side of the field, and even before they left the ship, they felt watched. They didn't wait for an escort, but walked alone across the field to the low building bearing Oso's sword-and-spiral symbol.

The uniformed Andro in charge of the office didn't bother with names and identification—the automatic transmitter on the ship was as nearly foolproof as it could get. "Your arrival was not posted. What is your purpose on Syrcase?"

"Curiosity." DonEel spoke, playing it out, already knowing the Andro's thought that the official interest concerned their connection with Stilks, but not sure why. "We wish to study the Builders' artifact."

"You are of Alb F?"

"Yes."

"Stilks is aware of the situation here, Albian. Surely you were warned this was a bad time."

"The jealousies of the Lane Lords in this sector have no effect on Alb F, Osoan."

The officer shrugged, thinking all Albians were insufferable. "The ship is yours?"

"She owns to me." Galen stepped forward, knowing there was a risk building here that had to do with Stilks.

"Under my charter." Galen and Pollo must have

nothing to do with the Osoans in the citadel, and the officer's thought was already touching there.

"As proxy owner, the responsibility is yours. You have the choice of lifting off within the hour—"

"I shouldn't think so," DonEel interrupted calmly. "If those ships we saw coming in are what I think they are, we wouldn't get to flash point one."

"—or reporting to the base commander for questioning and having the ship hangared until the situation stabilizes." The Andro was a bit tense about the interruption, but there was no threat in his mind; he was just doing his job.

"Neither Stilks nor Alb F is involved in this difference. I am no threat to your lane."

"Oso's authority rules here, Albian."

"Indeed." Not that it mattered; he wasn't planning on leaving. Silently, he instructed Galen and Pollo to return to the ship, knowing Pollo's inevitable protest was more worry than sense. There was no way the Delphan could be safe in the citadel.

He waited alone, ignored by the Andro, until a guide came to take him to the citadel. It was armed and alert and big, and Deon's memory told him the type was from a heavy world, big but quick and agile in what was for it only half-normal gravity. Silently following the guide through Port City, he searched its mind for information, but learned nothing that applied to himself. The mind was simple, containing little beyond a stolid loyalty and awareness of its own prowess.

He entered the citadel openly for the first time, not through the great doors, but through a slightly less ornate side entrance, coming into structured activity and tension as defenses were manned. He was motioned through wide, muraled corridors filled with activity, where his guide turned him over to an Andro, this one young and nervous, with a scurrying mind. They moved inward until the way became familiar and he remembered certain of the designs worked into floors and walls and ceiling. As they moved, the Andro's nervousness increased, and from the depths of his thoughts there came, reluctantly, an image, caricatured into reptilian evil, but familiar to him. Muset.

"Wait here. The base commander will come."

Here was a sort of deep niche off the corridor with no apparent purpose, a three-sided room furnished with couches and objects of art, a lot of it Prime, probably gathered from other areas of the citadel. Oso, it seemed, had an eye for the purely aesthetic. The art blended well with the ancient and indestructible colors and designs of the Builders. One piece in particular caught his attention, a large stone set in dark wood, light placed accurately to bring out the impossible intricacies of the pattern on the carved surface. Weirdling. Like his knife and the stone found on Eden. There was a connection here somewhere. The Zonas must have gotten the stone from Sa'alm or others from Jimo, probably as payment for bringing other Truemen to the mines. Kylee had lied intentionally about the stone he had, knowing it had not been made by a Plainer. But why? He could not possibly know of the Portal, or the citadel, or—

Icy attention blew conjecture from his mind, and for a minute he was scared. The Andro had returned, and with him the base commander, the Zniss Muset. Bad enough to touch that mind occupied elsewhere; now it was focused on him, curious, watchful, forming links of relationship. If the Andro's mind was quick and linear and logical, the Zniss's mind was pure, beautiful geometry, never still. And that was part of Muset's pleasure. DonEel understood it for a minute, then lost it in personal concern, realizing that right now was the hinge between past and any possible future he might have.

The Zniss approached without any greeting, mentally cataloguing, seeking clues to the situation that faced him. Details of posture, eye change, breathing rate—the things that men handled automatically, depending on observational ability and attention—were conscious additions to the multidimensional construct in the Zniss mind. A probable conclusion formed: This one does not want me near him, is uncomfortable . . . possible Andro natural reaction . . . fear . . . guilt . . . unknown reason. He did not stop at the reasonable confrontation distance for communication, but came subtly closer, challenging covertly to force reactions, to accumulate data to— The concepts must exist somewhere, but there were no human analogies DonEel could apply. He stayed still. Oddly, because his own attitude was changing with the understanding of what information was being picked up and analyzed, he seemed to reflect increasing calm and assurance with decreasing distance. Immediately the Zniss went still, rejecting the many possible conclusions that formed in the pattern of its thought.

"Your timing is bad, student. All who came to Syrcase in this time are suspect." The accusation, in a voice as smooth as the physical movements, was as open as necessary, and touching threat.

"My actions, so far, are not ruled by the power struggles of the Lane Lords. If another held Syrcase now, I would not be troubling Oso. I seek knowledge, and that is more permanent than who rules where."

"Knowledge of—" There was no flare of curiosity, only pushing buttons.

"The citadel, the Ancients. The Primes who did the work here and then disappeared."

"Why now?"

"Because my study has led me to it. I either come here or stop, and that would be neither useful nor intelligent."

Muset didn't respond, but kept his eyes riveted on DonEel. Behind those cold eyes DonEel sensed a racing, multisurfaced curiosity, waiting, forming no rigid conclusions, weighing what he had said against a more believable purpose and guilt.

Fascinated by the mental function and complete

absence of emotional shifts, DonEel also waited, seeking the direction of that alien mind. There was no way for him to know in advance how the Zniss would react.

"For now, you will wait in a safe place," Muset said finally.

It was no more than he had hoped for. At least he was in.

Muset did not speak to him again, but simply turned away, knowing DonEel would follow, taking it for granted. The uniformed beings in the corridors moved aside quickly to let the Zniss pass, giving more room than was necessary out of fear or some more complex feeling. Muset did not notice. It was a thing done for him. His attention had moved on to the preparations for battle and the scope of the coming conflict. He was involved but not personally touched by it. It was a thing that would come and pass. On the walk to his confinement, DonEel watched that mind and wondered why the Zniss had no concern for losing. The possibility was there in his mind, but as something that would concern Oso, not Muset.

He entered the room indicated, felt rather than heard the lock. It was a room almost identical to the one he had taken refuge in when he first came to the citadel through the Portal, but on a higher level. Curious, he followed the Zniss mind back through the corridors, frowning slightly at the wash of subjective feeling picked up concerning him. He had power here, and authority, but there was no warmth toward him, only fear and awe. For some reason, Muset was more of a power here than even Oso, by the mere fact of his presence. It was a wonder there weren't more thoughts of violence directed against him, but the thoughts DonEel touched on held no vengeful plans, only fear and caution.

Leaving the thoughts of the citadel, he looked around. There was nothing here to interest him, a place to stay for a time until someone should release him. Finally relaxing enough to realize how tense he had been with the Zniss, he reached out, away from the citadel, to the small, loud sound-feel that was Pollo and Galen together, focusing on him, a wordless touch, being here and there also, and knowing their worry for him balanced his eagerness to be doing and done with this. Satisfied they were with him, he flashed into the split-level feeling of the omnipresent song below his mind, or in his blood, the L'Hur, just there, a step of maybe a million million miles away. It was good like this, except now for missing the big solid reality of the Primes. He missed that, remembering having it, needing it to balance the Big Empty and the ever-long memory that was a Prime gift and burden. How good it would be to—

"DonEel, the ships are coming in!"

Dozing, he thought at first Zhan had called out to him, then realized they were still separated. The fascinating light that had dimmed as he lay down brightened smoothly as he rose from the bed. Had the Ancients made them? Or the Primes, the unremembered ones who had come to study and stayed, making this a home? Never mind.

He splashed water on his face, feeling outward from sleepiness into the mounting excitement of Oso's forces. The ships of Lindig and Rulf were indeed approaching. Communication flashed in confusion, point-counterpoint, and, trying to know everything, he caught only disconnected bits and pieces.

Leaning, eyes closed for better concentration, he did not hear the door open, was startled by the simultaneous word-intent, warm and female. "I heard the snake had his prize. Are you right?"

"Right?" Well, whatever. He nodded, wiping his wet face, eyes on the flame of her hair.

"Your cold captor meets now with Lord Oso. Don't stare; I meant only to be sure I saw you before he makes his game with you."

He didn't know what she was talking about, and

for a moment he didn't care, as long as she stood poised so, half-smiling, cat eyes measuring and admiring him. As they had done before. Did she know him? Could she have forgotten—

He shook his head. This was no time for errant thoughts. "I was asleep." Lame excuse. "Did Muset send you?"

She laughed at him, and he was glad for the sound of it. He knew now she did not remember him, but she was still delighted by her effect on him. "I came to warn you, Albian. The snake-man sees some connection between you and another Stilkser who came. That one betrayed a trust and died by Muset's cold hand. Now with all this happening to us, here comes another Stilkser. Track?"

He nodded, not looking at her because he wanted to think of something else. That Stilkser he had seen her with before, when he stole the tapes. Galen had said the man died accused of treason. He should have made the connection with Muset's suspicion of him. "He thinks I'm responsible for the trouble with Lindig and Rulf?" It was too close to the truth, but in a way they couldn't guess.

"Another's holding was destroyed. Oso is blamed, but he did not, see? Muset thinks—or says—Stilks managed to—"

He laughed at her. He couldn't help it. To think Stilks might go about destroying military bases.

"—to blame Oso and have an excuse to attack and take the citadel."

"Interesting."

"It is. With you coming from Stilks just now, before the attack threatens. It could say he has it right."

"So why warn me?" He looked into her cat eyes. *She came because she saw me and wanted to see me again.* A familiar flame warmed him, and she smiled.

"Don't team with Muset, Albian. He has already ordered your ship blown. You live safe here because he thinks you have something he wants. He is not on

Oso's side, or anyone's, beyond his own shedding skin."

"How does he think—" A shrieking siren cut into his words, and her head jerked toward the door.

"Don't run, Albian. It's death by order of Muset. But your gate is open." She moved to the door and through it, like a cat coiled for springing, leaving a slightly musky scent behind her.

Her departure woke his brain. The ship: *"Galen, Pollo, get out!"* They had followed the meaning, were already out and moving, and Galen's goal had the familiarity of the white and alien side of the citadel. There was probable safety there, and it was close to DonEel, making it the only choice. Something of the Duratheen nature came to the man, a predatory delight in the situation that even across the distance was clean and real, buoying him up.

A series of alarms rang through the corridors, building tension and fear and alertness. The mass of differing minds were caught and directed to become a tool wielded by Oso—or Muset. There was a sort of glory to it, catching the blood, making even DonEel want to become a part of it, to join them.

"Albian!"

The call snapped his eyes open to see a uniformed Andro standing in the open door.

"Lord Oso orders you to come."

They hurried though ranks of uniforms where orders came in sequence, and beyond, down fallchutes, deeper into the citadel, below ground level and toward the central core.

The great room was not meant for commanding a war—its size and beauty overshadowed the cluster of figures about the new, utilitarian machines, making them seem less than real. Oso was waiting for him, a study of contrasts, the mind schooled to calm action, the body overfleshed but solid, the face full and self-indulgent, on the surface more cruel than his Zniss commander. The woman stood beside the Lane Lord's chair, watching him approach.

"Lindig's fleet commander wishes to talk, Albian." The voice was somehow as overfleshed as the body, the mind curious and challenging. "Would you speak with him?"

"If you wish, My Lord. What would you have me say?" He played it like a pacifist, willing, but not too sure of himself. It startled Oso into looking sharply at his commander.

"Perhaps you can tell them who took their base, and why."

This was too much. He thought of telling them the truth, knowing they would not believe, but Muset's cold attention kept him straight. "I don't know if Stilks knows that, though you think they do. I believe Stilks would not want the citadel attacked."

"We agree to that." There was a silence of watching; then Oso turned to the one seated at the communication console. "Say we know nothing of the business on Weirdlil. Had we made the attack we would now occupy the base. Tell him also that our fleet has been recalled and will arrive in less than one standard day unit."

That, DonEel saw in the Lord's mind, was true. Oso believed the time too short for Lindig to commit himself to a ground battle before the patrol engaged his ships.

"Albian, if so you are, we are not entirely satisfied with this meeting. Perhaps you can tell our commander your true position here on Syrcase."

With no apparent feelings about it, Muset came toward him. Over the Zniss's slender shoulder he saw the look of frustration on the woman's face as she bent to speak into Oso's ear. Muset said nothing to him, only looked at him and walked by, and DonEel followed, wondering how it was the Zniss knew he would come.

They did not return to the room he had waited in

before, but dropped down several levels, coming to the one where he had found Pollo and later come for the tapes. Now it was deserted, with all the activity being concentrated on the ground level. In the record room, Muset finally spoke.

"You are no Albian, Andro." Always that uncluttered attention gauging responses, measuring. DonEel said nothing, ignoring the remark. "You do not get angry. Albians are noted for it. And pride."

"I am many things, as you are, Zniss." No score.

"You will tell me. In my time."

"My being what I am does not depend on your belief in it. You may have the truth and not know it." He felt himself smile and wondered why, because he was afraid of the Zniss. Not especially for himself; not entirely. It was just hard to believe that that cold, lucid touch of attention did not know him as intimately as he knew it.

"There is something here on Syrcase that is important to Stilks."

"The citadel, of course. Important to all because of the Ancients. Even Oso knows its importance."

"Oso has luck, and position by birth, but he is not—" A sudden bell tone cut him off, not in surprise, but more to assimilate the intrusion of new factors into his mental construct of the moment. "They choose a ground attack," he said quietly. "They must want Oso badly. Their codes bind them rigidly. If you are wise, Andro, you will not leave this place of safety. I will return, but now there are other duties."

Attack. His thoughts flashed to Galen and Pollo. Where were they? Muset's going left him momentarily drained with the effort of following and anticipating the alien structure of that mind. He sat down in the bell-punctuated silence, wondering why they chose a musical tone for the attack when all the warnings were harsh alarms.

"*DonEel, Durath fights with Lindig.*" Galen's bright thought touched him warmly, bringing battle excitement and Pollo-worry. With other Duratheen moving about, it would be easier to move toward the citadel. And if they needed it, help—at least for Galen—was a possibility. He let them know he was all right and urged them to caution in wordless touch and understanding. Waiting, he followed their movements through the engagement, the landed ships, the moving figures spreading through the city, flashes of loud light reaching for ships and machines and flesh, touching and leaving ruin. The weapons were the type first seen on Weirdlil. This, at least, had changed since Deon's time. He felt he moved through the battle with Galen, but here, where he could do nothing.

Keyed up, he moved about the room. There was almost certainly some kind of spy device watching him, but there were things he needed to know, and this was one of the places he might find some answers. He began going through the shelves of tapes idly, as though out of boredom. Many were copies of the works he had seen on Stilks, especially those of the last months dealing with the citadel. It was difficult to concentrate with the constant awareness of the battle making his hands damp, drawing his thoughts to seek for his companions. And why had Muset brought him here to be safe and apparently free?

Three times he nearly left the area, knowing the way to the central corridor. But he did not. There were things he could not learn by leaving, things he began to feel sure he must learn from the Zniss.

Then she was there, flashing the fires of conflict and victory, utterly female and wild, and as predatory as the cut she resembled.

"It goes well, Albian. They fall back, and the snake seeks to capture now, hoping for everything. He has not yet won you to him?"

"No." Her presence was a shock, drawing his thoughts and attention back from the distance to here and now in the room with her.

She came close, living bronze, and smiling. And

the scent of her reached him. He touched her mind, alert yet, still holding himself in the moment, then found the mysterious female duality of her excitement: sport and desire. His heart beat. He had fantasied this and she knew it, and he shared her knowing and it shook him loose from every consideration. Her hands were velvet on his face, daring him to touch, to master the wildness in her and claim his prize, saying he was male and she needed what he alone could give. Her mind was a storm of knowing and anticipation he had never touched, her mouth violent in its yielding, her body perfection without gentleness.

"This is not the time." His mind built the words, and she laughed deep in her throat, the hand moving on the front of his body calling him liar with unspeakable boldness. Unreal. This did not happen in the midst of battle. But her challenge raised a fire in him, a need to conquer her.

"Have you no name?" he asked through a blood-pounded throat.

"Sa'alm," she said or thought as she pulled his head down to her savage mouth.

"*No!*" Rage exploded through him. He knew it; yet his hands filled themselves with her yielding. Delirious, insane with the conflict in himself as she led him beyond knowledge, molding his action and thought so his conquest could be her victory.

This cannot be, his drowning mind whispered, helpless. Yet his hands, tearing at her, knew his goal: not nudity, not pleasure, only access and entry. He went into her brutally, hating, wanting to hurt. And she devoured him, drew him in, deaf and blind, doing as she willed until the tension culminated, bursting out in a rush that could be remembered only as agony, releasing him from hell, waking him to purpose. Fingers hard about her velvet throat, he squeezed, willing her dead for his shame, his helplessness, for Pollo's pain and humiliation, feeling her legs go limp, releasing him, wide cat eyes glazed. . . .

"No!" The hard word split his skull, and his hands leaped away. *"Losing us all for nothing."* Galen's thought rapped into him hard and hurting. *"Doing is past."*

Sick, he pushed her away and she fell heavily from the table. He forced himself to order, to straighten his clothing, aware now of deep scratches on hip and buttock and the taste of blood in his mouth. He was suspended in a curious nothingness with only Galen to touch sanely. Pollo, mercifully, was silent, screened away.

"You are too predictable, Sa'alm." The cool, easy voice struck like a whip. Unwilling, DonEel forced himself to turn, to watch Muset move into the room, his eyes on the woman on the floor. He was distantly surprised that she lived, pale now, lovely throat mottled with his handprints. She glared up at the Zniss, making no move to cover herself.

Muset paid no attention, looking now at DonEel. "I should have warned you. Your kind find her warm tricks irresistible. A talent her kind has."

The cold superiority was bracing, waking him, so he began to think, reaching for knowledge, learning. Her kind, the Ara'at, nonhuman in detail, but compatible.

"Go to your Lord, Sa'alm. Report failure if he ordered this. I could have told you he is more than you thought. Next time he will succeed in killing you." And to DonEel: "You have more pride than I saw. But it is as well you did not kill her. She is Oso's toy."

Mind racing away from the act completed, DonEel began to make sense of the cold thoughts. The Ara'at had a power to control men through that specific biologic function, probably on the emotional level because the Zniss were not affected, though they were physically compatible. A talent, then, like the Primes', but other-directed and -controlled. She had willed his arousal intentionally, unaware of his emotional commitment to revenge. He might well have killed her, but for Galen.

"The invaders have retreated to the port, hoping for a ship to run in and pick them up. Oso will allow it. The attack failed." The Ara'at was gone, unnoticed. "Your Duratheen ship was attacked and destroyed, so you seem to have joined our ranks. However, Sa'alm will put Oso against you unless you have a worth that outweighs her anger."

He was being manipulated, but to what end he could not tell. The Zniss's mind gave almost nothing he could understand. "I came to learn, Muset. Only that. I can't give you what I don't have."

Deep-set eyes glittered oddly as the Zniss looked about the room, noting the record tapes on the floor, swept there, forgotten, in the fury of his encounter with Sa'alm. He knew the Zniss did not believe him but was equally unsure of the truth and did not like it. But he was patient. "You will tell me sometime what you know of the Builders."

An alarm, faint at this level, broke into the Zniss's concentration. He turned to a communicator on the wall near the door, spoke briefly, listened. "The Lindig commander has contacted Oso a last time. They will attack the citadel itself. Oso miscalculated."

So did you, DonEel thought. They were after Oso after all. Then the meaning hit him. They would attack the citadel, the Portal. "They can't—" he began involuntarily, reaching to Galen and Pollo, knowing they knew, feeling Pollo's instinctive fear echoing his own, not personal now, but for the Portal. It couldn't be destroyed. It must not be. *"Go down now,"* he thought sharply. *"Through the Portal if you must."*

"They will." Muset answered him, but for a moment he did not remember saying anything, thought Muset had somehow heard— He pushed the thought away, listening. "They would do it for vengeance over a mistake." It was no more than the Zniss expected of Andros, and it was increasingly clear that he had no

273

thought of being caught up in it. Already a decision was forming. One factor gave him pause; then he gestured to the man to follow.

"There is a thing I brought to Oso to buy my position and his power." Symbols grew and dissolved in the fleet geometry of the mind, and part of it was from the Portal, then Oso, the histories, the one who uncovered the functioning power of the citadel. . . . And the Portal again.

Following rapidly, DonEel frowned, trying to make some sense of it. How could the Zniss have bought the Portal? It couldn't be that. The Portal was part of the citadel. "You found an artifact?" Leading question for his own probing thought.

"Of a sort." But the mind itself went beyond, made identification automatically. Jimo, artificial world-ship, with Portal. World. Ship.

They reached the spiral corridor and turned downward. Zniss made no effort, but DonEel had to stretch his legs to match the gliding stride. Jimo and ship. Muset must have a ship near Jimo. No wonder he wasn't worried.

"Is it possible, Galen?"

"Altogether. Jimo being ship. And another to leave."

Jimo meant safety to Muset. The geometric mind weighed the citadel and combined forces attacking, and calculated total destruction of the citadel. Following that cold logic, DonEel felt panic. It must not be. Maybe the Osoan patrol would arrive before the attack could be launched. Maybe it was a bluff. . . .

They would never know if Muset's estimate was correct. Rulf sent ships for the first attack, not to destroy but to get range and information on Oso's defenses. The first strike raised fire atop the mountain of the citadel, as harmless as the millions of years of weathering beneath the jade sky. Within the citadel the blast of sound was transmitted through the fabric of the structure, a gentle, muted gong-sound reverberating. Muset glanced up, calculating, always calcu-

274

lating, flashing a look at the man beside him that noted the sudden loss of hope, the pallor of desperation.

"They lose the more." The Zniss's voice was soft, hinting at some private victory.

The reverberation died away into a silence of waiting for the next blow, waiting. . . .

The keening hum was too high to hear. His first warning was a sharp look from Muset, then a sense of vibration shimmering the air, turning the constant light lighter, tending almost to blue. For a moment DonEel felt the change as a purely subjective experience, skull itching, vision fractioning, feeling the world tighten imperceptibly.

"*DonEel, what is it?*" Galen, more alert to sensation and threat, reacting to the reality before any, even the Zniss, translating the sensation as sound.

He did not know. Slowing, listening above the pounding of his heart. . .

It came down into his range slowly, sliding into focus, and the light was blue, as steady, but different, deepening. He began to find it, as though making it real by his effort. Beside him, the Zniss seemed watchful but unconcerned. It became painful to him, shrill and omnipresent, too bright against his brain. And he knew it was worse for Galen. It became a tone, more audible now; not loud, but more present, trembling bone and brain, irritating. He touched the curved wall, felt the vibration tingle against itching fingertips. It's real, he thought—maybe said, because Muset looked at him.

As full-surrounding sound, it came down the scale, reddening the light or vision, sliding slowly, a pure sound, taking the mind with it, catching all sensory antennae locked and helpless, down to hum tone, and down, faster now, becoming louder, imperative, God-voice of warning power, authority, deeper, until bones ached head swam vision cracked and jelled and split, too fast, kaleidoscopic nonattention, up and down or moving somehow, going sideways, belly-tensing with

no time to be sick or hurt or dizzy. *What's happening?*
What's happening? Thoughts reaching out, seeking,
touching panic and breeding panic, and the narrow
Zniss so close to him, back bending gracefully near the
wall. Touch the mind; find it calm, perfectly pat-
terned, curious, hearing and not being. . . .

Too low, too solid for sound, and like rushing too
fast through things shaking the very soul like floods
of thunder and storm and all the accusations of
heaven . . . He yelled at the peak of audible sound,
felt it in his throat, echoed by a hundred minds, stop,
stop, stop! A frail, human sound, unheard. But he felt
Muset's cold analysis of *that* reaction to sonics and
subsonics.

Subsound, terror reaction, and the beautiful golden
peace of the Portal room ahead. The Zniss stopped,
shimmering in the roar of silence that was the terri-
fying presence of sound too low for hearing, heating
the air, felt going down and down and when it gets
wherever something, some terrible thing is going to—

Muset was hurting from the inaudible noise, the
flood of silent sound, but not mentally, accepting with
the miracle of metaphor the cause and effect on his
body. But the trap once set by his own hand was a
greater threat. He bent and detached the device set
to protect the room from entry by anyone.

Scattered on the winds of his own reaction to the
sound, wide open, DonEel knew Pollo and Galen
were coming into the Portal room across from them.
He thought "*Hurry!*" against their minds, knowing
Muset meant no one but him to enter the Portal to
Jimo's safety.

Impulse moved before thought, releasing all the
sound-created tension and fear into attack. He leaped,
touching the cool slenderness, was shocked to reality
by something hurting as his own weight overcame
him, almost losing his grip on the unpleasant arm. He
rolled, bringing the coiling, sinewy body across his
own, aching from the sonic pummeling. "*Now, go*

through the Portal!" Pollo hesitated, locked in inde-
cision, but Galen knew the Zniss and the odds. They
went. And so did DonEel's hold on Muset. He tried
to move fast enough, reaching—

"Fool." The easy word slammed against his neck
with a hard hand, numbing everything but the understanding that he could not move, was helpless to
the arching foot exploding against his genitals, paralyzing him on the floor that swam with the voice of
the citadel.

Dark-glittered eyes measured him thoughtfully.
"You could have learned, Andro. You were almost
different enough." Bending, Muset took up the small
device, glanced up the corridor a moment, then turned,
running lightly toward the ornate gate of the Portal.

Watching, helpless, trying to make flesh and will
function together, DonEel saw him crouch beside the
Portal. No other fact had meaning now, only that.

He moved. He had to move, bent double, stumbling, trying not to breathe, ignoring the shouts behind
him, the flash of hot light. Felt the cool metal shape,
featureless, pulling it free, turning to—

The figure closest to him saw the thing in his up-
raised hand, launched himself with a cry of warning.
The impact caught DonEel above the knees, threw him
back, arms up. Only accident, helpless, blameless, feeling the weight leave his hand, thrown back, into the
Portal. That was the only thought in the forever time
of falling back and back, into—

Nowhere. Nothingness. No impact. Only the half-
sensed agony of fragmentation, of cessation.

NINETEEN_____

I *am—*
  I think—
  I don't—
  First thoughts. Impressions. Where?

Movement is another world. He knew that. But he didn't exist. He knew that, too, and so he wasn't able to—

Movement was—harmony. Distant bits, pieces, drifting in familiar mindsong of identification. L'Hur.

"DonEel!" Bell-tone, commanding. And he would come back, but he didn't know where—

"DonEel!"

—he was. Therefore—confusion. But knowing distant and absolute he had to be somewhere. He could feel—curious. Memory. Pollo. Pollo— Gone. Zhan Llir— That hurt. Remember. At the beginning. Smell of night and Blackwood, the sleeping face, one arm thrust out smooth and warm against the needle-strewn earth—

Where am I?

Everywhere. In the center of everywhere. All the wheres available, pulling, leading to—

He needed to see, to know, feeling the knot of here-bundling strands moving out—away—rivers to raft, taking him to—

Jimol Seeing the gate, the white room, washed by the violet energy release, tearing away base and steps and controls, making one more nothing-ended strand—

Syrcase? Seeing the knot of being about the Portal, led by the Ara'at, watching himself drifting backward, disappearing into—

Citadel? Outside. The howl of sound building, power and more power, and bright violet-gold beams springing up from the flat peak of the mountain it was, up, singing through air and space, seeking, reaching, touching the firefly ships of Lindig and Rulf, and there was no more threat, no ships, no enemy to—

Citadel! Timaret, and Harmond, and Primes coming, hearing words, and wrapped in knowing what. And how—

Citadel. Newer and more beautiful, and the wondrous winged men and women, the L'Hur, matching song for song, and—

Citadel—full and busy—
Citadel—and war—and—
Citadel—
"DonEel!"
Too far. He fled without moving, seeking some part
of himself, soaring wingless down spirals of power
cascading to nowhere he knew, seeing place and being
and knowing and part of it locked into it all, burdened
with the loss of everything—
Pollo, and Galen, and Eden, and the Primes— No
more, nevermore. And Ridl—the L'Hur—singing in—
his—mind—
Singing?
Mindsong—of—desire—for—
Union!
"Ridl!?"
Father! Blood-being—
L'Hur—
He caught the strands of song, familiar, being him,
and all being before him. Joyous? Becoming—pulling
him—falling—
Ridl! Help me—
Seeking—knowing a desire greater than any desire.
To be—
To be—
Back!

The absence of support sent him sprawling, drawing
forth a cry of protest a million million miles long.
Hard rock broke his fall, nearly broke his arm.

Gasping in relief, grasping at this tangible reality,
he moved, looked up through new firelight to the
dark-planed face bending down.

"You returned."

"Yes." The word hurt his throat. "The L'Hur way.
Again—"

Gentle hands explored his arm, knowing the hurt
there, lifted him gently. It felt good, this care.
"Father—" Wanting to tell all of it. "I know. I saw—"

279

"Yes. My son." The words carried him down the long slide into unconsciousness.

It made no sense now to fear the Zonas or Nomen, but the caution was there in them, so they moved away from the mines, back into the safety of the timber and the old camp. He was with them, but far away yet. The no-time of the Portal clung to his mind, turning his thoughts inside. I know, he had said to Ridl. And he did know.

He knew the citadel because he had been there in the building of it. He knew the graceful L'Hur and the pleasure of their creating, and the wisdom in them to prepare for other ages. And to protect. The citadel had not been destroyed. The mighty god-flames of destruction racing up from the cone of power, wakened by that first attack, had one task: protect the Portal. And that defense would outlast the time of the Lane Lords, maybe even the time of man.

"You, the L'Hur, are the Ancient Ones, the Builders," he said to Ridl.

"Were. You saw it. Long ago, before your race began counting time, we were the Builders. But all is change. We are not gods. We, too, came to a new beginning, and forgot."

And he knew more now. He knew the key to the awakening of the Primes. It was obvious now because he had somehow been there with Timaret and Harmond and the Prime scholars of Stilks, meeting in the gold room.

"It is done," Pollo said quietly, so DonEel turned to see the copper hair, the laughing golden eyes, sharing all in that look, knowing and understanding, forgiving even Sa'alm. The eyes darkened slightly, and the laughing mouth went still. "You might not have come back this time."

"I did."

"Aye." Laughing now and sharing it. "The Portal is

the way. Only that. Tim and the others knew it would be found someday and bring us back."

And so it had been. But not by Oso, holder of the citadel. DonEel had seen that other gate, Jimo, and Muset finding it, bringing it to Oso, but never really letting go.

"Jimo was the thing in the way. The energy flow had to be from the citadel to Eden, bringing the power here. Jimo made a cross—"

"Then Jimo is destroyed. And Muset."

"Gate only being gone," Galen rumbled, knowing the resilience of the Zniss. And the explosive device had not been large. "Portal opening now to citadel will have more danger in it." For it was always open here, pouring the fine song of power into the resonance of West Range now, a silent tone to wake the sleepers.

"Not so much. They won't trust it for a while. And the cave here can be resealed as before, so anyone coming will find nothing recognizable." In the first time it had been so, a chamber sealed in rock accessible only if one knew where to look. And was it, he wondered, solely coincidence that the miners had worked always toward the cave, perhaps unconsciously knowing....

It was done.

The fact of it settled over them, numbing, not yet making room for what would, what must, come next.

An errant thought uncurled somewhere between the two Primes, a memory touched once and forgotten during the trouble on Syrcase. *Phoenix*. The Prime-owned vessel, so like Galen's, hidden in a shallow riverbed, beneath the sand. The Duratheen picked up the thought, examined it. Yes. Very like. Yes.

And a new truth. The exile was ended. They were no longer bound to this world. The citadel would protect its reason for being, the Portal. Now they could, they must, think of what lay beyond.

"It begins for you," Ridl said quietly, standing beyond them, tall and more beautiful than any living thing could be, Eden fantasy, or a part of a reality they had never in their greatness approached. "Not alone for the men of Terra." He looked at them, including the Duratheen, sharing a vision of some future. Galen was needed, and not he alone. The new non-Terran telepaths would be needed beyond the Portal.

"Gate-keeping, us." He took the old phrase, made Duratheen in his way, and began to see how purpose could weld them together, close.

"It begins." There would be confusion and new trouble here. But healthy trouble, forcing growth. The Portal must remain accessible if only because Muset might somehow have escaped, might yet threaten their Eden. But not through the mines. The natural caves ran for miles through the mountains, branching, ending, beginning. . . . And one led south beneath the shade of Blackwood, a way traveled in the beginning of Oso's searching, to the green-gold light of a grove and a hollow marked with a white pillar. . . .

I will return to Scarsen soon, DonEel thought. First to Delpha where a son will be born to Pollo, a Terran Prime in more than potential. And Argath waited there, bound to him by a black-gold ring of twining ropes as never-ending, always-beginning, as forever.

First to Delpha, then.

Then to Scarsen, the beginning. And a future when a great white eagle would come sometimes at twilight into the grove, reminding of flight on the *Phoenix*, and the Big Empty, singing of distant stars, like the L'Hur singing in his blood.